BEAUTIFUL

by the same author
Disappearer
Colin Cleveland and the End of the World
Girl's Rock
The Eternal Prisoner
Rogue Males

Mark Hunter series
Beautiful Chaos
Sixty-Six Curses
Trouble at School
Mysterious Girlfriend
The Beasts of Bellend
Countdown to Zero

Beautiful Chaos

Chris Johnson

Samurai West

Published by Samurai West
disappearer007@gmail.com

Story and Art © Chris Johnson 2020, 2022
All rights reserved

ISBN-13: 9798293186150

All of the opinions expressed in this book are those of the author. Even the ones that contradict each other.

Chapter One
Sun is Shining, Trudie Rayne

It stops her in her tracks.

A sudden transition, a subtle shift in the atmosphere; an intangible feeling, registered by the brain, but too vague to be interpreted.

Nothing has changed that the girl can see. The street, part of her regular course to and from school, remains as it always has; the stone-flagged pavement; trees and lampposts at regular intervals; semi-detached houses distanced from the flags by low walls and perfunctory front yards. A quiet suburban street on a hazy spring afternoon.

The disjointed feeling shifts to alarm. Perhaps this strange feeling is a premonition, a warning of impending disaster. But there is nothing; nothing her senses can isolate as an immediate possible threat.

The girl relaxes, and, dismissing the feeling, resumes her walk.

Trudie Rayne is the girl's name. She wears the uniform of the local comprehensive, and carries a bag slung over her shoulder. Her figure is broad and athletic; the features of her face are strong, her hair short and dark, her jaw heavy, her eyebrows pronounced. She wears thick glasses; chunky frames supporting chunky lenses. To look at her, you might think Trudie to be a strong young woman, in both physique and in character; confident and bold.

And you wouldn't be entirely wrong; Trudie is a strong person, but has been guilty of a weakness, and she has fallen in her own esteem.

Reaching the end of the street, Trudie looks back, back at the spot where she had stopped in her tracks, expecting to see—she's not sure—maybe another her still standing there, frozen in that moment of time.

Trudie crosses the road, and steps into a supermarket car-park, another stage of her perambulation to and from school. Her route takes her past the supermarket entrance. Mr Dwight, her English teacher, steps out through the sliding doors at that moment, recognisable in his tasteless corduroy suit (with turn-ups.) He trips, either on a paving stone or over one of his own clumsy feet, and pitches forward, landing on his knees, spilling the contents of his two shopping bags. Some Year Seven kids, loitering outside the shop, howl with laughter.

The spectacle just makes Trudie sigh.

'Here, I'll help,' she offers, squatting to help pick up the groceries that have spilled from their bags. Trudie's voice, although cheerful and bright, has a discernible thickness to it; on account of this she is often affectionately addressed as 'you spazzy bitch!' by some of the younger kids.

She retrieves a jar of pasta sauce—garlic and herb—that has rolled across the pavement and defied its owner's usual bad luck by remaining intact.

'Thank you... er...' Dwight looks at her, awkward, embarrassed.

'Trudie,' says Trudie. 'I'm in your class, remember?'

Mr Dwight. Only in his twenties he is already completely bald on top. Glasses and a moustache make the lower part of his egg-shaped head seem very busy compared to the upper. Trudie wonders if his yellow suit and green bow-tie are just evidence of bad sartorial taste, or if they are some act of desperation—a terminally boring individual's sad attempt to appear more interesting.

Both bags are now filled. They stand up.

'Where's your car?' asks Trudie. 'I'll carry this one for you.'

'No, I can—' begins Dwight, reaching for the other bag.

'I don't mind,' insists Trudie. 'Lead the way.'

They set off across the car-park.

Mr Dwight has just started his first year of school teaching; and he is, professionally speaking, already a dead man walking. He was never cut out for the teaching profession. As awkward as he looks, and lacking either the charisma to engage with a class, or the authority to control one, his students, sensing this immediately, just walk all over him.

Poor bastard… Why the fuck did he choose a job he's totally unsuited for? wonders Trudie. Probably just earned his degree in English and realised there isn't much else he could do with it, career-wise. He won't be around for long. Word of his hopelessness has reached the staffroom—they probably worked it out from the volume of noise always coming out of his classroom. Rumour has it he's already been called to the headmaster's office.

Christ knows what he'll do when he gets the sack. Probably end up stacking shelves in that shop he just tripped out of.

They reach Dwight's car (characteristically shitty) and deposit the shopping bags in the boot.

'Thank you, Trudie,' says Dwight, tonelessly, avoiding her eyes.

'No problem!' says Trudie. 'See ya.'

Trudie turns away. There was no real gratitude in that 'thank you'. She knows she hasn't made a friend there. Probably resents her for being a witness to his clumsiness and having been laughed at by those kids. He'll be thinking she was laughing up her sleeve at him, even if she wasn't laughing out loud.

A black boy, dressed in the male version of her own uniform, stands there, regarding her with a puzzled look. It's Craig Denver, and as he happens to be one of the nicer boys in her year, she doesn't ignore him.

'What's up?'

'Why were you just helping Dwighty with his shopping?' he asks.

'Oh, he just came out of the shop and tripped over his own feet,' replies Trudie. 'Dropped all his shopping.'

'What a twat!' grinning.

'Yeah. I was just being the Good Samaritan and helping the poor bastard.'

'You going home now?'

'Yeah.'

'You know…' begins Craig.

'What?'

'Well…'

'Well what? Spit it out!'

'Sorry!' he laughs awkwardly. 'I just… wanted to tell ya that I'm here for you, y'know? If you need me. I'm on your side, know what I mean?'

Trudie looks at him, smiling. 'Are you?'

'Yeah! I mean it… You know… whatever happens…'

'Well… okay!' smiles Trudie, awkwardly accepting that which was awkwardly proffered. 'Cheers! Much appreciated!'

'Yeah… Well, see you later, then…'

Craig departs.

Trudie resumes her course. How much does he know? She's not sure how much of a secret her secret is anymore. Has he heard?

Maybe he doesn't know anything. Maybe he was angling to ask her out… Would have been nice, once upon a time… Yeah, she wouldn't have minded having a guy like Craig for a boyfriend, if things had been normal… But things are not normal; not anymore…

She would have to tell a crap-ton of lies if she ever wanted to keep a boyfriend…

A pedestrian way winding between the backs of houses takes Trudie from the supermarket onto the street in which she lives. She unshoulders her school bag and fishes out her smartphone. She needs to check to see if her evening tonight will be her own or not… No. It won't be. She has a message; as succinct and imperative as always:

You've got a client tonight. Be here at 8.

With a sigh, Trudie deletes the message and returns the phone to her bag. She wonders who the client will be this time.

The message comes courtesy of Martin Hammond, president of the Classical Music Club. The other members of the club are

Davey Sedgewick, Lucy Smith and Pattie Price.

Lucy Smith was formerly Trudie's best friend, but is a friend no longer. With the arbitrariness of youth, Lucy had one day, and for no discernible reason, decided that Trudie was no longer good enough for her to associate with; she had been 'unfriended,' to use the social media vernacular. At first it was the cold shoulder and spiteful comments; and then, when Martin and Davey had raped Trudie in the music room, Lucy had been the one standing there holding their coats for them.

When something like that happens, you can't help but feel that the honeymoon is well and truly over…

Trudie arrives home at the modest semi-detached in which she lives with her parents. Up the gravel drive, she unlocks the side door with her latch-key and lets herself in. She pulls off her shoes. In the kitchen fridge she finds a can of diet coke, pulls the tab, and proceeds upstairs to her bedroom, sipping the drink.

There is a girl sitting on her bed.

Blonde, elegantly beautiful, wearing a tartan-skirted public-school uniform, and a complete stranger to Trudie.

Frozen in the doorway, Trudie's mind races to find an explanation for this phenomenon, this apparition. Her mind just gives up and shrugs its shoulders.

The girl just sits there, calmly smiling at her.

'How did you get in here?' demands Trudie, finding her voice. 'All the doors were locked!'

'That doesn't matter,' answers the girl. Her voice is smooth, cultured.

'Doesn't ma—Just what the fuck do you want?'

'To see you, of course. Why else would I be here?'

The matter-of-factness is starting to grate. 'But I don't even know you!'

'True, but I know you. Your name is Trudie Rayne, age fifteen, student of Dale Street Comprehensive. An only child, your family is Jewish racially, although not religiously. Your hobbies include alternative rock music, computer games and reading; and you are currently working part-time as a prostitute. Although, as your "pimps" take all the money, it's perhaps more accurately sexual slavery rather than prostitution, as such.'

Trudie's jaw sags. 'How could you know tha—'

'It doesn't matter how I know. I just do. But I am a friend, I'm here to help you. I know my sudden appearance in your life must be disconcerting, but please sit down and I'll explain everything.'

Trudie finds herself sitting down on the swivel chair that supplies her bedroom writing desk. She knows she ought to be raging at this girl who has intruded in her personal sanctum; but the girl's words, the modulation of her speech, are compelling. She feels her anger evaporating; replaced by a desire to listen to whatever it is this girl has to say.

'What's your name?' she asks

'My name is Juliette Wainwright. I belong to an organisation that has become very interested in you. We're looking for recruits, you see, and we think that you're just the kind of person we want.'

'What organisation?'

'A covert one. An organisation opposed to the society we live in. We have rejected it and all its laws.'

'So, what: you're a terrorist group?'

'Well, we do commit acts of terrorism, but we're a lot more than just a terrorist group. For one thing, we have no political or religious agenda. We have no long-term goals. It is enough that we exist. We benefit ourselves and no-one else.'

The blonde girl reaches into her blouse pocket.

'Our card.'

She hands it to Trudie. It reads:

SEA

The SOCIETY of EVIL ACTIONS

Trudie looks up from the card to the affably smiling girl.
'This is a joke, right?'
'A bit tongue in cheek, perhaps. But the organisation is real

enough.'

'And did you come up with this name?'

'No, our leader came up with the name.'

'You're not in charge of this thing, then?'

'No, I was recruited. Our leader is a man called Vautrin. He found me. He's found you too, and he's sent me to recruit you.'

'Yeah? And how did he "find" me?'

'I'm not sure how he does it. He can sense people, the kind he's looking for, and reach out to them on some ethereal wavelength. We're all connected somehow; you, me, the other girls in the group…'

'How many of you are there?'

'Oh, a few. Vautrin says there will be eleven of us girls ultimately, so we're still recruiting at the moment.'

'Girls? So there's only girls in this thing?'

'Yes. We're all girls; all around the same age, too.'

'Why's that?'

'That's what Vautrin wants, I suppose. We're connected; we're special. He's concerned about our welfare.'

'Yeah, sounds more like he's building up a harem. Is this guy an old perv, then?'

Juliette shakes her head. 'No, he's actually fairly young. He has never mentioned his precise age, but in appearance he is mid to late twenties and he's remarkably handsome. As to his level of perversion, I couldn't say. He's very reserved about himself.'

'Do you have to fuck him?'

'No. He doesn't seem to be interested in that sort of thing.'

Trudie takes a swig of her coke. She observes the other girl's hands, slender, beautifully manicured. Her own hands, broad, with tombstone nails, look clumsy by comparison. The girl's uniform as well: the fitted blazer, the pleated tartan skirt, the knee socks… They make her own grey ensemble seem drab.

'Okay… Say I believe all this and that I'm interested,' says Trudie, slowly. 'What happens then?'

'Well, joining us would mean saying good-bye to your current life. You would have to leave this house, your family, forever, and come and live with us in our secret headquarters.'

'You've got a secret base?'

'Yes. Located in Limbo. Somewhere in Sussex. It's a pretty amazing place. You'll have your own private room and we've got a swimming pool, a sauna, home cinema, a video arcade... Everything you could want.'

'Everything?'

'Pretty much. It's a teenager's dream come true, our secret base: luxury and plenty and no-one to tell us what to do...' She looks at Trudie. 'You want to join us then? I can promise you it will give your life new meaning, and you'll make some good friends.'

'I dunno why I even believe you, but I do. This is all true, isn't it? What you're saying... I just know it is, somehow... You being here, and... How long do I have to think about this?'

'Well, I would rather you made up your mind right now. We believe in rash, impulsive action, you see. Dropping everything and coming with me would be your first rash, impulsive action.'

'Can I take anything with me?'

'You can pack a bag. Anything else you need you can buy later. We're not short of funds.'

Should she go? The reckless, living-on-borrowed-time buzz that has kept her going these last few months: has it all been leading up to this? And then there was that feeling she experienced earlier, on her way home from school; the feeling of a shift, a change... Here is that change; beautiful, blonde, smelling of expensive perfume, sitting on her bed, calmly telling her all these incredible things, inviting her to drop everything and start a new existence.

Juliette leans forward and takes Trudie's hand, looks into her eyes. 'You have to do it. You've been chosen. Vautrin never chooses the wrong person. He knows that you're one of us. Don't hesitate. Just do it.'

Trudie feels her heart racing, a broad smile spreads across her face. 'Yes! Yes, I'll go! Just let me pack some stuff.'

She springs to her feet.

'There's one more thing.'

She sits down again.

'The small matter of the Classical Music Club.'

Juliette opens the school satchel that has been sitting at her feet, takes from it an alarmingly large automatic pistol, shiny and new. She offers it to Trudie.

'Go on. It won't bite you.'

'That's one great big fuck-off gun,' says Trudie.

'Yes, it's a Magnum Desert Eagle, .50 calibre. Take it.'

Trudie accepts the gun, looks at it, then back at Juliette.

'What do you want me to do with it?'

'I believe you have a client tonight, at the usual venue for your sexual services. Take the gun with you.'

'You want me to…?'

'Clean up house. Think of it as your first act on behalf of the SEA, as well as giving you some personal sense of closure to that chapter of your life. You need to take control of your destiny, not let yourself be carried along by life.'

'Yeah, but I've never used a gun—'

'It's simple enough. You just have to take the safety off, point it, and squeeze the trigger. The Desert Eagle has no recoil, so it's a good gun for a newbie like you. And to make it easier for you, I've loaded the clip with soft-nosed bullets. Hit your target just about anywhere and they're dead. Have you ever read Octave Mirbeau's *Torture Garden*?'

'Never heard of it.'

'Oh, it's very good. You should read it. There's a delightful passage in which an English officer on a ship is telling his fellow passengers about the time they tested the original Dum Dum bullet in the city of that name. (That's where it gets its name from, you see? Dum Dum was in India back then, but in Pakistan since the Partition.) Well, what they did was, they made a dozen natives stand in a line and then they fired the bullet through them. You can just picture the scene, can't you? The Englishmen standing over all those ripped-open bodies—some of the victims perhaps still alive and vainly pleading for help—while they dispassionately discuss the results of their new bullet.'

'And that's "delightful" is it?'

An apologetic smile. 'Perhaps not for you, but you see I happen to rejoice in the condition Kraft-Ebbing, in his book *Psychopathia Sexualis,* designated "Sadism".'

'You're a sadist? Is that part of this SEA thing? Do we all have to be sadists?'

Another smile. 'Not at all. I'm the only clinical sadist in the group—and I never hurt my friends, by the way. Although I admit I am very pleased that I share my name with Marquis de Sade's fictional creation who was the embodiment of vice.'

Trudie's mind is not on literature. Her mind is on the gun, the Desert Eagle, cold and heavy, still cradled in her hands. Her finger on the trigger; the ultimate act of rebellion; the irrevocable act that would sever her from her past life; sever her from the normal run of society. Her mind is already adjusting to the idea. She just has to let go, and follow this girl Juliette to her mysterious leader Vautrin, and enter a new plane of existence. Life outside of life, with a completely new set of rules.

Eight O' Clock.

The lights are on in the house of Simon Hammond, Martin's older brother; the street is quiet in the gloaming. Trudie pauses at the end of the garden path.

Her bag packed, she had left her home with the girl Juliette. Her parents will have arrived home to find her absent, but probably won't start worrying until much later in the evening. Juliette had taken her across town to an expensive restaurant, and over a meal had told her more about Vautrin, the other girls, the organisation. And now she has returned to put a full-stop to the current chapter of her life, in order to begin a new one.

To clean up house.

The front door is unlocked for her as usual. She walks in, through the hall, into the living room.

They are listening to Mozart's *The Marriage of Figaro*. Strange that it should be this particular opera, tonight of all nights. This same piece of music had been playing that day in the school music room; the day that had marked the beginning of all this.

Martin lies stretched out on the sofa, hands behind his head, a picture of nonchalance; Lucy Smith and Pattie Price sit on the floor, sharing an ash-tray for their cigarettes; Davey Sedgewick occupies the arm-chair, reading while he listens.

Martin looks up at Trudie with studied disinterest. 'She arrives. Your client tonight seems a tad bashful, so be nice to him. He preferred to wait up there,' indicating the room above.

'He's going to be disappointed,' says Trudie calmly. 'I'm resigning.'

Lucy bridles at this impudence. 'Like fuck you are!'

Davey surfaces from his book. 'Looks like you're going to have to discipline the girl again, Martin.'

'Yeah, rape some sense into her,' concurs the charming Lucy.

Trudie reaches behind her back and produces the automatic from its uncomfortable lodging. She releases the safety.

Martin springs from the sofa.

'You have *got* to be kidding.'

'That's right,' says Trudie. 'And I guess the joke's on you.'

One gentle squeeze of the trigger and Martin's head splatters all over the place. Screaming, the girls bound to their feet. The second noisy bullet disintegrates Pattie Price's chest. Meanwhile, Davey has dived behind the armchair. Trudie just fires through it, precipitating a geyser of blood and upholstery.

That just leaves Lucy. Her former friend stands there, frozen with shock, shaking her head and whimpering.

'Please…'

Trudie briefly considers making a righteous speech about friendship betrayed—but then decides she can't be bothered and just blows the girl's head off.

Imperturbable Mozart plays on.

She passes back into the hallway. The slamming of a door upstairs reminds her there is still one person in the house. She walks purposefully up to the spare bedroom, a room she has become very accustomed to over the past few months. A quaking figure crouches in the far corner in the space between the bed and the wall. Trudie walks round to see who it is. A black boy, hands over his bowed head. She thinks she knows who it is.

'Look up.'

The crouching boy continues to whimper.

'Look. Up.'

He looks up. It is Craig Denver.

'Well well, so it's you,' says Trudie. 'So this is what all that talk about "being on my side" was leading up to.'

'I *am* on your side!' blubbers Craig, tears streaming down his face. 'I'm not like the others! I swear to God I'm not!'

'Right. So you were here to rescue me, were you? Coming to take me away from all this? Or were you just going to keep coming back for more? Giving me pep-talks while you were getting your money's worth?'

She levels the gun.

'Please don't kill me…'

The weapon roars.

Chapter Two
A Shady Customer

You can't help but notice the woman at the bar. A six-foot Juno dressed in black, the lines of both her face and her body are painted with a bold stroke. Her hair is black, cut short. Beneath the broken fringe a pair of frank grey eyes, a perfect Greek nose, a wide, full-lipped mouth, and a resolute jaw. A polo-neck sweater and faux-leather trousers hug the curves of her stately figure— from the regal neck and broad shoulders, plunging over the large breasts, following the torso clinging lovingly to the curves of powerful hips, ripe buttocks (which you can't see right now), and heavy pudendum (which you can); and down the long, healthy legs, terminating in two solid, substantial feet, boot-shod. (Small feet would have been an inadequate platform for this particular work of art.)

'The trouble with tall women is you never know what you're getting up to!' someone once said. (One of those jokes which sounds funny enough, but when you come to analyse it doesn't really mean anything.)

The imposing physical presence of this woman is amplified by a compelling aura. Intelligence, kindness and good-nature, confidence, self-sufficiency, boundless animal spirits: all of these things—everything you could want of an ideal friend, lover, or saviour—gloriously combine themselves in her pheromonal orbit.

Sipping a Southern Comfort held in a hand large and long-fingered, graceful and immaculate, the woman scans the saloon before her. Autumnal colours, muted lighting, low armchairs that you sink into, tables of the same chrome and glass of the bar and its fittings. The night is still young, and apart from herself there are just a couple of businessmen, poring over statistics; a group of aging socialites, bedecked with jewels and warpaint; and some noisy Finnish tourists, already half-seas over.

The woman drains her glass, strikes off purposefully across the room.

One of the business men looks up from his tablet.

'That's her!'

'Who's her?' asks his friend, an American.

'That woman!'

Following his friend's gaze, he sees Dodo's rear-view moving towards the exit.

'Yeah, and who is she?'

'Well, you might not know her over the pond, but she's Dodo Dupont, the TV psychologist. You see her on the box, setting the world to rights in these documentaries she does.'

The man watches her out of sight. 'Well whoever she is, she's got a hell of an ass on her.'

Dodo Dupont (For it is indeed her) crosses the lobby, takes the lift to the second floor. (Or the third floor to the appreciative

American in the saloon.) The same autumnal shades and subdued lighting prevail in the airy corridors of the hotel. Scanning the door numbers as she walks along, she stops before the one she is looking for, smiles up at where she surmises the camera will be, and walks straight in.

The suite, spacious, well-appointed, has but one occupant. Dressed in a chocolate brown suit, he slouches in a chair, feet up on the table beside an open laptop. A young forty, he has a handsome smiling face; affable hazel eyes, dark brown hair parted on the left. When he stands—and even when he doesn't—he measures three inches shorter than his companion. His name is Mark Hunter. He greets Dodo with a friendly: 'Good evening.'

Dodo scans the opulent room. 'Hello. You've certainly gone up in the world,' she remarks. Her voice is rich and warm.

'Yes, it is a bit roomier than my usual pad,' concedes Mark. 'Help yourself to a sandwich,' indicating an artistically arranged plate of those comestibles on the table.

'Ta.' Dodo picks one up, inspects the contents.

'So, what's the situation?' asks Dodo with her mouth full. (Speaking with a full mouth is something only elegant women such as Dodo Dupont can get away with without it seeming ill-mannered.)

Mark indicates the lap-top screen, showing a view of the corridor outside.

'Our first party has arrived, but not the second. Baxter, along with his bodyguard Jansen. So, we have the seller and we're waiting for the buyer.'

'Ah, the mysterious Mr Vautrin. When do you expect him?'

'I'm expecting him imminently. The meeting was scheduled for eight, so it looks like he's being fashionably late.'

'You still don't know what Baxter's selling?'

'Nope, but it's obviously too big a consignment to take up to the hotel suite. Baxter has a van in the basement car-park. Under surveillance, of course.'

'And the consignment is going to be armaments of some description?'

'Well, that's Baxter's business,' says Mark. 'Due to a convenient legal loophole, he can shift that kind of stuff under the banner of "security devices".'

'All in the name of Free Trade,' says Dodo. 'And, you know, it's the same establishment you work for that allows these things.'

'I don't make the rules, you know,' returns Mark. 'But yes, I do work for Whitehall, so I'm a cog in the Establishment machine. But then you yourself, Dodo, are a media whore, and unforgivably wealthy to boot. Yes… to the anti-establishment brigade, we're both "the enemy." Funny, that.'

There is a jug of coffee at hand; Mark pours himself a fresh cup.

'Good coffee they do in this place. None of your instant muck.'

'The "instant muck" is all you usually drink,' points out Dodo.

'That's because I'm an underpaid cog in the machine,' replies Mark.

'So, this Vautrin,' says Dodo, getting back to the subject in hand. 'I'm assuming he's not authorised to buy these "security devices", right?'

'Right. We've no idea who he is, but we know he's not representing any country. So yes, this is going to be an illegal deal, whatever's being sold. I've waited a long time to catch Baxter in a deal like this. He's an unpleasant piece of work and I'm looking forward to collaring him.'

'And this Vautrin is the one behind those bizarre terrorist incidents. At least, that's your theory, isn't it?'

'Yes, I'm sure it must be him. It's someone new who carried out those attacks; none of the usual suspects; and he's the new name in town. You know what happened—first we had that BBC executive: his front door booby-trapped so that when he put the key in the lock it gave him a massive electric shock; and then there was Chambers, the cabinet minister: it was no accident that spread glue over that zebra crossing and released the hand-brake on the steam-roller.

'And now we hear stories of this fellow called Vautrin and his mysterious organisation. He appears out of nowhere; and nobody knows a thing about him. I'll consider this sting operation worthwhile just to get a look at the fellow. I don't know who he is, what his agenda is, his resources, his country of origin; anything.'

'Mm. And if he's buying munitions from Baxter, it looks like he's planning to step up his campaign.'

'Yes it does.'

Dodo perches herself on the arm of a sofa. 'Life is never dull around you, Mark sweetheart.'

'You wouldn't help me out on my cases if they were dull, would you?' challenges Mark. 'Not that I'm complaining. You know I always appreciate your help. Things always seem to work out in the end when you're around.'

'Glad to be of assistance. But,' Dodo reminds him; 'don't forget the Peltdown Vale Incident. That one wasn't so successful.'

'Ah yes, the Disappearing Building. We never did find it, did we?'

Dodo smiles. 'And there are all those people who think that TV series *Spooks* is a realistic portrayal of life in the Intelligence business.'

Mark sighs. 'Yes, it does lack that air of verisimilitude. My life is more like *Voyage to the Bottom of the Sea.*'

Two figures appear on Mark's laptop screen.

He sits up. 'Hello, we've got something.'

Dodo joins him. 'It might not be them.'

'It has to be. This suite and Baxter's are the only ones occupied in this wing.'

The camera shows a fish-eyed lens view of a man and a girl walking down the corridor towards them. The man carries a briefcase. As they pass beneath the camera, the man, eyes hidden behind dark glasses, looks up and smiles.

They move on.

'Did you see that?' explodes Mark. 'Smiling straight up at the camera! He knows we're here and he wants us to know it!'

'Then hadn't you better move in now? He'll warn Baxter that

he's under surveillance.'

'No…' says Mark. 'I want to see which way they jump. If he knows we're here, why is he even going through with the meeting…? He's up to something…'

'We know he's eccentric, don't we?'

'He is that. What I don't get is why I haven't heard anything from the basement. I was sure they would have arrived in a vehicle of some kind, to take away the shipment.'

He puts on a radio headset.

'Collins? This is Hunter. Has another van arrived down there?'

Dodo puts her ear to Mark's to listen in.

'Nope. Two cars have left, none have arrived since my last report,' replies the voice.

'And Baxter's van?'

'Hasn't moved. Two men inside. One of them got out to stretch his legs and went back in.'

'And you haven't seen anyone else loitering around the car-park?'

'No. Only a couple of girls.'

'Only a couple of—then there *is* someone else!' Mark takes off the head-set. 'Dodo love, would you go downstairs and take charge of those idiots? I don't want to have to write letters of condolence to their mothers.'

'On my way.'

Exit Dodo, briskly.

Baxter doesn't know what to make of Vautrin.

He sits on the sofa facing Baxter, the coffee table between them. Vautrin appears about thirty years of age, dark hair with a low fringe, side-burns down to the angle of his jaw. Oblong-lensed tinted glasses conceal his eyes, his expression is unreadable. Cords, a red polo-neck sweater, and a wide-lapelled jacket complete his retro aesthetic.

His associate, the girl, remains standing. She has a sulky expression; short hair, dark with bright red highlights, fringe coming down over her left eye. She wears an army-surplus shirt, leggings, Doc Martens. The counterculture look is emphasised by the number of piercings: nose, lower lip, several in each ear.

Baxter sips his champagne. Dressed in an immaculate suit, a man in his fifties of slender build, white-haired, effete. His face, although furrowed with age, exhibits a softness which is somehow repellent.

On Baxter's left stands his bodyguard Jansen, a thin-lipped, dead-eyed automaton.

'I always like to conduct my business in opulent surroundings,' says Baxter. 'It's so much more civilised.'

'The actual transfer of goods will still have to take place down in the car-park,' points out Vautrin. 'And you realise they have CCTV down there?'

Baxter waves a dismissive hand. 'I've bribed the security staff. The cameras for the basement will have developed a fault. When you have money, Mr Vautrin, you can always get what you want. Speaking of money…?'

Vautrin slides his brief-case across the table. Baxter slips the catches, opens it, making a cursory inspection of the wads of fresh banknotes.

'Quite satisfactory. Are you quite sure you won't have any champagne? It really is excellent.'

'No, thank you.'

'And the "goods" you are purchasing: they are not for domestic use? I will sell to almost anyone, but only for export. I draw the line at muddying my own back-yard.'

'You don't have to worry there. The merchandise is for some little project on the continent I have planned,' says Vautrin mendaciously.

'Good.' Baxter pours himself another glass. 'I can tell that you are a man of means, Mr Vautrin; a man who knows what he wants. I am much the same. Yes, when you have money, you have power, and you can achieve anything. If anybody stands in your way, threats, bribery or blackmail will bring them into line. In the rare cases where none of these are efficacious, you simply eliminate the stubborn obstacle, and the person who takes their place is bound to be more amenable. Money is power, which is why the main Power in this world will always be big business; the controllers of the economy control the media, the wars; everything. The executive of a South American banana corporation has more clout than any transient US president. Governments and regimes rise and fall, but corporations will always thrive. We are the people with the true power, and when you have power, you have the luxury to take whatever you want. Anything at all. To give you an example pertaining to myself: there was an employee of mine; let's call him an accountant. There were some irregularities. They were brought to my attention. I threatened to ruin the man. He begged for clemency. This man had a son; a delightful boy of ten. I'd had my eye on him for some time. The use of his child was the price he paid in return for his reputation and livelihood. Oh, you should have seen the man cry! He pleaded with me to take anything else, but I insisted and of course he finally caved in. I knew he would; most people will sacrifice anything for financial security and an untarnished reputation.'

Baxter looks at Vautrin. The face is unchanged; no sign of approbation or concurrence.

A pause, uncomfortable.

Then Vautrin speaks. 'I've listened to your philosophy with great interest, Mr Baxter,' he says. 'Forgive me for taking you up on one point, but you say that money means power—and I'll grant that—but power doesn't make a weak man strong, and you are a weak man, Mr Baxter, a very weak man. Your father, a much stronger man than you, founded the Baxter munitions empire, you simply inherited it. You did not climb your own way to power by exerting your will over others; it was simply handed to you on a plate. You exercise authority, but yet you have no-one's respect. Your employees are all obliged to obey you, but they are secretly contemptuous of you for not being half the man your father was—and deep down you know this. Even your wife and teenage daughters despise you; they are well aware of your illicit sexual preferences, and they only put up with you because you are a convenient source of money to them. You desperately employ any means you can to bolster your fragile ego. The story of that child you have just favoured me with: boasting of how you took him from his parents; vain self-aggrandisement. Did you really think I would be impressed? No, you're a sad, puny little man, Mr Baxter, and I strongly object to you suggesting that we are in any way alike.'

During this speech Baxter's face has grown redder and redder. Now, he literally trembles with shame and impotent rage, almost in tears.

Petulantly, he pushes the brief-case back across the table, a child rejecting a toy.

'Take your money!' he screeches. 'The deal's off! Off, do you hear? You'll get nothing from me! Nothing!'

Vautrin just smiles.

'Oh, I'll get what I want,' he says. 'And there's one more thing you might like to know: in spite of your much-vaunted precautions, this meeting of ours is being staked-out by MI5. One of their top agents is in the suite just down the hall, and he has operatives stationed all over the hotel. I'm sure they've been waiting for years just to catch you red-handed in an illegal transaction, Mr Baxter.'

Baxter's rage turns to fear.

'You're lying!'

'I'm afraid not.'

'But it can't be. I—'

'Please don't concern yourself about MI5, Mr Baxter,' interrupts Vautrin. 'I can assure you they will not be a problem for you. Rachel.'

At this signal, an automatic appears in the girl's hand. The gun roars and takes off the top of Jansen's head, interrupting him in the act of drawing his own weapon.

She turns the gun to cover Baxter. He springs to his feet.

'No!' pleads Baxter.

'Good-bye, Mr Baxter. This concludes our business deal. I'm obliged to you.'

Rachel fires again and Baxter drops back onto the sofa, his silk shirt soaked red.

'Good work, Rachel,' says Vautrin, taking up the brief-case. 'Now we've got to move fast.'

They make for the door.

'I'm sending Dodo Dupont down to join you.'

'Oh good,' says Mike Collins when Hunter has signed off. 'Coming to teach us our job, is she? I mean obviously a TV psychologist knows more about the spy business than us mere trained agents.'

'I like her,' replies Daisy Fontaine.

The two agents sit in the back of the surveillance van, faces illuminated by a monitor, which, fed by a camera on the roof, provides them with a clear view of the target van across the car-park. Collins is square-jawed, mid-forties in age, hair grizzled; his companion a bright-eyed, elfin girl, with tousled hair cut short.

Collins snorts.

'Suit yourself. Personally, I don't go for posh birds.'

'She's not that posh,' defends Fontaine, 'Upper middle-class, I'd say.'

'Posh enough.'

Fontaine sips her Thermos coffee.

'Is there anything between them, then?' she wonders.

'Between who?'

'Hunter and Dodo.'

Collins snorts again.

'Them? No way. She's got a girlfriend for one thing. That Jap photographer bird.'

'Oh yeah? The one who photographed her for that book?'

'Yeah, her. And as for our Great White Chief, I reckon he's either impotent or gay.'

This stimulating speculation is cut short by a rap on the back doors of the van, which then open, admitting Dodo.

'Hullo, you two. Anything new?'

Fontaine answers 'Nope. The two men are sitting in the van.

No-one's come near them. So, what's happening upstairs?'

'A man and a girl—we're pretty sure the man is Vautrin—have arrived at the meeting. Mark's edgy; he thinks Vautrin knows we're here. And it doesn't look like he's brought a van to take away whatever he's supposed to be buying.' She looks at the monitor. 'What about those two girls you saw?'

'We haven't seen them again. They've probably gone.'

'Don't be too sure of that.'

Collins makes his favourite noise. 'They can't be anything to do with this; they were just kids.'

'The girl with Vautrin upstairs didn't look much more than a kid, either. Can you describe the two you saw?'

'One was in school clothes,' says Fontaine. 'Hair like yours and wearing glasses. The other one had a military look: camouflage trousers, khaki vest.'

'Hm. Neither of them is the girl we saw with Vautrin. They could be associates, though. We need to keep an eye out for those two.'

The radio buzzes.

'Collins?' comes Mark's voice. 'Vautrin and the girl are on their way down. There's been an incident up here. I think they're going to take the van by force. Stop them.'

'Right,' says Dodo, crisply. 'I'll try and intercept them. You two take the van and block the other one from leaving.'

'Right.'

They spill out of the van. Collins and Fontaine get into the cab, and Dodo strikes off across the car-park, weaving between the cars, keeping low. She hears the van behind her move off. The target van comes into sight. At that very moment two girls break from cover and close in on the van: a girl in combat trousers and khaki vest and a girl in school uniform, just as Fontaine described. Separating, the two girls make for the cab doors. From her position, Dodo can only see the combat girl; she has cropped blonde hair and a serious expression. The girl wrenches open the passenger side door, pulls out the surprised occupant, pins him to the ground and thrusts a knife into his chest; all in one neat movement. A loud gunshot alerts Dodo that the driver has also been dealt with. Simultaneously, the surveillance van pulls up with a squeal of brakes, boxing the other van in. School uniform fires at the van. Daisy Fontaine appears from the blind-side of the van and returns fire.

'Forget it!' yells the combat girl. 'Run!'

Dodo runs to intercept the girl. Seeing this new threat, the girl's eyes narrow and she lunges at Dodo with the knife. Dodo side-steps, kicks out, the knife is sent flying. Backing off, the girl aims a flying kick at Dodo with a sneakered foot. Dodo catches her ankle, twists. The girl falls, rolls with it, recovers, and runs.

Dodo gives chase. A car appears, swerving recklessly, headlights blazing. The fleeing girl runs towards it. The car brakes suddenly, a rear door opens, the girl dives in. The vehicle lurches forward, bearing down on Dodo. She dives out of its path. The car sweeps past, heading for the exit ramp.

Then it is gone. Silence returns.

Heaving a sigh, Dodo returns to the two vans, where Mark has joined Fontaine and Collins.

'They got away in a car,' she reports.

'Hm,' says Mark. 'They must have parked it here hours ago, just in case. They had all their bases covered, these people.'

'What happened upstairs?'

'Baxter and his bodyguard were both shot. Then Vautrin and the girl made a swift exit.'

'I wonder what they disagreed about…'

'Maybe nothing. Maybe Vautrin just planned to kill Baxter all along. It seems likely, when you consider the fact they never brought a van of their own to transfer the goods. Speaking of which—'

Mark opens the rear doors of the van. It is loaded with wooden crates.

'Open this one, Daisy.'

Producing her clasp-knife, Fontaine prises open the lid of one small crate. Mark brushes aside the usual straw padding. He whistles.

'What is it?' Dodo wants to know.

'Semtex. Enough to level a building. Now this is something you *cannot* get away with selling as a "security device".'

'Well at least Vautrin didn't get it.'

'Yes, but he got away, though. And if wants the stuff that badly, he'll find another seller.'

'That reminds me,' says Dodo. 'The girl I fought dropped her knife over there. You should get some prints off it.'

'Any leads are welcome.'

They move to retrieve the knife.

Chapter Three
'You're Fired!'

'...we cross live to our on-the-spot reporter, John Ashton, who will now repeat to you everything I've already told you. Isn't that right, John?'

'Absolutely right, Kate. I have absolutely no additional information to offer at this moment; I can only repeat—in my own words—everything you have already told the viewers.'

'So this live link is really a complete waste of time, isn't it, John?'

'It certainly is, Kate, just as you say. A complete waste of time.'

'And on top of that, you're not even a very good broadcaster, are you, John?'

'No, I am not a good broadcaster. You are absolutely right once again, Kate. I am, at best, only a mediocre television news reporter.'

'And I've heard that you're shit in bed as well, John, aren't you?'

'I'm sorry; I don't I think caught that last question…'

'Oh I think you did, John. I have it on very good authority that you're completely useless in bed.'

'Well, Kate, I don't know where you heard that one, but I feel I ought to—'

'It was your wife, John. It was your wife who told me.'

'I see. I didn't realise you knew my wife…'

'I know her intimately, John. Very intimately. And so does everyone else here on the BBC News team…'

'…Hunter here. Anything happening?'

'Yes, it's started raining.'

'I don't want a weather report, Daisy. Is anything happening at the house?'

'Nope. No-one has gone in, no-one has come out. No sign of movement.'

'Okay. Keep me posted…'

'…Hunter? We've got something! Three girls have just left the house, heading off on foot.'

'Yes, I've got them on the monitor. Zoom in closer… That blonde in the school uniform; I'm sure I've seen her somewhere… The one in the camouflage trousers; that's the knife girl you tangled with, isn't it, Dodo?'

'Yep. That's her.'

'And another girl in school clothes… Fontaine, you and Collins follow them. Group B will keep the house under surveillance…'

'…group of men boycotting the opening of the exhibition of famed Japanese photographer Mayumi Takahashi's erotic photography. We talked to their spokesman—'

'Spokes*person* please. We prefer non-gender-specific terms. We are Men Against Sexist Shit, and we are protesting against this degrading display of lewd photography, which objectifies women, reducing them to the status of lumps of meat for misogynistic males to fantasize over.'

'And yet the photographer in this case is a woman.'

'Yes, I am!'

'…And she's here with us now. Thank you for joining us, Miss Takahashi.'

'Yes.'

'What is your reaction to these men's comments?'

'Yes. I don't like what they say. My pictures very nice. Not degrading.'

'So you deny that this kind of photography objectifies women?'

'Yes. Objectify? What's wrong with objectify? Objectify is a good thing if it looks cute.'

'But then, why only women? Why do you never photograph male subjects? That's what some critics are asking.'

'Yes. I'm not interested in men. They don't pose so good. A lady, she can make any pose, and she looks cute. But if man gets in same pose, he just looks silly.'

'That just proves that women shouldn't pose like that either!'

'This is not so. Ladies are cuter, that's all. You Shitty Sex Men should go home now. You making an exhibition outside my exhibition…'

'…Collins here. They've gone into an underground garage. Fontaine's tailing them on foot…'

'They must be either using the garage as a shortcut to somewhere or they've got wheels…'

'…Fontaine here. The girls are getting into a red sedan.'

'Get back to Collins. When they come out, I want you to follow them.'

'But Guv, those girls have gotta be too young to have driving licences; couldn't we just nab them for—'

'No we can't, Collins. I'm more interested in where they're going than where they learned to drive…'

'…still with them, heading out of Hackney…'

'…City Centre. Christ knows where they're going; and the traffic's abysmal…'

'…what crashed into the Daedalus Crater on the far side of the moon. The official report tells us that it was a meteor, but some believe it may have been an alien spacecraft of some kind. Joining me in the studio are leading physicist Professor Phoebe Fleetwood—'

'Fifi, darling. Call me Fifi.'

'—Professor *Fifi* Fleetwood, and online conspiracy theorist Jason Sunday. If I can speak to you first, Jason; do you have any real facts to support your belief that it was actually an extra-terrestrial space vehicle which struck the moon?'

'I don't deal in facts, I deal in theories. The meteor is just a cover-story. It was a UFO which crashed into the moon. And some of the crew were still alive. These aliens have been brought down to Earth and are now being interrogated by the CIA.'

'Poppycock! Nothing could have survived a collision with the moon at the speed that thing was travelling. And it *was* a meteor. Astronomers were tracking its course for a long time and they had positively identified it as a meteor. So there!'

'But if that's the case, Professor, why has so little information been released with regard to the composition of this meteor?'

'Yeah! They're probably covering it up cuz it contained alien microbes or something!'

'Make your mind up, silly boy! Just now you said it was little grey men on a flying saucer, and now you're talking about microbes!'

'But this does sound more plausible, wouldn't you say, Professor? Similar discoveries have been made before.'

'Well yes, that's true enough. Perhaps they *have* found some bacteriological material in this meteor, or perhaps the meteor itself has some unknown elements in its composition…'

'…We've lost them, Guv.'

'You idiots! Where are you?'

'Canary Wharf.'
'Well keep looking for that car...!'

'...Victoria Bradley, the latest victim of the serial killer who has become known as "the Carpenter," on account of his use of a claw-hammer to smash the skulls of his victims. All of the victims have been young women. Police say the killer is an opportunist and are urging women in the North London area not to walk the streets alone after dark...'

'...Fontaine here. It's total chaos! They burst into Alan Sucrose's boardroom and opened up with machine guns!'
'Is Sucrose dead?'
'Everyone in the bloody room is dead, including a BBC film crew!'
'A *film* crew?'
'Yep. They were filming *The Apprentice*...'

'...breaking news. We are just receiving reports that business tycoon and television personality Sir Alan Sucrose has been murdered...'

Chapter Four
A Chapter Which Doesn't End in Shooting

A naked Dodo Dupont, bedroom scented, answers the door to Mark Hunter. Briefcase in hand, Mark is dressed in his usual chocolate-brown suit. Dodo has never seen him in anything else, and has long suspected him of having a wardrobe full of identical suits.

'Hullo,' she says. 'Step inside.'

Admiring the smooth-sculpted abundance of her buttocks,

Mark follows Dodo into the tennis-court sized living room of her penthouse apartment. A yawning Mayumi Takahashi emerges from the bedroom, in the same attire Dodo, with the addition of glasses.

'Morning, ladies,' says Mark cheerfully. 'Don't get dressed on my account.'

'We won't.'

'Just don't start love-making in front of me. Remember: it's not a male spectator-sport.'

'You're funny,' giggles Mayumi.

Acknowledging the compliment with a nod and a smile, Mark drops into his usual sofa, places the briefcase on the glass-topped coffee table.

'Coffee?' asks Dodo.

'I would love some, thank you.'

Dodo repairs to the kitchen.

The heiress's apartment is characteristically opulent, sporting a modernist style of furniture, a pastel colour scheme. The outer wall, glazed from floor to ceiling, offers an impressive view of the Central London skyline (and for that matter offers the Central London skyline an impressive view of Dodo's apartment.)

Mayumi seats herself on the sofa facing Mark. Of average Japanese height, her body is both curvy and petite, and she wears her raven hair very long, parted in the centre. Taking a packet of cigarettes from the coffee table, she extracts one, lights it.

Mark produces his own cigarette case from his breast pocket and follows her example.

'How's the exhibition going?' inquires Mark, exhaling smoke.

'It has been well-attended, thank you.'

'Glad to hear it.'

Mayumi is a photographer of great renown. From her beginnings as a junior idol photographer, she has risen to prominence in her own country, praised as a highly skilled erotic photographer. And it was her art that first brought Mayumi into contact with Dodo Dupont. Having discovered her work, Dodo was eager to film a documentary about Mayumi and her photography. Mayumi consented to the request, Dodo and her crew flew out to Japan, and the two women very quickly fell in love.

And the first fruits of this union were *Juno*, Dodo's first nude photobook, and Mayumi's first non-Japanese subject.

Dodo returns with the coffee tray.

'Filter coffee,' she says. 'None of your instant muck.'

She sets the tray down on the table, seats herself on the sofa next to Mayumi, and pours for everyone. Mark accepts his cup.

He sips his coffee appreciatively.

'Perfect as always,' he declares.

'Apart from my coffee, what brings you here this fine morning?' asks Dodo, lighting her own cigarette. 'I'm guessing there's news of some kind in that briefcase of yours?'

'Oh yes, my briefcase is brimming over with news,' confirms Mark. He takes up the case, places it on his knees, and flips the catches. He extracts a sheaf of documents.

'The Vautrin business. Some leads and some positive IDs.' He places a photographic blow-up on the table next to the coffee tray. 'Number one: the blonde girl in the school uniform, photographed outside the house in Hackney. I thought at the time I'd seen her somewhere before. She's Juliette Wainwright, only child of billionaire financier Rufus Wainwright, head of the Wainwright Corporation. Juliette is currently attending—or is *supposed* to be attending—Cynthia Imrie's exclusive girls' school in the Swiss Alps. It's their uniform she's wearing.'

'You said you recognised her; have you met the girl, then?'

'No, I've never met the girl,' says Mark. 'I must have just seen her picture somewhere.'

'What about the father? What sort of man is he?'

'About as unscrupulous and ruthless as they get. But for all that, I can't see him financing domestic terrorism.'

'Not even to please his little girl?'

'Not even for that.'

'So, what are your plans regarding Little Miss Wainwright?'

'First, check out the school; see if she's still attending, and if not, how, why and when she left it. And second, speak to her father. See what he knows.'

'Are you going to mention that she murdered Sir Alan Sucrose?'

'Nope. I intend to keep that little tit-bit to myself. I want to get an idea of how much *he* knows, first.'

Mayumi listens to this conference without speaking, smoking placidly, idly fingering her long pubic curls.

Mark places a second blow-up on the coffee table, pauses to sip his coffee.

'Ah. The knife girl,' murmurs Dodo. 'The one I briefly tangled with.'

'Yes, we got *her* records from Interpol. The finger-prints on the knife confirmed her ID. Name: Gina Santella, Italian by nationality and a former assassin for the Mafia.'

'An assassin for the Mafia. You're kidding! She can't be more than sixteen.'

'She isn't. Her story's an interesting one: A Mafia don named Santella discovered her as a small child, so the story goes; he'd had her parents killed or something. Anyway, acting on a whim it seems, he decided to "adopt" the orphan. He called her his niece, and he brought her up to be a killer. A knife is her weapon of choice; hence her attacking you with one. Interpol say she dropped completely out of sight a few months ago. Don Santella was eliminated in a re-shuffling of the Mafia hierarchy; it was assumed Gina had ended up an incidental victim. Her body was never found, but then the Mafia are experts at making people disappear without a trace. But now she turns up here in England, very much alive, and working for our man Vautrin.'

'The schoolgirl daughter of a billionaire. A Mafia knife-woman. Where's the connection?'

'Apparently none. But then we have these…'

Three more blow-ups.

'We haven't been able to identify these three yet. The girl who was with Vautrin when he met Baxter. The other girl in the hotel car-park. And this one, the third girl who left the safe-house in

Hackney.'

'All girls,' says Dodo. 'And young girls at that.'

'Yes, that seems to be the pattern. Maybe Vautrin's a what-do-you-call-it; someone who likes teenage girls…?'

'An ephebophile,' supplies Dodo.

'That's the bunny.'

'Five young girls, controlled by this man Vautrin. And there could be more, I'm thinking.'

'Yes, I'm thinking that too. But where does he get them? Did they find Vautrin; or did he find them?'

'Maybe he's recruiting over the internet,' suggests Dodo.

'We've been checking that possibility,' replies Mark. 'We haven't found anything so far…'   Dodo stretches luxuriantly, the rich growths of hair beneath her arms forming a triangle with the equally dense growth of her *mons veneris*.

'As for these three girls,' proceeds Mark, tapping the table-top. 'Identifying them may take time, especially as we have no intention of making any of this public as yet. This girl, the one in the glasses is wearing school uniform; we might be able to trace her through that. But it's a pretty nondescript uniform, no identifying marks visible in the pictures we've got. Ditto the third girl from the Hackney safe-house. And as I said, the girl who was with Vautrin at the meeting with Baxter we haven't been able to identify, either.'

'What about Vautrin himself? You got his picture too.'

'And a fat lot of good it's done us. There's nobody on our files who matches his appearance; nor is there with Interpol. We don't even know his nationality, and I'm willing to bet his name's an alias. You know your Balzac. "Vautrin" was the name of his Machiavellian anti-hero, one of his most well-known characters.'

'Yes, and I know my French, as well. The name doesn't really exist. The closest you'll find is "Vautrain".'

'Well, regardless of the name, we've now got his picture, but as I said, so far it hasn't done us any good. I had hopes that some of my informants might recognise him, that perhaps he's been in circulation under another alias. But no such luck. He seems to have just suddenly appeared out of nowhere. It's like he dropped from the sky.'

'So, that's all you've got so far?' asks Dodo. 'Or is there anything else?'

Mark smiles. 'Oh yes. There's one more thing. We searched the safe-house in Hackney. The girls didn't return there after the Canary Wharf bloodbath. They either knew we had the place staked out, or else they realised they were being followed. As I say, we went over the place. It was clearly not their permanent residence. There was food, bedding; not much in the way of equipment, apart from spare ammunition. But we did find this.'

Smiling, he hands a small business card to Dodo. She reads:

SEA

The SOCIETY of EVIL ACTIONS

Dodo laughs, half incredulous. 'Society of Evil Actions? Is this for real?'

'I know what you mean. I suspect that the childish sounding name is entirely intentional. I mean, if you think about it, there's been a childish element in a lot of these people's crimes, hasn't there? Booby-trapped doors, zebra crossings smeared with glue...'

Dodo passes the card back to Mark. 'And this was just lying around in that abandoned house in Hackney?'

'Yes, and lying there very conspicuously. I'm inclined to think the card was left intentionally for us to find. They're playing games with us, Vautrin and those girls. I'm sure of it.'

'Are you meant to say the word "sea" or pronounce the initials?' wonders Dodo.

'I think you're supposed to pronounce the initials. *The* SEA. Like CIA or IRA.'

Mayumi rises from her seat.

'Excuse me,' she says politely. 'I need to have a shit.'

'Oh. Right-o,' says Mark, for want of anything better.

Mayumi crosses the room to the bathroom.

'I've been thinking about that name,' resumes Mark. 'Society of Evil Actions. If the name means anything, it suggests that they commit evil acts just for the sake of it, and not with any objective in mind. That being the case, they've neatly eliminated the old dilemma of whether the ends justify the means, by just not *having* any ends.'

'And there's no pattern to their targets, is there? Business-men, politicians, media figures.'

'Yes, it seems that anyone is fair game. Anyone who's more or less a public figure.'

'And now these maniacs are after high explosives.'

'Yes... If they start a bombing campaign, God knows who they'll target. It's just as likely to be Buckingham Palace or the BBC Television Centre.'

'Well, we stopped them from getting that last lot of explosives. I'm guessing you haven't heard of them approaching any other sources to get the stuff?'

'Not so far. We've got our collective ear to the ground. And remember, there wasn't just the Semtex in that van: there were also automatic rifles, ammunition, hand grenades. It seems like these girls want to seriously arm themselves.'

Mark pauses to extinguish his cigarette. And then:

'According to my informants, there may be more of those safe-houses like the one in Hackney. That's another thing we're looking out for.'

'If they've set up temporary bases in London, that would imply that their main base of operations, if they have one, is somewhere outside the city.'

'Yes... Do they like to keep us on our toes by changing their headquarters all the time? Or have they got a main base somewhere else? I'm inclined to think the latter. I think they've got some nice, cosy hideaway, out in the country, perhaps...'

Mayumi returns from a satisfactory bowel movement, resets herself.

'So, as things stand, my main hope of collaring Vautrin is to be there wherever and whenever he tries to buy more guns and explosives to replace that first lot.'

'And apart from that,' says Dodo, 'your only real lead is the Wainwright girl.'

'Yes, and that's my next destination,' says Mark, snapping shut the catches of his briefcase. He smiles at the two women, one tall, one small, seated side-by-side on the sofa. 'So, as much as I hate to leave my two favourite people in the world, I need to be getting a move on. I have a plane to catch!'

In spite of the lousy pay, the instant coffee, and the awful knowledge that you're just a cog in the machinery of the state, working for MI5 can have its perks. An all-expenses paid trip to Switzerland would be one such bonus. An all-expenses paid trip to Switzerland to check out a girls' boarding school would be an even bigger one!

Mark Hunter steers his hired car through the gates into the grounds of the famed Imrie Academy. A sweeping driveway brings him to the imposing edifice of the school building. A slight haze makes the mountain backdrop look misty, insubstantial.

Stepping out of his car, Mark looks out across the grounds where some girls are playing hockey. Or rather, where they are not playing hockey. The girls are sitting on the hockey field, sticks discarded, gossiping and smoking cigarettes.

Cynthia Imrie's Academy for Young Ladies is an exclusive establishment. Only the very rich and powerful send their daughters here: film stars, aristocrats, business moguls, even royalty. If you are spoilt and rolling in money you are welcome to enrol at the Imrie Academy.

Mark proceeds into the building. His visit here is unannounced, intentionally so. He has wanted to give Juliette Wainwright no opportunity to make herself scarce—if she is in fact still here at all. He crosses a spacious lobby to the reception desk.

Can he see the headmistress?

No, he cannot. Not without an appointment.

He is with British Intelligence.
That is very nice for him.
It is rather urgent.
Urgent or not, he needs to have an appointment.
Can he make an appointment now?
He can.
Would immediately be convenient?
Yes, that would be fine. Straight down the corridor, and it's the last door on the right.

And so, Mark finds himself in the office of Cynthia Imrie, headmistress and proprietress of the school that bears her name. A sly, lubricious woman—this is Mark's first impression of her. In her mid-forties; she is small in stature; short russet hair, elegantly styled; a thin face, sharp features; arched, pencilled eyebrows; dressed in a smart tweed suit. Mark has read her file. Back in her debutante days, Cynthia had been an infamous wild-child. He gets the distinct impression that she has not mellowed with age.

What sort of a school would a woman like this be running? Judging from the girls on the hockey field, a very lax one.

'A spy? How thrilling!' enthuses Cynthia, looking at Mark's proffered identification. Handing it back, she drifts behind her desk, waving a hand to the chair opposite.

Mark sits down. Cynthia fits a cigarette into an elegant holder, lights it.

'So, what can I do for you, Mr Hunter?'

'It's about one of your girls—'

'Ah! Don't tell me! She's in danger! Let me guess: the daughter of a Middle-Eastern potentate. (We've got a few of those.) There are rumours of an uprising, and you've come here to protect the poor child from the rebels who want to abduct her.'

'No, actually. I just want to speak to Juliette Wainwright.'

'Juliette Wainwright?'

'Yes, daughter of the financier. She is a student here, isn't she?'

'Yes, of course she is. Delightful girl. A prodigy. One of my best students.'

'Then could you have her sent for? I'd like to speak to her for a few moments.'

'Quite impossible, darling. She's not here, you see.'

'Not here?'

'That's what I said. She's on a geography field-trip in Provence.'

'Provence?'

'In France, darling.'

'Yes, I know where Provence is; but are you sure she's actually there? We have reason to believe she may have run away.'

'Why on earth would she do that? No, she's there. The staff members superintending the field-trip call in every day to tell us that all is well. No absentees.'

She regards Mark through narrowed eyes, gauging his reaction.

'I see. Then it looks like I've made this trip for nothing.'

'It does rather, doesn't it? Try using the telephone, darling. Marvellous invention. Without your having to leave English soil, I could have told you that Juliette was not here in Switzerland. You didn't have to descend on us unannounced like this. Or were you hoping to catch us up to something nefarious?'

'Not at all,' smiles Mark. 'So you've had no problems with Juliette?'

'None whatsoever. As I said: she's a model student. Everybody loves her.'

'What about her politics? Does she have any extreme views?'

'Good heavens, how should I know that? I don't discuss politics with my girls. Dreadfully dull subject. No, girls in the flower of youth are far more interested in discussing things like lip gloss and eye-liner than that sort of nonsense.'

'And you haven't had any suspicious men prowling round the school recently?'

'Not until you arrived, darling.'

That seems to be that. Valedictions are exchanged and Mark departs. When the door has closed behind the spy, Cynthia returns to her desk and picks up the telephone.

'Hello? Cynthia Imrie here... You wanted to know if anyone came here asking about Juliette... Yes, I've just had someone. British Intelligence... No, he was a bit cagey... No, he didn't say... Right...'

(Mark, who knows from long experience that after leaving an interview with someone who is clearly holding something back, it is always a good idea to tarry and listen at the door, overhears every word of this.)

The office of Rufus Wainwright is a vast empty cavern of a room.

Ushered in through tall double doors, Mark is confronted with a wide expanse of polished floor between himself and the large mahogany desk at which the financier sits enthroned.

He sets forth, footsteps echoing on the parquet.

Rufus Wainwright: broad shouldered, iron-grey hair, double-breasted suit. Chairman of the board of several concerns, a major share-holder in dozens of others; a finger in every pie.

'No, I'm not interested,' he is saying into the phone. To Mark: 'Take a seat, I'll be with you in a minute... Well you can tell them what they can do with their diamonds...'

He slams the phone down, turned to his secretary, a thin, harassed looking man, standing by his side.

'We'll do no more business with International Diamonds; understood?'

'Yes, Mr Wainwright.'

'Find something on them and leak it. I want them ruined.'

'Yes, Mr Wainwright.'

'Global Titanium?'

'On the market, Mr Wainwright.'

'Then buy as many as you can. I'm expecting a boom.'

'Yes, Mr Wainwright.'

'How's our Carbon Base stock?'

'Falling, Mr Wainwright.'

'Why didn't we sell when it was up?'

'You didn't tell me to, Mr Wainwright.'

'Do I have to tell you to wipe your back-side when you've had a crap?'

'No, Mr Wainwright.'

'Good. Then we understand each other. You're fired.'

The secretary looks as though he's been slapped round the face.

'Sir, I—'

'Get out.'

'Yes, Mr Wainwright.'

Crimson-faced, the secretary exits the room.

Wainwright stabs the intercom button.

'I've just sacked my secretary. Do we have another one lined up?'

'Several, Mr Wainwright,' comes the voice of the receptionist.

'Then bring one in and brief him.'

He turns to Mark for the first time. Mark smiles.

'As you can see, I'm very busy, Mr Hunter. I only agreed to see you because I'm curious as to why British Intelligence should be interested in my daughter.'

'We're concerned that she may have disappeared. She's not at her school.'

'I know she's not at her school; she's in Provence on a fieldtrip.'

'Yes, that's what they told me. But are you sure she's there?'

'Of course I'm sure. She emailed me last night. Said she was having a great time.'

'Yes, but she could have emailed you from anywhere. For that matter, someone else could have sent the email in her name.'

'I'm not sure what you're getting at, Mr Hunter.'

'To be blunt, I think your daughter has absconded. I think her school is covering up for her for some reason. And I'm wondering how much you know.'

'That's ridiculous. I'm a widower, Mr Hunter; my daughter is all that I've got. Don't you think that if she was missing I would have informed the authorities?'

'Not if you think she might be up to something illegal you don't want to get her in trouble.'

'That's nonsense.'

'Then there's nothing you can tell me?'

'Nothing, except that you're barking up the wrong tree. My daughter is safe and sound. I'll bid you good-day, Mr Hunter.' He punches the intercom. 'Where's my new secretary?'

'Excuse me—'

Wainwright locks eyes with Mark; flinty grey eyes, cold and uncompromising.

'Good-day, Mr Hunter.'

Sensing the futility of persisting, Mark takes his leave, crossing the gymnasium floorspace back to the doors, where the receptionist is waiting to usher him out.

Not being able to loiter and eavesdrop on this occasion, Mark misses the following phone call:

'Research? Look up a Mark Hunter, MI5. Compile a dossier on him. I want to know everything there is to know.'

Chapter Five
Future or No Future

There is a traitor in the midst of the Brixton Anarchist Collective.

No, it's not one of those deep-cover police spies you sometimes hear about—one of those deep-cover agents who has spent years infiltrating the movement. Our traitor is just a teenage girl, a legitimate member of the group; and she is a traitor only in thought, not in deed; she just doesn't really believe in the cause she is following. She used to believe; but now she doesn't. Cynical disillusion has set in.

The Collective's headquarters is a small abandoned office building. The meeting room is a second-floor office, dusty, cobwebbed, lit by a naked bulb, furnished with an old table, a few rickety chairs, with wooden crates supplying the deficit of seating; the time, night.

Rachel Ramone sits on one of these crates. A skinny girl of average height, thin face with a pierced and pouting underlip lending her a sulky expression; short dark hair with red highlights, parted on one side, fringe coming down over her left eye. She wears an army shirt, leggings, boots. (Sounds familiar? We saw her with Vautrin in Chapter Two.) On Rachel's right sits her boyfriend Luke, a few years her senior, and the main reason for her being here in the first place. Rachel is as much disillusioned with him personally, as she is with the Cause. Luke prides himself on being the perfect Modern Man; feminist, eco-friendly, teetotal, and generally as Correct as he can Politically get. But then, when they are alone at their flat, and he loses his rag over some stupid little thing, starts verbally assaulting her and the throwing things across the room—then he doesn't seem so Politically Correct. He hasn't actually hit her yet, but she is sure he is quite capable of it; any man who can't control his temper is capable of it.

He always apologises afterwards, but—and this is what pissed her off the most—he always begs her not to tell the others what had happened. In the current climate any man guilty of domestic violence is generally considered to be worse than Hitler, and Luke just cares about his standing amongst his friends; how much he distresses her with his outbursts seems a minor consideration to him…

Rachel has thought about leaving Luke—of course she has; but at the moment leaving just seems like more hassle than simply staying where she is.

The Collective are meeting tonight to discuss what they were going to blow up. In a room across the hall, Jackson is working on some home-made explosives. These haven't actually been perfected as yet, but when the bombs *are* ready, they will certainly need to blow something up!

The question is: what?

Rachel listens without speaking. She rarely speaks out at these meetings. The other members of the group accept this, assuming her to be shy. In fact, her silence is more to do with a lack of interest.

And what a group they are!

The others are all older than her and Luke. First there is Jackson. He isn't their leader. Of course not. Being good anarchists, they do not acknowledge such entities as leaders. But any third person looking in on one of their meetings could be forgiven for thinking that Jackson holds seniority in the group. It is Jackson who discovered this derelict building, even getting hold of the keys from somewhere. It was he who installed a small generator and gave them an electricity supply. And it is he who is the chief chemist working on the explosives. Rachel considers Jackson to be the most sensible person in the Brixton Collective—at the same time acknowledging that that isn't saying much.

The rest of the group she considers to be cretins one and all.

There is Buzzard, a forty-year-old punk with a spiky orange mohican. Defacing walls with graffiti is his chief idea of positive action. 'If graffiti didn't make a difference, it wouldn't be illegal!' (Rachel remembers laughing on one occasion when she had seen one of Buzzard's usual 'Spread Anarchy!' slogans crossed out by a second graffiti-artist who had written underneath the slogan, 'Don't Tell Me What to Do!')

Next there is weasel-faced Sally Newton and David, her pussy-whipped non-entity of a husband. Sally has a major bee in her bonnet about pornography and wants nothing more than to see this pernicious material wiped from the face of the earth (and cyberspace). Naturally the source of Sally's moral stance is a personal aversion to porn, but she can give you plenty of statistics to back up her point-of-view, such as citing all those serial killers and sexual predators who are found to use the stuff. And if chooses to quietly gloss over the small matter of the zillions of other porn users who *aren't* serial killers or sexual predators, well, we can forgive her this small omission, can't we?

And whatever you do, don't make the foolish mistake of offering up any opinions on the subject of pornography that run contrary to Sally's! Sally is not very pretty when she is in a foaming rage and you wouldn't want to be on the receiving end of it.

Rachel herself is no porno fan, but she doesn't have any problems with it. A lot of men just need that visual stimulus when they want to jerk off; some women do, as well... She can remember her own first experience of porn: She had been eight at the time, and had one day snuck into the bedroom of her big brother (strictly off-limits!) and nosing around had found a pornographic magazine under the bed. She remembers thinking it was just funny, all these pictures of women with no clothes on, and that her big brother was a bit naughty having this magazine! One image in particular had stuck in her mind: a model, wearing only high-heeled shoes, posing with one foot on a chair... Now, this had puzzled the eight-year-old Rachel: to her childish mind your shoes were the last item of clothing you put on, and so she just couldn't understand why this woman was wearing her shoes and nothing else!

As for Sally's husband, David Newton... Well, he's Mr Bland; probably hand-picked by Sally as ideal material for the kind of husband she wanted: the pliable, easily dominated variety. If he has any opinions, he never ventures to air them; always leaving the talking to his wife. But still waters can run deep; Rachel knows how she herself is perceived as just an adjunct to her boyfriend. So, maybe deep down, David is starting to get as fed-up with his situation as she is with hers...

The final member of the gang present this evening is Crimp, the group's regulation psycho head-case. Crimp has an aversion to the representatives of law enforcement. In fact, his hatred of 'the pigs!' amounts to a pathological condition. Crimp is an anarchist who is just in it for the violence, the disruption. The Crimps of this world generally find their way into activist or paramilitary groups, right or left, religious or ideological. There will always be Crimps. Crimps are only interested in taking violent action and they rarely trouble themselves about the distant goals. The Crimps are doers not thinkers. If the object of any terrorist group were ever achieved, if the desired utopia was attained, and everything was rosy, the Crimps would be bored to tears. They would have to start up some new, counter-movement just to stir things up again.

Such are the Crimps.

Our Crimp, in the current discussion, is naturally strongly in favour of blowing up the local nick.

'Yes, but there's a National Front cell somewhere here in Brixton,' says Jackson. 'If we could find out where their base is, I'd be all for destroying it. Those people are the worst menace.'

'Nah,' insists Crimp. 'I say let's fry us some pigs.'

'We should find out where they store all the pornography,' speaks up Sally. 'There must be a warehouse full of the obscene filth somewhere. Raze it to the ground.'

Rachel rolls her eyes.

'Yes, but we don't know where this hypothetical warehouse is,' Jackson points out.

'We don't know where the National Front base is, either,' retorts Sally.

'But we know where the cop shop is,' says Crimp, triumphant. 'That settles that!'

'It doesn't settle anything!' snaps Jackson.

'I'd say all three of those are legitimate targets,' interjects Luke. 'We'll be making more than one bomb, won't we? Why not a campaign? Why not all of them?'

Mr Diplomacy, thinks Rachel. The peacemaker who sees all sides of an argument. They should see him at home—not so diplomatic when he's flying off the handle, yelling and throwing things at her.

What am I fucking doing here? she wonders, for not the first time. I don't like my boyfriend; I thinks his anarchist friends are a bunch of fucking idiots. Why the hell am I here?

She wonders if her new internet friend is serious. They have been communicating on social media for some weeks now. Her correspondent, who glories under the online name of Dizzy Hello, claims to belong to this new group—an exclusive group, an elite group; a group composed entirely of girls. She has been urging Rachel to join them. Dizzy Hello is somewhat vague as to this group's aims. Rachel isn't even sure if the group actually exists; it's quite possible this Dizzy Hello might be one of those online fantasists; a fake persona. But, as often happens online, Rachel has started to feel a strong connection with her correspondent, stronger than she feels with anyone out in the real world. Dizzy seems to understand everything about Rachel; about how she feels; there's real empathy. Rachel is almost sure that the girl, in some of her messages, has even referred to circumstances in her life that she doesn't recall having mentioned to the girl.

Rachel knows this feeling is not always to be trusted. She knows how fallacious this can be. You developed a strong bond with an on-line friend, someone you'd never even met; and based solely on the words and tone of their messages, you build up a personality of that person which is actually entirely your own creation; an image that is simply of what you desire that other person to be. She knows too, that face-to-face meetings with online friends can end in disappointment.

She knows all this, but yet she still believes in Dizzy Hello. Her vague hopes for the future are all pinned on this girl.

'Another target we could think about are the indoctrination centres,' Jackson is suggesting. (By this he means the schools.)

''Ere, we can't blow up a load of kids!' protests Buzzard.

'I know that! Obviously, we would blow up the schools when they were empty.'

Schools. Indoctrination centres. Yeah, right, thinks Rachel. The education system of this country is just clumsy and inefficient; it is not some well-oiled machine for churning out robots. The fact that we're all sitting here now proves that.

'Well, it's something new,' approves Luke. 'Targeting the education system.'

And then they hear the noise.

Jackson springs to his feet.

'What was that?'

'Came from downstairs,' says Sally. 'Sounded like glass breaking.'

'Could be a cat,' suggests Buzzard.

'Cats don't break windows, you moron,' grates Jackson.

They exchange worried glances.

Another sound; a thump.

'There's definitely someone down there,' says Luke, frightened.

'The pigs,' declares Crimp. 'A raid!'

'The law would just break down the front door,' says Jackson. He grabs his gun from the table. It's the only firearm the group possesses. 'They wouldn't try and sneak in. We'd better go down and see who it is.'

The seven of them step out onto the landing. Another naked bulb lights the landing; but below them the stairs angle round into darkness. Jackson holds a hand up for silence. They listen. A shuffling sound from below.

'I bet it's squatters,' hisses Crimp. 'The bloody nerve.'

As anarchists, shouldn't we be welcoming squatters with open arms?

'You might be right. Let's see.'

Jackson leads the way downstairs. When they reach the ground floor, he turns on the hallway light.

'Don't do that!' from Luke.

'It's no good if we can't see anything,' retorts Jackson. 'I think the noises were coming from the back.'

The group moves forward. Rachel feels her heart pounding. She feels as if a decisive moment is approaching. She can't explain the feeling; can find no logical reason for it. But something is going to happen that will change her life. Or end it.

More noises from the back room.

Luke clings to Rachel's arm. White-faced and trembling, he looks more scared than anyone else.

Jackson pushes open the door to the back room.

'Who's there?' he calls. 'I warn you I'm armed.'

He throws the light-switch.

There are four of them. Balaclavaed, dressed in black combat fatigues, the initials NF on the shoulders, the thick letters filled out with the Union Jack emblem. They hold assault rifles, aimed and ready

'Oh Christ, oh Christ,' whimpers Luke.

Almost casually, one of the men squeezes the trigger of his gun. With little sound the bullets perforate Jackson and Crimp's bodies. Again with no real urgency in the movement, the newly-made corpses collapse and fall to the ground.

'Run!' yells Rachel, her voice slicing through dazed horror.

The spell broken, they run screaming for the front door—but the gunshots must have been a signal. The front door comes under heavy assault, cracks and splinters appearing in the woodwork.

'Upstairs!' yells Rachel.

They scramble back up the narrow stairs. Bullets follow them, and Buzzard and David fall. Sally screams, turns to go to her fallen husband, but Rachel violently grabs her arm and pulls her onwards. They make it to the second floor. The gunmen are following, but, confident of their quarry, they aren't in any hurry.

Luke looks like he is about to run back into the meeting room.

'Forget it!' snaps Rachel. 'The roof!'

They mount the last flight of stairs, reach the door giving access to the flat roof. Rachel tries the handle. The door is locked.

The keys. Jackson had always kept the only set of keys.

Booted feet clamber up the stairs below.

'We're dead, we're dead,' whimpers Luke.

'Shut up!' snarls Rachel.

The sound of a key turning in the lock from outside; the door opens.

'Out here!' commands a female voice.

They pile out onto the flat roof, the door is shut and locked behind them.

Rachel studies their rescuers in the moonlight. Two teenage girls. One fairly tall, with short fair hair; the other very small, with a mop of dark tousled hair and large eyes. Both are armed with handguns.

The blonde girl steps forward, smiles at Rachel, takes her hand.

'Guess who?' she says.

'Dizzy!' Her online friend. Somehow Rachel knows it can only be her.

The smile widens. 'Right first time! We haven't got time to chat—those goons will realise you're up here soon. Snap decision time: come with me and Greta, or stay here and get killed. Everything I told you about is true. We have a team and we want you on it. That's why we're here.'

'Your name?' asks Rachel stupidly. 'What's your real name?'

A confused look. 'What are you on about? Dizzy Hello *is* my real name.'

'Look, who the hell are you?' cuts in Sally. 'What's goin—'

'Shut up,' snaps Dizzy. 'I'm only speaking to Rachel.'

This is it thinks Rachel. This is the decisive moment. The beginning of a new phase of her life.

Dizzy takes her hand, eyes flashing encouragement.

'Now or never…'

Come heavy blows to the stair-well door.

'I'll come with you!' declares Rachel. 'I don't fancy dying tonight.'

Dizzy looks jubilant. 'Wise career choice! Now over here, quick.'

They run to the edge of the building. A plank bridges the gulf between this and the adjacent rooftop. The small girl crosses first.

'Now you, Rachel.'

Rachel runs across the plank.

Luke and Sally move towards the plank. Dizzy levels her gun at them.

'I didn't say anything about you two.'

'What!' cries Luke. 'You can't—'

'I can and I am,' retorts Dizzy. 'We're taking Rachel out of this world; you two have to stay in it.'

She mounts the plank, backs across it, sure-footed.

'This is where you sever your links with your past life,' she calls back to Rachel. 'The moment I'm off the plank, pull it away.'

Dizzy, across the gap, jumps nimbly from the plank. Without pause for thought, Rachel takes hold of the plank and pulls. The plank, free from the other rooftop, see-saws, plummets.

'You bitch!' screeches Luke. 'You fucking bitch!'

'Come on,' says Dizzy. 'No time to hang around.'

They set off swiftly across the jumbled rooftops. Behind her, Rachel hears a door burst open, and then cries, and the ripple of machine-gun fire...

Chapter Six
They Didn't Get Her Boots!

'So, what are your views of Plato's theory of Ideas?'

'You mean the theory that every living object has an "Idea" or perfect form, and that we Earthbound mortals can only perceive imperfect copies of those perfect forms?'

'Yeah, that's it. What do you think about one?'

'Dunno...'

The speakers are two squaddies, Langton and Butler. They sit in the cab of a canvas-backed army truck, Langton at the wheel. Having delivered some equipment to a neighbouring base, they are returning to their own base at Westbirch.

Night has fallen and the two men are travelling a lonely road. (No, not metaphysically: there is no other traffic about.) The road they traverse intersects a forest; dark ramparts of pine trees rise on either side.

After that last exchange, one of those oft-quoted companionable silences has fallen between the two men, the only sound the steady rhythm of the truck's engine.

And then Langton speaks again: 'What do you think of Plato's argument against the system of democracy?'

'You mean his argument that democracy is an inefficient system in that it allows the people to select its own leaders; positing that the majority of the people are incapable of selecting the right leaders for themselves?'

'Yeah, that's it. What do you think about that one?'

'Dunno...'

That companionable silence establishes itself again.

Langton ruminates, wondering whether he should ask Butler for his views on Plato's belief that true love can only exist between men; positing that women are inferior creatures, unworthy of true love... Yes... Why not?

The words are almost on Langton's lips when one of those very same inferior, unworthy women runs out into the road, waving her arms madly.

Aside from a pair of Air Ware boots she is stark naked!

Langton stomps on the brakes. The truck skids to a halt a few feet from the girl.

'What the bloody hell...?'

Langton looks at Butler. Butler looks at Langton. Neither has an explanation to offer for this apparition. Forgetting, in their surprise, that according to protocol, they should first radio in this unscheduled stop, the two men climb out of the cab and approach the girl who stands in the glare of the headlights. Glasses; short, dark hair; a broad, athletic figure; she looks to be in her teens. A pale form in the glare of the artificial light, the dense growth of pubic hair clothing her groin a conspicuous patch of darkness.

The girl shields her eyes from the glare of the lights; she seems agitated.

'Who are you? I can't see...'

Her thick voice has a slight slur to it. Is she mentally deficient? Run away from one of those 'special' schools or homes or something?

'It's alright love,' says Langton. 'We're the army.'

'Oh, thank God,' sighs the girl. 'Please save me! I've just been gang-raped and I think they're still after me!'

'Raped? Who by?' demands Butler.

'Homeless men! Four of them, with dogs. Mangy, flea-bitten, smelly things, they were. And the dogs weren't much better!'

'What? And they attacked you? Where did this happen, love?'

The girl turns to face the tree-line. 'In the woods over there. That's where they grabbed me. When they'd finished with me, they wouldn't give me my clothes back. Said they were going to sell them for beer money. They wanted my boots too, but when one of them tried to take them off me, I kicked him in the face and ran for it. Only they seemed very serious about wanting my boots cuz they came after me! They were right behind me when I ran out onto the road…'

Butler scans the tree-line. 'Don't see anyone. Do you?'

'No. They probably saw we were military and cleared off,' surmises Langton.

The girl throws her arms round Langton. 'I bet they did! You scared them right off! You both look so strong and manly in those uniforms…'

'Er… thanks,' says Langton. 'But what the hell were you doing on your own in the woods at night in the first place?'

'I'm a botany student,' answers the girl, still embracing him. 'I was looking for this rare woodland flower, the *moistus vaginus*; it's a flower that only opens up at night. Have you heard of it?'

'No, I—' begins Langton. 'Hey!'

The girl steps back from Langton. She has taken his revolver from its holster. Butler reaches for his own gun; the girl shoots him on the spot.

      Then she shoots Langton.

Figures appeared from the density of the tree-line, seven more girls, some dressed in school clothes, some in casual wear…

'Nice work, Trudie,' congratulates Juliette Wainwright, immaculate as ever in her Imrie Academy uniform. 'Rachel, Albert, get those bodies off the road. Dizzy, you're with me in the cab; the rest of you in the back.'

The two dead philosophers are dragged off the road and left under cover of the trees. Dizzy Hello slides behind the wheel of the truck, Juliette taking the passenger seat. The others move round to the rear of the truck, lower the tail-board and pile in. A bench runs along each side of the interior. Rachel Ramone, Chrissie Wylde, Greta Garbo seat themselves along one bench; Trudie Rayne, Albertine Sagan, Flossie Farraday, the other. The SEA girls are out in force tonight.

The truck moves forward.

'Can I have my clothes back now, please?' requests Trudie,

looking at Rachel.

'Greta, give Trudie her clothes,' says Rachel.

'*Nein*, I do not haff her cloffes. Albertine hass them.'

'Albertine?'

'But *non*. I do not 'ave 'er clothes. I thought Chrissie 'ad zem.'

'Don't look at me. I haven't got them.'

Trudie groans. 'You've forgotten my fucking clothes, haven't you?'

This unfortunate oversight is soon confirmed.

'Sorry about that,' says sheepish Rachel. 'We can pick them on the way back. They're safe enough. Still; at least it's a warm night!'

So I've got to raid an army base in the buff, ponders Trudie—meanwhile Rachel can't help looking at the girl sitting opposite her, naked save for her footwear... It brings back childhood memories.

Since joining the SEA and meeting Vautrin, confidence has banished fear for our Trudie Rayne, as it has for the other girls. She has entered on a new plane of existence; her previous life has become an illusion. Note how quickly she adjusts to the prospect of participating in a paramilitary operation with no clothes on!

Trudie cares about her comrades, she cares about Vautrin; to everything and everyone else she has become merciless.

'Nearly there now,' announces Rachel, looking at the illuminated display of her watch.

The truck pulls up before the gates of Westbirch Army Base. There are two guards on duty and they are expecting the truck. One of them strolls up to the driver's side door. Dizzy shoots him with a silenced pistol. Juliette, jumping from the cab, takes care of the other guard in the same manner. She runs over to the sentry hut and throws the switch to open the gates, while Dizzy collects the two guards' rifles. The gates slide back, the truck drives in.

Plans of the base have been memorised. Dizzy drives straight past the administration building and deeper into the grounds, finally pulling up before the bunker-like munitions store. There are two more guards here, blinded in the glare of the headlights.

'Turn those bloody lights off!' yells one. 'What do you—'

Juliette and Dizzy's silenced pistols speaks quietly again, and the guards quietly die.

The tailboard is lowered, the other SEA girls pile out.

'Alright Greta; time to do your stuff,' says Juliette. She tosses one of assault rifles to Trudie. 'You know what to do. And why haven't you put your clothes back on?'

'Ask those idiots,' says Trudie.

She sets off at a sprint across the grass towards the lights of the nearest building. Reaching it, she flattens herself against the wall, peaks cautiously through the window. The window looks into a recreation room. Off-duty squaddies lounge about, nattering, smoking, drinking tea or coffee. Two are playing darts, while at one of the tables a poker game is in progress.

Comes a muffled explosion from the munitions store. Good. Greta has taken care of the lock.

Trudie kicks open the door in bursts into the ready room. A split-second of silence while everybody gawps at the naked girl with the SA80 assault rifle. Then Trudie opens fire, methodically fanning the room with bullets, cutting the soldiers down, one and all.

Her task completed, Trudie returns to the munitions store. SEA girls file through the open doors, carrying crates, which are swiftly loaded onto the truck. A box of grenades has been opened and lies ready. Raised voices from the direction of the barracks. Figures running towards them. An alarm begins its wailing cry. Dizzy and Albertine hurl grenades at the advancing figures. Two explosions brighten the night; screams, figures diving for cover.

Greta appears from the munitions store.

'It iss done.'

'Right. Everyone in the truck!' orders Juliette tersely.

Dizzy and Albert throw two more grenades, and they all pile into the truck. Even with the new cargo they have acquired there is still enough room for the girls.

The truck reverses, swings round, heads for the main gates, accelerating fast. They come under fire as they pass the administration building. Trudie, still brandishing the SA80, sends a valedictory fusillade from the back of the truck, mowing down the guards and officers.

And then they are out through the gates.

'Three...two... vun... zero!'

The bomb Greta has left in the munitions store explodes. Explosion follows explosion in a chain-reaction and the ground literally trembles as the entire cache ignites. The night sky behind them is illuminated by a tremendous fireworks display.

The girls whoop, and laugh, high-fiving and hugging one another.

Another job well done!

Little Greta Garbo hugs Trudie tightly round the middle, pillowing her face between Trudie's breasts. Trudie, delirious, buries her face in the girl's dark tousled hair, laughing and crying.

'Your breasts are so vorm,' murmurs Greta.

Trudie gasps as the girl's small teeth clamped lightly around her erect nipple. Greta starts to suck, while Trudie nuzzles and kisses her hair.

Chapter Seven
Two Girls: Extracted from Linear Time

Mark and Dodo sit once again on the sofas in Dodo's front room. On the present occasion Dodo is dressed, and Mayumi not present.

'Well, the terrorist attack on Westbirch army barracks was definitely them.'

'The SEA?'

'Yes. They managed to hijack a truck that was returning from a neighbouring base, and with this they were able to surprise the guards at the gates. There was CCTV covering the gates. The girls in the cab who killed the guards were our Julie Wainwright and one who's new one on us; a girl with short, fair hair. She wasn't Gina Santella. We don't know how many were in the back of the truck, but from survivor accounts, there were at least half a dozen of them, and they were all girls.

'The story we've released to the press is just that the munitions dump was blown by the raiders. But the truth of the matter is, they looted the place first. We have witnesses to that fact. I imagine they left the bomb behind partly so we wouldn't know what was taken, and partly as a parting gift.'

'And I'm assuming that there was Semtex stored in that place?'

'Right on the nose. I knew they'd try to get their hands on some somehow, but I never imagined they'd be so bloody brazen about it.'

'So we can expect a bombing campaign. Have you raised the Terror Alert level?'

'We don't have to: it's always set to "attack imminent" these days.'

'Well, after all that, have you brought any *good* news with you?'

'Yes, as a matter of fact; that's the main reason I'm here: I'd like you to help me with some sleuthing. We've identified two more of Vautrin's nymphets. We've been going through Scotland Yard's Missing Persons files—something I should have thought of sooner—and we came up with two matches. Our girl in the hotel car-park with the short hair and glasses is one Trudie Rayne. She upped sticks and left her parents' home a couple of months back. And the day she disappeared, five of her classmates were shot dead in an apparently motiveless massacre. Remember, it was all over the news.'

'Yes, I do remember. So she was the one responsible?'

'Seems likely, given what we know of her recent activities. The police were suspicious too, but as there wasn't a shred of evidence, and no sign of a motive, they couldn't issue a warrant for her arrest; so she was just listed as a Missing Person. From all accounts she was just an ordinary schoolgirl. Where would she get a gun from and why would she go on a killing spree? *We know* who could have supplied her with a handgun, but to anyone else at the time it would have seemed inexplicable.'

'And who's the other one you've identified?'

'The other school uniform. Our girl with the long brown hair who took part in the *Apprentice* massacre. Florence Farraday is her name. Her disappearance was if anything even more of an enigma. It seems she just vanished off the face of the Earth on her way to school one morning, just over a month back. She set off from the family home and was never seen again. No trace at all—until we caught sight of her.

'So we have two schoolgirls; both, as far as we can tell, perfectly ordinary, from perfectly ordinary families. Why did Vautrin select them, out of everyone, for his merry gang, and how did he know where to find them? The pattern is the same as with the other two, Julie Wainwright and Gina Santella. When he chooses a recruit, it seems like he uproots her completely from her previous life, and takes her we-don't-know-where. This is where I want your help: I'm thinking that if we do some digging into the backgrounds of those two girls Rayne and Farraday—the circumstances of their lives and their disappearances—we might just pick up some clue…'

'…Yes, we did get a call from one of her teachers. Her grades had been slipping. He wanted to know if there were any problems at home.'

The speaker is Lindsey Rayne, Trudie's mother. Mark has found her at home; her husband is at work. They are seated in the living room.

'And there weren't any problems at home?'

'No. Everything was the same as usual. We all got along fine.'

'Had she spoken of any problems at school?'

'No, but she didn't really talk about her school life or her social life with us. That's quite normal for a girl her age.'

'So, no changes in her routine?'

'Well, I did notice her bedroom was getting messy. She'd

always kept it very tidy before. And she'd been going out in the evenings more than she used to.'

'Do you know where?'

'No. She just said to see friends. We didn't press her for details. We just told her to be home by ten; she always was.'

'So she might have been going round that boy Martin Hammond's brother's house?'

Mrs Rayne's expression shifts to hostility. 'I get it. You think she killed those children as well, do you? I know the police were thinking that—asking us if we owned a gun, if it had gone missing... Of *course* we didn't have a gun and there was nowhere on earth Trudie could have got hold of one. And why would she want to kill her school-friends? The idea's ridiculous! There's no motive, no evidence; nothing.'

'I know, Mrs Rayne. It's just that we have the coincidence of your daughter running away from home that same evening. And all the evidence indicates that she *did* leave of her own accord. As you said yourself, there were clothes, possessions and a bag missing from her room.'

'Yes, but doesn't mean she wasn't tricked into running away, does it? Someone might have talked her into running away; maybe forced her to. My daughter's the victim here! She could have been taken by that maniac with the gun who killed those other kids! She might be dead by now!'

'We're fairly sure she's not dead, Mrs Rayne. There have been some sightings. Here in London...'

'...Have you some news, then, about our Florence?'

The tone is eager, the speaker Mrs Farraday. Her husband sits next to her.

'She's been seen,' says Dodo cautiously. 'At least, someone answering her description has been seen. That's all I can say at the moment.'

Disappointment on the faces of the Farradays.

'I can at least tell you that we're fairly certain your daughter ran away voluntarily; she wasn't abducted. It just seems very strange she should choose to run away first thing in the morning, when she was apparently just heading off to school. She didn't seem strange, excited, that morning?'

'No,' answers the husband. 'As we told the police, she was perfectly normal that day.'

'Was she happy at school?'

'We think so. She was on the hockey team...'

'You have two other teenage children, don't you? Didn't they commute to school with her...?'

Mr Farraday smiles. 'No. Eve and Nigel attend a different school...'

Dodo frowns. 'Why's that?'

A shrug. 'No particular reason. It just worked out that way... Is there really nothing else you can tell us? We've been very anxious...'

'I'm afraid not; we're still investigating the alleged sighting... I'd like to have a look at Flossie's room. I know the police searched it, but there may be something...'

Husband looks at wife. Then: 'Of course. It's the first door on the left at the top of the landing...'

Dodo makes her way upstairs. The house is a large one, the abode of an affluent middle-class family.

First door on the left...

She pauses in the act of opening the door... The smell of paint... Strange... Their daughter goes missing from home, and the family bother themselves with redecorating the runaway's bedroom...? Something's not right here...

Dodo hunkers down. Feeling the paintwork near the door handle, she detects a slight unevenness. Screw-holes that have been filled in and painted over. She inspects the door frame. Yes, the same; more filled in screw holes. A sliding lock has been fixed here previously... But, a teenage girl's bedroom in her own family home—and a door that can only be bolted on the outside?

Something's *definitely* not right here...

'...had you seen Trudie in the company of a man? About thirty, dark hair, long side-burns…'

It's home-time at Dale Street Comprehensive; the release of the prisoners. The usual gossiping groups of students loiter around outside the gates. Mark passes from group to group, asking the same question. He gets a lot of funny looks, a few jibes, but not many straight answers.

He observes one girl—standing by the railing, she has been watching him, a look of indecision on her face. She seems to reach a decision, because now she walks up to Mark, brushes past him, nudging him.

'Paedo!' she spits, quickly moving on.

The watching kids laugh at this.

Mark retreats from the school entrance, students jeering at him. The girl who bumped into him has left a scrap of paper in his hand. Once out of sight of the students, he stops, unfolds the paper. A girlish decorated sheet torn from a notepad; it bears the succinct message:

Meet me behind the bike sheds.

The bike sheds stand just inside the school gates on the left. Mark ambles back to the entrance. The chattering groups are starting to disperse. Mark enters the grounds and makes his casual way to the bike sheds. He skirts round to the back of them. Here he finds the girl who bumped into him: she stands alone amongst a litter of cigarette ends, leaning against a corrugated iron partition richly decorated with scatological graffiti. The girl—attractive, but with one side of her face martyr to an outbreak of adolescent acne—looks nervous, unsure of herself.

Mark smiles to put her at her ease. 'You've got something to tell me?'

'Yeah…' she says. 'I mean, you're for real, yeah? You're a copper, right?'

'More a spy than a cop,' says Mark. 'But yes, I'm genuine.'

He shows the girl his ID. She seems satisfied.

'Got a fag?'

Mark offers her his cigarette case, takes one himself. When they are both alight:

'What's your name then, young lady?'

'Lisa. You're looking for Trudie, right?'

'Yes. You know where she is?'

'No.'

'But you've seen her with that man you heard me describing?'

'No.'

'So, what do you know?'

'I know she was whoring,' announces the girl. 'Everyone knows it, just about, but they all decided not to tell. You know, after she disappeared.'

'Whoring?' echoes Mark. 'You mean she was being promiscuous, or she was actually taking money in return for sex?'

'I mean she was whoring. Martin Hammond and them others; they was pimping her.'

Mark begins to say daylight. 'You mean those students who were killed?'

'Yeah. Called themselves the Classical Music Club, but really they was pimping Trudie. She was doing it in that house where they all got killed; Martin's brother's place.'

Mark ponders. 'Then that might explain... But why would Trudie agree to sell herself like that? From what I know of the girl, it seems completely out of character. Or am I wrong about that? Can you tell me? Did you know Trudie well?'

'Not really. I never talked to her much. I reckon they must have been forcing her to do it, Martin and them others; blackmail porn or something. I reckon that's why she offed 'em. Got fed up with it, didn't she?'

'So you do think it was actually Trudie who killed those students?'

An emphatic nod of the head. 'Course it was. Fuck knows where she got a gun from, but, yeah, it must've been her.'

'Hm. What I don't understand is, why none of you kids told this to the police at the time.'

Lisa snorts, ejecting twin streams of carcinogenic smoke. 'Cuz half the boys in our year had been with her! They were all fuckin' paying to ride her; it was like a joke, or something. And they didn't want to get found out, did they? Didn't want to get in trouble. It was like everyone just decided to say they didn't know nothing.'

'I see... Well, thank you for coming out with this information, Lisa. So... have you told me all this just out of a sense of civic duty, are you hoping for some sort of payment...?'

'Well... maybe a couple of twenties...?'

'Seriously?'

'Seriously. I have no reason to think that girl was lying to me. In fact, what she told me explains a lot.'

Evening. They are back in Dodo's apartment, seated in the living area as before. The lighted room throws a reflection of itself against the plate-glass, blending with the twilit skyline.

'Christ,' says Dodo. 'I mean I've heard of schoolkids selling sex before, but a bunch of them actually forcing one of their own classmates...'

'I know. You could almost forgive the child for taking her revenge the way she did...'

'I think we can blame Vautrin for that. If she did really kill those kids, he will have been the one who put the gun in her hand.'

'True.'

'Well, for my part, I haven't found out anything concrete about Florence Farraday's disappearance—but I have a lot of suspicions. I think something very odd was going on in the Farraday household.'

She tells Mark about the evidence of the bedroom door.

'Hm... Well, if her parents were in the habit of locking her in her room, that would certainly be a motive for her running away. Anything else?'

'Yes. I spoke to a girl called Denise, a classmate of Florence's. According to the police report, Florence had gone round to Denise's house the evening before she disappeared, and her parents heard them having a very heated argument at the front door. I asked Denise what this argument was about: about a boy, she said. I wondered if the "boy" was actually a "man" and I gave her Vautrin's description. She didn't know him, and I think she was telling the truth about that; but her whole attitude was defensive, wary; she was holding back something, I'm certain of that.'

'Hm. I think we can assume that all was not well in Florence's life. That brings us back to the same old question: how did Vautrin get to know about her? He seems to pick girls in troubled circumstances and takes them away with him. Maybe in his twisted way he even thinks he's helping them. Trudie Rayne being prostituted. Gina Santella in danger because her Mafia protector had been killed. Florence Farraday: problems at home and/or at school, we don't know how bad yet.'

'What about Juliette Wainwright? We haven't heard that she was in any trouble.'

'Ah! But she might have been. I've had Cynthia Imrie's Academy put under observation; that woman is clearly involved to some extent. And one thing my man on the spot has picked up is that not very long ago there was a murder in the vicinity of the school—a young ski instructor who lived in the village nearby. Apparently some of the girls at the academy were in the habit of paying him nocturnal visits, for the usual reason. (It's always the sports instructor, isn't it!) But then one fine morning our ski instructor was found dead in his cabin; horribly tortured and mutilated. The police investigated; they even started sniffing around the academy. But then suddenly, and for no apparent reason, the investigation was shelved. It occurs to me that if Juliette *was* involved in this killing in any way, Daddy Wainwright might have used his influence to get the whole business hushed up.'

'If Juliette was in any way involved, we can assume Vautrin was as well.'

'That would be my assumption. The question is: is Vautrin still recruiting girls for his little *ménage*, or does he now have a full house...?'

Chapter Eight
Enter the Sub-Plot

Tonight is going to be the night.

Yes, tonight will be the night in which Robin Trent will finally come out of his shell, exercise those latent social skills he confidently believes himself to possess, and will actually make some friends! Lofty and noble endeavours, I'm sure you will agree.

The venue for this epoch-making event: a local pub of course; one particularly selected for being a favourite haunt of teenagers, those happy individuals just over and just under the legal drinking age. Robin himself is in his mid-twenties, but he still considers himself to be a teen at heart. Having squandered his own adolescence in bookish isolation, he now feels the need to belatedly live out his teenage life; to extend his youth by mixing with people of that enviable age-group. (This is a familiar pattern for those belated adolescents whose minds only start to catch up with their bodies when they're in their twenties.)

Robin Trent works as an office dog's-body, lives in a poky flat and spends much of his free-time online. He is a keen social-networker, but he knows that online friendships don't always translate very well into the real world. There had been this particular girl once: they had got on so well online, had built up a rapport, shared each other's problems, offering mutual advice and consolation… Finally and inevitably, they had decided to meet up in the real world. They were both Londoners, so commuting to a neutral meeting place would be no problem for either of them—It had been a disaster. Robin, unused to social contact, had been nervous and shy, and it had been obvious from the girl's behaviour that right from the start, right from the moment she had set eyes on him, that he was not living up to her expectations of him; she had been expecting something else and was clearly disappointed. And so, after an uncomfortable couple of hours in each other's company, she had made an excuse to leave. It had been the most miserable day of Robin's life; he had cried his way home. Of course he had then made the usual desperate and futile online efforts to salvage the wreck, pleading for a second meeting. A second chance... The result: the girl had just stopped replying to his emails, and had not only unfriended, but completely blocked him on the social networking site.

There are no second chances in these situations.

So here we have Robin Trent, lonely and disconsolate. In appearance, Robin is nondescript, so I won't bother describing him. He's just one of those people you see and then instantly forget. The world does not deliberately shun it's Robin Trents; the world just completely fails to notice them. Robin has recently made some attempts to make the world notice him, but he isn't entirely happy with these ventures and I won't go into them just now.

He has built up sanguine hopes for this coming evening at the White Swan; his first excursion of this kind for some time. He feels certain he is going to meet some new friends tonight; maybe even find that perfect girl! Robin constantly dreams of meeting that perfect girl, and like many people similarly circumstanced, his normally low mood will suddenly swing round to a ludicrous feeling of certainty that things are going to pan out the way he wants them to.

And so, showered, shaved, and in his best clothes, the sanguine youth sets off for the pub. It is a warm spring evening. There is a youthful buoyancy in the air, invigorating, elevating his mood, his hopes... His route takes him through a park. Teenage drinkers sit in groups, intoxicating themselves with the beer or liquor they have somehow managed to get hold of. These kids often avail themselves of the stands of shrubbery with which the park is supplied for bouts of alfresco sex. Sometimes, after dark, and if you are very quiet, you can spy on these casual couplings. But this is not on the agenda for tonight. No siree! Robin wants none of these vicarious pleasures tonight. He plans to actually participate in life, not to just watch from the side-lines.

He arrives at the White Swan, the popular haunt of youth and the people who want to sell drugs to them. Arming himself with a beer he ventures out into the courtyard beer garden, a huge enclosure, formerly the stable yard back in those Dickensian days when the White Swan had been a staging terminus. The coach house doors are still to be seen, now sealed shut, brightly painted, adorned with flower boxes.

Robin sits himself down at an unoccupied bench. It is fairly early as yet, and the place is still filling up. A group of teenagers sit a couple of benches away, talking loudly. There is one girl wearing a black mini-dress and high heels. She has these amazing legs, long and well-shaped. Of the girls in the group this one seems to be the alpha, the one getting the most attention from the boys. Robin wonders if she will turn round and notice him—if she will see him sitting there on his own, and feel compassion for him, and invite him to join her group. Surely if she knew how lonely he was, she would feel sorry for him. People have to feel sorry for Robin, don't they? He has a right to demand their sympathy! Poor Robin: he's had a hell of a life!

Two giggling girls sit down on a bench across from his. Overflowing with words and *joie de vivre*, they gush words, gabbling all over each other. They are quite touchy-feely, these girls, observes Robin. Lesbians? Robin purses his lips. They shouldn't be doing that. It's not natural. People like that should go to some other pub.

Crossing them off his list, Robin necks his drink.

Maybe if he goes to the bar right now to get another drink, the girl with the legs will notice him as he walks past her… He tries the experiment. It fails. The girl, too wrapped up in all the attention she's receiving, doesn't even notice him.

He feels the familiar stab of disappointment.

There's quite a scrum at the bar, and by the time he gets back to the courtyard, he finds that his bench has been taken over by a large group of people. The courtyard is now filling quickly. He locates another empty bench and sits down. That girl with the legs and the black dress is facing him now. He looks at her, hoping that his eyes might catch hers. Maybe she will smile at him...

And then three girls sit down at the further end of Robin's bench, two of them in jeans and t-shirts; the third, a vivacious looking girl with short curly hair, wears shorts and a vest. The girls, armed with pints, start gossiping about college and what their friends are doing... They seem to be Sixth-Formers.

Could this be it? wonders Colin. Will these girls notice him and invite him into their group?

The vivacious girl in the shorts looks round at Robin. 'Are you on your own? You can come and sit with us.'

'Thanks!' says Robin, shifting along the bench. He is now next to the vivacious girl. She smiles at him.

'What's your name?'

'Robin.'

'I'm Tina. This is Stella and Dora.'

Greetings are exchanged.

'Are you a student, then?' asks Tina.

'No. I work in an office,' says Robin. 'Pretty boring, huh?'

Tina shrugs. 'Oh, well. We've all got to do something. Do you live at home?'

'No, I've got my own place. Just a little flat.'

'You're independent. That's cool!'

'Me and Stella are at sixth form,' says Dora. 'Tina goes to art college.'

Robin looks at her with admiration. 'So, you're an artist?'

An embarrassed smile. 'That's what I want to be.'

'That's brilliant. I'd love to see some of your work.'

'You should do,' enthuses Dora. 'It's fucking good.'

'Dora!'

'Well, it is!'

'You like indie music?' Tina asks Robin.

'I love it.' Starting from this very moment!

'Cool! We're going on to an indie nightclub later. You should come with us.'

The other two enthusiastically support this decision, and Robin agrees to join them.

'Have you got a girlfriend?' is Tina's next question.

'Not at the moment.'

This answer seems to please Tina. She smiles at him. She is radiant, inviting. Robin is in love.

This is just the very situation Robin has come to the pub hoping for! The conversation flows, he hasn't made a fool of himself and one of the girls seems to particularly like him! Perfect! But on the debit side, the above conversation has taken place entirely in Robin's head, and, back in reality, the three girls, immersed in each other, have not even looked at him once.

And nothing does happen. A great big truck-load of nothing. Night descends. The courtyard overflows with chattering ebullient youth. When Robin rises to get his third pint, he returns to find his place at the bench has been taken by a group of boys. The vivacious girl and her two friends are chatting away with them eagerly.

He downs his last pint in the saloon. He decides to call it a night.

Out on the street he sees the three girls leave, along with the boys who had joined them; obviously going on somewhere.

'Watch out the Carpenter doesn't get you!' jokes one boy to a pair of girls who were setting off arm-in-arm.

The girls laugh at this. The Carpenter, the serial killer who has now killed four women, smashing their skulls with a claw hammer, is known to operate in this part of town.

Robin sets off back to his flat. At least *he* didn't have to worry about the Carpenter.

His night out has been a crushing failure. Nothing has happened the way he wanted it to happen... Why can't people just notice him? Why can't people just be friendly to him? Is it too much to ask?

Robin's thoughts, as they often do at these moments, start to drift back to his school-days. He had been a shy, awkward adolescent, particularly bashful around girls. The girls in his year had decided to take cruel advantage of this social handicap and had launched a campaign of merciless teasing; mock-flirting with him, air-kissing him across the classroom, flashing their knickers at him, pinching his bum in the corridor... The result of this teasing had been only to exacerbate Robin's nervousness around girls; it became a standing joke around the school. It reached the point where he literally could not say a word to any girl without blushing and stammering.

Those girls had ruined him for life.

Robin lets himself into his lonely flat, switches the light on. An old wardrobe stands against one wall. The skirting panel below the doors is loose. He tilts the panel, opening it like a drawer. Now he reaches his hand into the cavity and pulls out a package wrapped in a torn fragment of bedsheet. The sheet is stained with the brown spots of oxidised blood. He unwraps the sheet. Inside it is a heavy hammer. A claw-hammer.

It's no good, thinks Robin. He's going to have to kill another one.

Chapter Nine
Safe as Houses

The row of houses face a high embankment wall. The lane between the two is narrow, the sparse street-lamps shedding pools of orange light. Oblongs of light, muted by curtains, shine weakly from some of the windows of the houses—narrow-fronted, three-storeyed Victorian dwellings, each one long since divided into bedsit accommodation. Had it been daytime, you would have seen that the brick-work of both houses and embankment are blackened with smoke.

Mark Hunter stands in the shadow of the embankment, smoking a pensive cigarette. Apart from himself the street shows no sign of life. High above his head, a passenger train rumbles past.

The house he is currently concerned with is none of those in this gloomy lane. His target is one of a row which stand back-to-back with these dwellings; a street running parallel to this one. To approach his target circuitously is the reason for Mark being on this street. His target is an SEA safe house. At least, it is according to his informant, Perfect.

'They's there alright, Mr 'Unter. Some of them girls what was in them photos you showed me. The bloke, too. That geezer with the glasses.'

'The man? You actually saw him?'

'Saw 'im go in, I did; clear as day. Couldn't swear that 'e's still there now, o' course…'

He has left Perfect in a near-by café, left him with instructions to contact Dodo Dupont if he, Mark, does not return within one hour.

Finishing his cigarette, Mark crushes it under his foot and crosses the lane. He enters the narrow way between two of the buildings, windowless, pitch dark. From this he emerges into a back yard, long, narrow, stone-flagged, littered with junk. Several rusty bicycles lean against an out-house. A tarpaulin-covered motor-bike. Dust-bins. A dilapidated pram. Rotting planks of wood. Battered oil cans. Half-disintegrated cardboard boxes overflowing with discarded junk.

Mark cautiously peers round the edge of the nearest ground-floor window. The curtains are drawn. He can discern voices, music emanating from a television set. Sure-footed, he navigates the cluttered back yard. The wall at the far end is taller than he has anticipated—about twelve feet—but a coal bunker built against it makes reaching the top an easy enough matter. Hauling himself up, he is astride the wall when the back door of the house suddenly opens, spilling light and a human shadow across the flagstones. Mark quickly swings his leg over, drops to the other side, landing in thick weeds. He listens. The clutter of a dust-bin lid, a door slamming. No cry to suggest he has been seen.

He has landed in inky darkness. Wading through a tangle of weeds and briars, he comes to another wall, identical to the one he has just climbed over. This isn't good. He feels his way along the wall. No gate, and nothing to use as a stepping stone for scaling the wall.

He comes to an unexpected corner. Another wall. He feels his way along this wall. No gate. And then another right-angle, and realises he is back at the wall he has just scaled. He walks quickly along this wall, and comes up against another one.

I don't believe this.

He is in a box. Four brick walls, twelve feet high, enclosing a space of about twelve feet by thirty. A void; an extraneous unit of space; boxed in; forgotten; not even on the map.

Mark is trapped.

He gropes amongst the weeds, searching blindly for any object he might use as a step to mount the wall. There is nothing. No-one even uses this space as a dumping ground. It is a negative space in the middle of teeming London; a nowhere.

And I thought I was being clever, coming this way.

Not one to be easily discouraged, Mark returns to the wall marking the boundary of the property that is his target; the wall he needs to scale. He feels the surface of the wall. The surface is uneven, but the flaws he finds in the brickwork are too small to serve as foot-holds. Fine. Then he'll just have to create some foot-holds. He feels along the wall at waist height until his hand finds a brick that feels loose. The brick has cracked down the middle. He tries to extract the loose segment. No luck. From his jacket pocket he produces his clasp-knife. He works the blade between the brick and the mortar. It takes some time but he finally manages to pry the brick loose. Only half the brick, but the space freed ought to be enough for a toe-hold. He now gropes along the surface of the wall at eye-level. He discovers a second loose brick. Composing a silent prayer in gratitude to the natural decay of all matter, Mark tugs the brick from its lodging.

Placing his right foot in the lower foot-hold, Mark hoists himself up, his palms flat against the wall. He inches his left leg upwards; his foot attains the second foot-hold. Abandoning the first foot-hold, he slithers up the wall, extending his arms above him. His fingers curl around the lip of the wall. He heaves himself up, hooks his elbows over the ledge. The rest is easy and he soon he is straddling the top of the wall.

Recovering his breath, he examines his surroundings. The paved yard below, serving a larger house, is more extensive than that of the building opposite, and uncluttered with rubbish. There are several sizeable out-buildings. The three-storeyed house presents a blank façade. Lights show in none of the windows.

Dropping onto another helpful coal bunker, Mark gains the yard. Keeping to the shadow of the out-buildings, he makes his way to the back door, tries the handle. Locked. Stepping back, Mark surveys the façade of the house—and espies a possible way in. He climbs onto the dividing wall—much lower in height than the back wall—between this yard and the next. From this he attains the sloping roof of a projecting section of the house. Before him now is a window, and as he had observed from the ground, an open window. The room beyond is dark and silent. Raising the sash to its full extent, he climbs into the room.

Extracting a slim flashlight from his inside pocket, he switches it on. The beam reveals peeling wall-paper, patches of damp. The room has a musty odour. Up against the wall is a bed. The bedstead looks old, but the linen appears fresh and clean. The torch bean settles on a bed-side cabinet. On its surface are a small shaded lamp, an alarming dildo, a paperback book; apparently the room's current tenant is both a keen reader and a keen masturbator. Crossing the uncarpeted floor, Mark focuses his torch beam on the cover of the book. Appropriately enough, it is an old Penguin edition of Balzac's *A Harlot High and Low*.

Mark moves over to the door of the room, listens. Nothing. Extinguishing the flashlight, he cautiously opens the door. Darkness. He steps out into the corridor, advances slowly. He comes to another door, ajar. He looks inside. Bathroom. Very old fittings. The dripping of a tap. He moves on. Nearing a right-angle turn in the corridor, the low murmur of voices begins to reach his ears. He peeks round the corner. Further along this next arm of the corridor, a thin wedge of light bisects the floor—light from an occupied room, the door slightly ajar.

Flat against the wall, Mark sidles up slowly up to the door, conscious of the old floorboards, any one of which might treacherously announce his presence. Reaching the door, he squats down and peers into the lighted room. He can see very little. A table against one wall; standing on it a bottle of wine, some glasses.

'...all soaps and reality shows,' a girl's voice is saying in a tone of complaint.

'Yes, your television programming is rather depressing,' responds a male voice. (So Vautrin is here!) 'But it's what the majority wants, or those programmes wouldn't be there.'

'Yes, but we shouldn't care what the majority wants, should we?'

'Of course you shouldn't. All that matters is what you want, Jessica. If you want to blow up the *Big Brother* house or Albert Square, then please do so. I only want you to be happy.'

Mark listens on. Two other girlish voices join the conversation, casually debating a lunatic bombing campaign... And Vautrin; his voice smooth and placid, calmly tabling atrocities as though they were the most reasonable suggestions in the world...

Too late, Mark senses the person creeping stealthily up behind him. Before he can react something heavy descends with force onto the top of his head.

Now, there are those who say that out here in the real world it's just not possible to render a human being unconscious with just a single blow to the head. These people lie! Mark was out like a light.

Reality swims slowly back into focus.

His head throbs. He is seated on a chair; more than seated, tightly bound to it with ropes.

The first thing Mark's eyes focus on is Vautrin, leaning against a table, smoking a cigarette, smiling at him. Dressed in a polo-neck and jeans, and without the dark glasses he had worn that night at the hotel. The irises of his eyes are a piercing emerald-green.

'Welcome back, Mark,' he says smoothly. 'I hope you're not feeling too much the worse for your misadventure?'

'Oh, I'm fine,' Mark assures him: 'I've been hit over the head, and now I've been tied to a chair. Comfortably familiar territory for someone in my line of work. You know who I am, then?'

'Of course: the famous Mark Hunter, top troubleshooter for MI5: "the thinking man of action." I've researched your career with some interest; how you traded the East Anglian farmland of your childhood for the corridors of Whitehall, and quickly made a name for yourself as one of MI5's most accomplished field-agents. Quite a transition.'

Mark takes in his surroundings as he listens to Vautrin. He knows from the table with the bottle and glasses that he is in the room he was spying into before he was attacked. Aside from himself and Vautrin, there are four girls in the room. One, he instantly recognises as Trudie Rayne, still wearing her Dale Street school uniform. She stands near the table close to Vautrin. The second girl, leaning casually against the door, wearing jeans and t-shirt is the girl with cropped blonde hair he recognises from the CCTV footage of the raid at Westbirch. Of the other two girls, one is a small, bespectacled, freckle-faced girl with her hair in bunches; the other an even smaller girl with a tousled mop of dark hair and large brown eyes. Bunches wears t-shirt and cargo pants, her neighbour an army shirt and black jeans. Mark thinks he's seen the latter girl somewhere before, but can't immediately think where. These two girls sit side by side on a sagging, venerable-looking sofa. All four girls are observing him with keen interest.

Incongruously, a large poster of a naked Dodo Dupont has been pinned to the wall above the sofa. Mark recognises the image as one of Mayumi's studies of the psychology professor from the *Juno* collection. A colour shot—the images in the book veer between colour and monochrome—the subject bends forward slightly, a pose that accentuates the fullness of her buttocks. Looking back over her shoulder, she smiles with characteristic good humour... This vivid poster contrasts with the mildewed drabness of the room.

Vautrin follows his gaze. 'Surprised? Well, don't be. My girls are big fans of your Professor Dupont,' he explains. 'Of course, we know that she often assists you on your assignments. In fact, the girls have even started a Dodo Dupont fan-club. You should see our main base: pin-ups all over the place.'

'She's cool,' enthuses freckles. 'A real role-model for girls.'

'And buttocks you could eat your dinner off,' sighs short blonde hair.

'One of your girls attacked her with a knife,' objects Mark.

Vautrin shrugs. 'Well, the Professor was trying to prevent her from escaping. I don't say the girls wouldn't kill her if they really had to, but they're still huge fans. You're interested in my girls, aren't you, Mark? Well let me introduce you to the ones we have here: Trudie Rayne, Dizzy Hello, Jessica Harper, Greta Garbo.'

This last is the small, dark girl. Greta Garbo. Mark looks at her with renewed interest. He thought he'd recognised her! Greta Garbo, the child terrorist, poster girl of the RAF. (This RAF being the notorious Red Army Faction, not the Biggles brigade.) Some months ago, Greta had escaped from a maximum-security juvenile detention centre on the continent and had then completely disappeared.

'So, which of you ladies do I have to thank for this lump on my head?' inquired Mark, greetings having been exchanged.

'That would be me!' announces Dizzy cheerfully. She produces her gun, reverses it and mimes striking a blow. 'Pow!'

'You've got yourself quite a collection, here,' says Mark to Vautrin. 'Where do you find them? I mean Greta here's a celebrity, but to the best of my knowledge the other three aren't.'

'They were selected with great care, I can assure you of that. You see, I can sense things, Mark. My mind reached out to these girls.'

'ESP?'

'A resonance. Like-minds joining together on an ethereal wave-length. None of the girls had ever met each other before in the real world, but yet they were connected. I could see the thread that linked them, and so I decided to bring them together.'

'And just who are you, anyway, Vautrin? It seems like you didn't exist until a few months ago.'

'As far as you're concerned, I didn't.'

'You're not going to tell me you're an alien?'

Vautrin smiles. 'Let's just say "I'm not from around these parts."'

'And what's your real name? It can't really be Vautrin.'

'Oh, it is,' the other assures him. 'I mean, yes, I did choose it for myself—but as I've never had any other one, I think I can truthfully say that this is my "real" name.'

'And these girls: how many are there in your little coterie?'

'Eleven girls now. A full complement. The circle is complete.'

'With you at the centre of it.'

Dizzy lights herself a cigarette. She strolls over to Mark, sits herself on his lap.

'Want a drag?'

'I wouldn't say no,' says Mark.

Dizzy places the cigarette in Mark's mouth, let's him take a pull.

'Thanks. So, what's your story, Dizzy?' asks Mark. 'Why did you join Vautrin?'

Dizzy folds her arms around Mark's neck. 'My life was over,' she says wistfully. 'My mum died, you see. She was the world to me. I was about to kill myself, but Vautrin came along and offered me this new life. Now *he's* my world.'

Mark looks at Vautrin. 'You're quite the Svengali, aren't you? You've got your own little seraglio.'

'It's not quite like that, Mark. I never use or abuse the girls sexually.'

'Yeah, and doesn't that piss us off!' declares Dizzy.

Murmurs of agreement from the other SEA girls.

'And so you've taken a bunch of ordinary girls, extracted them from their lives, and turned them into killers.'

Vautrin shrugs. 'Several of them were already killers when I met them. That saucy minx sitting on your knee is one of them.'

'Yep!' confirms Dizzy.

'Me too,' says Jessica. 'But only by accident.'

'And Greta is a well-known killer,' adds Vautrin.

'Yes, but what about Trudie there?' argues Mark. 'She wasn't a killer until you put a gun in her hands, was she?'

'Well, no; she wasn't,' concedes Vautrin. 'But do you know what was going on in her life at the time?'

'Yes, I do,' replies Mark. 'I've heard that she was being prostituted against her will. But if you knew about that, Vautrin, you could have rescued her from that situation without turning her into a killer.'

'But I *like* being a killer,' speaks up Trudie. 'I love being in the SEA. I'm more happy now than I've ever been before.'

'The SEA,' repeats Mark. 'The Society of Evil Actions. I found one of your calling cards at the Hackney place.'

'We left it there for you,' says Vautrin.

'That's what I thought. From the name I take it you have no political agenda?'

'Nope. None at all. I gave up on politics a long time ago, and the subject bores my girls witless. Democratic politics are a joke that's not even funny anymore. Look at this country: you elect your politicians into office, and then you proceed to uniformly despise them and belittle them at every opportunity. I mean yes, your politicians are continually saying and doing things which invite ridicule and contempt—but it's still a ridiculous situation, isn't it?'

'So you people of the SEA do what you do just for the sake of it?'

'We just want to shake things up a bit.'

'And have fun while we're doing it,' appends Dizzy. 'That's what's most important.'

She rises from Mark's knee.

'And now you're going to start a bombing campaign with those explosives you helped yourselves to at Westbirch,' says Mark. 'I heard some of your conversation in here before I got knocked on the head.'

'Yes, we've limited ourselves mostly to single executions up until now,' explains Vautrin. 'And the girls are starting to get restless. They want to branch out onto larger-scale acts of terrorism. Something loud and vivid.'

'Yep! There's nothing like a big bang,' agrees Dizzy.

The girls giggle at this.

'I can see you don't have anything resembling a conscience, Vautrin,' says Mark. 'Maybe that's normal wherever you come from. You're just reshaping these girls in your own image. Making them think the way you do. You're not doing it for them, at all: you're doing it for you.'

'Now there you wrong me, Mark,' demurs Vautrin. 'My intentions are entirely altruistic.'

'You've got stop this madness, Vautrin.'

'I thought that was your job, Mark?' counters Vautrin. 'Which brings us to our next question: Now that we've got you, what are we going to do with you?' says Vautrin. 'I admit you surprised me being here tonight. I wasn't expecting this visit.'

'I suppose we'll just have to kill him,' says Trudie, a tone of regret in her voice.

'*Nein, nein*!' from little Greta. Launching herself from the sofa, she throws her arms around Mark's neck, showering his face with childish kisses. 'I like him. He'ss so sweet!'

'Unhand me, young woman!' from Mark, indignant. 'I'm old enough to be your dirty uncle.'

'I thought Mark was our arch-enemy,' speaks up Jessica. 'Who's going to be our arch-enemy if we just kill him?'

'Yes, that is a bit of a dilemma,' agrees Vautrin. 'Ought we to kill our adversary this early in the game?' He claps his hands. 'This calls for a conference. Downstairs, I think. Mark shouldn't be present while we're deciding his fate.' To Mark: 'You will excuse us?'

'Take as long as you like.'

Vautrin and the four girls file out of the room.

Left alone, Mark waits while their footsteps retreat down the stairs. From moving about he has already established that the chair he has been tied to is a very rickety one. He might be able to work himself free. The back feels loose, the legs feel loose. His hands are tied to the vertical bars of the back-rest, his ankles to the front legs. He leans forward, pulls, hoping to pull the back away from the seat completely. The chair creaks, but doesn't give. Maybe the other way. He leans his weight against the chair-back. He leans too far. The chair over-balances, one of the back legs gives out, and chair and Mark Hunter crash to the ground, the back-rest coming away from the seat.

Mark listens, expecting to hear footsteps pounding up the stairs. Nothing. Have they not heard him? Either way, there is no time to lose. Turning onto his side, he wriggles his hands loose from the struts of the chair. Now he is able to untie his ankles.

And then the light cuts out.

The room is windowless, so Mark finds himself in almost pitch darkness. What has happened? Has the light-bulb just died? A power cut? He listens. No sound of a commotion downstairs. He climbs to his feet and moves over to the table against the far wall. He had observed before that his gun and the contents of his pockets have been placed here. Feeling with his hands, he finds his belongings. Wallet, torch, keys, phone and clasp-knife he returns to his pockets; the gun he keeps in his hand.

He steps out of the room. The corridor is still in darkness. He advances, reaches the head of a staircase. A large window, uncurtained, looks out onto the street. He sees street-lamps; lighted windows in the opposite houses. No power cut, then. Slowly, he descends the stairs, gun at the ready, finally alighting in a spacious hallway. Still no sound. Where has everyone gone? The front door beckons. Should he just get the hell out of here while he can?

But then he does hear a sound. A door creaks. Mark follows the sound to the rear of the hall. A door stands ajar. He pushes it open. It creaks. He steps forward into the room.

Suddenly his gun-arm is clamped by an unseen assailant, and before he can react he is knocked off balance and thrown adroitly across the room, to land heavily on the uncarpeted floor.

'Who's there?' he demands.

'Is that you?' speaks a familiar female voice.

Mark pulls out his torch, flicks the switch. Transfixed by the beam, one Dodo Dupont standing beside the doorway, eyes shielded, smiling at him, her silhouette climbing the wall behind.

'Sorry about that, sweetheart; you didn't announce yourself.'

Mark climbs to his feet. 'Quite alright, I assure you. How did you get here?'

'Your Perfect informer informed me.'

'Ah, yes! My sixty minutes must have expired. Where're Vautrin and the girls?'

'I haven't seen Vautrin or any girls. Unless they're hiding upstairs, this place seems deserted.'

'They're not upstairs; I was up there and they came down here. Were the lights out when you arrived?'

'Yes.'

Mark tries the light switch near the door.

'There's a bulb up there, but no power. They must have turned off the supply at the fuse-box.'

'What precisely is going on here?' Dodo wants to know.

A wry smile. 'Another one of Vautrin's jokes, I think. And I'm the stooge.'

The fuse-box is located, the lights restored, and a rapid search of the premises reveals, as Mark has suspected, that Vautrin and the girls have decamped.

Coming to rest in the room in which he had enjoyed his conference with the SEA, Mark brings Dodo up to speed.

'He's the most charming homicidal maniac I've ever met,' he says, referring to his recent captor. 'I can't figure him out at all. Maybe he really *is* an alien. And he has some magnetic influence over those girls—a sort of lethal personal charisma.'

'Yes, but he chooses susceptible subjects for that magnetism of his,' says Dodo. 'Those girls he's picked up all seem to have been vulnerable in one way or another.'

'Yes... Trudie Rayne is a case in point... You know, she admitted it was her who killed those classmates of hers; the ones who were pimping her—admitted it cheerfully.'

'And he said it's all some big game that they're playing, did he...?' Dodo nods to the poster of herself. 'And that we're both part of it...'

Mark nods. 'Yes, whether we want to be or not. And to milk the metaphor further: we're going to have start making our own rules for this particular game to have any chance of winning it before things get out of hand.'

Chapter Ten
Interlude in Paris

Phillipe Sagan met Claudette Lantier at the *Sorbonne*, where they were both studying History. He was a tall young man, lanky and awkward, bearded. She was a redhead, with aristocratic good looks. Both were quiet and studious—knowledgeable, but naïve in terms of life-experience. The two slowly built up a friendship, studying together, and in their free time visiting museums and galleries, or enjoying country walks. They didn't mix well with the other students, and eschewed the drinking and partying lifestyle; disdained it, in fact. After graduating, Phillipe and Claudette decided to become man and wife. It seemed the natural and inevitable thing to do. Both came from strict Roman Catholic families, and so the nuptials were solemnised under that church. Their honeymoon was in Italy, but was strictly speaking nothing more than a cultural sight-seeing tour, as the marriage remained unconsummated. They returned from this excursion and settled in their native Paris, where Phillipe found work as a research assistant, and Claudette took up teaching. They were reasonably happy together and talked freely about all subjects except one. Things went on in this comfortable but unsatisfactory way until one night when walking home after working late, Phillipe was approached by a man, a stranger. The man spoke to Phillipe and Phillipe listened to him. And then he followed the man to a garret apartment. When Phillipe returned home that night, he made love to his wife for the first time. Nine months later, a daughter was born to them. They named her Albertine. As the child moved from infancy to childhood, it was Phillipe, who, enjoying more flexible working hours, performed most of the work of raising Albertine. At nights Phillipe would often absent himself from his wife, saying he liked to go out walking after dark as it gave him time to think. Albertine, who inherited her mother's red hair and green eyes, and her father's thin features, was a precocious child, quick to learn, quiet like her parents. She remained an only child. One day, when Albertine was twelve, Phillipe and Claudette announced to their daughter that they would no longer be living together. When asked by them which parent she would prefer to live with, Albertine without hesitation chose her father.

Father and daughter moved to another part of Paris, close to the Catholic secondary school Albertine was due to start attending. One day, early the following year, Phillipe brought home a man named Jean, a handsome, amiable young man some ten years younger than himself. Time passed; Jean became a frequent visitor. And then, Phillipe announced to his daughter that Jean would be living with them from henceforth. Jean was a 'special friend.' Albertine, now fourteen, and who had learned as much from her fellow students at school as she had from her habited instructors, knew exactly what the term 'special friend' implied. She accepted the addition to the household without protest, merely taking the opportunity to announce to her father that she had taken up smoking, and would it be permissible for her to smoke in the apartment? Her father acquiesced.

Soon after this came the defining night of young Albertine's life. Sleep was eluding her, and she left her bedroom needing to relieve herself. Traversing the darkened landing, she heard sounds emanating from her father's room. The door to this room was usually firmly closed when Jean and her father had retired for the night, but tonight it was ajar. Albertine approached the door, crouched before it, and peered into the room. A bedside lamp shed a soft glow over the room. Her father and Jean were lying on the bed, side-by-side, talking softly. Both were naked; her father thin and angular, pale and smooth. By contrast, Jean was bronzed, toned, hirsute. He seemed like a strong, aggressive animal. Her father seemed fragile. At this point Jean stood up, revealing to the girl's eyes a rampant state of arousal. Albertine gasped at the vision. They had talked about such things at school, she and her classmates, but she had never actually seen one before. She thought it monstrous, yet compelling. Projecting from a jungle of hair, a vast pole taut with veins; the purple crown slick like an internal organ, and at the root, two ripe plums, sheathed in skin. Her father sat up on the edge of the bed and she observed his erection, much smaller in size, unsatisfactory-looking by comparison. She watched as her father arranged himself on the edge of the bed—presenting himself, proffering himself. Her pulses raced, for she knew what this presaged. And sure enough, Jean moved around behind her father, and guided his member between those bony buttocks; pushed and penetrated. Albertine, enraptured, followed the motion of the now copulating couple with a rhythm of her own, performed with her hand between her legs. As the violence of Jean's thrusts increased, so did she rub herself harder. All three of them climaxed simultaneously.

After this epiphany, she would often spy on the lovers; whenever she found the bedroom door ajar—and it invariably was—she would become a third participant in their activities. She discovered her father to be a passive lover, much preferring to be taken rather than to take, while Jean was the far more virile, aggressive lover. What excited her the most was the sight of Jean's huge member. Her at first conflicting feelings had resolved themselves, and she now deemed it the most beautiful thing in the world. Just to see it was to fill her with emotion, and set her heart racing. To see it in the glory of eruption would almost bring tears to her eyes. Watching her father fellate and caress Jean, she began to feel the pangs of envy; *she* wanted to be the one taking that penis in her mouth; *she* wanted to be the one holding and caressing it.

One weekend, when Phillipe was away, Jean had come into Albertine's bedroom. He revealed to her that he knew she had been spying; that it was he himself who had been purposefully leaving the door ajar to facilitate this. He now offered the girl this chance of taking a leading role. Upon her acquiescence, Jean had unzipped himself, his partially-distended penis soon rising to its full glory. Albertine had approached it at first with trepidation, and then with reverence, falling to her knees before her god, for the first time close enough to feel its heat, to breathe its odour, to taste it in her mouth; she had performed the rites of worship with expert hands, bringing her god to a crisis, and imbibing its warm effluence, the eucharist of her religion… Naturally, the loss of her virginity had followed soon after this; and from that time onwards, she would invariably find Jean waiting for her at home when she returned from school in the afternoons. On those occasions, they would always have a clear two hours before her father's return from work. As a sodomist, Jean preferred to take Albertine analy, and she indulged him in this, but she derived more pleasure from virginal intercourse—but most of all she liked her divinity to be right before her eyes and to hold in her hands; to taste and caress; to cap the geyser and feel the thrilling pressure of its discharge…

Albertine did not love Jean; in fact, she despised the man for betraying, while still living off, her father—moreover, she was confident that she was not the only additional sexual partner in his life. She deemed him shallow, vain and conceited, and his conversation—when not pertaining to sex—vapid. No, she did not love Jean; only one part of him: this she adored, speaking to it with words of love that she would never have addressed to its owner. Like a New Age witch, Albertine worshipped the penis—but she did not worship the men they were attached to.

And then Albertine came to realise that Jean's penis alone was not enough for her. She hungered for intimacy with others; she craved variety. It was at a party that she found her first opportunity. One of her rich school-friends, her family being absent for the weekend, invited a number of her classmates, including Albertine, to a Saturday night party. There would be boys, she promised. There had indeed been boys, and Albertine had taken all of them. She had assumed complete command of the event, transforming her friend's party into an orgy of phallic worship. Jean's fit of infantile jealousy when she had informed him of this marathon had been most gratifying.

And now we come to the crisis point.

Albertine lies on her bed, smoking a post-coital cigarette, basking in the afterglow of a satisfactorily torrid bout of sex. A tall, oval-faced girl, slender of build; her russet hair cut short; haughty green eyes sit below arched, satirical brows; a long, pointed nose, and one of those thin-lipped mouths whose pouting tautness hints at insatiable appetites barely contained. Her breasts are small and conical, her pubic thatch of a russet shade, her hands and feet long and thin. She wears her navy-blue stockings, the only undivested part of her school uniform. Jean reclines next to her, tanned and muscular, leaning on one elbow, watching her.

'So, do you still not love me, Albertine?' he asks coyly.

'No, you are a pig,' replies Albertine, exhaling smoke through her nose and not turning to look at him. 'I admire your penis and your ability to put it to good use. That is all.'

'But I was your first lover, Albertine,' Jean reminds her. 'I was your teacher in the art of love. Do you not owe me a debt of gratitude for that?'

'None at all. I agree that you were my teacher, but you taught me only to gratify yourself, not for my benefit. And do not fail to recollect that another word for "teaching" is "grooming". That is how they would describe the matter in a court of law.'

'You are so cold, Albertine,' protests Jean.

His whining tones irritates her.

'Cold to you, yes, because I have no warm feelings for you. Never expect me to fawn all over you like a love-struck schoolgirl. You are just a vapid gigolo, kept by Papa, and you can't even be constant to the man who feeds and shelters you.'

'What would you have me do? As you say, he feeds and shelters me; in return I satisfy him as a lover. What I do the rest of the time is surely my affair?'

'You think that because you are so completely selfish.'

'What about you, Albertine? I never forced you, not even the first time. You gave yourself willingly to your father's lover.'

'I gave myself to you because my body urgently required it. Do not think that because of all this I have no respect for Papa. I love him, as much as I can love anyone. He needs me because he is weak. That is why I chose to remain with him when my parents separated.'

'But I don't see how you can—'

'Silence! Your conversation bores me.'

She continues to smoke her cigarette. Jean turns over on his back, hands cupped behind his head. When she has finished her cigarette and extinguished it, Albertine climbs on top of Jean, straddles him, lowers her foam-flecked vagina over his face. Cunnilingus is the one sexual act Jean does not particularly care for, so it amuses Albertine to make him perform it. She lies down over him, bringing her own face level with his genitalia. She takes the soft, inert limb in her hand; it soon begins to stir, and, seemingly with an existence separate to the body it is attached to, it rapidly grows; gaining length, breadth and solidity.

After this, two mouths are at work, one tasting heaven, the other endurance...

And then the bedroom door opens. It is Phillipe.

Albertine leaps from on top of Jean, pulls the sheets over herself. Jean sits up. Both are terrified, speechless. They have been so complacent in their afternoons of lovemaking, they have just never envisaged this happening.

Phillipe just stands there staring, mortified disbelief written on his bearded face. Then he turns and flees the room.

'Papa!' cries Albertine.

Jean turns on her, his expression savage. 'You stupid bitch. If you hadn't started this last stupid game—You knew he would be back soon.'

'Shut up, you prick,' snarls Albertine. 'All you care about is the loss of your bread ticket. Did you see Papa's face? I have never seen anyone look so completely crushed.'

And then they hear the gunshot.

They find Phillipe Sagan lying on the floor in his bedroom, the revolver at his side. Albertine screams, falls to her knees.

'Pathetic bastard,' mutters Jean, bitterly. 'I'm out of here. You can tell the police what the hell you like, but I wasn't here. Got it?'

He returns to Albertine's room for his discarded clothes. He has just finished putting them on when Albertine, tears streaming down her eyes, appears in the doorway.

'What do you want now?' And then he sees the gun in her hand. 'You crazy bitch! What did you pick that up for? Do you want the police to think you killed him?'

Albertine raises the gun, levels it at Jean's head.

'Fuck you, Jean.'

'No—'

She fires.

Albertine runs out into the street. She has thrown on her school clothes, her satchel slung over her shoulder. She has put the revolver in the satchel. There had been residents out on the landings as she ran down the stairs. They had heard the shots. Albertine had left the door of their apartment wide open. The police would be along soon.

She runs on blindly, putting street after street between herself and the tragedy. Finally, reaching a park, she stops, dropping exhausted onto a bench.

Wracked with guilt, she bursts into fresh tears, burying her face in her hands. She has killed him. She has killed him. It is not Jean of whom she thinks; Jean was a pig who got what he deserved: it is her father that occupies her thoughts. She has killed Papa, driven him to a pathetic suicide.

To her annoyance, she senses someone sit down on the bench by her side. She ignores him. Probably just some park pervert wanting to pick up the girl in the pinafore dress and navy-blue stockings.

But then the newcomer speaks. 'Don't cry, Albertine.'

She looks up at him. A beatnik type with low fringe, long sideburns, polo-neck sweater. He is a stranger to Albertine.

'How do you know my name?'

The man smiles. 'I know everything about you, Albertine. I know that you have a gun in that satchel and that you're planning to do away with yourself with it.'

She is startled. 'How can you know this?'

'I told you: I know everything.'

'And what business is it of yours?'

'It would be a terrible waste.'

'That would be my affair.'

'You really don't have to do it.'

'Who are you, anyway?'

'My name is Vautrin.'

'But your accent is English.'

'It's an adopted name. I took it from one of your country's greatest men of letters.'

'And are you, like Monsieur Balzac's character, an emissary of the devil?'

Another smile. 'I could be. But right now I'm here as your saviour.'

A hollow laugh from Albertine. 'If you know so much about me then you must comprehend that I am beyond saving.'

'I know it must seem like that. Your father has taken his own life and you blame yourself. (We won't even mention that idiot Jean.) You can atone for your perceived crimes either by killing yourself or submitting yourself to the law. I'm here to propose a third option. Come with me and I promise you a completely new life; a new start.'

'In England?'

'In England. I'm starting a little organisation; a movement of sorts; just for girls like you.'

'And what are we to do in this organisation of yours?'

'Whatever you want, Albertine. Complete freedom guaranteed. No past, no future; an organisation dedicated to living for the moment…'

'You jest with me, monsieur.'

'I'm very serious. You're a link in the chain, Albertine. You, and other girls I'm assembling are all connected, special. And myself, I'm the catalyst; the catalyst who brings you together.'

'And are you going to speak of this being "destiny"?'

'No. Nothing is cast in stone. We can each forge our own destiny. Come with me, Albertine—I promise you a whole new life…'

Vautrin takes her hand. She feels something pass from him into her. A connection. She looks into his compelling green eyes and knows that her destiny lies with him.

Chapter Eleven
Inside the Headquarters of the SOCIETY of EVIL ACTIONS! (Nefarious Plots, Intrigue and Danger!)

Now I know the patient reader has been gagging to take a tour of the SEA's secret headquarters, located somewhere in Limbo, Sussex. You have, haven't you? Thought as much. Well, your accommodating narrator is here to oblige. But where to begin? It's such a vast and sprawling complex. I could speak of the endless corridors of futuristic design and uniform white in colour; corridors illumined by some undetermined light source. The luxury suites in the central hub occupied by the various SEA members could be described in detail. The plethora of entertainment facilities, from the giant water park to the well-supplied video arcade could be listed in full. The team of scientists working under duress and in captivity in a remote sector of the complex could be tantalisingly alluded to… All this and much more could be delineated at length, but I know that my reader is an individual of refined taste and intellectual cultivation, and respecting this I have a notion you would much prefer to be taken straight to the base's main recreation room, which at the time of going to press is occupied by eleven young ladies in the flower of youth and disporting themselves in various states of undress.

I hear murmurs of assent.

The SEAbase recreation room is spacious, supplied with chairs and sofas so comfortable and luxurious that they could not have come from IKEA—as well as a profusion of bean bags and cushions. Upon these our heroines sit, sprawl and slouch. A huge LED TV dominates one wall; the production being screened is the French classic *Baise-Moi*, a particular favourite of the girls. They have seen it loads of times before, so they chat freely amongst themselves, but without completely ignoring the film. (When there is a television switched on in the room, people will look at it. This is a modern fundamental truth of human nature.) The rec room is further supplied with a pool table and a jukebox, not in use at present. The white walls are enlivened with a plethora of colour pinups of Dodo Dupont, enlargements of images from her Mayumi Takahashi photobooks.

This evening, all eleven of the SEA girls are present, if not exactly correct. Alcohol is being consumed, and the girls are attired as for one of the raunchier of girlie sleepovers. Let me introduce you: first, we have Trudie Rayne. Trudie swigs her fourth can of Foster's, a bag of cheese puffs within easy reach. She sits on one of the luxury non-self-assembly sofas previously mentioned, wearing a peach-coloured silk chemise. With one leg drawn up on the sofa, her exposed delta of Venus smiles vertically at everyone.

On the other side of the bag of cheese puffs, Rachel Ramone sits with her legs tucked under her, cigarette in hand, and sipping a gin and tonic. Since her timely rescue from those straight-edge losers of the Brixton Anarchist Collective, Rachel has grown quite fond of alcohol. Her new best friend Dizzy Hello has introduced her to these beverages. Dizzy has also introduced Rachel to eye-pleasing underwear, and likes nothing more than to dress-up the one-time political activist. Thusly, we see Rachel sporting a black basque corset with matching thong, stockings and suspenders.

One person not sparing a glance for the film is Jessica Harper;

her of the glasses, freckles and twintails, seen here clad in a gauzy negligee. Her tip-tilted nose is buried in a book—to be exact, Emile Zola's novel, *Truth*. (This being the third book in the great writer's 'Four Gospels' tetralogy; which is actually a trilogy as the fourth book was never written on account of the author rather inconsiderately dying the night before he was due to start work on it.) Jessica, although engrossed by the story, occasionally looks up from her reading to admire her friend Sophie Harris, stretched out on the floor in front of her. 'Wait a minute!' I hear you cry; 'Sophie! Sophie Who?' Relax. You are not losing track (which would be understandable enough anyway, with eleven murderous heroines to keep in mind); Sophie is one we haven't met before. Sophie is an athletic girl with a flapper's bob of black hair, curled up at the ends, bangs ruler-straight. Laying on her tummy stretched out over two big cushions, she is dressed in a simple white petticoat, which, more through squirming and inattention than from wilful exhibitionism, is currently riding up around her waist and displaying two shapely buttocks. I know what you're thinking; but don't jump the gun here—It is not those terrestrial hemispheres which keep distracting Jessica. To find the source of her persistent interest we have to travel further south, along those supple, athletic legs, the type that are of an almost uniform thickness from thigh to calf; past the thick ankles with which they terminate, and onto the broad heavy feet—here we arrive at our destination. Yes, it is these nether extremities, which that hussy Sophie swings about in a most lewd and provocative way, that attract Jessica's attention! Those large pink feet, languidly swaying, curled and pointed. The large oval of her great toe, the round buds of her smaller toes; the voluptuous folds of skin along the sole—all of these indicative of a pleasant aroma to the nose and a pleasing tartness to the tongue. You see, as well as being the SEA's chief bookworm, Jessica also fills the important function of being the team's premier foot fetishist. And not being Chinese, Jessica doesn't favour tiny feet. No siree, ma'am. As far as our Jessie is concerned, the bigger the better; hence her intense admiration of Sophie's perfectly formed size tens. Please don't think this a monomania on Jessie's part. Nothing of the sort. Jessica is a girl of many and varied interests, and she only occasionally lifts her eyes from her book for refreshing look at Sophie's feet—and then it's eyes down again and attention returned to anti-Semitism and the iniquities of the Roman Catholic Church.

On another sofa sit Juliette Wainwright and Chrissie Wylde. We know Juliette, the elegant and refined heiress, and absentee student of the famed Imrie Academy. She looks every bit the dominatrix tonight in black leather bra and knickers with thigh-boots to match; a Nazi officer's peaked cap sitting jauntily on her blonde head. Kneeling at her feet is her slave for this evening, Flossie Farraday. Flossie has a collar around her neck, Juliette idly holding the lead. Flossie—you may recall Mark and Dodo investigating her disappearance—is a beautiful girl with long, straight chestnut hair. She wears a flower-patterned bra and knickers set. Struggling to escape from the former are the largest pair of mammaries in the SEA.

Chrissie Wylde, as you probably don't recall, was one of the participants in that thrilling raid on Westbirch army base—but alas, I neglected to describe her at the time. She is a tall, vivacious girl, with a generous smile, sparkling eyes, and abundant brown hair collected at the crown in a pony-tail. Tonight she is modelling for us a lacy black bra and thong. Fizzing agreeably from the beer she has been necking, she giggles merrily at the antics of the charming heroines of *Baise-Moi*. (You can't see it because she's sitting on it, but Chrissie is also the owner of the fattest bottom in the SEA; twin hemispheres of prodigious proportions and the source of much good-natured joking, slapping and fondling from the other girls.)

A third sofa is occupied by Gina Santella and Albertine Sagan. Toying with her ubiquitous knife, Gina wears a cropped version of her usual khaki vest. Being nude from the belly down, you just can't help noticing that, although the hair on her head is a silky honey blonde, the forest of her *mons veneris* is undeniably dark brown in hue. Now, it is not for me to suggest that Gina is not a natural blonde, just because her collar and cuffs don't happen to match. Having no evidence to support it, I make no such claim, and merely remind the reader that nature is infinite, mysterious, full of wonders to behold, and that these administrative errors do sometimes occur.

Albertine—the only lady present who doesn't have to look at the film's subtitles—sits cross-legged, smoking cigarette after cigarette, sipping gin and tonic. She wears an egg-shell blue silk camisole, bordered with lace, and shorts to match. (And as I only just described Albertine's physical appearance in the last chapter, I ain't doing it again.)

Dizzy Hello rises from the beanbag on which she has been reclining and crosses the room to fix herself another drink. Dizzy, being the healthy animal she is, prefers to wear no clothes at all as often as possible. She loves to 'revel in her animal nakedness'—a juicy line from Bram Stoker's *Lair of the White Worm*, that my mind has long retained. (And in using this comparison, I am not implying that our Dizzy is covered in body-paint; that was just Amanda Donohoe in the film version.) Dizzy moves with the grace and ease of someone who only sees clothes as an incumbrance to moving with grace and ease—someone for whom to walk nakedly is to walk naturally. Her figure is an exquisite short-legged hour-glass; her breasts and bottom are both rounded perfection—and boy does she know it! A table across the room, stacked with cans of beer, bottles of spirits, bottles of mixers, plus numerous bags of munchies is her destination.

Sweet little Greta Garbo, also in search of refreshment, follows Dizzy to the table. Greta is dressed sensibly in a plain white sports bra and knickers.

Dizzy fixes herself a vodka and coke.

'Want one?' she asks the German girl, holding up the bottle.

Greta raises her hand in a gesture of firm refusal.

'*Nein.* I neffer drink alcohol. I must remain sober for the good off the causse.'

(The others have long since given up trying to explain to Greta that they don't really have a cause as such.)

'I vill just haff a coke.'

'Coming up.'

Dizzy pours out a glass of coke, and then, making sure the little terrorist isn't looking, adds a generous measure of vodka.

'*Danke*,' says Greta, accepting the proffered glass. 'I am very thirsty.'

She downs it in one. Her cheeks instantly redden, her large eyes grow even larger.

'That vos good! I vill haff anoffer!'

Dizzy is happy to oblige.

'…Yeah, but almost any girl is a male fantasy these days,' Trudie is saying to Juliette. 'Even sadists like you and Dizzy.'

Juliette holds up a hand. 'I will have to dispute with you on one point, Trudie dearest: I am the only qualified sadist here; Dizzy is just bloodthirsty.'

'She's a couple of Pakistani men short of a grooming gang,' opines Chrissie.

'All of us here fantasies to some men,' says Flossie.

Juliette gives Flossie's collar a tug. 'I didn't give you permission to speak, slave. But yes, you're right. The clinical sadist, the bubbly psychopath, the cute bomb-maker… We would all be fantasies to some of those men who are aroused at the idea of women encroaching on the traditionally male preserve of perpetrating violence and bloodshed.'

A triumphant Dizzy returns, towing Greta, who is clamped around her waist.

'I luff you!' Greta is saying.

'And I love you, sweetheart,' responds Dizzy, ruffling her hair.

'Greta, you're hammered!' exclaims Chrissie.

Releasing Dizzy, Greta sways on the spot.

'*Nein, nein*. I neffer touch alcohol.'

She runs over to Chrissie, throws her arms round her neck.

'I luff you!'

'Dizzy, you're mean!' laughs Chrissie. 'You've got her shit-faced!'

'You're never too young to start,' asserts Dizzy. She slides onto the sofa next to Albertine, takes the French girl's cigarette and helps herself to a drag.

Greta has moved on to Gina, hugging the seated girl's waist, cheek pressed against that dark pubic thatch. 'I luff you!'

'*Grazie*,' says Gina, patting Greta's head. 'I am also quite fond of you.'

Dizzy starts to fondle Albertine. The French girl remains aloof.

'I want none of your lesbian fumblings,' she says. 'I only fuck cocks.'

'Then you *are* fucked,' responds Dizzy brightly. 'Vautrin's the only one with that kind of equipment around here, and he doesn't seem like he's interested in using it.'

'There are the scientists,' Rachel reminds her.

'They're out of bounds,' says Dizzy, her hand also out of bounds in Albertine's shorts. 'Anyway, who ever heard of a scientist who was good in bed?'

'I luff you!' says Greta to Rachel.

Dizzy, on her knees before Albertine, starts to pull off her shorts.

'No, I say!'

'No, you say,' mimics Dizzy, exploring with her hand. 'Down here it's a different story. You're gagging for it, my little *grisette*.'

She buries her face between Albertine's legs.

Meanwhile, Jessica has finally succumbed to temptation. Zola has been tossed aside and she straddles Sophie's back, industriously licking the girl's feet. Jessica is in no way to blame for her actions here: she is simply obeying her natural instincts. The guilt and responsibility lie with Sophie: she was asking for it, flaunting her bare feet like that!

Greta has now fallen at Trudie's feet.

'I luff you most off all *mein liebling*,' she says. 'You are so strong and healthy!'

And before you can bat an eye-lid, Greta's tousled mop is tickling Trudie's thighs as she burrows away like an eager terrier. Trudie—very vocal at these times—broadcasts her approbation to the room.

Juliette, beginning to feel left out, tugs Flossie's collar, points imperiously to her own leather-clad crotch...

At this point, we have to take reluctant leave of this innocent and charming *vignette*. We have to leave our virtuous heroines and turn our attention to a scientist; and a male scientist at that. I know! and I apologise profusely—but this story does have a plot of sorts, and occasionally it needs to be nudged along; and our scientist has a brief but very important role to play in this regard.

However, not wishing to mar a delightful chapter, one that will certainly be remembered by literary history alongside the likes of 'The Devil—Ivan's Nightmare,' from *The Brothers Karamazov*, I shall consign our boring scientist to the ensuing chapter.

Chapter Twelve
The Guy Had Guts!

They've cracked the code on the door and now Herriot has escaped from the lab into the complex.

And now... well he can't really say that he is lost; in order to become lost you have to have known where you were starting from in the first place. Herriot's starting point was the lab; but the precise location of that lab is an enigma to him. An escaped prisoner, his destination is freedom, but he has no idea in which direction that objective lies, or how long it will take him to reach it. He has been walking for some time now, traversing these endless white corridors. This base or whatever it is seems to defy logic: an endless maze of intersecting corridors; corridors for the sake of corridors.

Herriot ploughs on, half-walking, half-running. Has he been missed yet? Is he being searched for? No audible alarm has been raised. He hasn't seen a soul. Can such a huge complex really be occupied solely by that madman Vautrin and his gang of psychotic girls?

He has to find a way out of this nightmare.

Being the youngest and fittest amongst the hostage scientists, Herriot had been selected by Professor Norton for this escape bid. Desperation has set in. They just couldn't go on much longer. Being forced to work for Vautrin, working for all they knew against the interests of their own country—their own planet, even. Refusing to obey Vautrin's mandates is not an option. They had tried that once at the beginning: refused to touch the machinery, to continue the research; demanded their freedom. When they had given Vautrin this ultimatum, he had simply sighed and called in three of his girls. 'Non-essential personnel'—administrative staff, janitors—had been separated from the group and the girls had killed them all; gunned them down there and then.

Refusing to work is not an option. But the work, the captivity, is slowly driving them up the wall.

And where are they? How were they abducted and brought here? From the absence of windows, they assume the place must be somewhere underground, but even this is no more than supposition. They don't even know if they are still in England. Not one of them can remember how they had been brought here. A blank space obstructs recollection; a void of missing time.

Where are these corridors taking him? To freedom? Or will he perversely end up back where he started from?

And then, turning yet another corner he hears sound for the first time since leaving his friends behind. Talking. Multiple voices. Female.

He sees a pair of doors ahead, on his left. The sounds seem to issue from the room beyond. He sidles up to them. The doors are supplied with circular panes of glass. He peers inside. Some sort of recreation room. A huge television screen faces him on the opposite wall, showing a subtitled film. And there are those sick little girls, immersed in a clearly drunken orgy.

Good. At least they're occupied.

Herriot passes quickly on. He has found his way to the inhabited part of the base; logic dictates that the way out should be nearby. In the next corridor he comes to a pair of sliding metal doors, their red colour seeming to confirm their importance. A key panel is fixed to the wall beside them. Lift doors. Herriot's heart pounds. Is this it? Has he finally found the way out of this nightmare?

He presses a button on the panel. The doors slide open, reveal the angular vacancy of a lift compartment.

He steps inside. The doors close. Without any prompting, the lift starts to ascend. Yes, upwards! Upwards to freedom. It seems a long ascent, but finally the lift comes to a halt. The red doors part. Facing Herriot are a second pair of doors, wooden, old-looking, firmly closed. Sudden panic. Were they going to be locked? Would a key be needed to open them?

No. He pushes the doors, and they open with gratifying ease. Beyond, darkness.

Herriot steps through the doorway. The light from the lift car illumines a dusty living room—a few sticks of ancient, cobweb-shrouded furniture; boarded-up windows; a solid-looking door... Behind him, the lift doors close, extinguishing the light. And then the wooden doors slam shut.

Herriot spins round. It seems unnatural, this shutting of those doors; more the work of a phantom than of electronics. Experimentally, he turns the handle, just to see if the door will still open. The door *does* open, and flabbergasted Herriot finds himself looking into the cobwebbed darkness of another musty room! No bright red lift doors stare at him. No lift. It isn't possible! Could the entire lift shaft have descended into the floor? He drops to his knees, examines the floor. Bare floorboards, thick with dust and decay—Not a sign of a hatch or concealed opening of any kind.

Wait. Never mind this enigma—He needs to be getting a move on! His escape may already have been discovered.

Dusting off his hands, he runs back to the first room and to the door that looks like an exterior door. He turns the handle; the door opens. And yes, he is outside. A star-filled sky, fresh air, rolling grassy countryside. He feels giddy. Blessed freedom! He had thought he would never see the sky again. He breathes in the cool night air, scented with turf. Before him is a rutted yard; beyond this, rising grassland. He sees a patch of whiteness against the hillside, and realises it is a huddled group of sleeping sheep. Setting off, he runs towards the top of the drive, and looking back sees that the building he has just left appears to be an old farmhouse; rambling, decrepit, not a light showing.

Beyond the gates, a track running to left and right. Which way? Either. He just has to get as far away from this house as possible, before they notice he has gone.

He sets off.

'So the Disappearing Building has turned up, then?' asks Dodo, at the wheel of her Jaguar. Mark Hunter sits beside her. They are travelling down the motorway.

'No, but one of the scientists who was in it has,' answers Mark. 'Dr William Herriot. In the early hours of this morning he stumbled onto a road somewhere between East Grinstead and Tunbridge Wells. A lorry driver picked him up. He'd been wandering on the downs all night and was suffering from exhaustion. He's been taken to a hospital in Tunbridge Wells. The police have tried to get a statement from the man, without result. Apparently he seems very agitated, traumatised, even. Said he would only speak to someone in authority; someone high up. That'll be me.'

And why are you taking this assignment?' queries Dodo. 'Haven't you got your hands full enough with the Vautrin Affair?'

'Yes, but I rather want to know what happened to that man and his colleagues. The whole Peltdown Vale case was one big question mark, and we never did get anywhere with it. If Herriot is alive does that mean the other scientists are as well? Where did they go when the lab building vanished? Where have they been all this time?'

'Well, the fact that even one of the staff is still alive means we can cancel our theory that the building was destroyed.'

'Yes, we left that case with just two possible explanations, didn't we? The instantaneous transportation of the building to some other location, or the complete destruction of matter leaving no residue. As you say, Herriot turning up alive would seem to knock out that second theory.'

'Although maybe not,' says Dodo, on reflection. 'He might have been removed from the building before it happened.'

'Yes, that's also a possibility. Hopefully we're on our way to finding some of the answers.'

They arrive at the cottage hospital. The doctor in charge meets them in the lobby.

'He's getting worse,' in answer to Mark's inquiry. 'Frankly, I don't know what's wrong with him. He's feverish. His pulse and body temperature are dangerously high. It's more than just nervous shock. We've tried drugs to bring the fever down, but nothing seems to work. You can speak to him if you must, but I doubt you'll get much sense out of him.'

William Herriot has been placed in a private room. Mark and Dodo find him in the condition the doctor has described; pale, drenched in sweat, wild-eyed.

Mark informs the man of his identity.

'Thank God,' gasps Herriot. 'You've got to rescue the others!'

'The others? The rest of your team from Peltdown Vale? They're alive, then?'

'Peltdown Vale?' confused. 'Where's that?'

'It's a research establishment. You were stationed there. Don't you remember?'

'Peltdown Vale... it sounds—No, it's all hazy...'

'Well what do you remember? Where have you been these past months?'

'Prisoners! Forced to work on some project... Madman... Vautrin...'

'Vautrin!' urgently. 'Did you say Vautrin?'

'Yes... Underground base...'

Mark and Dodo trade looks.

'Vautrin behind the Peltdown Vale Incident? That's a turn up,' murmurs Mark. To Herriot: 'This underground base. Where is it? If we're going to rescue the others, we need to know.'

'There's a farmhouse on the downs... secret lift...'

To Dodo: 'We'll have to wait till he recovers to get any coherent directions from him.' To Herriot: 'What sort of project was he making you work on?'

'Solanite particles... particle accelerator...'

'That makes sense,' says Dodo. 'We know they were examining that meteor at Peltdown Vale.'

'But, what does Vautrin want with solanite energy...?' Looking at Herriot: 'Do you know?'

Feverish shake of the head. 'Experiments... Transference... Just did what Vautrin told us to...'

'Who else is at this base? How many guards?'

'No guards... Just a bunch of girls... sick... killers...' He starts to writhe violently, screaming, clutching his head. 'You've got to get them out of there!'

'Nurses, quickly!' orders the doctor, running to the bedside. 'I must ask you two to leave. His temperature is hitting the roof.'

Mark and Dodo retreat into the corridor.

'So Vautrin kidnapped those scientists and is forcing them to work on experiments with the solanite material from the meteor,' says Mark. 'What's his interest? Solanite is an unknown element to us—Does Vautrin know more about the stuff than we do? Maybe for him it's *not* an unknown element...'

'At least now we know that the building wasn't destroyed,' observes Dodo. 'But how the hell did Vautrin make it vanish?'

'I haven't the foggiest. Maybe it wasn't Vautrin. Maybe it was something they did with that meteor...'

'But they still ended up in this underground base of Vautrin's...'

The sound of a small explosion from the room behind them. And then screaming, swearing, pandemonium.

Mark and Dodo rush back inside.

It looks like an abattoir. The bed is crimson, occupied by a mess of bones and entrails that was once William Herriot. The hospital doctor and three nurses are saturated with blood and gore. One of the nurses has Herriot's intestines draped all over herself. She doesn't look too happy about it.

Chapter Thirteen
A Room with a View

Gustave is dead.

He lies sprawled on the floor of the hotel room, a knife in his back. So much Mark Hunter sees when he slips into the room and turns on the light. The room has been ransacked. Furniture overturned, clothes scattered, the bed denuded of its linen. Had Gustave talked? Had he been knifed before or after the ransacking of the room?

Mark crosses to the bathroom, pulls the light cord. The cabinet has been pillaged; bottles and containers litter the floor. The searchers had obviously considered the cabinet the only possible hiding place in the bathroom and hadn't searched any further. The tiles above the bath-tub have not been disturbed. Good. Mark knows the sign to look for: a tile slightly chipped at the bottom left corner. He finds such a tile. He prises the tile loose. In the hollowed-out cavity behind it is a small black note-book. He flips through the pages, finds what he is looking for, pockets the book. So far so good. Now all he has to do is get out of here and make his way to the embassy.

Mark's hand is almost at the door when the handle begins to turn. He flattens himself against the wall on the blind side of the door. He unholsters his automatic, holds it by the barrel. The door opens. A gun appears, followed by a man, entering cautiously. Black suit, black trilby, dark glasses. One of Lousteau's goons. Mark hits him on the back of the head with his gun. The goon joins Gustave flat on the carpet.

Mark slips out of the room and is halfway to the lift at the end of the corridor when two more trilbies appear, blocking it. He makes a one-eighty turn, hurries the other way. The fire escape is his only chance now. But the move has been anticipated. Another two trilbies appear, blocking the fire doors. They advance towards him. He turns again. The two at the lift are closing in as well. An intersecting corridor offers itself. He darts down the corridor, knowing it terminates in a dead-end. He goes straight to the first apartment door. Locked. He moves on to the second. The door opens. He ducks inside, flattens himself against the door.

And then he gapes.

The woman before him is bending low, just stepping into a pair of knickers, and presenting to Mark a vast expanse of smoothly sculpted posterior, long, long legs with powerful thighs and strong calves. Her skin is perfectly smooth, of an exquisite strawberries-and-cream complexion. The onlooker's attention is drawn by contrast to the one region of darkness in the centre of that ivory landscape: the dark fringe of hair that grows abundantly along her buttock cleft—parting to form a border of verdant leafage around the lush pink flower of her pudendum.

Mark's eyes take in this majestic tableau in far less time than it takes to describe; and meanwhile the woman quickly hoists her knickers, straightens, and turns to confront the intruder, revealing breasts as abundant as her posteriors. A tall woman, her hair is short and black, her features regal and well-defined and currently expressing alarm; the eyes wide and brows elevated; the lips parted and clearly on the brink of utterance—

Mark holds out a restraining hand. 'Please don't scream,' he begs.

'I wasn't going to scream, ' is the calm reply. 'I was going to say "Who the bloody hell are you?" '

'Oh, you're English!' says Mark. 'Well, no time for explanations. Some very dangerous men are after me. I need to hide in your wardrobe. They didn't see me come in here but they're bound to start checking every room.'

'And why should I hide you? Are these men the bad guys or are you?'

'I assure you I'm the one on the side of the angels.'

'Get in the wardrobe, then. I'll believe you for now. I know I shouldn't judge by appearances, but you have an honest face.'

'Yes, I like to think it reflects my nature,' says Mark, crossing the room to the built-in wardrobe.

'And what do I do when these men come in?' asks the woman.

'Just do what you didn't do with me: start screaming; kick up a fuss; threaten to call the *concierge*.'

Mark ducks into the wardrobe, slides the door shut.

Moments later the apartment door opens, a black trilby looks in. As requested, the woman shrieks, (rather unconvincingly, thinks the concealed agent), and covers her chest with her arms.

The headgear is doffed. 'A thousand apologies, ma'moiselle. I am a police officer. We are looking for a very dangerous man. We are searching every apartment on this level. He may have come in here.'

'Well, he didn't come in here, did he? I think I would have noticed.'

'Of course, ma'moiselle. Once again, my apologies.'

The door closes. The woman walks up to it, listens, locks it. She crosses to the wardrobe.

'You can come out now.'

Mark emerges from his hiding place.

'Thank you for trusting me.'

'I don't trust you. I want an explanation first.'

'My name's Mark Hunter, and I'm with British Intelligence.'

He shows her his card. The woman takes it, looks at it, then looks at Mark.

'You don't look like a spy.'

'Nevertheless, I am.'

'And if you're with MI5, what are you doing in Paris? I thought your lot were only supposed to operate on British soil.'

'Well *technically* we are, but sometimes… Look, it's a long story. By the way, what's your name?'

'Dodo.'

And never was a woman more aptly named, thinks Mark.

'You look vaguely familiar…' he says.

'You might have seen me on the telly.'

'Oh! An actress.'

'Actually no; I'm a professor of psychology.'

'Profess… Of course! Professor Dorothea Dupont, the pop psychologist! Pleased to meet you.'

He shakes her hand with vigour. Dodo finds herself smiling at him.

'Why are those men after you, then?' she asks.

'For a notebook I have in my possession. It contains a code that's vitally important to us. It could prevent a cyber-war. I have to get it to the British Embassy.'

'Well take it there, then. The embassy's not far from here.'

'I would, but that's more easily said than done. Those gentlemen in the black hats will be swarming all over this hotel. Every exit will be covered.' He considers. 'You know, a plan is forming in this active brain of mine...' He looks Dodo up and down, she smiling sardonically at this brazen appraisal. 'Yes... With a little assistance from you, I think I might just be able to get out of here...'

Everyone in the hotel lobby notices the nurse pushing the old man in the invalid chair.

The nurse is six foot tall. Her crisp white tunic-dress clings tightly to her contours. She walks with a hip-swaying rhythm that unavoidably draws all eyes—male and female—to those magnificent hindquarters. But even had the nurse been of unremarkable appearance, attention would still have been drawn in her direction on account of her charge: the man in the wheelchair. In his case, however, it is volubility rather than physical characteristics which command people's attention. Brandishing a walking stick, he delivers a steady stream of crotchety verbal abuse, hurling imprecations at everyone he passes. The old man wears a heavy raincoat, and a tartan rug covers his legs. A low-brimmed hat, dark glasses and a grey beard all but conceal his face.

'Out of the way!' he yells. 'Haven't you any respect for an old man and an invalid? Out of the way!' He fetches one well-dressed woman a smart slap across the rump with his cane. 'Make some room, you baggage!'

'Please, sir! You shouldn't be so rude!' protests nurse, reprovingly.

'I'm a paying guest of this establishment, aren't I?' retorts the invalid.

'Yes, but think about your blood-pressure!'

'*They* should think about my blood-pressure, and stop annoying me all the time!' To a woman with three youngsters: 'Madam, kindly get your wretched brats out of my way!'

A number of Black trilbies are stationed at the hotel's main doors. Grinning at the scene, they stand aside for the cantankerous old codger and his erotic nurse.

Out in the night air, they take the wheel-chair ramp adjacent to the steps, and descend to the street. Another trilby stands at the foot of the steps. The dark glasses seem to be trained on Dodo.

'That's the one who came into my room,' says Dodo out of the corner of her mouth. 'I think he's recognised me.'

'There's a taxi pulling in,' responds Mark through his beard. 'Let's grab it.'

The trilby starts walking towards them.

'It isn't a disabled taxi,' points out Dodo.

'Never mind that!' Mark throws the rug aside, leaps from the chair, and dives into the taxi, with Dodo right behind him.

'British Embassy!' orders Mark. 'And step on it!'

The taxi lurches forward. They look back, see trilbies piling into a black car.

'This is going to be close,' says Mark, shedding his disguise.

'At the clip we're going, they'll have a hard time over-taking us.'

'Yes, but unfortunately they'll know where I'm headed so they might—'

A second black saloon shoots from a side-street, blocking the road ahead. Their cabbie stamps on the brakes.

'—try and cut us off at the pass.'

The first car pulls up behind them, penning them in. Trilbies pour out of each vehicle, surrounding the taxi, covering it with their guns.

'Driver. Stay where you are and you won't get hurt,' says one of them, crisply. 'You two in the back: get out.'

Mark and Dodo get out.

'Hands in the air.'

They comply. Mark is relieved of his gun.

'Get in.'

A pointed gun indicates the car in front of the taxi. Dodo and Mark climb into the back seat. A trilby slides behind the wheel. A second takes the passenger seat, turning to cover them with his gun. The car sets off.

'Who are these men?' Dodo wants to know. 'French Counter-Intelligence?'

'I wish. No, they are the henchmen of one Monsieur Lousteau, a buyer and seller of secrets by trade. I imagine you will be meeting him presently.'

They cruise through nocturnal Paris, finally turning in through an arched gateway into the courtyard of a large mansion.

'Yes, this is Lousteau's pad,' confirms Mark.

The two captives are escorted inside, across a hall, and into a vast salon; antique furniture, huge fire-place, old masters on the panelled walls. A man reclining on a chaise-longue rises to his full four feet when Mark and Dodo are presented before him. The man is stoutly-built, bald on top, his black hair long at the back and sides; his smooth round face adorned with a clipped moustache. He wears a patterned silk dressing-gown over his clothes and sips cognac from a bulbous glass.

Ignoring Mark, he approaches Dodo. 'Magnificent!' he declares, gazing up at her. 'A veritable monument sculpted in living flesh; a living monument to the goddess Woman. Allow me to introduce myself: Jacques Lousteau, at your service.'

He takes her hand and implants a respectful kiss.

'Dodo Dupont,' says Dodo.

'Ah! Then you are French?'

'Half French. On my mother's side.'

'And a nurse, as well! An honourable profession.'

'Actually, I'm not a nurse. This is a disguise.'

'A disguise? You don't work for him, do you?' disapproving, inclining his bald dome at Mark.

'Not until this evening.'

'Ah, say no more! I see it all! You are some poor innocent that Monsieur Hunter has dragged into his ridiculous escapades, inveigling you with his smooth tongue; and without consulting your wishes, without so much as a passing thought for your safety.' Lousteau looks sideways at Mark. 'As for you, Monsieur, you annoy me; you annoy me intensely.'

'Yes, you have had occasion to mention that in the past,' says Mark.

'Quite so.' He extends a pudgy hand. 'The notebook, if you please.'

'Notebook?'

'Yes. The one you appropriated from Gustave's room.'

'I'm afraid I don't have it.'

Lousteau clicks his fingers; a trilby glides forward.

'Search him.'

The trilby efficiently frisks Mark, but comes up with nothing save his wallet and cigarette case.

Lousteau turns to Dodo. 'My dear, if this nincompoop has made you conceal the notebook somewhere on your exquisite person, I implore you to surrender it at once. He has dragged you into something that is none of your affair, this man; you owe him nothing. Please, I beseech you, just surrender the notebook to me now. I do not want to have you… searched.'

'I'm afraid I don't have the notebook, Monsieur Lousteau,' says Dodo.

'My dear: I beg you to reconsider,' pleads Lousteau. 'The notebook has no value to yourself. Just hand it to me now and, I promise you, you are free to go.'

'That's very decent of you,' says Mark.

Lousteau shoots him a withering look. 'The offer does not extend to you.'

'I honestly don't have the notebook,' insists Dodo.

Lousteau sighs. Turning to his minion: 'You: search the mademoiselle And don't look like you are enjoying it.'

The trilby frisks her, not neglecting to look under her nurse's cap. He shakes his head.

'What did you do with it?' Lousteau demands of Mark.

'Do with what—Oh! the notebook. D'you know, I can't remember what I did with it. Do you remember what I did with it, Dodo?'

'Nope, I don't remember.'

'That's funny that... I know I had it back at the hotel...'

'Perhaps you dropped it somewhere...'

Lousteau scowls. 'You play games with me. Very well. Lock them in the cellar.'

Mark and Dodo are escorted across a hall, through a narrow door and down a flight of wooden steps into a vast wine cellar. Wine-racks stretch across one wall, while a row of huge horizontal barrels stand in the middle of the room. Dodo and Mark are guided into a small adjacent room, the door locked behind them. The room, illumined by a naked bulb, is furnished as a cell: a palliasse, a wooden chair, a wash basin.

Mark sits down on the bed; Dodo takes the chair.

'This is turning into a hell of a night,' remarks the latter. 'I was supposed to have been going to a psychologists' conference.'

'Yes, I'm sorry I got you mixed up in all this.' Mark produces his cigarette case, offers one to Dodo, lights it for her, and then lights another for himself.

'It's an experience, anyway,' says philosophical Dodo, blowing out smoke. 'I'll say that much. So does this kind of thing happen to you often?'

'Getting locked in cellars? Yes, all the time.'

Dodo contemplates her new acquaintance with a wry smile. Look at him, sitting there calmly smoking as though this is all in a day's work. Obviously it *is*, for him. He bursts into her room, gets himself an eyeful of her unintentionally mooning him; then he hijacks her life and drags her into this improbable spy story without a second thought. What is going on in that head of his? He has that look about him of being always quietly amused by the world... He would make an interesting character study...

'What's going to happen now?' she asks.

'Now? I should think they'll go back to your hotel room and search for the notebook. As neither of us appeared to have it, they'll think that we may have hidden it there.'

'And when they search my room?'

'They'll find it. I stuffed it under the mattress of your bed. Very obvious hiding-place. When they bring it back to Lousteau of course, he will discover that the vital page containing the code has been torn out; and then, I imagine he will send his men down here to search us more thoroughly.'

'And when that happens?'

'And when that happens, we make our escape.'

'You've got a plan, then?'

'Dodo love, I always have a plan…'

The lock turns and two armed trilbies come into the cell.

Mark sits on the bed with his head in his hands, a picture of guilt and dejection; Dodo stands against the opposite wall, flushed and distressed, cap askew, dress torn open at the front, displaying attention-grabbing cleavage. She is in tears.

'How could you have locked me up with this monster?' she wails. 'He tried to rape me!'

Trilby one moves forward to assist her. 'Mademoiselle…'

Dodo grabs him by the wrist, delivers a chop to the back of his neck. Simultaneously, Mark leaps up from the bed and socks trilby number two under the jaw. Both trilbies go down.

'You know self-defence?' Mark asks Dodo.

'Yes, I have a black-belt in karate,' is the reply.

They pick up the guards' automatics and hurry outside. More trilbies are in the cellar. One of them, armed with a machine-gun, opens fire. Dodo flattens herself against a supporting column; Mark dives behind one of the giant barrels. Bullets spray around them, the noise of the gun echoing around the cellar. A lull, and Dodo fires off one shot, killing the machine-gunner.

Mark looks at her questioningly.

'I've practiced target shooting,' says Dodo.

The other two trilbies run forward, firing automatics. Mark

dispatches one of them, Dodo the other. The coast is clear. Breaking from cover, they run across the cellar, Mark scooping up the machine-gun. Two more trilbies appear at the top of the wooden staircase. Mark turns the machine-gun on them. They tumble down the steps.

Leaping over them, our two heroes race up the staircase. Bullets whizz through the door from the hall beyond. Mark sweeps the hall with bullets and two more trilbies go down.

Lousteau stands in the doorway to the reception room. He does not move as they approach him, his smooth face expressionless. Mark, suspicious, catches a flicker of his eyes, spins and fires a salvo at a trilby taking aim at them from the grand staircase. The man flops down the stairs a corpse.

Taking fright, Lousteau disappears back into the salon. Mark and Dodo find him cowering behind the chaise-longue.

He rises to his feet, arms aloft, quivering. 'P-please don't kill m-me...'

'It's tempting...' says Mark. He looks around the room. 'Now let me see... Ah!'

Handing the gun to Dodo, he moves over to a large drinks' cabinet, unlocks it and commences removing the bottles.

'What are you doing?' asks Dodo, puzzled.

'You'll see.' He removes the last of the bottles. 'Bring him over here.'

Nudged by the machine-gun, Lousteau joins Mark at the drinks' cabinet.

Mark points to the interior. 'In.'

'In there?' protests Lousteau, haughtily. 'You jest, of course.'

'In!'

Capitulating, Lousteau reluctantly squeezes his four-foot frame into the cabinet.

Mark hands him a bottle of scotch. 'This'll keep you going.'

Lousteau hands it back with disdain. 'The cognac, if you please.'

Mark hands him the cognac, closes the doors, turns the key in the lock.

He turns a smiling face to Dodo. 'Now I suggest we make a swift departure before the police arrive.'

When they are out in the street: 'Oh! The code! Do you still have it?'

'Of course.'

Dodo lifts the skirt of her tunic, slips a hand down the back of her knickers, into the cleft between her buttocks, and from its ample depths withdraws a folded sheet of paper. She hands the paper, warm and fragrantly scented, to Mark.

'*Merci, mademoiselle,*' says Mark, with a bow. And then, contemplating her thoughtfully: 'You know, Dodo, you're a pretty handy lady to have around in a scrape. Resourceful, skilled in unarmed combat, can handle a gun. Yes... If you ever—'

Dodo holds up a restraining hand. 'No, thank you.'

'But we make such a great team!' protests Mark. 'That instant rapport—'

'Forget it! Instant rapport or not, this is the first and last time— I am not getting drawn into your silly adventures again. We part now: I will go my way, you will go yours. I'll admit it's been fun—just for one evening; but no, never again. Our paths will not cross. This is good-bye, Mr Hunter; farewell. My services will be at your disposal no more... Why are you smiling like that...?'

Chapter Fourteen
How Many *Doctor Who* Fans Does It Take to Change a Light-bulb?

Welcome to the one-day extravaganza that is WhoCon!

The auditorium is packed. There are stalls selling *Doctor Who* merchandise of all descriptions, from video cassettes going for a song, to novels and trading cards going for a mint... There stands an exhibition of monsters from the television series: from the vicious Mandrel of planet Eden, which upon death rapidly decomposes into an addictive drug, to the ant-like Zarbi, denizen of the planet Vortis, who produce an eerie chittering sound as well as displaying a propensity to run straight into cameras... There are *Doctor Who* celebrities seated at tables around the auditorium, signing autographs and posing for photographs. These notables include Sixth Doctor Colin Baker, two companions from the 1960s who are remarkably still alive, and the woman who knitted the Fourth Doctor's scarf... A cinema-sized screen placed high against the rear wall of the lofty auditorium is screening the recently re-discovered classic missing story 'Marco Polo'... In one corner of the venue a large paddling pool has been filled with foam—fans are invited to dive in and re-enact their favourite scenes from 'The Seeds of Death' and 'Fury from the Deep.'

Dodo Dupont, clad in cargo-pants, t-shirt and boots, and wearing a discreet headset, a badge marked 'security' conspicuous on her ample chest, surveys the crowd. With WhoCon being a convention devoted only to the classic *Doctor Who* series, there are not so many children or families present—the attendance seems to be composed chiefly of men in the twenty-five to forty-five bracket. Many of them are overweight.

A group of geeks amble past Dodo, deep in conversation.

'...If the TARDIS telepathic circuits are supposed to translate all languages, why didn't they translate the Foamasi's speech in "The Leisure Hive"?'

'Yeah, and what about the aliens in "The Ambassadors of Death"?'

'Yeah, but that wasn't during the Doctor's exile on Earth, when the TARDIS wasn't working properly...'

Some people really need to invest in an existence, muses Dodo.

'Dodo?' comes Mark's voice in her ear.

'Yep?'

'Just checking with everyone. Seen anything suspicious?'

'I've seen a lot of sexually-inhibited men displaying an unhealthy preoccupation with a kids' TV series, but apart from that; nothing.'

WhoCon is being staked-out as it is believed to be the SEA's next intended target, possibly the first subject of the group's threatened bombing campaign. It is unknown whether the SEA girls have an aversion to *Doctor Who*, or only to *Doctor Who* fans... The venue has already been checked from roof to basement prior to opening its doors; but no concealed bomb, or any other device, had been discovered. Regardless of this, the convention's security has been taken over by MI5, with Mark Hunter—who still expects trouble—coordinating the operation. No-one can guess what form the anticipated attack might take. With the SEA it could be almost anything. Everyone is keeping their eyes peeled for SEA girls, but so far, nothing has happened, no sightings have been made; and it is now well into the afternoon.

As a psychologist, Dodo is concerned for the mental health of some of these *Doctor Who* fans. She is certain that at least some of these people are completely fixated on *Doctor Who*, to the exclusion of all else. They live, eat and breathe *Doctor Who*.

Now, while it is fine to have one central interest in life, Dodo would tell you that you should also have at least one or two other interests to back it up, lest that main interest become a monomania and you start campaigning for it to be officially recognised as a religion.

Dodo espies a guy who looks more like a slacker—lumberjack shirt, Nirvana t-shirt—wending his way through the crowd, his bored-looking girlfriend in tow.

'Haven't you seen everything, now?' asks the girl, Tanya.

'I want to have a look at the stalls,' says the guy, Curtis. 'They might have some of the novels I haven't got.'

'Please bear in mind that I'm only here reluctantly,' Tanya reminds him. 'And that I'm bored out of my fucking skull.'

'I know, honey,' says Curtis. 'And I appreciate your sacrifice. But think how sad I would have looked, coming here on my tod.'

'Oh, so you just wanted me along to show to everyone you're that rare animal "a *Doctor Who* fan who's actually got a girl-friend"?'

It is true that Curtis thinks himself superior to all these geeks milling about. He likes alternative rock music, he doesn't have a boring office job (nor any job, for that matter), he doesn't spend all day online, he has a sense of humour, he enjoys socialising and he appreciates the beneficial effects of alcohol.

Two geeks nearby are getting dangerously close to an argument. One of them has ventured to suggest that the 1965 television story 'The Romans' was funny.

'I don't like it when it tries to be funny,' declares the other, sulkily. 'It's not supposed to be funny.' (These fanboys, like anyone else unblessed with a sense of humour, are more to be pitied than censured.)

Weaving through the crowd, Dodo finds Mark watching the big screen. A lot of fans' eyes are glued to the screen. This newly recovered story (discovered in a Quonset hut in an abandoned WWII airfield in New Guinea) has only just been digitally-restored and isn't even out on blu-ray yet!

'Still nothing?' she asks Mark.

'Nope. I've told everyone to look hard at any young females they see around. Our girls may try to infiltrate the place in disguise; dressed as companions or something.'

'Lucky for us there aren't that many women here!' says Dodo.

Meanwhile, Curtis and Tanya have reached the book stall. There is a large selection on offer. As well as the ubiquitous Target novelisations, there are a selection of the *Doctor Who* novels from the 90s; some of these books, had they been televised productions, would have probably carried '18' certificates.

'They've got *So Vile a Sin!*' cries Curtis. 'This one was delayed for months because the author's computer crashed.'

'Really?' says Tanya, not even pretending to sound interested.

'Mm-hm. Yeah, and he was so pissed off about it, he didn't want to go back and write out the whole thing again—so another author took over and wrote it instead.'

'Fascinating,' says Tanya. 'Tell me, why is it you want to read stupid *Doctor Who* books? I thought you liked proper books?'

'These *are* proper books,' Curtis insists. 'The *Doctor Who* novels of the nineties and noughties carried the baton for contemporary British fiction. They weren't meant for kids, these books. But then the TV series came back and killed them off. Now they put out these crappy little novels for kiddies to read... Makes you think: If they hadn't brought back the TV series, they'd still be bringing out decent *Doctor Who* books...'

Curtis heaves a sigh.

'Fucking load of rubbish,' declares a new voice.

They look round and see a scruffy-looking man regarding the display of books with contempt. Curtis identifies the type immediately: the 'Oi!' *Doctor Who* fan; the *Doctor Who* fan with attitude. This type gets his back up even more than the sad geeks.

'I bet you've never even read any of them,' challenges Curtis.

The fan looks at him.

'Don't want to read 'em,' he replies. 'Fan-written wank.'

'Really? Well if that's true then every episode of the new TV series written by Russell T. Davies, Paul Cornell, Gareth Roberts, etc, would have to be "fan-written wank," as well.'

'Look at them. Most of 'em about the fucking Seventh Doctor,' says the Oi! fan, changing his line of attack.

'And what's wrong with the Seventh Doctor?' demands Curtis, his tone dangerous.

'Sylvester fucking McCoy? What's right with him? He was fucking rubbish!'

'Actually, he was the best Doctor.'

'Like buggery was he! He couldn't act, he had no charisma...'

'He could act and he had plenty of charisma, thank you.'

'Oh, yeah? Compared to Tennant and Smith—'

'Tennant and Smith are all performance! There's no naturalism.'

'What? you expect them to play the Doctor bollock-naked?'

'I said "naturalism" not "naturism," you gonad-brain.'

'Fuck off.'

The Oi! fan shoves Curtis. Curtis shoves the Oi! fan. The Oi! fan shoves harder. Curtis falls back against the book stall. The table—a trestle—collapses under his weight. Curtis picks himself up and launches himself at the Oi! fan. The crowd falls back as they lay into each other, tumbling around the floor. Tanya just rolls her eyes.

And then Dodo Dupont wades in, separating the combatants and picking them up by the scruffs of their necks. Both exhibit nose-bleeds, cut lips and incipient black eyes.

'That's enough!' she declares. 'What the hell were you clowns fighting about, anyway?'

'We, er... had a disagreement,' says Curtis.

Dodo looks from one combatant to the other. 'Sylvester McCoy?'

'Yes.'

Dodo sighs. 'Really, you two. The McCoy debate isn't worth coming to blows over, is it now? You both have your opinions on the subject and you're both entitled to them. There's no right or wrong in this, is there? An opinion is an opinion, not an empirical fact. Why can't you just agree to disagree on the subject?'

'Yeah, I s'pose,' grumbles Curtis.

'Whatever...' grumbles the Oi! fan.

'Good! Now we've got that cleared up, I'm pleased to announce that you're both banned from the remainder of this convention. Allow me to show you the way out.' And taking the two men in arm-locks, Dodo marches them to the exit—with an embarrassed Tanya following at a distance.

After ejecting the two combatants, Dodo walks back inside. She notices a group of fanboys gawping at her.

'What's wrong?' Dodo wants to know. Do they recognise her? She wouldn't have thought sci-fi fanboys would be viewers of her own brand of television.

However, it is not Dodo Dupont they recognise, but someone else.

Says one of the fans: 'You look like a pre-Lisa Bowerman Benny Summerfield.'

'A pre-Lisa how-much?'

'Benny Summerfield, companion to the Seventh Doctor in the New Adventures novels,' explains the fan. 'First appeared in 1992. In recent years portrayed by Lisa Bowerman in the audio format.'

The fan shows her a paperback book. The book is called *Love and War*, and the gun-toting heroine painted on the cover does indeed bear a resemblance to herself.

Oh great. So now she's a fanboy's wet dream.

There is a commotion at the door.

'ATTENTION, HUMANS! YOU ARE OUR PRISONERS!'

Three Daleks glide into the room.

The attendant from the door rushes up to them.

'Here! You haven't paid!'

'WE ARE THE DALEKS! WE ARE THE SUPREME RACE OF THE UNIVERSE! WE ARE NOT REQUIRED TO PAY ADMISSION!'

'You bloody are!'

'SILENCE! YOU WILL BE EXTERMINATED!'

'EXTERMINATE! EXTERMINATE!'

Mark, who has been watching this with amusement, has a sudden alarming thought.

'Scramble everyone!' he yells into his mike. 'Get those Daleks out of here!'

MI5 agents spring from all directions, grab the Daleks, and start running to the exit with them.

'OI! WHAT'S GOING ON?'

'CANNOT CONTROL! CANNOT CONTROL!'

'THIS IS ONLY THE BEGINNING!'

They stop once they have them safely outside, clear of the building.

Mark regards them with triumph. 'I thought you would try to get in in disguise, but disguised as Daleks—But then, nothing you girls do ought to surprise me... So what do those guns fire? Bullets? Gas?'

'OUR WEAPONS FIRE SUPERIOR DALEK ENERGY BEAMS! THEY CAUSE MASSIVE MOLECULAR DISRUPTION OF HUMAN TARGETS!'

'Ray guns, eh?' says Mark. 'Get the lids off. Let's see who we've got.'

The tops of the Daleks are removed... Revealing not a single SEA nymphet! Instead three pudgy fanboys are squeezed into the casings.

'We made them ourselves,' says one of them, proudly.

Mark's face falls. Dodo pats him consolingly on the shoulder.

'Oh well. It was a good guess...'

'Can we go back in now?' asks one of the fanboys.

'No, you can't!' rages Mark. 'You're banned! Push off!'

The convention continues. By now, nobody is queueing up for Colin Baker's autograph. He sits engrossed with his smartphone. Being such a regular attendant at these functions, just about everybody and their uncle already has his autograph.

When the event is finally over, the guests departing, and nothing has occurred, Mark sits over a dolorous cup of coffee in the refectory.

'I don't get it,' he says to Dodo. 'Why the no-show? We searched that safe-house, found that ticket for this convention...'

'Well, *I* get it,' avers Dodo. 'That ticket was planted by the SEA just for us to find. Don't you see? They just wanted to trick us into spending all bloody day at a *Doctor Who* convention!'

Chapter Fifteen
Fahrenheit 999

'...was no mechanical explosive inside Dr Herriot. My guess would be some kind of chemical reaction. A foreign substance introduced into his system...'

'...Leader, I am pleased to report that everything is going according to plan; the Earth will soon be ours.'

'Excellent...!'

'...And in other news, the Government are proposing stringent new rules to penalise people who write silly answers for their religion on their census forms...'

'...Now the question was what is two plus two... And you've gone for answer B which is four—Are you sure you don't want to call a friend...?'

'...Holly Jesus Christ on a fucking rubber bike, Batman!'
    'Yes, Robin; this looks like the work of that arch-fiend of urine, the Piddler...!'

'...starting to receive reports that there has been a massive explosion at Guys Hospital, London...'

'...I've just finished *The Fallen Leaves*, Part One... So when's Part Two coming out...?'

'...Leader, I am pleased to report that the time-traveller known as the Doctor has walked straight into our trap, just as anticipated.'
    'Excellent...!'

'...Breaking news. Guys Hospital has been devastated by a massive explosion—Wait a minute; news just coming in... Yes, we are now receiving reports of a second explosion, this time at Great Ormond Street Hospital...'

'...Captain, permission to spend the entire series talking like I've got a blocked-up nose?'
    'Permission granted, Mr Sulu...'

'...It's faces, George. Faces with shooters. It's a blagging. They're after the readies.'
    'Say that again in English, Guvnor...'

'...now been four massive explosions in the Greater London area, all of them at hospitals. London Bridge, King's College, Great Ormond Street and Guys have all been hit...'

'...Chaos here in Central London. Four thick columns of smoke are filling the sky. You can see one of them behind me. The sound of sirens is everywhere...'

'...Coming soon, the new Hammer Horror film, *The Beast with Two Backs*. "You Never Know if it's Coming or Going...!"'

'...I want a team covering every suspected SEA safe house in London. See anyone there, I want them taken. Alive if possible, but taken...!'

'...worst disaster to hit London since the Blitz. There's no word as yet as to who is responsible for these atrocities...'

'...Leader, I regret to report that all of our plans have gone tits-up and this base is about to be destroyed!'
'Excellent...!'

'...Collins here. We've got them, Mr Hunter! Four of the little bitches...!'

Chapter Sixteen
From Bad to Worse for Flossie Farraday

They have won the after-school hockey match. Flossie Farraday, the chief goal-scorer, helps put the equipment away. Flossie Farraday: a top student as well as sportswoman. Flossie Farraday, who, with her long chestnut hair, large bust and long legs, looks like a fashion model. Flossie Farraday, the popular, but largely unobtainable, object of the Year Ten boys' desires. Flossie Farraday, who conceals her misery behind a cheerful smile.

Back in the changing rooms, Flossie strips out of her hockey kit, grabs her towel and hits the showers. There are only two other girls in the communal shower cubicle; the rest of the team are already getting dressed and departing. Facing the wall, Flossie leans back and lets the hot water pour over her pleasantly tired body. The other two girls leave. On the field, playing a match, she had felt happy. Right now, under that invigorating shower and in the afterglow of victory, she feels happy. Flossie knows how to make the most of these brief moments.

She turns around to let the spray hit her back—And sees Denise Richmond, flanked by two other laughing girls, pointing her smartphone camera at her.

Flossie screams, one hand flying to cover her crotch, her other arm shielding her breasts.

The three girls scream with laughter.

'Stop that! You can't take pictures of me like this!'

'We're not taking pictures,' replies Denise. 'We're filming you. Gunna make you an internet star, girl!'

'Stop it!' screams Flossie, frozen to the spot.

'Yeah, I reckon we got enough,' agrees Denise. She switches off her phone. 'Come on; let's get out of here.'

Flossie flies at her. 'Give me that phone!' she screeches.

One of the cronies shoves Flossie, and she slips and falls back into the shower cubicle. The laughing girls make for the exit.

Flossie, naked and bedraggled, splatters after them.

'Please! You can't do this!' she pleads. 'Delete that film!'

Denise, at the door, turns back, smiling scornfully. 'What, and disappoint all the guys, who think you're oh-so-wonderful? Just think—You'll be even more popular now!'

'You cow!'

She moves to grab Denise, but the girl backs through the door into the corridor.

'You can come out here and get me if you want.'

The door closes. Flossie slides wetly to the floor, draws her knees up to her chest and hides her face, sobbing piteously.

Me. Always me. Everything happens to me. Everyone's out to get me. What have I ever done for this to happen? Nothing. I've never done anything wrong. But it all fucking happens to me. Always to me.

Flossie often has these introspective moments.

Her tears subsiding, she climbs to her feet. The changing room is empty now. All the other girls have gone, none of them stopping to offer Flossie any support. She has to get that film erased. All the boys seeing her like that would be the final humiliation. She would never be able to show her face in school again…

Well, she'll find that evil bitch Denise. She will go to Denise's home. She will tell the girl's parents. What Denise has done is a crime.

Quickly drying herself off, Flossie starts to dress. Her clothes are neatly piled on the bench beside her bag. Wait a minute. She can't find her knickers. Did she put them in her bag with her hockey kit? She looks in her bag. No knickers. She looks on the floor. No knickers.

Her knickers have gone. Someone has obviously taken them, thinking it would be an hilarious joke.

Just another kick in the teeth.

Dressed, Flossie sets off, tearful but determined. She will go round to Denise's house and make her delete that recording. Denise has always had it in for Flossie. None of the girls really like her, but with Denise it has become a vendetta. Flossie has been democratically elected by the male contingent most attractive and desirable girl in her year—Flossie has thick, sensuous lips which boys really like; and she has big tits, which boys like even more. This approval of her male classmates has only served to make Flossie even less popular with her female classmates.

Flossie has never really had any friends amongst the girls at school. She has done nothing wrong. She has no disagreeable personality traits.; she's not bossy or stuck-up or self-centred. She doesn't have bad breath, smelly feet or any other personal hygiene problems. But, in spite of everything, she has always been disliked.

And, regardless of her standing in the desirability stakes, she hasn't actually had many boyfriends either. She has been out with a couple of the boys in her time, but never for long. It didn't take her long to realise they were only interested in her body.

As well as good looks and a pleasant personality, another complaint against Flossie is that she comes from a much higher-income family than most of the students at this state comprehensive. The girls often joke that Flossie must be 'slumming it' by going to an ordinary comprehensive, while her older brother and younger sister both attend an expensive public school.

Flossie walks on through the busy streets. She feels uncomfortable and exposed with no knickers on. The sensation seems to contribute to her feeling of barely-suppressed panic; like everything is spiralling out of control, and she has to fight to keep the lid on it. She feels sure people can somehow tell she is going commando, even though her skirt is long enough to conceal this fact from passers-by.

Her thoughts turn to Juliette, the one proverbial beacon of hope in her life. Her one friend. She has never even met Juliette. Juliette isn't even an internet friend. Juliette had just appeared out of nowhere on her mobile phone. (A regular mobile phone; Flossie doesn't have a smartphone.) First there had been text messages; and then voice-mail. A mysterious correspondent who had found out her number she doesn't know how, and who seems to know everything about her life. Flossie had at first been suspicious of this phantom caller, suspecting a prank from one of other of her classmates. But Juliette herself had driven those thoughts from her mind; convinced her of her identity. Listening to her messages, Flossie has fallen in love with that cultured, somewhat clinical, voice. She knows by now it can't be any girl from school disguising their voice: Juliette says things that make it clear she is much smarter than any of them. This girl is like a political scientist or something!

Flossie has tried speaking to Juliette directly, but whenever she has dialled her number, she is always put straight through to voice-mail. Juliette tells her it is not yet time for them to communicate directly. But that time will come soon.

Denise lives on a street that is a long way out of Flossie's way, but she finally reaches it. Number sixteen. She knocks on the front door. Denise herself answers. The girl affects a look of mild surprise.

'What do you want?'

'What do you think I want? I want to see you delete that film from your phone.'

A malicious smile. 'Why should I? I'm only going to show it to the guys. You should be pleased! The guys'll love you even more after your first naked shower scene.'

'You can't do this! Fucking bitch!'

Denise scowls. 'Don't call me a bitch, you stuck-up little whore.'

Desperate, Flossie turns to pleading. 'I'm sorry! Look; I'm begging you: just delete that film. Please.'

'I will. Sometime. Or maybe I'll just post it on-line…'

'Don't you dare!'

'Come on, you'd like that, wouldn't you? All those internet perverts wanking off to you…?'

'Denise, for Christ's sake…!'

'"For Christ's sake!"' mimics Denise. 'I'll do what I fucking like, okay? If you don't like it, then go to another fucking school.'

'Oh, please…' tearfully.

'Oh, shut up whinging!'

'But—'

'I'm in the middle of my dinner, so fuck off.'

She slams the door.

Flossie turns away, crushed. She has tried to be assertive for once, and she has failed. And she despises herself for her failure.

The Farraday family -minus our Flossie- are having dinner. The dining room is like the rest of the Farraday residence, redolent of old-fashioned elegance.

Mr Farraday is speaking. '…So I was saying to Dave at work:

"The only way forward is through a more aggressive, dynamic approach." That's the key to sound marketing strategy.'

'And coercive,' says his wife.

'Absolutely. Dynamics and the aggressive/coercive approach. Demographic factors just don't come into it.'

'But if people want the product...' speaks up Nigel, Flossie's older brother, aged seventeen.

'It's not about the people who want the product,' explains his father. 'You need to target the people who *don't* want it. You have to convince those people that they *do* need the product, even if they have no use for it.'

'Redundant utility,' observes Eve, Flossie's little sister, aged thirteen.

'That's right,' concurs father. 'Redundant utility, dynamics and the aggressive/coercive approach.'

'And did Dave understand your argument?' asks Mrs Farraday.

'Dave didn't understand. I think I'm going to have to go over his head on this one...'

The family are eating roast duck. Each of them has a glass of vintage red wine. A good-looking family, straight out of a commercial.

'We're playing a concert in Vienna next month,' announces Eve, violinist in her school orchestra.

'That's wonderful, dear,' enthuses her mother. 'We'll certainly be there to watch you, won't we dear?'

'Without a doubt. You know how proud I am of you, Eve.'

'Yes, Daddy.'

'I've got some good news as well,' says Nigel. 'I've been accepted into King's next year.'

A surge of enthusiasm, everyone congratulating the young scholar. At this point the front door slams, a disconsolate Flossie walks into the room. As if a switch has been flicked, the convivial expressions vanish from the faces of the family, looks of antipathy and aversion taking their place.

A pregnant silence. Then Mr Farraday speaks, his tone ominous.

'What time do you call this?'

'I-I'm sorry,' whimpers Flossie. 'I had a hockey match after school...'

'Your ridiculous hockey game was taken into account,' says her mother, sharply. 'You're still twenty-five minutes late.'

'I know, but I had to go round Denise's...'

'That's a lie,' snorts Eve. 'Denise is on your team, isn't she? You could have said whatever you had to say to her before she went home.'

'It was something urgent that came up...'

'Like what?'

'What's it got to do with you?' snaps Flossie.

'How dare you speak to your sister like that!' shrieks Mrs Farraday.

'Send the brazen creature up to her room,' says Nigel. 'She disgusts me.'

Mr Farraday rises from his chair, towers over his daughter, his expression savage.

'Apologise to your sister at once.'

'But—' begins Flossie

'But *nothing*.'

He shoves Flossie violently. She falls down hard on her hindquarters, legs apart.

Sharp intakes of breath from the Farradays.

With her fall, Flossie's skirt has ridden up revealing her lack of underwear—her exposed vagina is the cynosure of all eyes!

A heavy silence follows those gasps of horror.

Father is the first to speak; his voice is quiet, ominously so.

'You. Little. Whore.'

'So that's why she was late,' pronounces Eve, with disgust.

Poor Flossie, covering herself, shakes her head hopelessly. 'No, it's not that. I-I just lost my pants in the changing room.'

'Lies!' screams Mr Farraday. He delivers a smart penalty kick to Flossie's crotch with his slippered foot.

'Lies! Lies! Lies!'

Each repetition is accompanied with another kick.

Flossie howls with agony, curling herself up in a ball.

'You richly deserved that,' snaps her mother, lips curled with disgust. 'Husband, take the filthy wretch up to her room. I can't stomach the sight of her.'

Brother and sister vehemently second this decision.

Mr Farraday picks up the still moaning Flossie by her hair, drags her upstairs, shoves her into her room, locking the door. Flossie's bedroom door is unique in the Farraday house: it has a bolt on the outside.

Flossie lies on her bed for some time. Her tears have dried up. A listless resignation has settled over her. She almost thinks she doesn't even care if Denise shows that video to the boys at school. What does anything matter anymore? She is hated by her own family. Always has been. Has she ever done anything wrong? No. Or rather, *everything* she does is wrong, in the eyes of her family. They are so baneful to her that being locked into her room at times like this actually comes as a relief. (She has made sure never to let them know she enjoys this solitude; they would only have found something worse to replace it!)

She has heard Nigel and Eve come upstairs some time ago and go into Nigel's bedroom—that nest of incest and statutory rape, indulgently over-looked by the loving parents.

Her crotch feels sore.

And then her mobile phone buzzes. She picks it up. A text message. Could it be...? Yes, it is! She eagerly reads the message:

> *It's time to leave your old life. I'm*
> *waiting at the end of your drive.*
> *Come and join me. Juliette. X*

Time to leave her old life! It seems as if this mystery girl knows exactly what has just happened to her; how she is feeling right now. She feels something surging within her; a reckless joy at the prospect of the new life this girl Juliette has been promising her. It is there, now; waiting for her! All she has to do is reach out and take it.

Flossie may be locked in her room, but this is no obstacle for her leaving the house. Her room is at the front of the house, her window directly above the thatched roof of the porch. She has often considered this as a viable escape-route, but she has never actually availed herself of it before tonight—before tonight she has never had anywhere to escape to.

Flossie pulls on a fresh pair of knickers, pockets her phone and wallet, lifts the sash of her bedroom window. Night has fallen. She climbs out onto the porch roof. From this she lowers herself over the edge, till she is hanging by her fingers, and then drops to the ground. She peaks in through the diamond panes of the living room window. Mum and Dad are watching television.

Good-bye forever.

Flossie runs down the drive towards the street. A figure emerges from the shadows, a girl in school uniform. She is smiling; a smile of welcome such as Flossie has never experienced before in her life.

Chapter Seventeen
The SEA Devils

The interview room is a small parlour of the country house; carpeted, furnished with a table and chairs. Outside the window the sun smiles on the extensive gardens. The location of this stately home is Surrey. The Department uses it for entertaining—and protecting—special guests, as a venue for conferences, or, as in this case, for housing special prisoners.

Mark Hunter regards Trudie Rayne with interest. Although a prisoner, and having committed a terrorist atrocity, the girl seems relaxed, unconcerned. Her eyes, behind those chunky lenses, are not afraid to meet his.

He offers her a cigarette.
'No thanks. I don't smoke.'
'Do you mind if I do?'

'Go ahead.'

Mark ignites his cigarette, exhales.

'So, Trudie; why did you do it?'

'Do what?' innocently.

'The hospital bombings.'

A smile. 'Can you prove that we did do it?'

'Not as yet, but I'm sure we'll find something. You can't move around in Central London without being caught on CCTV. We've got a lot of footage to sift through. And what with you all being minors, we've kept you out of the news. The public still don't know about you.'

'You know what I don't get—Why did you take us alive? Your guys could have killed us; they caught us by surprise, and they looked angry enough to do it.'

'They had orders from me to take you alive. Aside from any humanitarian argument, I wanted you alive so that I could have a talk with you. I admit that you fascinate me, you and your friends. I've come up against all sorts in my time, but I don't understand you lot at all.'

Trudie smiles. 'So is this an interrogation or just a child psychology session?'

'Maybe a bit of both. I want to know why you do what you do, Trudie. This lunatic organisation of yours... I want to know more about that man Vautrin. When did he approach you? Was it the day you killed your four classmates? Before that?'

'He didn't approach me—not personally; it was Juliette. But yeah, it was that day I killed Lucy and the others.'

'And where did you meet Juliette?'

'In my bedroom. She was just sitting there when I got home from school that day.'

'And was it she who put you to killing your classmates; the ones who were pimping you? I assume she gave you the gun?'

'Yes, she gave me the gun.'

'Juliette must have made a very appealing offer, for you to just up sticks and go off with her and join Vautrin.'

'You know what was happening to me Mark,' smiles Trudie.

'I'd've gone to Syria with Juliette if that was what she'd offered. Anything was better than where I was then.'

Mark taps the ash from his cigarette. 'So you joined this lunatic terrorist group; and now it's led to this: blowing up hospitals.'

A shrug.

'We only blew up four, and we probably won't do it again.'

'And of course, you did it for no reason. You'd got hold of some Semtex and you had to use it on something. Why hospitals?'

Another shrug. 'Just for a change. I mean normally, when there's a bomb attack, they take the casualties to the hospitals, don't they? So we thought "What do they do if it's the hospitals that get bombed?"'

'So you chose hospitals just to be ironic?'

'Yeah, I guess. Why not? It's all childish and silly, anyway. Throwing bombs, making planes crash... I mean, look at those 9/11 bombers.'

'They were religious fanatics.'

'So what? That's just an excuse. They were still being childish.'

'Okay, so it's all childish and silly. What makes you any better?'

Trudie smiles. 'Cuz we actually *admit* that it's childish and silly. That's the difference. You talk about "better" and "worse," but those are just your values. Us girls—we're like outside of all that. We just don't care.'

Mark exhales cigarette smoke. 'But it's over for you now, isn't it? We've caught you.'

Trudie giggles. 'It's not over! You're our designated arch-enemy, Mark. Vautrin says so. It's your job to try and stop us; to catch us. This time you caught us; but who says we're going to stay caught?'

'You think you can escape?'

'No, I *know* we can escape. You can't keep *us*, Mark,' as though explaining to a child. 'The game's not finished yet. We're going to get away sooner or later.'

Mark studies her pensively. 'Has it occurred to you that you've changed? Think about how you were before, in your previous existence…'

'Yes, I know I've changed.'

'But don't you wonder why?' urgently. 'It's Vautrin. He's put a spell on you; corrupted you.'

Trudie just laughs again. 'So what if he has? I don't mind. I like being like this.'

Mark sighs. 'Then there's nothing I can say… Nothing I can do to help you…'

Trudie places a hand over his. 'It's nice that you want to help me, Mark, but I don't need help. Not like that. I'm happy. We all are…'

'I can't believe it!' gushes Sophie Harris. 'I'm actually in the same room as Dodo Dupont!'

Dodo indicates a seat, sits down herself. Another parlour, very much like the one occupied by Mark and Trudie.

Sophie's face, framed by her black bob, glows, her eyes sparkling as she laps up the TV scientist. Sophie's figure is athletic and she wears an anime t-shirt, cargo pants and brightly coloured sneakers.

'You look even more amazing in person,' she gushes. 'They say us women are getting bigger since we were emancipated, so you're like the latest thing from evolution!'

A wry smile. 'Well, there are taller women than me in this world, so I can't be *quite* the latest thing. But let's move the conversation away from me and onto that small act of genocide you and your friends have just committed.'

'Okay! If you want to,' brightly.

'Whose idea was it?'

'Oh, Vautrin's!' she replies. But then, reflecting: '…Or it might have been Juliette...'

'And how do you feel about what you've done?'

'Oh, super! Went with a bang, didn't it?' She giggles.

'No feelings of remorse, then, for those hundreds of dead?'

'No, I'm afraid not. But then, they were hospitals we bombed; so a lot of the people there would have been dying anyway!'

'And that makes a difference?'

'Not really. I was just trying to be philosophical—like you always are!'

Dodo opens a file on the table before her. 'Could you tell me how and why you joined Vautrin? You're listed as a missing person a couple of months back, but there doesn't seem to be any major event coinciding with your disappearance…'

'No, not like some of the other girls, right?'

'Your father had just returned from abroad. You vanished from home while visiting him. You know the police suspected him of having murdered you? It seems he was the last one to see you. They arrested him twice, but had to release him due to lack of evidence.'

Sophie nods. 'The lack of evidence being the absence of my raped and naked corpse? I hope Daddy wasn't put out too much.'

'So, why did Vautrin choose you for the SEA?'

'Because I was the right sort of person. Don't ask me how I was. Vautrin just knew who was right for him. He could sense us. We're all somehow connected, us girls, even before we'd ever met. At least, that's what Vautrin says. That's a delicious fragrance you're wearing. I bet it's expensive!'

Dodo smiles. 'Thank you, and yes, it is. Turning the conversation round again: so there was no tragedy in your life, no big problem?'

Sophie looks at the floor. 'Well…' stretching the word. 'I *did* have a problem of sorts…'

'What sort?'

A nervous giggle. 'I'd rather not talk about it, actually. It's a bit embarrassing. Vautrin called it an "Unfortunate Condition." But anyway, he cured me! I'm perfectly fine now.'

'How did Vautrin "cure" you?'

'Oh, he just did. Magic, I suppose…'

'Do you know where Vautrin comes from?'

'No, none of us know that. He's a very private man, and we don't like to pry. Personally, I think he just appeared because me and the other girls were all subconsciously wishing for him. We wanted a handsome man to come along and save us all. Yes, we wished him into existence...!'

'...Take a seat, Albertine.'

Albertine takes a seat, accepts a proffered cigarette.

Mark makes a show of consulting a file. 'You are Albertine Sagan, daughter of Phillipe and Claudette Sagan?'

'*Oui.*'

'You're fourteen years of age...'

'*Oui.*'

'And you disappeared from your home in Paris three months ago...'

'Is it zat long? 'Ow times flies!'

Mark closes the file, and looks at the girl in the gym-slip uniform.

'I'll be frank with you, Albertine,' he says. 'Maybe I can't pin any of the hospital bombings on you, but I could have you deported. The French police have a warrant out for your arrest.'

'I know.'

'They think you killed your father and his boyfriend.'

'I did.'

'So—what if I handed you over to them?'

Albertine shrugs. 'It does not signify. Whether I am in zeir custody or yours, I shall escape all ze same.'

'So, I suppose I would be wasting my breath offering to make a deal with you?'

'Of course you would, Monsieur 'Unter. You can offer nothing to one who 'as everything.'

'You have everything?'

'*Oui.* Ze 'ole world and everything in it.' She smiles. 'You *could* offer me sexual congress in return for information,' she suggests. 'But I warn you in advance, after you 'ad performed your part of ze bargain, I would renege on mine.'

'Thank you for your honesty, but sex is out of the question.'

She blows smoke at him, smiling archly. 'A great pity. I think Vautrin would find it very droll that I 'ad fucked our designated arch-enemy…'

'*Fraulein* Dodo!'

Little Greta Garbo throws her arms around Dodo, burying her face in that worthy's ample bosom. Dodo find herself stroking the girl's tousled head. Another adoring fan. She prises herself free of the little terrorist and guides her into a chair. Greta is dressed as always in an army shirt, black jeans and heavy boots.

Dodo lights one of her occasional cigars, Greta watching her with eager admiration.

'I'm curious about your change of allegiance, Greta,' begins Dodo. 'For several years you were fanatically devoted to the Red Army Faction. What made you switch?'

'*Herr* Fautrin confinced me. He showed me that I vos just a symbol to the RAF. That they vere using me. He showed me that hiss organisation vos vhere I belonked.'

'And was he right?'

Oh, *ja*. I haff been so happy since I joint the SEA. I haff found my true friends.'

Dodo exhales Cuban smoke. 'You're an expert bomber. Was it you who set the explosives in the hospitals?'

'*Nein*; not all off them. Ve ver assigned vun each.'

'But there were five of you.'

'Juliette vos coordinator.'

'So which one did you blow up?'

'Great Ormond Street.'

'And don't you feel remorse? Killing all those children?'

Greta rises to her feet. 'I am sad that thosse sick and dying chiltren had to perish! But they died for the Causse, and I salute them!'

And she does just that.

'And precisely what cause did they die for?'

'The Causse of Anti-Social Behaffiour and Self-Gratification!'

'And that's a cause?'
'*Ja*, a ferry good vun…'

'…I get the impression that you're second-in-command of the SEA,' says Mark to Juliette Wainwright.

Juliette pulls a non-committal face. 'There's nothing in writing, if that's what you mean. We don't have an official pecking order. That sort of thing is for your ridiculous structured society. But yes, I suppose I possess natural leadership skills, and people listen to what I say. It all comes down to personalities, doesn't it?'

'So the others don't object to taking orders from you?'

'No. Especially when they know they don't have to obey them if they don't want to.'

'How did you meet Vautrin?'

'In Switzerland. He just appeared one night. I'd been out; I came back to my room and found him sitting there. He talked. I listened. I liked what I heard. I went with him.'

'And what about your father? Is he financing the SEA?'

Amused surprise. 'Daddy? Why on earth would he finance us? He only funds things he can make money out of. There's no money in what we're doing.'

'But you are still in contact with your father?'

'I am not! When you join Vautrin you part company with your previous existence. It has to be that way. It's a kind of a temporal shift.'

'So, who supplied the money to build your underground base?'

'No-one did. No-one built it. It's just there.' She looks at Mark. 'I'm curious. How did you know our headquarters was underground?'

'From a man called Dr Herriot.'

'Oh! He must be that scientist who escaped.'

'And there are other scientists being held prisoner at your base, yes? The rest of the Peltdown Vale team? What does Vautrin want with them? Why is he experimenting with solanite particles?'

'Even if I knew, I wouldn't tell you. That's Vautrin's business.'

'And I suppose, like your friends, you see your current incarceration as just a temporary state of affairs?'

'Oh, yes. We'll get out somehow. It's inevitable.'

'And what atrocities will you commit next?'

'I don't know that, do I? We don't plan things in advance like you people do. We're spontaneous. You'll just have to keep on our trail, won't you? That's your role in this game…'

Mark and Dodo sit in the mansion's drawing room, coffee and sandwiches on the table between them.

'I didn't get through to any of them,' Dodo is saying. 'It's like they're on a completely different wave-length to normal human beings.'

'Hm,' agrees Mark. 'Most subversives see themselves as being outside the normal run of society, but these girls are completely off the scale. They acknowledge no connections at all with the world they once inhabited. And they talk about that base of theirs as though it were some little pocket universe.'

'Maybe it is.'

'Yes. But however separate it is from our plane of reality, there has to be an interface, a door between one and the other.'

'That house on the Downs that Herriot mentioned…'

'Yes. That's our only lead. A house on the Downs, presumably isolated, presumably untenanted. There must be quite a few.'

'You'll have to start a search.'

'I will. And the search will radiate outwards from the Peltdown Vale research establishment. We know there's a link between Vautrin and what happened there.'

'Maybe you could get one of the girls to talk.'

'They won't tell us anything they don't want to. Or are you suggesting torture?'

'I was thinking more along the lines of truth drugs.'

'Yes, I'd thought of that, and it might be worth trying. But I wouldn't be surprised if whatever magic Vautrin has worked on those girls has rendered them impervious to the effects of the usual truth serums.'

Mark sips his coffee cup.

'So you really think Vautrin has worked some magic on those girls?' asks Dodo.

'He must have done something. I can't believe that all of them were that callous before that man got hold of them. Juliette, perhaps; and obviously Greta was already an active terrorist. But some of the others...'

'Have we identified all eleven of them now?'

'Nope. There are the five upstairs. I met two others that time I was captured in their safe-house: a Dizzy Hello and a Jessica Harper. That's seven. We know there's a Florence Farraday and the Italian girl Gina Santella in the group. Nine. That leaves two more: the girl with Vautrin at the hotel—who we still haven't been able to identify—and one other.'

'So, what's next?'

'Well, I'm going back to London for instructions. You might as well come with me. We've got their confessions of guilt—but what do we do with them? The higher-ups might not what this one made public—that a bunch of kids are the ones behind the hospital bombings.'

'You've got their room bugged? Have they said anything?'

Mark pulls a face. 'Oh yes, we're listening. They just sit there discussing clothes, cosmetics, food, sex, films, music. They're acting like schoolgirls at a Summer Camp.'

'No escape plots being furtively hatched?'

'Not a whisper. They freely admit that to them this whole thing is a game; and whether we like it or not, you and I are players in that game. I am their "designated arch-enemy," and you they've started a fan-club devoted to. I see Vautrin's hand in this. *He* selected us, not the girls.'

'In your case, that would have to be true. Those girls may already have known about me, but none of them could have known about you.'

'Right.' He rises. 'Let's be making a move. I'll tell the guards to keep on their toes. Apart from escape attempts, there's the possibility that Vautrin and the other girls may attempt a rescue.'

'Do you think he knows his girls are here? We haven't exactly broadcast the fact.'

'Yes, but Vautrin seems to know a lot of things he shouldn't know. And don't forget, he spoke to me of having some sort of sympathetic link with the girls. I wonder if that means he always knows where to find them...?'

Day is giving way to night when the two men in suits stroll purposefully up the avenue to the manor house. They wear bowler hats, and their swing umbrellas in unison. As they come within view of the house, they wave to the two armed men standing at the portico.

The newcomers come to a halt at the foot of the steps.

'We're from the Ministry,' announces one bowler hat. 'Here by Mr Hunter's instructions. We've come to interrogate the prisoners.'

'Have you got authorisation?' demands one of the guards, suspicious.

'Of course we have,' replies bowler hat. 'Otherwise your men at the gates wouldn't have passed us through, would they?' He turns to his companion. 'Show them our authorisation.'

Second bowler hat raises his umbrella to the horizontal. There are two muffled thuds; the guards collapse. First bowler hat whistles. Six men, dressed in military black, appear from the cover of the shrubbery. They carry silenced pistols; one has a satchel, another a gas canister strapped to his back. The eight men mount the portico steps and enter the house.

There are two more guards in the main hall. They are given no time to react before they are shot dead.

The raiding party quickly ascend the main stairs. They cross the gallery, and turn into one of the branching corridors. Two guards are stationed at a door up further down the corridor. Espying the newcomers, these guards react more quickly. One of them fires off a shot, stopping one of the black sweaters. But then the two umbrellas speak softly, and the guards crumple.

Ignoring their fallen companion, the remaining raiders reach the now unguarded door. The black sweater with the canister on his back detaches the hose and inserts the slim nozzle into the door's key-hole. He turns on the gas. Black sweater with the satchel hands out gas masks. These are quickly donned by the raiders, the two umbrellas resuming their bowler hats when they have put on theirs.

At the expiration of a minute the gas is switched off, the nozzle removed from the key-hole. First umbrella takes a set of keys from one of the fallen guards, finds the correct one, unlocks the door.

The room, originally a master bedroom, has been fitted as a small dormitory, with six beds facing each other in two rows. Five girls in their underwear sprawl unconscious on and around the beds.

'Why not just take Miss Wainwright?' comes the muffled voice of second umbrella.

'No,' replies first umbrella. 'It must be all of them. Our master wants her friends, as well.'

He clicks his fingers. The black sweaters each hoist a girl over their shoulder. The raiding party marches out of the room.

Chapter Eighteen
The Keller Ray

Eckerton, muses Mark Hunter, looks like a pot-bellied simian in a Hawaiian shirt: Brawny, hairy arms; hair sprouting from the open collar of his shirt; a large blue jaw, cigar clamped between tombstone teeth; eyes hidden behind dark glasses; a straw sun hat on his bald pate; below the pot belly, beige bermuda shorts, huge feet encased in canvas shoes.

They sit in deck chairs on the after-deck of Eckerton's luxury 100-ton motor yacht, moored amongst the many vessels in Alexandria harbour, beneath a cloudless Mediterranean sky. Present is Dr Keller, Eckerton's pet scientist; Hassan, representing the Ayatollah; Cheng from North Korea; Estevez from one of the

Columbian cartels; and not forgetting Mark Hunter, representative of a sinister—and completely fictitious—European consortium. Each man—apart from Keller—sips a cocktail from a tall, frosted glass.

Eckerton checks his gold-plated Swiss wrist-watch. 'Relax and take your time, fellers. Demonstration's not till 11:05.'

'Why must we wait?' demands Hassan, a clean-shaven Arab in a Western suit. 'We are all here.'

'Because I have in mind a little demonstration,' replies Eckerton. 'Actually, it'll be one hell of a demonstration. Just so's you all can see that the gizmo does what it's supposed to.'

'A demonstration is agreeable to me,' says Cheng, cooling himself with a paper fan.

Something else very agreeable strolls onto the deck at this moment; one six-foot Juno in a black and white bikini. All eyes turn and focus on the statuesque apparition.

'My gal,' announces Eckerton. 'An intellectual broad. Psychologist or somethin'. A limey. That two-piece she's wearin' is straight off a Paris cat-walk. Cost me ten grand.'

Reaching her sun lounger, Dodo Dupont (don't tell me you didn't recognise her!) casually peels off the ten-grand bikini, casts it aside and arranges herself, stomach down, on the lounger.

'Can one of you gentlemen do my back, please?' she asks.

Looks are exchanged.

'Say, Hunter, why don't you have the honour?' suggests Eckerton. 'You bein' a fellow Brit an' all.'

'My pleasure.'

Rising from his chair, Mark strolls over to supine Dodo, picks up a bottle of sun lotion from the table beside the lounger. He pours the gel onto his hand, applies it to Dodo's back. Like everything else about her, Dodo's back is ample and tremendously erotic; the angle of the shoulder blades, the cleft along the lower spine, the plains of soft, yielding skin. He slowly massages the oil onto her, from her shoulders down to the growth of downy hair at the small of her back.

'What's this demonstration about?' asks Mark, under his

breath.

'I don't know. Eckerton won't tell me; says it's a surprise,' replies Dodo in the same tone. 'From hints he's dropped, it's going to be something pretty spectacular.'

'Which will probably mean involving a spectacular loss of life.'

'I think so. Unless we do something to stop it. Can you do my legs, please?'

Dodo's position as Eckerton's current woman is a purely nominal one. No sex is involved. She is there purely for show. Eckerton is incurably impotent and therefore he likes to have a woman with him a) to look at; and b) for everyone to *think* he is having sex with.

Mark rubs the oil into his friend's long, healthy legs; from the ankle, along the smooth calves, over the powerful thighs; that perfect balance of flesh and muscle; first the left leg, then the right.

'All done!' he says.

'No, you've missed a bit.'

'Oh. There as well?'

'Yup.'

Obediently, Mark squeezes more lotion onto his palms and set to work on the ripe hemispheres of her *gluteus maximus*, kneading and caressing them all over until they glisten with oil, running his thumbs deep into the cleft, matting the thickly-growing hair.

Dodo purrs with delight.

'Done now?' asks Mark, wiping his hands on a towel.

'Done,' sighs Dodo. And then, in a louder voice: 'Thank you. You're very good with your hands, Mr Hunter.'

'The pleasure was mine, Professor.'

Rising with some difficulty, Mark limps back to his chair, sits down and crosses his legs, wincing as though in pain.

'Quite a dame, huh?' remarks Eckerton.

'A remarkable specimen,' agrees Mark.

He observes that Hassan cannot tear his eyes off that supine female body. But then Hassan hails from a world which demands that a woman must be covered from head to toe at all times—because if she displays so much as a bare ankle a man will not be able to control his aggressive natural urges. And of course the fault would all be the woman's for exposing said ankle!

'Before the demonstration, could Dr Keller please give us some more details about the device?' suggests Cheng.

'Sure,' acquiesces Eckerton. 'Give 'em your spiel, Doc.'

Keller is a sorry looking specimen. Weedy, limp hair heavily streaked with grey. Mark has read his file. The man had been expelled from the British scientific community when his unfortunate predilection for pre-pubescent girls had become known. He had been exposed by a nosey colleague, who, raiding Keller's computer for scientific data, had discovered instead an abundance of kiddie-porn. After his disgrace, Keller had disappeared off the radar for some time, and it had been believed he had headed for parts East looking to indulge his vices. But now Eckerton has somehow got hold of him and made him his tame scientist, giving him funds and equipment to work on saleable projects, as well as keeping him supplied with outlets for his vice.

'The device is a focused energy beam,' begins Keller. 'Fired at an aircraft such as a military jet or a commercial airliner, it will completely disrupt all the craft's electrical systems, inevitably resulting in a crash. Its range is much greater and more focused than any regular ECM jamming device.'

'And just what is the range of the beam?' Hassan wants to know.

'Sixty thousand feet is the maximum for full disruption. It can reach the ceiling of any aircraft. Any higher and the effect of the beam becomes diminished.'

Eckerton looks at his watch again. 'Say, Doc: I guess it's about time you were setting things up for our demonstration.'

Keller leaves his chair and moves to the stern of the yacht where the equipment has been set up—a bulky control console and a device resembling a swivel-mounted artillery gun, but much more sophisticated in appearance. Thick cables run from the console down into the boat's interior.

'May we ask now what the demonstration is to be?' inquires Mark.

'Sure. At exactly 11:05 a passenger airliner bound for Rome will take off from Borg al arab airport right here in Alex. From where we are we'll see it clearly. The Doc is gunna fire his gizmo at it, and you'll see it drop out of the sky.'

'If the device works,' says Estevez.

'It'll work.' Eckerton rises heavily from his deck chair. 'Let's go watch the action.'

There is a general move to the rear deck.

'Just building up power,' announces Keller, manipulating the controls.

'The plane should be taking off just about now,' says Eckerton, consulting his watch once more. 'We'll see it over there to the west.'

'The device is aimed at the correct coordinates,' says Keller. 'Once the target comes into range, it will lock in automatically.' He points to a monitor on the control panel. 'This screen shows the weapon's rangefinder.'

'I see you only have the power dials set to fifty per cent,' observes Mark. 'If you increased them to maximum wouldn't that increase the maximum range of the beam?'

'No it would not,' returns Keller pettishly. 'If the power was increased to maximum, the circuits would overload.'

Mark finds himself wondering why the power settings can be increased to a strength that would overload the machine. Presumably this follows the same brand of logic which equips all domestic electrical toasters with a setting that burns the bread to charcoal.

He looks back at Dodo. Propped up on her arms, looking back over her shoulder, her eyes meet his inquiringly. Mark nods his head towards the boarding steps. At the foot of these the launch in which himself and the other guests had arrived is still moored. Dodo signals her understanding of the message.

The sound of jet engines.

'Here comes the plane,' announces Eckerton.

'I'll just check the device is correctly calibrated,' says Keller.

He moves over to the ray emitter and Mark takes advantage of his absence to discreetly turn the power controls on the console to maximum. The power, which has been a steady hum, immediately increases to an alarming whine. Mark backs away from the console.

'The power!' screeches Keller. He runs back to the console. Smoke starts to rise from it. 'What have you done? I can't reduce the power! The circuits are locked!'

Eckerton turns on Mark. 'You lousy spy! Kill him!'

Hassan, Estevez and Cheng reach for their guns, but Mark already has his in his hand. He fires. The three men dive for cover. Mark runs for the boarding steps. At the top he fires off two more shots.

The smoke on the rear deck thickens while the electrical whine rises to an hysterical pitch.

'We've got to get out of here!' yells Keller.

Mark hurries down the steps to the launch. Dodo is already at the wheel and has the engine running. Mark unties the painter.

'Let's go!'

The launch surges forward across the bay. Behind them comes a huge explosion as the console ignites A second blast follows when the feedback blows the yacht's generator. The boat becomes a blazing inferno and thick black smoke rises into the azure sky.

'Scratch one death ray,' remarks Dodo, satisfied. 'Heading for shore.'

Mark regards his naked assistant pensively. She catches the look.

'What?'

'I'm just wondering how I'm going to get you back to my hotel without the local population chucking rocks at you!' he says.

Chapter Nineteen
Juliette Wainwright Accepts a Proposal

Juliette's eyes open, admitting daylight and returning consciousness. There is a moment of confusion. The room is unfamiliar, unexpected... No, wait, she *does* know the room. Yes, it's the bedroom that is kept permanently at her disposal in the penthouse of the Wainwright Building, her father's corporate temple. How does she come to be here? Memories are disentangled, shaping themselves into a linear thread... They had been captured: Trudie, Albertine, Greta, Sophie and herself. They had allowed their guard to drop in the elation of the success of their bombing campaign... Mark Hunter's agents had taken them, and they were being held prisoner in a country house somewhere; under interrogation. The last Juliette can remember, it was evening; confined to their room, they had been sitting on their beds, talking. Then had come the sounds of a commotion out in the corridor; a gunshot... And then she had suddenly felt very sleepy; incredibly sleepy. So had the others. She remembers seeing them overcome by inertia. Gas. It must have been gas. A jail-break. And judging from her present location, the whole operation has to have been her father's doing.

She throws back the covers and rises from the bed. She is wearing the same bra and knickers she had been wearing the night before. The night before? Daylight streams in through the window. It surely has to be only the following morning, unless she has been intentionally kept under for longer for some reason. The clock on the wall says nine. She feels an armpit experimentally. The skin is still smooth from depilation the evening before.

Juliette crosses the room to the wardrobe. The clothes that are kept here for her are all present. Discarding her underwear, she wraps herself in a silk dressing gown.

There comes a respectful knock at the door, which then opens, admitting a man in waiter's livery pushing a breakfast tray before him.

'Good morning, Miss Juliette,' he says. 'Shall I set the things on the table?'

'No, just leave it by the bed,' says Juliette. The servant is familiar to her. Simpkins? Simmonds? Something like that. 'How long have I been here?'

'I believe you arrived sometime last evening, miss.'

'And where's my father?'

'I couldn't say, miss. In his office, I presume. Is there anything else?'

'No. You may go.'

The man departs.

Juliette sits herself down on her bed and pours herself a coffee. There is also orange juice, toast, marmalade, a boiled egg.

'And how are you today, darling?'

Juliette looks up. Her headmistress, Cynthia Imrie stands in the doorway, dressed in her usual tweed suit, regarding her with a sardonic smile.

'Miss Imrie!' exclaims Juliette, hardly believing her eyes. 'What on earth are you doing here?'

'Your father sent for me, darling,' replies the other. 'He wants me to try and talk some sense into you.'

She pulls up a chair on the other side of the breakfast trolley, fits a cigarette into its holder, ignites it with her gold lighter.

'Talk some sense into me?' echoes Juliette. 'What does dear Daddy mean by that?'

'Well, he wants you to come back to school for a start,' says Cynthia. 'And speaking for myself, I was most offended when you upped sticks and left like that, without so much as a goodbye letter. What's so bad about my school, I'd like to know? You were practically running the place, anyway. All the girls adored you; you had them eating out of your hand.'

'I'm sorry, Miss Imrie,' Juliette, her mouth full of toast. 'I had no complaints with your school, honestly.'

'Then come back, dear. All the girls miss you dreadfully. And if you're worried about that unfortunate business with Karl; don't. It's all blown over. The police have stopped investigating the case; your father saw to that.'

'I'm afraid I can't go back, Miss Imrie. Not now. That chapter of my life is closed. I've moved onto something much better.'

Cynthia snorts carcinogenically. 'Better? Killing people? Blowing things up? Childish nonsense. I don't pretend to understand politics, but whatever silly cause do you think you're fighting for anyway?'

'No cause, Miss Imrie. We just kill people and blow things up.'

'Well it's got to stop, my dear. Sooner or later you're going to get caught—What am I saying? You *were* caught. It's only thanks to your father that you're now at liberty again.'

'Naturally I'm very grateful to dear Papa for his timely rescue operation, but as soon as I've finished my breakfast I shall be leaving here.'

'You won't be, you know,' demurs Celia. 'Do you think your father's just going to let you walk out of here? After all the trouble he's been through to find you? Not on your nelly. You're going to be kept on a short leash from here on in, young lady.'

'But how can I go back to my old life, even if I wanted to?' asks Juliette, sucking marmalade from her fingertips. 'Surely I'm a wanted terrorist by now…'

Cynthia waves a dismissive hand. 'Oh, your father can hush up all that.'

'What, the hospital bombings?'

'No, darling; he can't hush those up. They're still all over the news. But he can hush up your involvement in them.'

'So, he can keep my name clean. And then what?'

'Back to school, for you. But before that, he wants you to see young Cuthbert.'

'Him! What for?'

'I believe the young rascal is going to propose to you. It's all been arranged. Candle-lit dinner for two in the penthouse suite tonight. You'll be very charming, and he will get down on one knee.'

'We're both too young to marry.'

'Yes, but you can be engaged. You can tie the knot after you've finished school.'

Cuthbert Quentin is the son and heir of the Quentin Corporation. Rufus Wainwright has long envisaged this marriage in the way of a company merger.

'Cuthbert is very sweet, but I really don't want to marry him,' says Juliette.

'My dear, it's just a business arrangement,' replies Cynthia. 'Once you're married there's nothing to stop you bedding whoever you like. Let's be honest: Cuthbert is not exactly your dominant male; you can wrap him round your finger. You'd be as free to do whatever you want as you were before.'

Juliette shakes her head. 'Can't do it. I just don't belong here anymore. School. Corporate marriages. That's the old world. I have a new life now. Father can't force me back into my old one.'

'He can, you know.'

Cynthia gets up and moves over to the widescreen television set with which the room is supplied.

'Are we going to watch TV?' asks Juliette.

'Yes, my dear, there's a very good programme on CCTV right now. It's called "Four Naughty Girls in their Knickers." '

Picking up the remote, she switches on the set. The image that appears is of a room spartanly furnished with two bunk beds. Lounging on the beds are Greta, Trudie, Sophie and Albertine, still in their undergarments as they were the previous evening. The sound is muted, so nothing can be heard of their conversation.

'Where are they?' demands Juliette.

'Oh, somewhere in the bowels of this building,' answers Cynthia. 'To discourage escape attempts, they haven't been given any clothes. Still in their undies, just like you were when you were brought here.'

Juliette smiles at this naivety. Even if they had been stark naked, the girls would still make a break for it the first chance they get.

'So, father is using my friends as hostages,' she says.

'That's more or less the idea. You need to realise how ticked off with you your father is, young lady. If you do anything to put his back up now, he'll start killing those friends of yours.'

Juliette reflects.

'Then I'd better start thinking about what I'm going to wear for my dinner date this evening.'

Cynthia smiles. 'That's the spirit.'

The luxury penthouse suite is sumptuous. The main room occupies two storeys, floor-to-ceiling windows along the outer wall looking out on the night-lit London skyline. Opposite, a spiral staircase ascends to a broad gallery and the suite's upper rooms.

A candle-lit table for two has been placed in the middle of the vast living space. The electric lighting has been muted, creating a cosy atmosphere for the two diners. A (recorded) violin concerto plays in the background.

Juliette, flawlessly regal in a shimmering shift-dress, looks between the candles at her dinner partner. Dressed in a tuxedo, a ruffled shirt and bow-tie, Cuthbert Quentin is a handsome enough boy, but his good looks are compromised by the obviously shy and awkward demeanour of their owner. Appearance and personality do not match, as though the result of some mix-up; the mind having been decanted into the wrong body.

'It's awfully good to see you again, Julie,' says Cuthbert for the fifth time. 'Remember that time when we were kids at your pater's place, and I fell into the lake?'

Juliette sips her wine. They have finished their soup and are awaiting the main course.

'You didn't fall in; I pushed you,' she says.

'Did you? Well, I'm sure I would have fallen in anyway. I was such an awful klutz back then.'

'Yes, and I'm glad to see you haven't changed.'

Cuthbert laughs merrily at this witticism.

'Very good! ...So, you've been away from school for a while?'

'Yes. What do you know about that, Cuthbert?'

A shrug.

'Not much. Your old man just said you'd been away from school. Up to anything exciting?'

'Yes. I've made some wonderful new friends and we've been having the most exquisitely delightful time.'

'These friends... Not boys, are they?'

'Oh, no. It's very much a girlie thing.'

'Ah! Good! So what sort of larks have you been up to?'

'Well, we blew up four hospitals.'

Cuthbert laughs awkwardly, inwardly thinking it might be a bit too soon for jokes about that one.

Changing the subject: 'Remember that time you spent a whole summer at our place?'

'Did I?'

'Yes! Must have been four years ago, now.'

'Oh, yes! I remember. That was when you'd just been given that puppy.'

Cuthbert's face falls. 'Oh, yes. Scamp. We never did find out what happened to him.'

Juliette smiles privately. *She* remembers very well what happened to Scamp.

The lift doors open and the waiter drifts in with the main course. He lifts the lid to reveal a roast pheasant. He starts to carve.

'Cuthbert, why don't we just serve ourselves?' suggests Juliette, suddenly. 'It'll be more cosy without the waiter hovering around.'

'Good idea! Let's do that!'

'You can go, Simmonds,' says Juliette. 'I'll give you a buzz on the intercom when we're ready for dessert.'

The waiter bows. 'Whatever you wish, Miss Juliette.'

The lift doors close on the waiter.

'I'll do the honours,' says Cuthbert. He gets up and slices the pheasant with the carving knife, then serves up the vegetables.

They eat in silence for a while.

'It's awfully good to see you again, Juliette,' says Cuthbert at length.

'So you keep saying.'

'I mean, we haven't seen that much of each other lately, with you being in Switzerland. But I've been thinking about you a lot.'

'That's nice.'

'The thing is… I think we would be good together… I know our paters both want it, but that's not the point for me—No, it's because I'm so awfully fond of you…!'

He rises awkwardly from his place, fumbling in his pocket for a small box. He drops down on one knee at the side of Juliette's chair, proffers the box.

'Will you marry me, Juliette?'

'Oh, Cuthbert!' gushes Juliette.

Cuthbert opens the box; it contains the inevitable diamond ring.

'It's beautiful!' exclaims Juliette.

She takes the ring from its setting and slips it on her finger.

'I accept, Cuthbert; I accept!' she says, holding her hand out, admiring the jewel.

And having made this announcement, she picks up the carving knife and slashes her betrothed across the face.

Cuthbert staggers backwards, blood gushing from the wound. Shocked incomprehension written on his gashed features, he puts his hand to his face, then stares at the blood on it.

Juliette rises from her chair, moves towards him with the carving knife. Cuthbert extends his hands, palms outwards, a vain defensive gesture.

'No… stop…'

Juliette slashes at his hands with the knife.

Whimpering, Cuthbert backs away from her, hugging his bleeding hands to his chest, staining the white tuxedo with vivid red.

'Oh, Cuthbert,' says Juliette. 'I know we're going to be so happy together.'

She plunges the knife into his stomach.

The gentle music plays on.

Cuthbert collapses to the floor, one hand clutching at his wounded stomach. Whimpering piteously, racked with pain, he feebly tries to crawl away from his assailant.

'We'll have a honeymoon in the Bahamas,' proceeds Juliette. 'And when we get back we'll have lots of corporate babies to carry on our fathers' good work.'

She stabs him between the ribs.

Cuthbert's terrified eyes look at her with blank incomprehension, imploring her for mercy.

'I know my actions must seem contradictory to my acceptance of your marriage proposal,' says Juliette apologetically. 'But this dichotomy can be easily explained by my sadistic nature and refined sense of irony.'

She stabs him again. And again. And again. Cuthbert just gives up trying to understand his fiancée and dies. There isn't much else he can do.

Carrying the bleeding knife, Juliette sashays over to the intercom beside the lift doors.

She flicks the button. 'Simpkins? We're ready for the dessert, now. Could you bring it up, please?'

Chapter Twenty
A Rescue? A Capture? Or an Escape?

It is in the evening that Dodo arrives at Mark's apartment. She is dressed for action, wearing the same black ensemble as when we first met her back in Chapter Two. The walls of the living room, modest in size, are almost entirely taken up with bookcases; from floor to ceiling, venerable hardbacks stand shoulder-to-shoulder, parading their gilt and decorated spines. All the great philosophers and historians, all the classic tellers of tales, are represented on those shelves, arranged for the reading pleasure of the bibliophile secret agent.

'So what's the news?' ask Dodo, when they are both seated.

'We've identified the body of the raider who was killed in the attack on our safe-house,' says Mark. 'I should have guessed who was behind this really—it didn't seem likely that Vautrin would hire thugs to rescue his girls: he would have just sent in the other girls to get them out. No, our dead raider worked for Rufus Wainwright.'

'Ah, Juliette's father! He wanted his little girl back.'

'Yes, and that man has enough contacts in high places to have been able to find out where we were holding her. What I don't understand is why he bothered having the other four girls taken as well... There were traces of an anaesthetic gas in the room the girls were sleeping in, so we know that they didn't leave with the raiders voluntarily. So, that being the case, why not just take Juliette and leave the others behind?'

'You'd have to ask Rufus Wainwright that one.'

'Precisely what I'm going to do,' announces Mark; 'and why I called you over. We're going to pay a visit to Wainwright's corporate headquarters, and find out what he's done with those girls.'

'And what if Wainwright doesn't want to talk?'

'Then we shall employ whatever gentle means of persuasion that become necessary.'

'Wainwright carries a lot of clout. Won't your superiors object to you just charging in there?'

'They might, which is why I haven't told them what I'm planning. Our little visit will be completely unofficial...'

Dodo and Mark walk briskly into the brightly-lit foyer of the Wainwright Building and approach the reception desk. At this late hour there is only a single receptionist on duty. She regards the smiling visitors with a look of puzzlement.

'Can I help you?'

'Yes, we'd like to see Mr Wainwright. At once, if you please.'

'I'm sorry, sir,' replies the receptionist. 'Mr Wainwright doesn't see anyone after six o'clock, and certainly not without an appointment.'

'He'll see me. Tell him it's Mark Hunter, here to speak to him about his daughter.'

The receptionist puts through the call. 'Put me through to Mr Wainwright, please... Mr Wainwright, sir, there's a Mr Hunter to see you... He says it's about your daughter... I see...' She looks up at Mark. 'I'm sorry, but Mr Wainwright can't see you right now... If you could come back in the morning, I can book you in...'

'Thank you!' says Mark. 'Glad to hear it! We'll go straight up!'

Mark and Dodo head for the lifts.

A lorry drives down the access ramp into the basement storage area of the Wainwright Building; it turns and neatly reverses into one of the loading bays.

Dizzy Hello, Chrissie Wylde and Gina Santella emerge from the cab. Some workers hauling crates espy them. The truck is expected, but not its youthful occupants.

'Hey! What are you girls—'

And then the three girls have guns in their hands and shots echo through the concrete cavern.

Mark and Dodo march into Wainwright's huge office, crossing its gymnasium floorspace at a brisk pace. They had been met by two security guards when they had emerged from the lift. Dodo has dealt with them, relieving one of the men of his side-arm. The tycoon sits behind the desk at the far end of the room, just as Mark had seen him on his previous visit.

Startled by the intrusion, Wainwright stabs a button on his intercom. 'Security—'

'Don't call anyone,' adjures Mark. 'My friend has a gun.'

'You can't just barge in here like this,' grates Wainwright. 'Let me see your warrant.'

'You know, I think I may have left it at home.'

'I'll have your job for this, Hunter.'

'You're welcome to try. But not till I've got those girls back.'

'What girls?'

'Let's not mess around, Wainwright. Your daughter and four of her friends. You abducted them from MI5 custody last night.'

'You can't prove that.'

'Actually, I can. You shouldn't leave the corpses of your minions lying about; they can be traced back to you. I imagine you've got the girls somewhere in this building: you're going to take us to them.'

'Like hell I am.'

'Dodo…?'

Dodo moves around Wainwright's desk and put her revolver to the tycoon's head.

'I'm going to count to ten,' says Mark. 'And if you don't start cooperating, Dodo is going to put a hole in your head. She can be quite ruthless, you know…'

The lift doors of the penthouse suite open and the waiter glides out, pushing the dessert trolley. The sight of Cuthbert Quentin lying on a blood-soaked carpet brings him up in his tracks.

And then he feels a carving knife pressed against his throat.

'You're going to tell me where my friends are, Simmonds,' says Juliette. 'If you don't, I'll cut your throat open…'

Dizzy, Chrissie and Gina cross the basement to the main lift. The doors open and three security guards rush out. Two are gunned down on the spot.

'Drop your gun,' orders Dizzy to the third.

Stunned, the guard complies.

'Good. You are holding five of our friends in this building. If you want to keep on living, you'll take us to them…'

It's high time they escaped.

They have been good little girls all day, have Trudie, Greta,

Sophie and Albertine; so hopefully the guards who bring them their meals will by now have decided their prisoners aren't planning to cause any trouble.

The four girls sit on their bunks, Trudie and Albertine swinging their legs from the upper bunks, Greta and Sophie occupying the lower. Having hopefully lulled their captors into that well-known false sense of security, they are planning to make their move now. Little Greta, being the youngest and cutest, has been selected for the seducing-the-guard routine; going by the understanding that most men like them sexually mature but otherwise as young as possible.

'He'll be back to take the trays away any minute,' says Trudie. 'So just act sexy and seductive. Okay?'

'*Ja*,' says Greta.

'It might help if you take your knickers off.'

'Off course.'

Greta peels off her nether-garment and lies back on her bunk, legs parted.

A key turns in the lock. Trudie, Albertine and Sophie throw themselves flat on their bunks, assuming attitudes of studied nonchalance.

Leaving his companion at the door, the guard comes in to collect the trays. The first thing he sees is little Greta and her invitingly open legs. His eyes goggle.

'Pleasse to serffice me,' says Greta. 'I require sexual relief and an injection off semen.'

Trudie winces. *That's* supposed to be sexy and seductive?

Apparently it is; at least, it works. The guard—with the nodded approval of his companion—moves to join Greta on her bunk. Greta, smiling sweetly, takes the man's head in her hands and neatly snaps his neck. Trudie leaps from her bunk and serves the second guard the same manner.

They grab the men's guns.

'Come on. Let's get out of here.'

The lift doors open. Rufus Wainwright steps out followed by

Mark and Dodo, the latter with her gun in the tycoon's back. They have descended to a sub-basement; here the corridors are functional, displaying none of the corporate opulence of the upper floors.

'Lead on,' invites Mark.

They advance. Reaching a junction of corridors, they suddenly find themselves facing four SEA girls in their underwear who have just stepped out of a room up ahead: Trudie, Greta, Albertine and Sophie (with Greta noticeably lacking any nether garments.) Simultaneously, Juliette, in an evening dress, appears from the corridor on their right, leading the terrified Simmonds (or is it Simpkins?) with a carving knife at his throat. And then, if that's not enough, *three other* SEA girls—these ones in their usual clothes—appear from the corridor on their left, leading a security guard with a gun in his ear: the girls are Dizzy, Gina and a third whom Mark does not recognise.

Joyous are the greetings exchanged by the fortuitously reunited SEA nymphets! Dizzy blows the guard's brains out, Juliette slits open the waiter's throat, and the girls rush to embrace each other!

Then they turn to face Mark's group.

'I don't suppose you'd consider surrendering?' asks Mark hopefully.

'We appear to have more guns than you, so I'll have to say "no",' replies Juliette. She turns to her father. 'I'm afraid the marriage is off, father dearest. Cuthbert has met with a fatal accident with a carving knife.' She holds up her glittering left hand. 'But he did give me this ring! Wasn't that sweet of him?'

Wainwright's face is a mask. 'You're a monster.'

'Well, in your own sweet way, dear father, so are you,' replies Juliette. 'Don't try and find me again. The next time we meet will be when I come to kill you.'

'You could kill him now,' suggests Chrissie, always helpful.

'What, and save him the embarrassment of having to explain Cuthbert's murder to Quentin senior? Oh, no! Let's just leave. I assume you have transport?'

'Back this way,' confirms Dizzy.

'Mark; Dodo; please don't try to follow us,' warns Juliette. 'We don't want to kill either of you, unless you force us.'

'Very decent of you,' says Mark. 'Can I just ask the name of the young lady with the pony-tail? She's the only one of your little group I haven't encountered before.'

'Don't tell him your name, Chris!' quips Dizzy.

And with this the SEA girls depart, giggling merrily.

The departure of the girls brings with it a heavy silence. Mark, Dodo and Wainwright just stand where they are for several uncomfortable moments.

'Well, this is awkward,' says Mark, finally.

'Just a bit,' agrees Dodo.

Wainwright says nothing.

'Perhaps we should just toddle off,' says Mark.

'I think toddling off is our best option at the moment,' agrees Dodo.

Off Mark and Dodo toddle.

Wainwright glares at Mark's retreating back, and if looks could have killed, our hero would have been annihilated on the spot.

Chapter Twenty-One
A Day in the Life of Jessica Harper

Jessica Harper awakes to the sound of her mum calling her from downstairs.

'Will you get a move on? You'll be late for school!'

Jessica looks at her alarm clock. Seven-thirty! Crap! She swings pyjamaed legs out of bed, fumbles for her glasses, picks up the clock and examines it with interrogative, accusing eyes. She had definitely set the alarm for six o'clock. The alarm has failed to go off; she couldn't have slept through it; the alarm did not ring when it should have rung. The clock has betrayed her. Typical! Now she won't have any time for reading before going to school. And she is in the middle of a really good book! It's a novel called *Resurrection* and she had hoped to get a couple of chapters in before she had to get up; hence the setting of her alarm.

Oh, well. Tolstoy will just have to wait till her lunch break. She puts the book in her school bag. What day is it? Jessie searches her memory... Wednesday! Yes, it's Wednesday. She will need her Maths, Chemistry and Geography books. Oh, and her PE kit. It's gym class today.

She pulls off her pyjamas, rummages in the drawer for some clean undies. Jessica is a smallish girl, with a round, freckled face, and goofy gap-teeth. She has a trim figure and little dumpling breasts, which, to the critical she claims are 'still developing.' But in her heart of hearts she suspects that those boobs of hers aren't going to get any bigger. And why does she suspect this? Why, from the simple fact that she wants them to get bigger! Ergo, they won't. You see, things have a habit of not going the way young Jessica wants them to.

'Are you up yet?' yells Mum.

'Coming!' calls back Jessica.

Dressed in her school clothes, she puts on her glasses and arranges her long, brown hair in its customary twin-tails. She rushes out of her room. A top of the stairs Jessie trips over the school bag she is dragging along, and pitching forward, noisily descends the staircase via the arse-over-tit method.

'One of these days you're going to break your stupid neck!' yells Mum from the kitchen.

A dishevelled Jessica staggers into the kitchen, rubbing her tail bone. Mum and her big brother Trev are seated at the breakfast table. Jessie sits herself down in front of her bowl of cereals, reaches for the carton of milk. Pouring the milk onto her cereals, a headline on the tabloid newspaper behind which her brother is hidden catches Jessie's attention. The tabloid, in an uncharacteristic outbreak of prudishness, is criticising a former Disney starlet for having just made a very raunchy music video.

'For God's sake, Jessica! Look what you're doing!'

Jessica looks. Distracted by the newspaper story she hasn't

noticed that her bowl is overflowing with milk.

'Sorry, Mum!'

Trev looks over the top of his newspaper. 'She can't help being a klutz,' he announces, not unaffectionately.

'A klutz?' snorts Mum. 'She's a walking bloody disaster.'

Jessica slurps up the milk in which her cereals are now swimming.

The letter-box rattles.

'That'll be the post,' says Mum and goes into the hall to pick it up. She returns with a padded envelope for Jessica.

'For you.'

'Oh great!'

It is the music CD she has ordered online. She tears open the envelope and extracts the CD. In spite of the padded envelope the plastic jewellery box has cracked, the lid having come away completely. Jessica's face falls. She has yet to order a CD through the post that has arrived with jewel case unbroken. She had been hoping—as she always hopes—that this time would be the exception; because in spite of the mountain of evidence to the contrary, Jessica is possessed of a streak of optimism; optimism that one day something might just turn out the way she wants it to…

Breakfast over, Jessie rushes back upstairs to wash her face and brush her teeth.

Back downstairs again: 'I'm off now!'

She steps outside into the bright spring morning. She checks her watch, finds that in spite of having risen so late she is actually early! The mad rush through her breakfast and ablutions has paid off: she ought to have no trouble catching the bus today.

However, as she rounds the corner from her close to the main thoroughfare, the bus, a green double-decker, is already at the bus-stop.

'Hey! Wait for me!'

Repeating this entreaty, she runs for the bus—and of course the bus, ignoring her plea, pulls away, some of her schoolfriends on the back seat laughing and waving ironic farewells through the window. Jessica sighs. The one day she's early setting off, the bus has to be early as well!

Oh, well.

She crosses the road and sets off across the park. She can still make it in time for first bell by taking this short-cut. Strolling along, she hears what sounds like a bus's diesel engine on the road behind her. She looks back. Yes, there is another bus pulling in at her stop! She realises now that the bus she has missed must have been the previous bus running very late. And now, her normal bus has arrived on time.

She briefly considers running back, but knows she won't get there before the bus pulls away... Yes, there it goes!

Sighing again, Jessica walks on. (You would sigh a lot, if you were Jessica!) She feels something land on her head. Oh, great. Now it's going to start raining, and she isn't even wearing a hooded coat... She looks up through the interlacing tree branches overhead. The sky is clear. A few patches of cloud, but nothing that looks threatening. It must have just been one random rain drop. Either that or she just imagined it.

Always looking for the bright side, Jessica calls to mind the fact that Games today is indoor Games. In her gym class most of the girls opt to go bare-foot, and Jessica never tires of admiring all those naked female feet! They're just so sexy! All those soles! All those toes...! Very prudently, Jessie has never let on about this lamentable sexual aberration of hers. If the other girls knew about it, they would be uniformly grossed-out and would immediately start wearing trainers in gym class!

Thus far in her life, the only toes Jessica has got to suck have been her own. And this she had found to be a delicious autoerotic experience, with the one draw-back that, not being that supple of limb, she really needs both hands to bring her foot up to the vicinity of her mouth, and this makes it rather difficult, if not impossible, for her to masturbate herself at the same time. (She had once fallen off her bed attempting this manoeuvre.)

And now Jessie arrives at her school. Crossing the school-yard she can't help but notice people looking at her and smiling. She hears stifled outbreaks of laughter behind her back. What is it this time? Has the story of her running to catch the bus already been passed around? Probably. Poor Jessica is used to being the school laughing-stock.

The bell rings for registration, and the students file into the school buildings. Reaching her form room, Jessica sits herself at her usual desk. People are still looking at her and sniggering. She feels her freckled cheeks burn with puffed-out indignation. Okay, so she missed the bus! Bloody hilarious!

Mr Bright, their form teacher walks in.

'Alright; what's all this mirth about?' he inquires. 'It's far too early in the morning for levity.'

And then he sees the object of the class's amusement. He pulls a face.

'Jessica, I think you need to go to the bathroom.'

'The bathroom?' echoes Jessica. 'I don't get it.'

'Just go to the bathroom and take a look in the mirror. All will become clear.'

So Jessica goes to the bathroom and looks in the mirror and sees what they have all been laughing at: bird crap. A bird has dumped on her head. That 'rain drop' she had felt in the park!

Even the birds have got it in for her.

She cleans her hair with wet toilet roll; and this proves an awkward operation as toilet paper is designed to disintegrate when it gets wet. By the time she has finished and got all the bits of toilet paper out of her hair, the bell has rung for first lesson. First lesson is Chemistry today. She hurries over to the Science building and into Mr Williams' classroom.

Much to surprise, she finds the room full of Year Seven kids.

'What do you want, Jessica?'

'Er... I thought it was Year Ten Chemistry...'

Mr Williams sighs. 'That's tomorrow, Jessica.'

'But today *is* Wednesday, isn't it?' defensively.

'No, Jessica, today is Tuesday.'

Exit Jessica, pursued by laughter.

Oh, great. If it isn't Wednesday that means she has packed all the wrong books and needlessly brought her PE kit! It also means that she should be in English right now, and Mr Lensfield is a very strict teacher. She walks into his class at the worst possible moment. Several students have forgotten to do their homework assignment, and Lensfield is thundering at them.

'Sorry I'm late!'

He glares at her. 'Sit down.'

Jessica sits down.

'And have you "forgotten" to do the homework I set as well?' he inquires.

'Oh, no, I've done the homework!' says Jessica brightly. Her face falls. 'Oh no, but wait a minute. I've forgotten to bring it…'

'You've done it but you forgot to bring it.' Mr Lensfield's voice drips acid. 'I could tell you what I think of that excuse, but I won't embarrass you. You can join the others in detention after school.'

'But you see I thought today was Wednesday so I brought the wrong books and—'

'Detention!'

At lunchtime, Jessica sits herself on a secluded bench on the edge of the playing field. Opening her lunch box, she discovers that her carton of fruit juice has somehow sprung a leak; the box is swimming in it and her sandwiches and biscuits are soaked. Sighing, she empties the contents of the box into a nearby bin and takes out her Tolstoy. At least she still has this food for the mind. She has reached an amazing chapter in the book, where the convicts have to march across the town in leg-irons. Jessie is soon engrossed in the classic tale.

So wrapped up in the moment is Jessica that she completely forgets that no moment of unalloyed pleasure can last long for her, and that she ought to be keeping a weather eye alert for the approach of the next disaster. But alas due to her inattention that next disaster approaches unobserved, and the hapless one only becomes aware of it when she feels fizzing liquid being poured over her head, and even worse, cascading down onto the pages of the open book. Coke. The caffeinated brown liquid soaks into the pages of her precious paperback.

Jessica springs to her feet. The culprits are two of her classmates, Hayley and Connie.

'There was still some bird shit on your head,' declares Connie. 'I just cleaned it off for you!'

The girls laugh.

'Look what you've done to my book!' explodes Jessica. 'You've ruined it! You bitches!'

'Ah, diddums.'

'Cunts!'

'Ooh, strong language from Miss Klutz! I'm gunna tell your mum!'

Their work done, Connie and Hayley depart, spluttering with laughter.

Jessica seethes.

After lunch, comes Physics. Jessica manages to short-circuit a battery and cause an experiment to melt. Business as usual.

Finally the last lesson arrives, and it is Art. Outside the Art building she meets three Year Nine girls with whom she gets along quite well. One of the girls, Linda, is showing off a jewellery box she has just finished making in pottery class: shaped like a casket, glazed and beautifully painted.

'Pretty good, isn't it?' says Sandra, passing the box to Jessica.

'It's fantastic!' enthuses Jessica, inspecting the box. 'How did you—oh!'

The box slips from her fingers, smashes to pieces on the ground.

Linda bursts into tears.

'You stupid bitch!' rages Sandra. 'Do you know how long it took her to make that? You know, people warned us we should keep away from you cuz you're a walking disaster; we should have fucking listened to them!'

Crimson with shame, tearfully apologising, Jessica flees.

After Art, detention with Mr Lensfield.

When this is over, Jessica walks back home in the

gathering dusk feeling wretched about her day, her ruined book, and especially about Linda's jewellery box. It's bad enough when she breaks her own things, but when it's other people's… And it looks like she's lost three more friends into the bargain. Was her book being spoilt a punishment? If it was, then the retribution had been enacted before the crime. That doesn't make sense, but then nothing in her life does. So decides Jessica, miserably. For not the first time she wonders if she is being punished for crimes in a previous existence. This bad-luck that constantly follows her in her wake: it hasn't always been like this. Her early childhood had been very happy and free from all but acceptable levels of juvenile clumsiness and misadventure… It had all seemed to start along with her menstrual cycle, when she was eleven. The change in her body seemed to have simultaneously triggered some change in her karma.

Now, Jessica has read up extensively on the subject of the menstrual cycle, both online and in library books, but chronic misfortune and butter-fingeredness are neither of them recognised side-effects of this process. In fact, for all her rigorous online scrutiny, she can find absolutely no record of any other woman reporting similar symptoms.

Our luckless heroine reaches home without further misadventure. Her out-of-work brother is stretched out on the sofa watching Freeview TV.

'A bit late, aren't you?'

'Detention.'

She ascends to her room, changes out of her school clothes into cargo pants and a t-shirt.

Mum arrives home late and in a hurry. She has an evening class to attend later.

'What's for dinner, Mum?' asked Jessica.

'Spaghetti Bolognese. Just let me get changed.'

Jessica goes into the kitchen. Mum's rushed off her feet; she'll just help making dinner. She knows Mum doesn't like her doing this sort of thing—last time Jessica had tried to cook a family meal it had been a disaster—but it can't hurt to just start things off. She goes to their cooker and turns on the gas. The cooker is an old one and the hobs do not ignite themselves. Matches… Where are the matches? And the big saucepan. And the pasta. She finds the saucepan first. At this point, Mum rushes in.

'What are you doing?' she demands, alarmed.

'Starting the dinner,' says Jessica.

Mum snatches the saucepan from her hand. 'Well don't. If you want to make yourself useful, empty that bin,' pointing to the swing bin in the corner.

As her mum fills the saucepan with tap-water, Jessica pulls the bin-liner from the bin. The thin plastic splits, and the bag sheds its contents over the floor.

Her mum growls with something close to despair. 'Can't you do anything?' Putting the saucepan down, she peels off another bin liner from the roll in the drawer and together they transfer the contents of the first bag into the second. Mum ties it off at the handles. 'Now go and take it outside. The black bin, remember?'

'Yes, Mum.'

Trev, cigarette in hand, slouches into the room. 'Has anyone seen my lighter?'

'Not me,' says Jessica, passing him. Pulling on her trainers, she goes out the front door and to the wheelie bins at the top of the drive. She dumps the bag into the black bin.

And then the back of the house explodes.

Stunned and rooted to the spot, Jessica watches as the plume of black smoke rises into the evening sky. Motion returns, and she runs round to the back garden. The kitchen is in flames, thick smoke billowing from the windows, up into the air. Then comes a second explosion, knocking her off her feet. The top floor of the house collapses onto the kitchen.

Mum. Trev.

Jessie stares at the inferno. The horror of it is too much for her to take in.

Then she remembers. The gas. She'd turned on the gas.

With an animal cry of despair, she throws herself down, buries her face in the grass.

And then she feels a hand on her shoulder. Bleary-eyed, she looks up. A handsome man, thirtyish, with long side-burns, hunkers down beside her.

'It's not your fault, Jessica,' he says. His voice is calm, caressing.

'It is!' retorts Jessica, wretchedly. 'I turned on the gas...'

'It's not your fault,' he repeats. 'Any of it. All your bad luck. All the accidents. It's not your fault. It's all an illness; a medical condition.'

'An illness? But it's not! I looked it up—'

The man shakes his head. 'It's a condition that human science has yet to identify. You won't find it documented anywhere.'

'Then it might as well not exist! If there's not any cure—'

'There *is* a cure, Jessica. I happen to have it. That's why I'm here. I've come to take you away from here, Jessica. I want to cure you; to make you better.'

There is something hypnotic about his voice.

'Who are you?'

'My name's Vautrin. I'm a friend.'

'You can cure me...?'

'I can. I can take you to a new life. We have a base, you see; a complex. Top-secret and underground. You'll have your own room. There are other girls already there. They're all waiting for you; girls your own age. They'll be true friends to you; and I promise you'll never again bring bad luck upon yourself or anyone else.'

He helps her to her feet, rests his hands on her shoulders.

'But we have to go now. If we wait for the fire brigade and the police, you're going to be taken into care; you might even be prosecuted for criminal negligence or involuntary man-slaughter. *I* know that you're innocent, but the authorities might not look at it that way.'

'But if I run, they'll just find me—'

Another shake of the head. 'Where I'm taking you, you'll be safe from the police. Safe from all authority.'

'But I deserve to be punished!' insists Jessica. 'Mum...

Trev...'

'You don't deserve punishment, Jessica. Please don't say that. It's time to move on. Will you come with me?'

She looks up into his eyes, sparks of light from the blaze dancing in the irises.

'Yes...' she says.

Chapter Twenty-Two
Don't Make Any Plans for Nigel

Flossie Farraday, dressed in her school clothes, bag over her shoulder, pauses at the top of the drive. She looks at the half-timbered house, that symbol of her miserable previous life. Flossie has come home. She has some unfinished business. Looking back on her old life from its new, altered perspective, she finds it hard to understand how she could have put up with it for so long; that unrelenting barrage of abuse and contempt from the rest of her family; the constant bullying at school... It was like Juliette had once said to her: given time, you can become accustomed to almost anything.

She had endured it because in all her life she had never known anything different. She had endured it because she had grown up to think that somehow *she* must have been the one at fault.

All that has changed now. Juliette and Vautrin have come into her life and given it new meaning. Now, she is happy. Now, she has been reborn. She enjoys a life of blissful self-indulgence; she has real friends who will support her; her home, the leisure and luxury of the SEA base; money is no object; they can buy, buy, buy, all the worldly possessions they desire. And none of the girls concern themselves over the dichotomy of, on the one hand, waging war against society, and on the other hand, being avid consumers of the media products and commercial goods of that same society—This is one of the beauties of living by no rules: you can be as contradictory as you like!

And now for that unfinished business...

Flossie crunches up the gravel drive to her former home. The front door is unlocked. She just walks straight into the living room where her parents are sat watching TV.

'Hello Mum. Hello Dad,' she greets them, as though she has just returned from a trip to the shops.

Her parents gawp at her, blank incomprehension written on their features.

Mr Farraday finds his voice first.

'You,' he says.

'Yes; me,' confirms Flossie, brightly.

The parents exchange looks, expressions of alarm, perplexity, mute inquiry chasing themselves across their features. This situation, their daughter's casual reappearance, is clearly one for which they are unprepared.

Mustering himself, Mr Farraday stands up. Assuming the familiar tone of curt authority he has always reserved for Flossie, he says: 'You've got some explaining to do, young woman. Walking out without so much as a by-your-leave. Where have you been all this time? You realise we had to call the police after you vanished?'

'Yes, it must have been very inconvenient for you, my running away like that,' replies Flossie airily. 'But I notice you did your best to cover your tracks and cover up the trail for the police. You told them you last saw me the morning *after* I actually disappeared, didn't you? Said I vanished on my way to school. I read about that in the papers. And I'm guessing you've removed the lock from my bedroom door, haven't you? *That* would have taken some explaining.'

Mr Farraday looks down at his wife. She looks back up at him. Something is wrong. This is their daughter, sure enough; looks the same, sounds the same—but she has changed. Her body language is all wrong; her expression, her demeanour. She sounds relaxed, confident, completely unafraid.

'Where have you been all this time?' repeats Mr Farraday, in a quieter tone. He reseats himself beside his wife.

'I've been with my new friends,' says Flossie. 'We've been

having a lovely time. Sorry I forgot to send a postcard.'

Mrs Farraday then speaks. 'Why did you come back?'

Her tone is challenging, bitter.

'Oh, I'm sorry, Mum,' returns Flossie. 'I know this must be a disappointment for you. I know you must have hoped so much that I was lying dead in a ditch somewhere. But don't worry; this is only a flying visit; I'm not back to stay. I just wanted to ask you something.'

'Ask us what?'

'I'd like to know what I did wrong. What did I do wrong for you to all hate me and make my life a misery?'

Mrs Farraday's face becomes stone. 'I never loved you from the day you were born,' she answers, her voice a dull monotone. 'I felt nothing for you, nothing at all. You're like the kitten in the litter that the mother cat rejects. Only I couldn't just abandon you. Oh no, I've had to put up with you all these years.'

Her husband takes up the thread. 'Everything you said, everything you did, every little thing about you just infuriated us, grated on our nerves. We had a lovely home, a beautiful son and a beautiful daughter; and then you were always here to spoil everything; a blot on our existence.'

'I'm so sorry for being a blot on your existence, Dad, Mum,' says Flossie. 'It must have been hard for you. But, why didn't you just kill me?'

'Don't think it didn't occur to us,' answers Mr Farraday. 'If there was some way we could have done it; some way we could have quietly disposed of you and escaped the consequences, we would have done it.'

'But then you wouldn't have had the pleasure of making my life a misery,' points out Flossie. 'And it *was* a pleasure, wasn't it, Dad? But you were entitled to it, weren't you? A payback for having been burdened with me in the first place.'

A short silence.

'Why don't you just go?' says Mrs Farraday. 'Go back to where you came from.'

'I will, but there's something I need to do first.'

Flossie reaches into her bag and produces a handgun; a desert eagle, the same weapon Juliette had presented to Trudie on the day of their first meeting.

'I suppose I should tell you a bit more about my new friends. We're an organisation. We've been very busy; you'll have heard about us. We've killed lots of celebrities and VIPs. We even blew up some hospitals. You could say we're dedicated to chaos and destruction.'

She points the gun at her horrified parents.

'Flossie, dear…' says Mrs Farraday, imploring.

'Oh, Mum!' protests Flossie, an indulgent smile in her voice. 'It's a bit late now for "Flossie, dear." '

She shoots her parents where they sit, decorating the upholstery with their blood.

Flossie allows herself a few moments to savour her revenge; she then returns to the hall and mounts the staircase. Eve, in her underwear, has appeared on the landing, drawn by the sound of the gunshots.

'Florence!' she yelps. 'What's going on?'

Flossie holds up the gun. 'Hello, Eve. I've just killed Mum and Dad.'

Eve screams and runs back into Nigel's bedroom. Flossie follows her, kicks open the door. Nigel is there in his boxer shorts. He and his sister cower on the bed.

'Please, Flossie…' whimpers Eve. 'It was mum and dad! It was them who made us be mean to you! We didn't want to be like that! It was them!'

'Yeah, whatever.'

Flossie fires off two shots and the incestuous sheets are stained red.

Flossie leaves her family house, walks back down the drive, crosses the road and calmly waits for the bus. She feels better for what she has just done; she has achieved a sense of 'closure.' Of course, she could have just left them be; after all, they were part of a life she had finished with anyway. But violent and gratuitous revenge is definitely an SEA 'thing.' The other girls have been very enthusiastic in encouraging her to pay this flying visit to her past life. As the ever-practical Dizzy Hello had said: 'If you've got issues with your family, then all you've got to do is kill your family—Problem solved!'

Now there is somebody else Flossie has to see. Just one other person with whom she needs to reach the same understanding she has attained with her family. The bus arrives, the familiar red bus that had daily taken her to school in her previous life. She even still has her Oyster card. School is not her destination this time; she gets off a couple of stops short, and makes her way to Denise's house. Remember Denise, that budding amateur filmmaker?

The girl herself answers the door. Her eyes saucer.

'You!'

'Yes, me.'

Out comes the desert eagle once again.

Denise squeaks and runs back into the house. Flossie follows her into her living room, where Denise's parents and younger brother are also present.

'She's got a gun!' shrieks Denise.

'What's going on?' demands Mum, looking at the handgun, uncertain.

'It's her! It's Flossie Farraday!'

'Yes, it's me,' confirms Flossie. 'Sorry for the intrusion, but this is just between Denise and me. Nothing to concern you.'

And to ensure their unconcern Flossie calmly shoots Mum, Dad, little brother. Blood geysers all over the living room.

She turns to Denise.

'That's better! Now we won't be interrupted.'

Denise is screaming hysterically, clutching and shaking her head. Flossie slugs her round the face with the heavy gun. Denise collapses, blood streaming from a gashed cheek.

'Not so tough now, are you, bitch-queen?' observes Flossie, pointing the gun at the whimpering girl on the floor. 'Tell me: what did you do with that film you took of me in the shower? I looked for it online, but I couldn't find it anywhere.'

'It's gone! I deleted it,' sobs Denise. 'After you disappeared, I panicked. So I deleted the film; I deleted it! I never showed it to anyone, I swear.'

'I believe you,' allows Flossie. 'Mind you, I wouldn't really care if the whole world had seen it. The old me would have cared, but not the new me.'

She levels her gun at Denise's head.

'Please don't kill me…' blubbers Denise.

'You know, that's really sad,' says Flossie, meditatively. 'Here I've just killed your whole family, destroyed your home, and you still want to live. Selfish or what?'

'Please…'

Flossie's finger tightens on the trigger. Then it relaxes.

'You know, I *will* let you live,' she decides. 'I came here for some payback and I think I've got that now. And don't worry: you won't be seeing me again, Denise; so have a nice rest of your life.'

And she leaves the girl with the wreckage of her family.

Chapter Twenty-Three
The House on the Downs

They are looking at a hole in the ground. A vast rectangular excavation, it looks like a trench that has been dug to receive the foundations of a new building. However in this case, time has reversed itself: this trench all that remains of a building that once stood here. Not a building demolished or burnt down, but a building that one fine day had simply vanished, winking out of existence without a sound or a ripple.

The location is, or *was*, the Peltdown Vale Research Establishment. The station has officially closed down; an inevitable action given the loss of the main laboratory building and the team of scientists who staffed it. The electrified fence marking the boundaries of the compound, now just protects a couple of out-buildings and one great big hole.

Mark Hunter and Dodo Dupont stand on the verge of the cavity. They have been here before; summoned to the spot immediately after the 'incident.' On that occasion they had been unable to find the missing building and its occupants, or even any clue to explain the loss. Today, they have returned.

'Somehow, it all started with this,' says Mark. 'A research building, with over twenty people in it, suddenly disappears. Nothing is heard, no progress is made, and the case gets shelved. Then out of the blue, one of the missing scientists reappears, raving about having been held prisoner in some huge underground complex. He gives us the name of his captor: Vautrin. The other missing scientists are still there. This spot is the epicentre; this is where it all started. Somewhere out on the Downs, in an abandoned, isolated house, is the entrance to the base. And that's what we've got to find.'

'Couldn't your department have spared more people for the search?' inquires Dodo. She indicates the two parked cars behind them. One is her own vehicle. Against the side of the other, recline agents Daisy Fontaine and Mike Collins.

'Apparently they couldn't,' replies Mark. 'To be honest, my superiors are sceptical as to the existence of this alleged base. I mean, I don't have much proof, do I? The garbled account of one very sick man who then exploded. They think I'm wasting my time; that I should be scouring the capital looking for Vautrin and those girls; anticipating their next attack. Either way, I've got to come up with some results soon, or I'll be out of a job.'

'They can't do that!' protests Dodo.

'I only wish that were true; but unfortunately, my track record on this case has been somewhat less than impressive—I stopped the SEA from acquiring a supply of munitions; they just got them from somewhere else. I captured five of the terrorists; then I let them be taken out from under my nose. And on top of that, so far I haven't prevented a single one of their attacks.'

'But do they think anyone else could have done any better?

You've always got results in the past.'

'Yes, but I think that might just make it worse for me: a blemish shows up all the more on a spotless record. Also, I have a lurking suspicion that I may have Rufus Wainwright to thank for my current unpopularity upstairs. That man has some very influential people on his friends list, and what with one thing and another, he's not terribly fond of yours truly.'

Smiling ruefully, Mark stares down into the excavation, as though hoping he can extract some hint or clue from those planes of compressed earth.

'Just what happened here?' he murmurs. 'The building disappeared and now the scientists are prisoners of Vautrin. But did he cause the building to vanish, or did they do it themselves?'

'Themselves?'

'Yes, we know that they were experimenting with material of extra-terrestrial origin, an element previously unknown to us. Maybe something went wrong with one of their experiments. You know, it's a fact that the first whispers of Vautrin's existence weren't heard until after the Peltdown Vale Incident. So, what happened? Did they go to him? Did he come to them? Or did they meet in some middle ground, some limbo?'

'You mean they might have actually done something to bring Vautrin here from wherever it is he comes from? Dragged him in like a magnet with that solanite stuff?'

'Well, *something* happened to bring him and those scientists together, didn't it? And it's no more unlikely than the idea that those eleven girls just subconsciously wished him into existence.'

'And we know that Vautrin is making the scientists continue their work under his guidance. I wonder what his interest in solanite is... What is he making those scientists work towards?'

'It won't be anything for the good of humanity, if his past record is anything to go by,' says Mark.

They return to the cars.

'Let's look at the map,' says Mark. He unfolds it on the bonnet of Dodo's car. 'According to Dr Herriot, the entrance to the SEA headquarters is in an abandoned farmhouse somewhere on the downs. We're here. Herriot was picked up by the lorry driver here. Between those two points we've established the existence of twelve possible locations. We need to check them all. As we've only got two cars, we'll take six of them each.'

'What's that?' asks Dodo, pointing to a symbol on the map.

'Oh, that's a government installation. An old nuclear bomb shelter or something, built back in the fifties. The installation is still staffed, so I don't see how Vautrin could be using it as his base... Okay. Collins, you and Fontaine take those six houses to the west; Dodo and I will take the ones to the east.'

They climb into their cars and set off, Dodo at the wheel of her own car; Mark relaxes in the passenger seat. An almost cloudless firmament smiles down on the rolling grassland, many of the slopes populated by grazing sheep.

'It occurs to me,' says Mark, apropos of nothing, 'that the absence of facial hair would be a far more effective disguise than the addition of it. Don't you think so? Yes... really, a spy ought to wear a false moustache all the time, and then just take it off whenever he wants to disguise himself.'

'You should have thought of that one earlier, then,' says Dodo. 'You've been walking around clean-shaven for too long.'

'I wonder how I'd look with a false moustache...?'

'Just as handsome as you would with a real one, sweetheart.'

They drive on.

'There should be turning on the right,' says Mark, presently. 'Our first location is down there.'

They turn off the road onto a farm track and presently arrive at an old farmhouse, grey bricked, windows boarded up, garden a jungle of weeds.

Dodo drives up to the house; they get out of the car.

'Well it matches Herriot's description,' says Mark. 'But then, they probably all do. A farmhouse is a farmhouse, really. Let's check the barn first. If this is the place we're looking for, there ought to be some transport lying about. I can't see Vautrin and those girls walking all the way to the nearest bus stop every time they want to go anywhere.'

'Tire tracks in the mud,' observes Dodo as they approach the barn. 'Someone's been using this place.'

'Yes, and they look like car tracks as well,' says Mark. 'They're not the marks of farm vehicles. But how recent are they? It's hard to tell with the ground being so dry.'

They find no vehicles at all in the barn. They move on to the house. Finding the front door unlocked, they step inside. The murky front room contains nothing more than a few rickety pieces of furniture. Mark opens a door under the staircase.

'Cellar. Let's take a look.'

Armed with torches, they descend to the cellar, damp and bare. They examine the walls, the floor; no sign of a hidden entrance presents itself. Back upstairs, they pass through double doors into the back room, perhaps once the dining room but now completely devoid of furniture.

'Here's something.' Mark picks up a wallet from the floor, opens it, shines his torch on it. 'Well, well. It looks like we've struck gold first time. This belongs to William Herriot, our exploding scientist.'

'So this is the place...'

'Must be.'

'Then where's the entrance to the base?'

'It must be very well concealed.'

'So, what do we do now?'

'Well, I don't know about you, but I'm feeling a bit peckish. Why don't you get the Thermos and sarnies from the car? I'll dust off a couple of those chairs and we can have our lunch in here.'

'Alright.'

Dodo returns with the coffee and the sandwiches. They seat themselves on two wooden chairs Mark has made presentable. Dodo pours out the coffee and they tear open the wrapping on the sandwiches.

'One thing that puzzles me,' says Mark. 'What was the wallet doing in that back room? Herriot escapes from the SEA base, presumably comes out from the cellar (even though we couldn't find the entrance.) The cellar steps bring him out into this room. If it was me, not knowing how close pursuit might be, I'd have been out that front door and over the green hills and away, before you could say Will Robinson. Yet Herriot apparently decides to have a look at the back rooms of the house, somehow managing to drop his wallet in the process. Seems a bit odd.'

'Maybe the front door was locked on that occasion,' suggests Dodo. 'If he couldn't get out through the front, he would have gone through to the back to look for another way out.'

'Yes, that's a possibility...' Mark sips his coffee thoughtfully.

'You know what I'm wondering?' says Dodo.

'What are you wondering?' asks Mark.

'I'm wondering what you'd do with yourself,' says Dodo. 'I mean, if they actually gave you the boot.'

'Good question. Here I am, forty-years-old, and nothing on my CV apart from "Spy." Unless I defected to the Russians or something, there aren't that many job possibilities out there for an ex-spy.'

'You could always become a private detective,' smiles Dodo.

Mark returns the smile. 'Oh yes. That "other" career choice for the overgrown boy. Is that how you see me, then?'

'Well, no. I said when we first met that you didn't look like a spy, remember...?'

'Fondly.'

A smile from Dodo. 'I'm sure. Well, if I didn't know any better I'd've had you pegged as an academic; a university lecturer or something; that's what I mean.' She looks at him. 'So, why *did* you decide to become a spy? You've never told me.'

A wistful sigh from Mark. 'Why indeed? I think it was just destiny.'

They finish the food and the coffee. Mark lights a cigarette, Dodo one of her cigars.

'I wonder what those girls will do next,' says Dodo, exhaling reflectively. 'I mean, they're not even following a standard pattern of escalation. You might have expected them to follow up the hospital bombings, but instead it's just this SEA Paparazzi thing.'

The SEA Paparazzi has recently become the terror of the Establishment, exposing the secret vices of a number of civil servants: a cabinet minister who relaxed himself by taking trips away from his family to indulge in paraphilic infantilism (pretending to be a baby); an eminent high-court judge who hired high-class prostitutes for satisfying his coprophiliac tendencies… Vices that are not criminal, but are deeply embarrassing when made public, and which have led to resignations. Had the offenders been merely media celebrities, public opinion might have forgiven them their private peccadilloes, but civil servants possess a demeanour of spotless respectability which they have to maintain, and if they fail to do this, then public opinion is merciless…

'Yes,' says Mark. 'Those girls are unpredictable. About the only thing you can really say the SEA's attacks have in common is that they all have that air of being very bad-taste jokes.'

The two friends smoke in silence for a while.

His cigarette finished, Mark crushes it under his foot, looks at his watch.

'No, it looks like it's not going to work,' he murmurs.

'What's not going to work?' inquires Dodo.

'My plan.'

'What plan would that be?'

'I thought perhaps we might be under surveillance. I was hoping the SEA girls might pop out from somewhere and take us prisoner.'

Dodo laughs a hollow one. 'Thanks! You could have warned me you were planning to let us be captured by a bunch of adolescent sociopaths!'

'Well, I thought that at least one of us ought to look surprised if it actually happened. I didn't want them smelling a rat.'

'And now that it *hasn't* happened…?'

'Back to the car, I think.'

They return to the car.

Dodo turns the ignition key. 'You'll have to send in excavators to start digging the place up, if you want to find the base.'

'Perhaps not,' says Mark, buckling his seatbelt. 'Another possibility occurs to me: the SEA will know, or at least guess, that we know from Herriot that the entrance to their headquarters is in an isolated empty house, and in this general area...'

'I think I get it. So they could have just planted that wallet in the wrong house to mislead us,' finishes Dodo.

'It's a possibility.'

'Great. So does that mean we have to check out those other five houses after all?'

''Fraid so.'

'And what if we find wallets in all of them?'

'Then it will be time to say "Back to square one!"'

Chapter Twenty-Four
NEET Untidy

The bedsit of Curtis, our friend from the *Doctor Who* convention, looks as untidy as you would expect it to be. The room is small, with a lot of bed and not much room for sitting, unless it's on the bed itself. This bed is permanently unmade and the linen emits a fragrance suggesting it hasn't seen the inside of a washing machine for some time. Clothes, books, CDs, DVDs, are strewn all over what floorspace is available. A permanent odour of beer and cigarettes hangs in the air. A neglected electric guitar, propped against an amp in one corner, speaks of its owner's now discarded ambitions in the arena of rock stardom. On a coffee table before the curtained bay window, sits Curt's TV set and stereo system. To the right this, a venerable bookcase displays the tenant's media interests. Books, displaying a cultish taste: JG Ballard, Albert Camus, William Burroughs are prominent, with the nineteenth century chiefly represented by Dostoyevsky. CDs, vertically stacked: Curtis's collection of alternative rock CDs, started when he was fifteen. DVDs, all in the arena of cult TV: individual *Doctor Who* titles, complete series boxsets; all bought—like his book collection —second-hand from charity shops and market stalls.

A man is his hobbies, muses Tanya, seated on, or rather sunk into, the room's dilapidated settee. A man is his hobbies. So what does that make Curt? An indie-rock slacker with a nerdy fanboy trying to get out?

Her boyfriend sits on the dishevelled bed, looking pretty dishevelled himself. His tousled hair urgently requires the attention of a pair of scissors, and he sports a five-day beard growth, and the remains of a black eye from that little set-to at WhoCon.

The couple swig cans of Budweiser; music from the stereo speakers forms a background to their rather sporadic conversation. (The band are Trumans Water, a math-rock ensemble originally from the '90s, but who, in common with most bands from that decade, have since re-formed.) They don't seem to be connecting this evening, Curt and Tanya. London is still in shock from the recent bombings; perhaps the prevailing sense of gloom is affecting them both…

'You know you reek,' Tanya tells Curt. 'When did you last have a bath?'

Curt shrugs. 'Few days ago… Anyway, I don't reek. I can't smell anything.'

'You'd have to be really ripe before you started to notice it yourself. At the moment, it's just other people who have to suffer.'

'Shall I just run myself a bath right now, then?' suggests Curt, irritably.

'No, not now—but you shouldn't let yourself go like that.'

'Let myself go?'

'Yeah, like the not shaving or getting your hair cut; and your room being like a pig-sty. You need to tidy up a bit. It's not good for you to live in a mess like this.'

'Yes, mother.'

'I'm serious, Curt. How do you expect to get a job looking like that?'

'What job? There aren't any bloody jobs.'

'Yeah, not when you're looking like that, there aren't!'

'I can smarten myself up if I need to.'

'You should smarten yourself up all the time; it's called personal hygiene. You're getting into bad habits.'

Tanya and Curtis have been an item for going on three years now. Music is the interest they have in common; they had met at a gig at the Garage. They had been standing next to each other at the venue's bar and they'd both tried to shout their orders at the same time. Tanya works as a nurse; Curtis, generally speaking, doesn't work. In all the time Tanya has known him, she has never seen Curt hold down a job for more than a week; he can never seem to knuckle down to anything. And worst of all, he just doesn't seem to care; he seems quite happy just being on the dole.

'Wanna watch *The Man from U.N.C.L.E.*?' ventures Curt.

Tanya groans. 'No I don't. And you always try and change the subject whenever I'm trying to have a serious conversation with you,' she complains.

'But I've just got the American movie boxset. It's got all eight of the films on it. The English one only had five of them.'

'Why didn't they put the other three on while they were about it?' Tanya stops herself, winces. 'Argh! That's beside the point! We were talking about you.'

'I don't want to talk about me.'

'Well, I do. How old are you?'

'Thirty, same as you.'

'Then don't you think it's time you grew up a bit? Started taking some responsibility in your life?'

'Ah yes, Jean-Paul Sartre's "age of reason"!' says Curt. 'That time when you stop acting like an overgrown teenager and start behaving like an adult.'

Tanya flares up. 'You see! You've just done it again! Changing the subject!'

'It wasn't changing the subject!' protests Curt. 'What I said was very relevant to what you were saying!'

'Yeah, but you were still deflecting the conversation away from yourself! You can't face up to things, can you?'

'Do you want another Bud?'

'No. And you should cut down yourself. You're starting to get a beer gut.'

'I am not!'

'You bloody are!'

Craig looks down at his stomach.

'Doesn't look that big to me,' he says.

'It wouldn't when you're looking down at it like that; but you just try looking at it in profile in a full-length mirror. You'll see a different picture then.'

Curt lights a cigarette. 'You're in a funny mood tonight. What's up? You still worried about those terrorists?'

'Of course I'm still worried about those terrorists; I work in a hospital! The whole bloody world's going to hell in a handbasket... And our relationship feels like it's going the same way...'

'What are you on about? Our relationship's fine. Same as it always was.'

'Is it? When was the last time we had sex?'

'I dunno... Last week...?'

'Three weeks ago. And that was the first time for a month. Just how much recovery time do you need?'

Another shrug. 'I can't be in the mood all the time. If that's all you want from me...'

'It's not all I want from you, Curt. But I'm just saying it's all part of a bigger problem... Like your mind: its crammed full of trivia.'

'What's that supposed to mean?'

'I mean like when you regale me with facts like "Did you know the last two seasons of *Voyage to the Bottom of the Sea* were almost entirely studio-bound?" or "Did you know that *Department S* director Leslie Norman was the father of Barry Norman?" Things like that.'

'I'm sorry if I bore you,' sulkily.

'It's not that; I'm just saying you need to think about people more, and less about your hobbies. You need to think about me, and you need to think about yourself.'

'Yeah, can we postpone this conversation? Let's just watch something.'

'Curtis!'

'Well, why not? It's what we usually do. Fuck, it's what *most* people do.'

Why is she being like this? Can't she understand he just isn't in the mood for this kind of soul-searching discussion? Not right now. He doesn't see that anything even needs to be discussed. They are getting on fine, aren't they? Things have coasted along nicely for them for three years now. Nothing has changed. Nothing needs to change... When you start to have those 'serious discussions' about your relationship—doing that's what fucks things up in the first place!

He looks at Tanya as she sits there. Slender and short-haired, her face is thin, with a wide mouth, a sharp nose, very pale blue eyes; the features in repose have a sardonic cast to them. Tanya's parents are both Scottish—although being born and raised here in London, Tanya has not inherited the Scottish accent—and on account of this Curtis considers Tanya's to be a Hibernian visage—in which he is wrong on two accounts, because 'Hibernian' refers to things Irish, not Scottish; and not all Scottish women happen to look like Tanya.

Looking at her now, Curtis recalls this one surreal incident, only a few months back: they had arranged to meet at the pub one evening when Tanya finished her shift at work; Curt had arrived first; he had been sitting alone at a table, nursing a pint, not really thinking of much... And then suddenly she had appeared, standing over him, smiling that warm smile of hers that gave the lie to those sardonic features... And he had looked up at her and there had been this strange moment of disconnection; it was like he hadn't known who she was. He had found himself thinking: 'Who is this woman? Why is she smiling like that at me? Why does she want to be with me? With me of all people?' The moment of unreality had passed, but it had left an impression. He has never mentioned it to her...

Looking at her at this moment brings the memory back to Curtis. Perhaps if he had mentioned it now; perhaps if he had told her about that strange moment, it might have altered the course of this uncomfortable evening for the better…

Unfortunately, Curtis doesn't mention it—instead he says:

'How about *The Spy in the Green Hat*? It's got Jack Palance and Janet Leigh in it.'

Tanya puts down her beer can, unfinished. 'I don't care about Jack bloody Palance!' She stands up. 'Christ! It's impossible trying to have a serious conversation with you.'

'What are you doing?'

'I'm going; that's what I'm doing. This isn't working tonight. We're just getting on each other's nerves. It's better if I go.'

'You don't have to do that. We can just watch something.'

'I don't want to watch something. I want you to start taking some responsibility in your life.'

Curt groans. 'Oh, stop sticking your nose in!'

'Sticking my nose? I'm your girlfriend. I *care* about you, for Christ's sake!'

'Alright, but that doesn't give you the right to disrupt my routine.'

'Your routine is the problem, Curtis. You're stuck in a rut.'

'Yeah? Well I'm perfectly happy, thank you very much.'

'Well, you shouldn't be! You need to get up and do something!'

'I don't want to "do something"! I don't have to be the same as everyone else! This is me; this is who I am, and if you don't like it, you can fuck off!'

Silence. Tanya looks like she has been slapped.

She finds her voice. 'If you're going to be like that—' She makes a hurried exit from the room.

Curt buries his face in his hands. Why did he go and say that? He's never sworn at Tanya like that before. But why had she had to start preaching at him like that? And at the worst possible time… Why couldn't she have just let things be?

And now she's walked out… Should he run after her and

apologise? But then it might just lead to another scene, another argument...

No...

No, he'll leave it till tomorrow; he'll give her a call tomorrow.

It is a decision he will regret for the rest of his life.

Outside, Tanya hurries down the lamp-lit street, her mind seething. He can be so bloody exasperating! Couldn't he see that she was trying to help him? That she was concerned because she loves him? Well, he is going to get some major guilty treatment for that 'fuck off.' She'll want a full, grovelling apology for that one...

Sometimes it feels like he takes her too much for granted. He's slipped into this comfortable, apathetic groove. He's scared of making any change in his life; that's what the problem is...

She stops at the end of the street, looks back at the house she has just left. No, he isn't coming after her... Is he still angry? Or is he already starting to feel ashamed?

She walks on.

Some of Tanya's friends would say she should leave Curtis. Some of her friends *have* said that; likewise her parents. But they don't know how she feels—His smile. His voice. His smell (even if it sometimes gets a bit *too* much!) He's comfortable, that's what he is; like a warm and cosy jumper. He has taken up a large place in her heart, in her being. She can't just let go of him like that. She doesn't *want* to let go of him. He works so hard at being laid-back, unflappable, does Curt; but she knows that underneath he's insecure...

He needs her... She needs him...

A footstep behind her, and then a building drops on her head. An explosion of pain, blinding light before her eyes. Staggering, she turns, sees a raised arm, a hammer clenched in the fist. It descends. She hears her own skull crack... Darkness blankets her vision... Nausea... The pavement jumps up and slams into her...

The last thought to pass through her stunned and stricken brain: This can't be happening; not this; this can't be happening to me.

The hammer comes down again.

And then, oblivion.

Chapter Twenty-Five
Dizzy's First Time

Dizzy Hello, deflowered, inseminated, lying on the mattress in post-coital bliss, reflects the subject of sex—the subject understandably uppermost in her mind at this moment.

The missionary position; her first bout of sex has been performed thusly. Do most people do it that way the first time? And why do they call it the missionary position, anyway? Is it because this was the position in which woman missionaries had traditionally been raped by lusty black savages? (Nice guess but wide of the mark, Dizzy!) It's the most submissive position for a woman, she reflects... You lie down on your back and you spread your legs open; you are totally exposed, vulnerable. Then the man looms over you, pinning you down; he has you at his mercy, and he forces his cock between your thighs, penetrates and pounds into you, inflicting pleasure on you, the weight of his body on top of yours. And what can the girl do? Well, you can either lie back passively and take it, while perhaps thinking fondly of England; or you can—as Dizzy has just done—wrap your arms and legs around him, desperately embracing the savage beast who is pounding away at you, gripping his body with all the assertion of ownership with which your cunt grips his cock; underlining that he's as much yours as you are his...

From this, her thoughts wander on to the plethora of other sexual positions she has yet to experience; which one would she like to try next...? There is the cow-girl position, the one in which the woman takes the most active role while the man remains fairly passive. Don't the feminists call this position 'empowering' because you are fucking the guy instead of him fucking you? (If by 'fucking' you specifically mean the actual aggressive act, rather than 'fucking' simply to mean two people having sex.) And of course lazy guys like the cow-girl position because they don't have to do anything. It's like they are lying on their backs masturbating, without even having to use their right hands. Yeah, it's like you are jerking the guy off with your pussy... Then there is doggy-style, and its more comfortable counterpart, facedown. There's something very casual about that one, muses Dizzy. It's the way the animals do it. It's like you just present yourself to the male, arse in the air, and he moves in and inserts himself, pumps away at you and then shoots his load. You can't see your partner, he can't see your face, and there's the minimum of physical contact aside from the conjoined genitals. Being taken from behind is, Dizzy decides, the most natural position, convenient for an alfresco quickie with a stranger—Wham, bam, thank you, ma'am, and no awkward eye-contact!

So ruminates post-coital Dizzy.

The venue for Dizzy's first night of sex is not an impressive one. Doug's bedsit is a tip, the 'bed' just a mattress on the floor. Doug lies by her side, smoking a post-coital cigarette. Doug is dark, lean, floppy-fringed; Dizzy—as I'm sure you haven't forgotten—is a well-made girl with short blonde hair, a smiling face, lively blue eyes.

'Well then, first-time girl,' says Doug. 'How was it?'

'It was totally yummy, Doug,' enthuses Dizzy. She takes Doug's cigarette from his mouth, inhales a lungful. 'I can't wait to tell Mum. She'll be really pleased!'

'What?' from Doug, incredulous. 'You can't tell your bloody mum!'

'Oh, I can,' Dizzy assures him. 'I don't have any secrets from Mum. We're very close, me and Mum.'

'Yeah? Well, don't mention my name. I don't want to be done for statutory.'

'Oh, don't worry about that. Mum isn't bothered about the age thing and she won't care less who it was I was with.'

'Charming. So, is your mum as spaced-out as you, then?'

'No,' says Dizzy. 'She's not like me, really. She's just very... motherly.'

Doug retrieves his cigarette.

'I was only fifteen the first time, as well,' he tells her. 'It was this anarchist chick I met at a demo. In her twenties, she was. She showed me the ropes.'

'That's the most sensible way,' says Dizzy, nodding sagely. 'The women should teach the boys sex, and the men should teach the girls. Didn't they do it like that back in pagan times? I think I heard that somewhere. Yeah, it makes more sense that way, being shown the ropes by someone who knows what's what—and not just having two complete newbies trying it together for the first time and making a hash of it. You know: a bad first time can be psychologically damaging.'

'Did you hear that somewhere, as well?' asks Doug, a smile in his voice.

'Yes, I think I did.'

Dizzy has been seeing Doug for a few months. Doug is this lone-wolf anarchist slacker, living alone in this pokey bedsit. Since hooking up with him, Dizzy had put off letting him have sex with her for some time: partly to tease him, and partly because she wanted to build up to the main event, to explore all the avenues of foreplay. And so she had tantalised him with her best striptease dances, she had blown him, golden showered him, jerked him off with her hands and with her feet; and she had let him lick her out, rim her, suck on her tits, kiss and lick her body all over, come all over her... And now tonight, she decided it was finally time to reward Doug for all his patience and forbearance...

And it has been well worth the wait.

Doug is a good guy. He's not all preachy and pedantic about his politics. Doug's anarchism seems to mostly involve wanting to cause as much violence and disorder as possible, but he is still dedicated to his cause, and Dizzy admires him for this.

She snuggles up to him, feeling his wiry, muscular arm. 'How about a second bout? *Ding-a-ling!* Round two!'

Doug sighs. 'You're new to this. Let me tell you about something called "recovery time." '

'What does that mean?'

'It means you've got to wait a bit.'

Dizzy pouts.

'Tell you what!' says Doug, suddenly. 'I've got something to show you.'

He picks up a box from the floor beside the mattress, grinning with pride.

'Oh, Doug!' gushes Dizzy, delighted. 'You shouldn't have!'

'It's not for you, you nelly,' Doug tells her. 'I'm just showing you it. I got this from the dark net. Had to save up a lot of dole money to pay for it, I did.'

From the box he produces a shiny new automatic pistol.

'Wow!' gasps Dizzy, her eyes saucers.

'This little beauty is a Walther P99, Second Generation, AS model,' he announces, proudly.

'So it's the real thing, is it?'

"Course it is! It's not a fucking water-pistol.'

'And what does "AS" stand for?'

'Anti-Stress.'

'Oh, I get it! So, if someone's causing you any stress, you just shoot them with this gun and then the stress goes away!'

(Dodo's conjectures are always as original as they are wide of the mark.)

'No,' says Doug, heavily. 'It refers to the trigger mechanism.'

He passes the gun to her.

'Wow!' says Dizzy again. She caresses the weapon, grips it, curls her finger round the trigger. She has never held a gun before today, but somehow it already feels like an old friend. (If a firearm is a phallic extension for a man, then for a girl like Dizzy handling a gun is more a case of ardent phallic worship.)

'Is it loaded?' she asks.

'Yeah, there's a clip in it, but don't worry; it's cocked.'

Dizzy giggles. 'Ha-ha! Yeah it is like a cock! A big metal cock!'

'You slide that catch there to uncock it. You can also have it half-cocked.'

More giggling. 'Yeah, but you're not one to go off half-cocked, are you?'

'Funny.'

'Still; it's really cool. What are you going to do with it?'

Doug smiles his lazy, lady-killing smile. 'I'm gunna shoot me some pigs,' he announces with pride.

Dizzy leaps up from the mattress, striking a pose with the gun. 'Bang! Bang! Take that you nasty policemen!'

Doug sits up on the edge of the mattress, looks at his girl with admiration. 'Oh, yeah. Naked chick with gun. Fuck, yeah. You're pretty damn sexy, Dizzy.' He makes a viewfinder of his hands. 'Strike a pose, baby!'

She strikes a James Bond pose, gun raised.

'Something sexy!'

She gets down on one knee, holding the gun two-handed.

'That's good!'

She points her bottom at him, aiming the gun behind her.

'Oh, yes!'

She lies down on her side, the gun between her thighs.

'That's it! Give me more, honey!'

On all fours, she rubs the gun along her buttock crevice, sniffs the barrel appreciatively.

'Oh, yeah! The camera loves you!'

Back on her feet, she bends over, pointing the gun at him.

'Give it to me, baby!'

She shoots him in the knee-cap.

'Arrgghh!'

He collapses to the floor, screaming, swearing, blood gushing from his knee.

'Oh, whoopsie!' says Dizzy. 'Have I just gone off half-cocked?'

'You crazy fucking bitch!' screams Doug. 'You've fucking shot me!'

Dizzy fires again, shooting him in the stomach.

'Oops! There I go again! I think I must be fully cocked tonight!'

Doug gapes at her with blank incomprehension, clutching his stomach.

'Mm, that's got to hurt,' muses Dizzy. 'Your stomach acid must be leaking out into the rest of your body. Nasty.'

'You're fucking insane…' gasps Doug.

'No, I'm just very happy,' demurs Dizzy. 'This is a lot of fun.'

She points the gun at him again. Whimpering, Doug makes a futile effort to escape, crawling with his hands and his one good leg.

'Look at you!' giggles Dizzy. 'You're like a little animal, hopelessly thinking you can still crawl away from danger! Well, I tell you what: I don't think you're going to make it, Doug!'

She shoots him in the spine, paralysing him.

She squats down by his side.

'I definitely approve of your purchase, Doug,' she tells him. 'You have not wasted your hard-earned dole money.'

Doug's mouth moves, vainly trying to articulate.

'I know, sweetheart,' says Dizzy, her voice soothing. 'This is a happy time for me, as well. You've taken my virginity, and you've given me a gun. You don't have to try and say anything. This special evening is just too big for mere words to describe.'

She shoots him in the head.

Humming a ditty, Dizzy quickly dresses, storing the gun and all the spare ammunition in her bag. She skips out of the apartment. She exits the building without being seen and sets off home along the darkened streets.

She can't wait to tell Mum!

Dizzy and her mother inhabit a bungalow in a quiet suburban close. It's just the two of them; Dizzy has no brothers or sisters, no father. She arrives home to find her progenitor sitting up in bed, reading. Dizzy's Mum is a very motherly mum: tall, ripe and stately; with long luxuriant blonde hair and a warm, caressing voice. Dizzy—little pagan herself!—thinks her the embodiment of a pagan Matriarch.

'Oh, Mum!' blurts Dizzy, joyfully, rushing into the room.

'What is it, dear?'

Throwing down her bag, Dizzy tears off her clothes and jumps into bed with her mother, snuggling up to her.

'I've done it, Mum! My first time!'

Mum, putting her book aside, strokes her hair. 'What have you done, sweetness?' she inquires indulgently. 'Is it that young man you've been seeing? Have you surrendered your virginity at last?'

'Well, yes; that as well,' says Dizzy 'But something much more important: I've killed my first man!'

She gazes at her mother, eyes sparkling, searching for approval.

Dizzy's Mum answers her with a look of heartfelt approbation. Tears well up in her eyes; she throws her arms around her daughter. 'Oh, my darling! I'm so happy for you!' she sighs. 'Who did you kill? Was it the young man who deflowered you?'

'Yes Mum, it was Doug.'

'And how did you kill him, sweetness?'

'I shot him, Mum! *Bang! Bang!* Four times!'

'But that's wonderful, darling! Where did you get the gun from?'

'Oh, it was Doug's. He'd just bought it. He wanted to kill some policemen because he's political. I was just playing with the gun, holding it, and then it just came over me—I started shooting him! A spur of the moment thing, really.'

'You should always follow your impulses, darling. Did it make you happy, killing the nice young man?'

'Oh, yes! I mean I'll miss Doug, of course, but yes, it was really yummy killing someone like that!'

'I'm so proud of you, my dear,' says Dizzy' Mum, kissing her daughter's hair.

Dizzy looks up at her mother with adoring eyes. Her mother looks back at her, her own eyes—blue like her daughter's—brimming with maternal love. Their lips meet in a passionate prolonged kiss.

'You're growing up just the way I knew you would...' breathes the fond parent.

'Yes, Mum...' replies Dizzy, her voice also dropping to a whisper.

'You're special; you know that, don't you?'

'Yes, Mum...'

'Yes, you're my secret weapon, my darling daughter. I created you, gave birth to you; and I've shaped you, I've moulded you; just to make you what you are now. Tonight my love, you have finally blossomed, you've reached your full potential. I'm so very, very proud of you. And now you've come of age, and it's time; time for me to unleash you on the world...'

'Yes. Mum...'

'My darling daughter, I love you so, so much...'

'I love you, Mum...'

Dizzy's mother now arranges Dizzy on the bed, just as Doug had arranged her short hours before. She kisses her daughter's neck, her breasts, her stomach, her legs, her feet. And then she comes to rest upon the mound of Venus, her long blonde hair fanning out around her daughter's thighs as she kisses that delicate flesh so recently violated...

For Dizzy, her mother is her entire world. For Dizzy's mother, Dizzy is her entire world. A symbiotic relationship. Mother has been obsessively devoted to daughter from the day the latter was conceived. For her, Dizzy is not just special, but unique; a prodigy. She has raised the girl lovingly, has watched over her, moulded her, corrupted her; sculpted her into the perfect weapon with which to wreak havoc on an unsuspecting world.

Yes, for Dizzy, her mother is her world.

And today that world will come crashing down.

She has been to the pictures with some of her classmates from school. (Dizzy can still enjoy doing normal things with normal people; she's adaptable!) Returning home from this after-school outing, she finds the house in unexpected darkness. Her first thought is that her mum must have gone out unexpectedly for some reason; but then she walks into the kitchen and sees the body lying on the floor.

'Mum!'

She runs to her. The woman's body is limp, unresponsive. Instinct tells Dizzy that what she holds is just a husk, an empty shell: her mother, the being that inhabited and animated this human clay, has gone; no longer exists.

She vents a moan of animal despair.

The rest is a blur. The anguished phone-call. The trip to the hospital. The anxious waiting. And then the doctor, sombre-faced. A heart-attack. An undiagnosed condition. There had been nothing they could do.

And then hearing herself discussed. An only child. No relatives within reach. The Child Welfare Agency needs to be summoned. The girl will have to be taken into care.

When backs are turned, Dizzy slips away. She flees the hospital, runs back home. Unfamiliar emotions assail her. Mortification. Rage. She wants to hit back at the world that has taken her precious mother away. The people she passes in the streets: how can they all be alive when her mother is dead? How dare they? These people are nothing. Insects. She loathes them all.

What is she to do? Her mother had given her life meaning. Without Mum, her life has no meaning. There's just nothing left; nothing save for an aching void.

Back at the bungalow, no longer a home, she rushes into her bedroom and pulls the box with Doug's gun—her gun—from her chest of drawers. She will take this gun and go out onto the streets, and she will kill as many of those stupid people—those insects—as she can before turning the weapon on herself.

She pushes an ammunition clip into the Walther. Only then does she sense that she is not alone in the darkened room. A shadowy figure sits on her bed, completely still, completely silent.

Springing to her feet, she aims the gun at the intruder.

'Who are you?' she demands.

'Don't worry,' comes the reply, gentle, masculine. 'I'm not from Child Welfare.'

Keeping him covered, Dizzy backs to the door and switches on the light. The man sitting on her bed is thirtyish, handsome; long fringe and long side-burns, retro clothes.

'Who are you?' she repeats.

'You can call me Vautrin,' he says. 'I'm here as a friend.'

'A friend? I don't even know you.'

'No, but I know you, Dizzy Hello,' says Vautrin. 'Certain things in linear time can be predicted. I knew you were approaching a crisis point. Believe me, I know how you feel. Your mother was your life. You lived for her, as she did for you. Now that she's gone, you feel that your life is over. And you're right: it is over. Your old life, at any rate. But I can offer you a brand-new life; an alternative to oblivion.'

Dizzy lowers the gun. 'A new life? What sort of life?'

A disarming smile. 'I'm assembling a little group, you see. An organisation. It will be composed of girls; girls like you; girls who are special.'

'Why would I want to join your stupid organisation? What do you do: fund-raising?'

'No, not fund-raising. This group will be a very active, anti-social group. Basically, you can do whatever you want.'

'Can I kill people?'

'You can kill all the people you want to. Whatever makes you happy.'

'And these other girls; are they like me?'

'Yes and no. You're all different, all distinct individuals, true originals; but you have a connection, you and the other girls. There's a thread that binds you, a special kind of resonance.'

'And how many girls have you got in this group?'

'There will be eleven all told; but I'm still assembling the group.'

'And who exactly are you?'

'I'm the catalyst. I'm the means of bringing you together.'

'Yeah, but what are you getting out of it?'

Vautrin shrugs. 'Your happiness is mine, Dizzy. I have no ulterior motive.'

'And we can kill whoever we want…'

'Join us. I'm sure it's what your mother would want…'

Yes; her Mum! What her mother had always wanted her to become: it is being offered to her on a plate right now. Mum wouldn't want her to just destroy herself; Mum would want her to carry on: to follow the course destined for her; the result of her mother's careful nurture. Yes; she owes it to her Mum's memory to realise her dreams, her expectations—to be what Mum created her to be.

Perceiving the look of new purpose on her face, Vautrin smiles. 'You're interested, aren't you? Here, let me show you my card.'

He hands a business card to Dizzy. She reads:

SEA

The SOCIETY of EVIL ACTIONS

Dizzy looks up from the card, her smile broadening.
'You like the sound of it?' asks Vautrin.
'Yes...'

Chapter Twenty-Six
Where is Everybody?

Mark Hunter awakes with the sensation that something is not right. He tracks the sensation and arrives at an explanation. He is lying in his own bed, the covers over him, but he is fully clothed; dressed in his usual brown suit—even wearing his shoes. As has already been said, Mark's brown suit is ubiquitous; he is rarely seen wearing anything else. But, as a rule, he does generally wear it to bed.

What on earth had made him go to bed like this? He would have to have been extremely drunk to have climbed into bed like this; but even in that state he would have expected himself to have at least remembered to take off his shoes... *Has* he been drinking? It would be a long time since he had allowed himself to get *that* drunk... Moreover, he doesn't feel hungover. No dehydration; not even a trace of a headache.

No, he cannot have been drinking.

So, what has happened? As nothing short of being a condition of complete befuddlement would have caused him to voluntarily climb into his bed fully clothed, the only alternative that presents itself is that someone *else* has him to bed this manner...

Mark struggles to recollect the events of the previous night. And he finds that he *can't*. His searching mind comes up against a brick wall.

So, what *can* he remember? What is his last clear thought...? He drags up a host of memories; but it's all a non-linear jumble...

He attempts to disentangle the thread...

The case he has been working on: Vautrin. The SEA girls. The attacks. His attempts to locate their base. He can recall all of this, but he just can't sort the memories out. He just can't arrange them into a neat order, one that will show him which memory is the most recent.

It is morning now at any rate. The sun shines in through the bedroom window. He looks at his watch. 10:30. That itself is unusual. He doesn't generally sleep that late, regardless of how late he might have turned in. What *had* he been doing last night? What events had led to him ending up in his own bed fully clothed like this? He sifts again the jumble of memories, but something tells them that none of those accessible memories relate to the evening before. In fact, he has the feeling that all of the memories he can bring before his inner vision are fairly old memories; and then, after them, there is that barrier; that brick wall. What has happened to his most recent memories? Has somebody stolen them?

Mark climbs out of bed, straightens out his crumpled suit and walks through to the living room. Empty. No guests, welcome or unwelcome.

Then something strikes him. The silence. The sound of the traffic passing in the busy street outside, one of those everyday sounds his mind usually filters out, is absent. He goes to the window and looks out. There is no traffic. Nor is there a single pedestrian to be seen. Not a soul, not a movement. It's unnatural. Even if it had been a Sunday—and according to his watch it isn't—there should have been some traffic, some passers-by.

Something is very wrong here. Mark feels unaccustomed fear tugging at him. He returns to the bedroom, picks up his smartphone and calls Dodo. What is this? No connection. He tries calling the Department. No connection. And no internet access either. Is his phone on the blink? Or is this a symptom of a larger problem?

Back in the living room, Mark powers up his desktop computer. Maybe there will be something on the news that will explain all of this. But his desktop proves to be as uncooperative as his phone; no internet connection.

He squats down to check the internet hub beneath his desk. The light on the device is blue—blue means connected. But connected he certainly isn't.

Yes, something is very wrong.

After another look out through the window—still no-one and nothing moving—Mark steps out of his flat. He knocks on the door of the apartment opposite. No answer. He calls his neighbour's name. No answer. He tries the door. Locked. He descends to the next floor, tries another apartment. And another. Same result... Down on the first floor, he finds a door that is unlocked. He opens it.

'Hello? Anybody home?'

No reply. He walks into the flat. Not knowing all his neighbours, he cannot remember who inhabits this one. He finds everything is neat and tidy—no sign of any hurried evacuation—But no-one is home.

Mark walks out into the forecourt that fronts his apartment building. A sunny morning, the slightest of breezes. But that silence reigns; that complete, unnatural silence. And it's not just the absence of traffic, but also that other background noise you normally don't notice: birdsong. The trees and rooftops are silent. There are no birds.

No shortage of parked cars; both here in the apartment building's carpark, and out on the street. If there had been some sort of mass civilian evacuation, you would have expected all the cars to be gone...

He needs to get to Headquarters. If anything in London is still functioning, it ought to be there, in Whitehall, in the very infrastructure of the Establishment. That is where he needs to be; where the answers will be found.

Armed with a purpose, Mark sets off along the street. The sound of his own footsteps seems unusually loud. Not having a car of his own, Mark has no choice but to walk; he very much doubts that the Underground will be operating.

Has everyone gone? Worse: is everyone dead? A gas attack, perhaps. Could that explain everything? But then there would be bodies everywhere. And for that matter how could he himself have survived the event? Being asleep or unconscious would be no protection—Unless he hadn't been there when the attack happened; that someone had placed him in his bed afterwards. But still, no bodies. So, had everyone been safely evacuated before this hypothetical attack? Perhaps they were all evacuated by the military, and in trucks...? That would explain his neighbours' cars being still here... But what about the birds? If there had been any kind of chemical or biological attack, the streets ought to be littered with feathered corpses. Unless the birds themselves had sensed the danger and had managed to flee the danger-zone...

These streets. All so familiar, but yet how unreal they seem now. The silence, the stillness... *Am I dreaming? If I am, this is the most vivid dream I can ever remember experiencing...*

...No, face it; you're awake, Mark Hunter. However unreal it seems, it is *real. This is no dream.*

He comes to a thoroughfare lined with shops. Still not a soul in sight. None of the shops have their shutters down; all look to be open for business. He tries the doors of several; all are unlocked. An idea occurring to him, Mark steps into a newsagent. He scans the newspaper display, taking in the headlines. No; none of them are carrying any story that would account for the absence of people in the capital. No warnings of imminent disaster. No sudden outbreak of war. Just the usual vice, crime and gossip. He looks at the date on the papers, checks it against the date on his wrist-watch. They match. Unless his watch has been tampered with, then the newspapers before him are today's morning editions. But how the hell could that be? The city of London apparently completely deserted, and yet the morning papers have somehow still been printed and distributed as usual…

He leaves the newsagent. A movement catches his eye: the plate-glass entrance doors of a shop down the street swinging shut. Mark starts running. Those doors hadn't moved by themselves. He's not alone, after all.

He bursts into the shop, a clothes boutique. Silence and stillness greet him; the escalators facing the entrance motionless.

'Hello?' he calls. 'Is there anyone there?'

No answer.

'Come on! I know you're in here!'

He moves towards the escalator. Comes a noise from above; something being knocked over. Mark runs up the escalator. Half way up, he stumbles. For a moment, the sudden sensation that the escalator was actually in motion. Just for a moment. Puzzled, he proceeds to the top. The menswear department. He scans the shopfloor. He can see no-one.

'Come on, whoever you are! I heard you! I know you're up here somewhere. I just want to talk to you. If you're confused about what's happening, so am I.'

He moves through the aisles of clothing. They have to be here, somewhere. Hiding. Who is it? Why are they hiding? Are they scared of him—or are they toying with him?

He hears a door shut, runs towards the sound. A fire-escape. He bursts through the door. A concrete emergency stairwell. The sound of rapid footsteps echoing down the stairs.

'Hey! I just want to talk!'

Receiving no response, he vaults down the stairs, hears another door swing shut below. The ground-floor exit. Reaching the doors, Mark passes through and finds himself in an open yard, the store's delivery area.

And there, at the far end of the yard, a girl is perched high on the wall, waiting for him.

The girl seems to be dressed for a burlesque party: black leather thigh boots, all straps, buckles, chunky soles; basque, front-laced, also in black leather; a thong of the same colour and material completing the ensemble. The girl smiles at him. She has short dark hair and very chunky glasses.

Trudie Rayne.

Trudie!' gasps Mark. 'What's going on? Where is everyone? Is this something you've done? Is Vautrin responsible for this?'

Trudie's only reply is a peal of merry laughter.

'Well, answer me!' snaps Mark.

More exasperating laughter.

'Look, I am really not in the mood for games, young lady,' says Mark, advancing towards the girl.

Trudie allows him to reach the foot of the wall, then, quick as a flash, she swings her legs round and jumps from the wall on the other side.

'Hey!'

Mark looks helplessly up at the wall. It is high. There is no way he can scale it. How had she got up there? He turns to the yard's gates, finds them unlocked. Beyond them, a narrow access road, serving the backs of all the row of shops. He sees Trudie. She is almost at the far end of the lane, running like a hare.

'Trudie!'

She turns, laughing mockingly, dances a pirouette, and disappears round the corner.

Mark runs after her. When he reaches the corner, the girl is already more than half way down the next street. How has she got so far ahead? How can she even run so fast in those clunky boots? Mark resumes the chase. He has to catch up with that girl. She is the only one here. She must have the answers.

The chase soon becomes a nightmare. Every time Mark closes in on his quarry, she disappears round a corner, and by the time Mark reaches the same corner she is already halfway down the next street. It happens every time. The girl seems as light as a feather, taunting him with her merry laughter. Frustrated, Mark doggedly keeps up the pursuit. He is starting to tire, his breath raw in his throat. She is always just out of reach, always the same distance ahead of him… But he needs to catch up with her; he is desperate to catch up with her. She has become his sole object, his obsession; he *has* to catch up with that girl; nothing else matters. Everything else can wait. But the way she constantly laughs and eludes him! It's enough to make him cry…

Trudie leads Mark all the way from Pimlico to Hyde Park, and then into Oxford Street—that sweeping thoroughfare, usually thick with traffic and pedestrians, with noise and pollution, now a yawning, empty gorge. Up ahead, Trudie stops at the doors of a shopping mall. Giggling, she beckons to Mark, and disappears through the doors.

Panting and exhausted Mark follows her. Inside the arcade, he sees her haring up the motionless escalator to the food court.

Breathlessly, he follows her up the escalator.

Trudie has finally stopped running. She has brought him to where she wants him to be, standing by the side of a lone man seated at the only occupied table in the food court.

'Hello, Mark. I'm very glad you could make it.'

Vautrin.

Chapter Twenty-Seven
A Slippery Customer

Night has fallen with tropical suddenness.

From her vantage-point high in the branches of a mahogany tree, Dodo Dupont surveys the rebel compound. Behind her, the jungle, dense, impenetrable; overhead, the stars shine with equatorial brilliance against the ebony firmament. The ceaseless calls of nocturnal nature fill the air; silence never reigns in this teeming wilderness—from the vine-choked forest come rustlings, slitherings, constant movement; somewhere, not far away, a leopard growls. The European woman, straddling a bough of the tree studies the layout of the compound before her. Enclosed by a tall wooden palisade, a large area of ground, swept clean of vegetation, forms a central parade ground. Surrounding this open area, a collection of huts, some large, some small. Lights shine from the windows of several of the buildings, while others are in darkness. From the largest structure, an elongated building at the furthest extremity of the compound—which Dodo deduces to be the troops' quarters and mess hall—issue the sounds of revelry: raucous laughter, screams and whoops, from voices both male and female; and the muffled beats of music from a stereo. A motley assortment of vehicles around the compound's water tower: canvas-backed military trucks, jeeps, a battered pick-up truck, a sedan car... Occasionally, a moving shadow can be seen, as a human form passes from one hut to another...

There are no guards patrolling the fence. Security—apart from a couple of men stationed at the main gate off to Dodo's right—seems pretty much non-existent. But then, strict guard would seem hardly necessary to the inhabitants of this retreat, who doubtless feel secure in the knowledge that no one in their right mind would come anywhere near the lair of General Katanga and the Kimba rebels. And in the normal course of things, the rebels would have been correct in this assumption; Dodo Dupont is an exception. Although in full possession of her faculties, she has every intention of penetrating the rebel compound, of braving this lions' den—Mark Hunter is in there somewhere; and she has to get him out.

Posing as a Dutch arms dealer named Van Driessen, Mark had infiltrated the Kimba base. But then something had gone badly wrong. The real Van Driessen had escaped from detention, and it was a fairly safe bet that he would have made straight for Katanga's headquarters. If this has indeed happened, then Mark's cover must surely have been blown by now. Dodo needs to go in there and get him out—if she isn't already too late.

Having now familiarised herself with the terrain, it's time for Dodo to make a move. First, she quickly divests herself of all her clothes; then, from her ruck-sack, hanging for convenience from a branch above, she extracts a plastic jar containing a brown,

TROOPS' BARRACKS AND MESSHALL

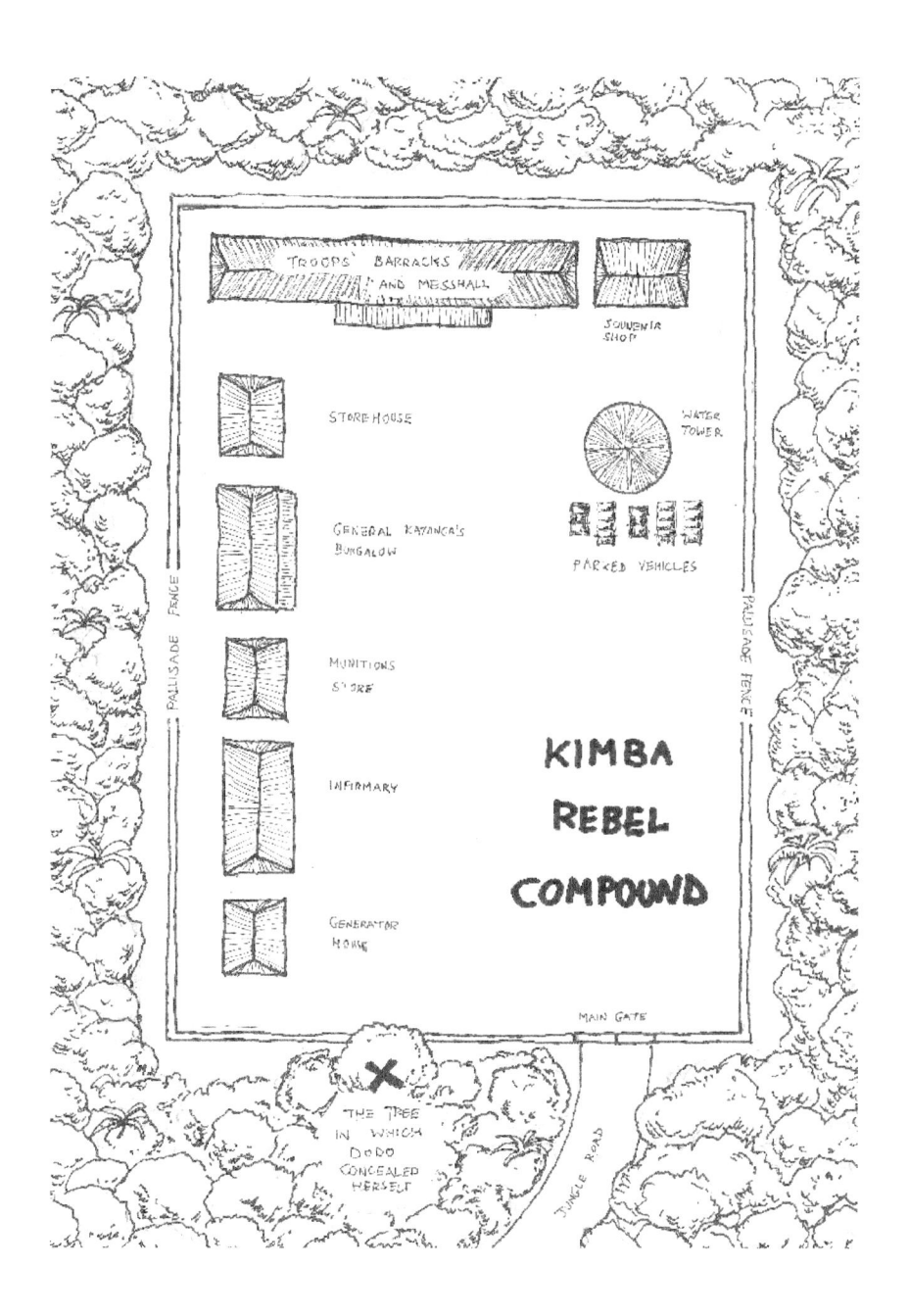

SOUVENIR SHOP

STOREHOUSE

WATER TOWER

GENERAL KAYANGA'S BUNGALOW

PARKED VEHICLES

MUNITIONS STORE

INFIRMARY

KIMBA REBEL COMPOUND

GENERATOR HOUSE

PALISADE FENCE

MAIN GATE

✗ THE TREE IN WHICH DODO CONCEALED HERSELF

JUNGLE ROAD

gelatinous, substance. With this she proceeds to methodically cover her limbs, her face, her torso, until her body is entirely coated, leaving her skin a walnut brown in hue, wet and glistening in the starlight. This gel serves a two-fold purpose: it serves as camouflage and more importantly renders her as slippery as an eel, making it almost impossible for her to be caught hold of or restrained in any way. This lubrication of the body is a tactic employed of old by assassins in the East. She wipes her hands clean with her discarded shirt, and takes from her bag a sheathed knife; this she straps to her thigh. Now she is ready.

The bough Dodo has made her vantage-point extends over the stockade fence and into the compound. Dodo has selected it for this reason. She now crawls along the branch until she is over the compound, and, lowering herself by her arms, drops to the ground. Crouched and ready, Dodo scans the nearest buildings. No sudden movement. No cry of alarm. Her arrival has gone unnoticed. The parade ground separates Dodo from the nearest huts; the hard-packed soil, retaining the heat of the African day, is warm beneath her feet.

She darts across to the nearest building, a small hut showing no lights. From within she can hear the hum of an electrical generator, the compound's power source. Dodo is about to move on when a dark figure appears from around a corner of the building. Dodo flattens herself against the wall. The figure, not observing her, shambles awkwardly along. It is a rebel soldier, bearded, naked to the waist. As Dodo watches, he pauses, raises a bottle to his lips, takes a long swig. The man laughs quietly to himself and then pitches forward onto the ground, dropping the bottle and spilling its remaining contents. He starts to snore loudly.

Dodo smiles grimly at this display. If everyone on the base is this hammered, it will make her job easier. She's not at all surprised at this undisciplined behaviour. When General Katanga had sought to assemble his rebel army, he had, as is invariably the case in these situations, attracted some of the most violent and degenerate young men his country had to offer; aside from their other activities, the Kimbas are infamous for their dependence on booze and drugs.

Dodo moves on to the next hut, peers through the unglazed window from which electric light issues. It is the ward of a medical centre. The row of beds are empty, the room's only occupant being a doctor, wearing a much-soiled white coat over his combat fatigues. Seated at a desk, he is drinking rum, reading a magazine.

Nothing for her here.

The next hut is much larger, windowless, the door padlocked. Dodo surmises this to be the camp's munitions store. She moves on, but suddenly, two men appear from behind a parked truck. Dodo freezes, but too late—the men have seen her. Two more rebels: both intoxicated, both stripped to the waist. Broad grins spread over their faces as they survey the naked intruder.

'Say, what've we got here?' chuckles one of the men, leering at Dodo. 'You come to join our army, pretty lady? Tha's good: we need more women.'

'An' she's come dressed for the party,' says the second man, appreciatively.

Relaxing her stance, Dodo steps forward, smiles invitingly at the two Kimbas. With her strong, well-fleshed frame, her skin tinted nut brown save for the palms of her hands and the soles of her feet, the men have apparently taken her for a local girl.

'You strip for the guards so they let you in, huh?' says the first man. 'That figures.'

'She must wanna join us real bad…'

'Right. Come 'ere, baby. Let's have us a party for three right here an' now. You can meet the other guys later…'

The first man approaches Dodo, extracting from his open fly an already semi-tumescent penis. The Kimba Rebels always keep themselves unzipped and ready for instant offensive action! (This tends to be standard military procedure in warzones the world over.) Favouring Dodo with his alcohol breath, the aroused rebel tries to take her in his arms—but she slips out of his embrace like a bar of soap.

'What the fuck—'

Before the man can even understand what's happening, Dodo unsheathes her knife and plunges it into his ribs. With a choking sound at the back of his throat, the rebel collapses, his life extinguished.

The second man, his senses befuddled by booze and hash, reacts too late. The cry of alarm is on his lips when Dodo pounces and silences him with a slash of the knife across the jugular. He falls, spraying Dodo with his blood. Dodo quickly drags the two corpses into the deep shadows behind the munitions store. And then, crouched and alert, she scans the compound. No-one in sight; the Kimbas are unaware that their ranks have been reduced by two.

Dodo feels no remorse for these two casualties: she knows all too well some of the crimes of which will have been guilty. It is standard practice for the Kimba rebels, when they descend on a village or township to burn and pillage the place, to systematically rape all the women-folk. It goes without saying that even young girls are not spared—if anything they are given preferential treatment. The young boys, likewise. (The men, of course, are just slaughtered.) Being raped has become such a common occurrence in this part of the country, that the women here have come to simply refer to it as being 'grabbed.' ('Did you get grabbed today…? Really? So did I!')

The sounds of revelry continue unabated from the troops' quarters at the rear of the compound; Dodo wonders how many of those women whose shrill laughter and coital cries she hears initially came to this place as voluntary camp followers—and how many are captives who have just drunk or drugged themselves into a kind of reckless resignation.

Rising, Dodo sheaves her knife, and relieves one of the dead rebels of his sidearm. Armed with this, she moves on to the next building; a larger structure with a veranda. This looks promising. It might be the general's quarters. The first window shows no light. Dodo peers inside; it looks to be a bedroom, the bed protected by a mosquito-curtain. She moves stealthily on, past the door, to a lighted window at the far end of the veranda. She peers cautiously inside.

The first thing she sees is Mark. Facing the window, the agent is tied to a chair, his safari suit torn and blood-stained. His left eye has swollen almost shut, the lower part of his face bloody from a pistol-whipping. Standing over Mark, a bull of a man in a beige military uniform, peaked cap, dark glasses. General Katanga. The luxury of a ceiling fan, and an imposing desk with a large map of the country pinned to the wall behind it, indicate the room to be the rebel leader's office. In a corner, leaning against a filing cabinet and smoking a cigarette, a thin-faced European in a grubby cotton suit. Dodo recognises him as Van Driessen.

'For the fiftieth time, I'm not working for anyone,' Mark is saying, head bowed, his voice dry and cracked. 'I stole the consignment and took Van Driessen's place because I thought I could make some money out of it.'

'Bullshit,' retorts Katanaga. 'You're a spy. A British spy. You're in cahoots with M'Boma.' (The county's president.)

'Never met him,' says Mark.

Van Driessen speaks. 'If you wanted to make money out of my consignment, then where is it? Why didn't you just bring the stuff here?'

'I've got it hidden in the jungle. I thought it better to strike a deal before I produced the merchandise.'

'Yeah, right. You haven't got the merchandise; the government's got it. Like they had me until I escaped. You just pretended to be me to get into this camp.'

'You British make me puke,' declares Katanga. 'Always stickin' your noses in other people's business. You'd like to come back and colonise us again, wouldn't ya? Think us niggers were better off when you were runnin' the show, huh?'

Katanga unholsters his pistol and clubs Mark savagely across the temple.

'Fuckin' white trash!'

Dodo has seen enough. She goes back to the main door, quietly opens it and steps through it into an unlighted entrance hall. The door on her right is ajar, spilling a wedge of light across the wooden floor. Dodo, swift but silent, moves to the door, looks inside. Katanga has just re-holstered his pistol. Now is the time. She opens the door and steps into the room, gun at the ready.

'Nobody move.'

The command is almost superfluous. Both the General and Van Driessen stand frozen, gaping with slack-jawed disbelief at this sudden apparition; this blood-splattered naked jungle woman with the air of an avenging goddess. To Mark, on the other hand, she is an immaculate angel descended from heaven.

Dodo is the first to break the silence.

'You two. Take out your guns and throw them on the floor. Slowly.' She doesn't know for sure that Van Driessen is armed, but assumes that he is. In this she is right. Driessen lifts his jacket, slowly removes a revolver from his trouser belt, drops it on the floor. Katanga does the same with his automatic.

'Who the fuck are you, woman?' demands the rebel leader, looking fit to explode now that his surprise has passed. 'How the hell did you get in here?'

'Shut up,' snaps Dodo. 'Not a word from either of you. You.' She points her gun at Van Driessen. 'Untie your prisoner. When you've done that, go and stand next to the General.'

With a resigned shrug, Van Driessen complies. He unties the ropes securing Mark to the chair, then joins Katanga by the desk. His arms and legs free, Mark rises unsteadily to his feet. Taking up the two guns, he joins Dodo at the door.

'Are you okay?' she asks, keeping her eyes on the two men.

'Getting better all the time, now that you're here,' replies Mark. 'I'll admit my life expectancy wasn't looking too healthy until just now.'

'Yes, I can see the bastards have put you through the wringer.' She levels her gun at Katanga, murder in her eyes.

'Don't shoot him, Dodo,' adjures Mark. 'With Katanga dead, his men would just go on the rampage. Let's tie them up and gag them.'

'Okay,' acquiesces Dodo. 'Down the floor, you two; flat on

your stomachs.'

'You fuckin' bitch!' snarls Katanga. 'Do you know who you're messin' with—'

'Down on the floor or I'll kneecap you,' snaps Dodo. 'You've got five seconds.'

Katanga and Van Driessen get down on the floor, the latter resigned, the former swearing and foaming at the mouth with suppressed rage. Mark picks up the ropes that so recently bound himself, and securely pinions their arms and legs. With Dodo's gun trained on them, the two men have no choice but to submit.

Finally, Mark gags their mouths using handkerchiefs.

'Right!' he says, rising to his feet. 'Time for us to make a brisk exit from this den of iniquity.'

Once they are outside: 'Thank you, Dodo. You really saved my bacon this time.'

'My pleasure,' Dodo assures him.

'And have got our escape route sorted out?'

'Naturally. There's a plane waiting for us at the abandoned airstrip about five miles from this place.'

'Excellent. Do we walk?'

Dodo looks at him. 'Well, we could, but you don't look like you'd make it five miles in your present condition. How about we help ourselves to some transport?'

'Good idea!'

Keeping to the shadows as much as possible, they cross the compound to the nearest group of parked vehicles, selecting an open-topped jeep. The music and roistering continue unabated from the long hut behind them. No-one is in sight.

'Where are your clothes, by the way?' inquires Mark.

'Up a tree, and we won't have time to collect them.'

Dodo jumps behind the wheel of the jeep, guns the engine. Mark climbs in beside her and the vehicle accelerates towards the main gates of the compound.

'Any idea how we're going to get through those gates?' inquires Mark.

'I thought I'd fall back on one of your favourite ploys,' replies

Dodo: 'Look like we own the place.'

Nearing the gates, she sounds the horn. The two guards on duty spring to attention. Unsuspicious, they lift the bar and open the heavy gates.

Dodo floors the accelerator; the jeep shoots through the gateway like a bullet. Exclamations from the guards. Whether it's the white man in the passenger seat, the naked woman at the wheel, or merely the clip the jeep is moving at that rouses their suspicions, they clearly realise something is wrong. Cries for them to stop, and then shots are fired as they accelerate down the unsurfaced jungle road.

'They'll soon be after us,' observes Mark, as though commenting on the weather.

'We've got a decent head start,' replies Dodo. 'We should be able to keep ahead of any pursuit, and we haven't got too far to go.'

Mark holds on tight as the jeep bounces and rattles at full pelt along the rutted dirt road, the beam from the headlights picking out the enclosing jungle vegetation as it streams past on either hand. The road is winding and they have soon left the compound behind and out of sight.

'I think I can see headlights through the trees behind us,' reports Mark, at length.

'Soon be there,' is the brief reply.

Presently, Dodo swings the jeep off the road onto an even bumpier track; this one clearly unused, and steadily being reclaimed by the jungle. The track is narrow, the jungle foliage meeting overhead. And then they emerge from this tunnel onto the open ground of an abandoned dirt airstrip. The buildings and canvas hangars that serve the runway are in ruins. A single-engined light aircraft stands on the runway, ready for take-off. Dodo skids the jeep to a halt close behind it.

They run for the aircraft. Mark opens the cockpit door, climbs in.

'Where's the bloody pilot?' he yelps.

'*I'm* the bloody pilot,' retorts Dodo. 'Budge up.'

Her lubricated body slides smoothly into the pilot's seat. She starts the ignition. The rotor blades whir into life.

'I forgot you've got your pilot's license,' says Mark. 'I'm obviously still a bit groggy.'

'That's understandable after what you've been through,' says Dodo.

Headlights appear at the edge of the field.

'Company!' warns Mark. 'Time to get us airborne, Worrals.'

'Here we go.'

Dodo opens the throttle, and the aircraft moves forward across the airstrip, gaining speed. The pursuing vehicles—a truck and two jeeps—are closing in. Shots are fired. Then the plane's wheels leave the ground and they are airborne. The pursuing vehicles halt, fire wildly at the retreating aircraft. They are soon out of range.

'They haven't punctured our fuel-tanks or anything, have they?' asks Mark.

Dodo checks the gauges. 'No; we're fine.'

Mark sits back in his seat, breathes a sigh of relief.

'There's a brandy flask in the pocket next to your seat,' Dodo informs him. 'Help yourself.'

'Ah yes, brandy; the universal panacea.'

Mark finds the flask and takes a grateful swig of the contents.

'Thanks once again, my dear. Fly me straight to a nice hot bath, if you would.'

'I could do with one myself. Want to share?'

Mark looks his friend up and down. He runs a finger along her upper arm, picking up some of the unguent covering her skin. He rubs it between his fingers.

'While I thank you for the kind offer, I think I'd prefer to bathe alone on this particular occasion…'

Chapter Twenty-Eight

Love and Singularity

In some primitive societies, claims Dizzy Hello, that well-known anthropologist, people will select their mates guided entirely by scent. In some societies, the participants at the pairing ceremonies would even be blind-folded, so as not to be influenced in any way by physical appearance. These people believe that only by olfactory examination can you determine your ideal mate: and it's a good long sniff of the assembled men's wedding tackle that will inform the bride-to-be which of those eligible males is the man for her... In this regard, Dizzy has evolved a theory: Admit it or not, everyone likes the smell of their own arse, right? But conversely, the smell of other people's hindquarters aren't always so agreeable to us. Accepting this proposition, Dizzy theorises that someone whose arse smells appealing to you, must, on a basic biological level, be a good match for you.

Simple, right?

The foregoing is necessary in order to explain to the reader why, when we now look into the recreation room of that notorious band of terrorists, the Society of Evil Actions, we find ten of the girls kneeling in front of sofas, upper bodies resting on the seats, and with their backsides thrust out for inspection. As you can see, two of the sofas have been placed side-by-side so that the girls can form an uninterrupted row—ten noble females, willing guinea pigs gallantly proffering their posteriors in the name of expanding the horizons of medical knowledge.

Naturally, it is the inceptor of the project, Dizzy Hello, who will be conducting the experiment. She is also stark naked; perhaps this is just to put her subjects more at their ease.

Before embarking on this ground-breaking endeavour, Professor Dizzy pauses to admire the display of derrière before her. (What happened to the blind-folding ceremony?) Now, according to one of history's leading pygophiliacs, the female posterior is to be seen at its very best when the subject is standing and with the upper body slightly inclined. And this may well be the case for a purely visual inspection—looking at it from an entirely aesthetic stand-point. Dizzy would be the last one to argue with that. But for her proposed olfactory inspection, the subjects placed as they are, with the upper bodies perpendicular to the thighs, the buttocks thrust out—this provides greater room for the olfactory assessor to gain deeper access and thus obtain a more comprehensive sample for analysis.

Trudie, for present purposes known as Subject No.1 by virtue of being the first in the row (from left to right), looks back over her shoulder.

'Are you going to get on with this, or just spend all day gawping at our arses?'

'Silence, Subject No.1!' says Dizzy. 'I'm mentally preparing myself. And remember the rules: no farting while I'm down there. And that goes for all you, got it?'

Ten subjects voice weary acquiescence.

'Especially you, No. 7. I've got my eye on you. No funny business!'

'Why me?' protests Subject No.7, otherwise Jessica Harper. 'I'm not the one who farts the most around here! What about—'

'Silence! You're interrupting my mental preparation!' Dizzy takes a deep breath, exhales from the diaphragm. 'Right! I am now mentally prepared!'

And, brimming over with mental preparedness, Dizzy steps forward and commences her fascinating scientific experiment, this glorious endeavour to cross the boundaries of human knowledge, a process with involves her progressing along the row of her friends' variously-sized posteriors (from left to right), burying her nose between the cheeks, inhaling, and then, like a wine-taster, thoroughly assessing the aroma with her keen olfactory senses—and then exhaling.

This she does. And, obedient to the rules, none of the test subjects pass wind.

'Okay; done! You can sit up now!'

The SEA girls rise from their knees and reversing themselves, seat themselves on the sofa.

Dizzy faces them, standing with arms folded and a triumphant smile upon her face.

'Well?' demands Rachel, after Dizzy has stood there for some time without saying anything.

'Well, indeed,' says Dizzy, solemnly.

'So, who's bottom smell did you like best?' asks Sophie.

'Drum roll, please!' cries Dizzy. She pauses, and then: 'Rachel, Greta, and Albertine!'

'Us!' in chorus.

'Yes, you! And now for the final proof of the compatibility test, we now have to reverse the experiment!'

Dizzy now positions herself on all fours, presenting her own rear to the other girls.

Another pregnant silence

'What are you doing?' asks Trudie at last.

'I'm waiting for one of you to grow a penis and fuck me— what does it look like I'm doing?' is Dizzy's irritable reply. 'Form an orderly queue, Subjects 1-10, and inhale a nose-full of Professor Dizzy's derriere.'

'You never said we had to do that!'

'It's the final stage of the experiment, isn't it? Come on; you first, Subject No.1!'

Sighing, the girls form an orderly queue as instructed, and in turn each of them take a good sniff of Dizzy's buttock crevice. And which of the girls find the odour most appealing? None other than Rachel, Greta and Albertine! In other words, a perfect match! The experiment is a success! Congratulations, Dizzy! We look forward to reading your paper on the subject!

'Hello, ladies,' comes a new voice. 'I hope I'm not interrupting anything.'

'Vautrin!' cry eleven ecstatic voices.

The eager nymphets swoop on their leader, laughing, hugging him. Vautrin pats them, ruffles their hair, returns their greetings— seemingly entirely oblivious to the eleven girls' vigorous nudity.

'Where have you been all day?' Chrissie wants to know.

'Yes, we haven't seen you for ages!' adds Sophie.

'Oh, I've been exploring,' replies Vautrin. 'Mapping out more of the base.'

Even Vautrin doesn't know the full extent of the SEA headquarters complex. He has warned the girls not to stray too far from the central area, as they might get lost. Vautrin sometimes sets out on these mapping expeditions, in order to increase his knowledge of the dimensions of the base.

The girls guide him to a sofa, sit him down. They surround him, some of the girls placing themselves beside of him, the others at his feet, all of them gazing on him adoring eyes—a throned prince surrounded by his devoted concubines.

'So, what have you young ladies been up to?'

Several voices at once proceed to tell him about the scientific experiment in which they have just been engaged; Vautrin remains placid under this barrage of overlapping voices, merely nodding his understanding. They ask him if he approves.

'I approve of everything you girls do; you know that,' he assures them.

'Haff you any new jobs planned for uss?' Greta inquires.

'Well, Greta, I don't like to make plans for you girls,' says Vautrin. 'Nothing that's cast in stone, at any rate. I might occasionally suggest something, but you're free to reject the idea if you don't like it. Don't plan for the future. Be impulsive. Take each day as it comes. Most importantly: have fun.'

'But you make plans, don't you?' argues Juliette. 'Those scientists you've got working for you. You must have something planned with that?'

'Yes, I do have a plan of sorts,' confesses Vautrin. 'Those scientists are working on a little device for me. A sort of side-project to the main research. When the thing is ready, I'm thinking of trying out its effects on our friend Mark Hunter. I think it will be quite amusing.'

'Tell us more!' the girls chorus.

'Well, my current researches are geared towards perception and reality. I mean, what is reality? Basically, reality is what you perceive it to be. Reality is the world around you, interpreted to you by your mind and senses. Now, what I would like to find out is: if you could alter someone's perceptions, could you also alter their physical surroundings? This is what I'm hoping to achieve. To see if the physical world can be completely overwritten simply by adjusting an individual's perception of that world.'

Vautrin reaches into his jacket pocket, produces a packet of cigarettes, extracts one. Instantly there are eleven ignited lighters under Vautrin's nose, jostling for position. Vautrin simply chooses the nearest flame to light his cigarette.

'And what's this solanite stuff got to do with all that?' asks Sophie. 'That adjusting reality thing?'

'It has everything to do with it, I hope,' replies Vautrin. 'At least, I hope so. I believe solanite will be the key to unlocking the doors of perception.'

Vautrin draws on his cigarette before proceeding, 'You girls know how proud I am of you, and what you're doing.' (They do.) 'Furthering the cause of Selfish Individualism is very important work. Here we have arrived at the perfect arrangement. You form a group, you become fast friends with each other—'

'—And to heck with the rest of the world!' concludes Dizzy, brightly.

'That's right. This world you inhabit is fast becoming a singularity, and if that happened, you would lose your precious individuality; everything that makes you what you are.'

'A singularity? What's that?' asks Flossie.

'It's basically the whole world and everyone in it functioning as a single unit.'

'Like an ant colony?' from Trudie.

'Yes, that's a good comparison. Humankind is already drawing in on itself. You have evolved the internet, a means of bringing people at opposite ends of the world into instantaneous communication. All the knowledge and experience of humankind is recorded as data in that same system; cyberspace is becoming an extension of humankind's collective unconscious. A time could arrive in which that electronic web envelops everybody, guiding people, controlling their every thought and physical action.'

'Could that really happen?' wonders Jessica.

'Very easily.' Vautrin pauses, tips the ash from his cigarette into one of the waiting ashtrays. 'Let me tell you about a place I know of where what I've been describing has already happened: a world where everybody thinks and functions as part of a single unit. If you saw that world, at first glance you might think it wasn't any different to the world you live in now. You would see people moving around, performing day-to-day activities, just as they do in any population centre here on Earth. Yes, at a first glance it would seem to you that everyone you saw had free will, and could perform individual action. But you would be wrong: it would be an illusion; it would be merely a façade—all on the surface. In truth, there is a predetermined place and function for every single person on this world. They perform as a unit, a gestalt; they have no individual autonomy... But sometimes a mistake might occur. Sometimes someone might be born who does not fit in, who cannot or will not perform their allotted task. Usually, any abnormalities like this will be spotted in infancy and corrected—but sometimes, one of these anomalies will slip through the net and be suffered to grow to maturity. That individual would become a danger to the function of this society, it could corrupt the whole system, spreading disharmony, like a cancer, throughout this world. Therefore, the abnormality would have to be dealt with; they would have to be expunged from the system, and quickly, before they could cause irremediable damage.'

'So do they get killed?' asks Trudie.

'Killed or banished.'

'Does a world that's a singularity 'ave a leader?' inquires Albertine.

'No. It's a self-governing unit. The whole is the sum of the parts. There's no dictator. No god.'

'So, there is no religion?'

'None. Religions are clumsy attempts by disorganised humans to create a singularity. They create a deity, invent a set of rules, and they seek to convert the world. But these badly built machines inevitably fail. They impose too many unnatural restrictions, deny basic pleasures and functions; and the staunchest adherents of these religions often become sick, unhealthy people. That's why even now in your own world we see this reaction against complicated, organised religions in favour of primitive fertility cults. But really this kind of neo-paganism is just about being true to yourself as a human animal; following your desires instead of repressing them. Look at you girls: you're intelligent, thinking beings, but you also enjoy your basic bodily functions; eating, laughing, defecating, copulating. Human nature is a combination of the animal and the rational; the two should work in harmony, not be at odds with each other. And you see, you girls have got it right. Most people have got it wrong.'

'And killing?' says Dizzy. 'That's natural.'

'Of course it is. Killing is prohibited by your laws, so most people do their killing at second-hand. Your entertainment forms are geared to the vicarious enjoyment of death and violence; films, television, books, comics, computer games. Some say it's catharsis. You girls have simply elected to enjoy the real thing instead of the simulated substitutes.'

'You know when something is right...' says Sophie thoughtfully. 'It just *feels* right. Inside. All this; what we're doing: it just feels right to me.'

'And you should embrace those feelings,' Vautrin tells her. 'Never despise them.'

'But *you*, Vautrin,' says Dizzy. 'I worship you. We all do. Doesn't that make us as bad as all those religious idiots?'

'Well, for a start, I'm not a god,' smiles Vautrin. 'And I'm sure your feelings for me are as much hormonal as anything else, and therefore entirely natural. And of course, I have that ascendancy over you that comes of age and experience. But you know, you only need me as much as you need each other. We're a team; that's how we work together. We're all here for ourselves and for each other.'

Vautrin finishes his cigarette.

'I've got some further news for you girls. In my exploration of the complex today, I found something interesting...'

'Ooh, what was it?' cry eleven voices.

'Another portal. Another way out of this base. And it leads somewhere very interesting…'

Chapter Twenty-Nine
A Knife in the Back

Scipioni is a nervous man.

The Organisation is relentless. Tracking down and exterminating a traitor is to them a matter of 'honour.' As well as being sound business practice. They will always be searching for Scipioni as long as he remains alive. But, with the deal he's made with the cops, he should at least have a head-start, and with plenty of dough to throw around, he can always escape and move on if ever they track him down. Hell, he could even have plastic surgery… Yes, Scipioni is nervous, and he knows that he'll always have to be nervous, always alert, always suspicious—but he has weighed up the pros and cons and he's decided that the money and seeing that bastard Castanelli put in the slammer are worth it.

Picture a seedy man in a modest hotel room. A small, round-shouldered man with a ferret face; wet, protruding lips; pop-eyed. This is Scipioni. He sits at a table playing black-jack with Fillipo, his police bodyguard. A bottle of bourbon stands on the table. Scipioni has been helping himself liberally, Fillipo abstaining.

Fillipo shows his cards. A five-card trick. Scipioni throws his own hand down in disgust.

'Jesus! You've cleaned me out again!'

Fillipo sweeps the crumpled pile of Euros to his side of the table. 'Well, you can afford it, Luco; can't you?' he reminds his companion. 'You're a rich man now!'

'Yeah, if I live long enough to spend it,' returns Scipioni. 'When are we getting out of Rome?'

'Patience. The instant the escape route is finalised, we'll be on the move. Your pals won't be able to intercept us if the timetable is only decided at the last minute—No time for any information to leak out, *comprende*? Another game?'

'Sure. I got nothing else to do in this crummy joint.' Scipioni pours himself another drink. 'Just these cards an' the booze; that's all I got...'

'And the pleasure of my sweet company,' grins Fillipo.

'Oh yeah, great. I'd rather have a broad. Why can't I have a broad? Just for a crummy half hour...!'

'I told you why not. And what's all that about a half hour? You figure you could last that long?' Grinning, Fillipo deals the cards.

'Ah, Jeez, stop it—you're killing me.'

A knock at the door. Scipioni jumps.

'You expecting anyone?'

'Would you relax?' Fillipo moves to the door, hand on the butt of the revolver holstered under his arm. 'Who is it?' he calls.

'I've come to change the towels, signor,' comes a female voice.

Fillipo looks through the peephole: a fish-eye view of a pretty blonde maid, clutching fresh towels.

'It's just the maid,' he tells Scipioni. He opens the door. The maid enters. She is fairly small, very young, with an attractive but expressionless face.

'Thank you, signor.'

Fillipo turns away from her. And then his body tenses, his features contorting. He utters a weak cry.

Scipioni springs from his chair. 'What is it? What's wrong?'

Fillipo collapses. Behind him the maid, brandishing a bloody knife. Stepping over the body, she advances towards the terrified Scipioni.

'No, no...' he pleads, backing away. 'Let's talk about this. Did Santella send you? Look, I got money, now—lots of it. Name your price. Anything.'

'I do not accept bribes,' the girl informs him, advancing.

'C'mon, sweetheart...'

Scipioni backs against the wall, quaking with fear. He looks into the girl's eyes; and he sees nothing: no eagerness or bloodlust—but no mercy or pity either.

'I'm begging you…'

'I do not react to pleas for mercy, either,' says the girl. 'I'm here simply to kill you. That is my duty.'

Tears stream down the informer's face. 'I don't wanna die…' the most wretched words in the world.

Gina plunges the knife into his chest.

Gina has worked for her Uncle, Don Santella for most of her young life.

When she was four years old, she had witnessed her parents being executed in their own front room, while Santella looked on. But then, and almost on a whim, when the young witness had been discovered, he had not only spared Gina's life, he had decided to take her in and raise her. Santella had declared the girl his 'niece,' leading some of his colleagues to erroneously suspect she must really be his illegitimate daughter. Although never the most openly affectionate of guardians, he had had the girl well-brought up, given a classical education by the best private tutors. He had also brought her up to be a killer. Gina had learned to handle a gun proficiently by the age of seven, but it had soon emerged that she had a particular affinity for knives. She loved knives: she learned to throw them with skill and precision. It was with a knife she had carried out her first execution at the age of eight. Since then she has killed dozens of people on behalf of the Organisation. Gina isn't certain if it is love she feels for her guardian, or just gratitude and loyalty; either way, she always obeys him implicitly. And although she still remembers the night she had witnessed her parents both shot in the back of the head, she harbours no hidden feelings of rancour on account of this. She has been brought up to believe in the Mafia way; her parents had been traitors: therefore they had had to die.

Gina reclines on the bed in her room at the Santella villa one afternoon, bathing herself in the music issuing from the speaker of an antique gramophone—*Rienzi*, Edward Bulwer-Lytton's novel put to music by Richard Wagner. Dressed as always in camouflage trousers and a khaki top, Gina is a girl of medium height, with short, honey-blonde hair; her face beautiful but unmarked with character or expression.

A discreet knock at the door.

'Come in,' says Gina.

The butler enters.

'Don Santella wishes to see you in his study, Signorina.'

'Very well.'

Rising from her bed, Gina takes the needle from the record, switches off the gramophone, and makes her way down to her uncle's study—high-ceilinged, sculpted in the elaborate Renaissance style. A row of tall arched windows along the rear wall look out onto the gardens of the mock-Florentine villa.

Gina makes her way across the marble floor to where her uncle is seated at his desk. A vigorous man in his sixties, iron grey hair, tanned complexion, his expression is grim. Gina can tell that something is wrong. At Santella's shoulder stands his lieutenant, Silvestro, eyes hidden as always behind mirrored lenses, directing at her a smile that doesn't bode well for Gina. Gina has always disliked Silvestro and she knows full well that the feeling is reciprocated. The third person present is Peppi. He stands facing his employer.

He looks terrified.

'I wanna ask you a question, Gina,' commences Santella without preamble. He indicates Peppi. 'Has this piece of trash ever raped you?'

'No, Uncle,' answers Gina.

'Okay. Has this piece of trash ever had consensual sex with you?'

'Yes, Uncle,' answers Gina.

'How many times?'

'Many times, Uncle.'

Santella fixes Peppi with a look of undiluted malice.

'You slimy bastard,' he grates. 'You piece of fucking garbage…'

'B-but it's like she said, boss,' stammers Peppi. 'I never forced her. We just—'

'I don't give a shit about that, you son of a bitch!' yells Santella. 'Helping yourself to something that's mine, behind my back? Treating her like your personal whore—a girl I gave the Santella name to…? You think I can just overlook that, you lousy garbage?'

Silvestro's smile broadens. Gina realises he must be responsible for all this. How the man has found out, she doesn't know. She and Peppi had always been careful, discreet, in their assignations. Her uncle has always been jealous of Gina's chastity; warning off his men with dire threats from ever 'trying it on' with her—But Silvestro bears a grudge against Gina; some small matter of her killing his cousin. (The fact that she had been ordered to do this didn't seem to make any difference to him.) Doubtless, by spilling the beans to Don Santella, he has been hoping to get herself into trouble as well—to cast her off for having allowed herself to be 'polluted'; but Uncle's wrath seems to be directed solely at Peppi. Poor Peppi. She likes Peppi; he is agreeable, he gives her pleasure—but it would never have occurred to her for one second to lie to her uncle in order to protect him.

'But, boss, it's not like that; we're in love, Gina an' me,' protests Peppi.

'Love!' spits Santella. 'Don't give me that horse-shit.' He turns to Gina. 'Are you in "love" with this man?'

'No, Uncle,' responds Gina.

'Sure you are, honey,' says Peppi, turning to her, pleading. 'We're in love. Tell him…'

'I'm sorry, Peppi, but I'm not in love with you,' says Gina. 'And if you're in love with me, you've never mentioned it to me.'

'So much for the love bullshit,' sneers Santella. 'What I see is a sleazy little rat, taking advantage of his employer's trust, having sex with his employer's niece behind his back, treating her like his personal whore. I can't forgive that, Peppi.'

'It's not like that, boss, I swear! I'm loyal! Have I ever done a thing wrong before?'

'Maybe you haven't, but that doesn't count for squat right now. I can't allow you to go on living, after this.'

'Boss, please, for Chrissakes…!'

'Gina?'

'Yes, Uncle?'

'I want you to kill this man.'

'Yes, Uncle.' Obediently, she extracts her knife from its sheaf on her belt.

Peppi looks at her with horrified disbelief.

'Gina… Honey…You couldn't… After all we've meant to each other…You couldn't…'

'I'm sorry, Peppi. I have to do what Uncle Santella says.'

'No… No!'

He turns and runs for the French windows. Gina's knife-arm moves with lightning speed, and Peppi pitches forward, the blade buried between his shoulder blades. Gina walks up to the prone body, extracts the knife, wipes the blade clean, returns it to its sheaf.

'Get rid of that trash,' says Santella to Silvestro.

'I'll see to it right away, boss.' Silvestro departs.

'Come here, Gina.'

Obediently, Gina approaches Santella's chair. He takes her hand.

'You kept something secret from me, Gina…'

'I never lied to you, Uncle.'

'I know you didn't, but you still kept something back from me. I want no more secrets between us, okay?'

'Yes, Uncle.'

'Okay. You're a good girl. Off you go.'

'Thank you, Uncle.'

Arturo Gambella parks his car in the drive of his suburban family home. He is an investigative journalist, a very busy man; but like most people returning home from work, right now he is just thinking about what he'll be having for his evening meal; that meal he always shares—whenever work allows—with his beautiful wife and two children.

Crossing the garden, he sees that the front door is ajar. Strange. Have the kids been playing out here…?

With a sudden vague sense of alarm, he hurries to the front door, passes through into the hallway.

'I'm home!' he calls out. 'Papa's home! Everything okay?'

Silence. Not even the sounds of the television set.

He steps into the living room. And he freezes. His mind refuses to accept what his eyes saw: his children, Julio, five, and Angelina, seven: lying on the floor, clothes saturated with blood. And their faces; oh, sweet lord, their faces…

Moaning wretchedly, he drops on his knees beside them. Both bodies are warm, but the children are quite dead, their faces both horribly mutilated.

'No, oh no, oh no…' he whimpers. He looks round wildly, yells his wife's name: 'Sophia!'

He races back into the hall and then into the kitchen. Further horror greets his eyes: his wife on the floor, her blood pooling over the linoleum. And a girl: blonde, young. She squats over the dead body, calmly gouging out the eyes with the point of her knife. She looks up, regards the newcomer with no surprise, no expression at all…

She stands up, faces him.

Arturo goggles at her, his frantic mind struggling to find an explanation. A girl… Has some teenage psychopath broken into their home?

Her first words dispel this theory.

'I have been instructed to kill you, Signor Gambella,' she says, tonelessly.

'You killed my family,' rasps Arturo, his lip quivering.

'Those also were my instructions,' replies the girl. 'Your exposés on Organisation links to the Entertainment Industry have caused considerable embarrassment; leading to a number of forced resignations and a substantial decrease in profits. This is unacceptable, and it has been decided that you should be made an example of; so that other journalists will understand that although we allow considerable freedom to the press, that there are limits, and that you are not immune from retribution should you step over the line.'

'But my wife... my children...' gasps the horrified journalist. 'They didn't have anything to do with this! You didn't have to—'

'Their deaths were also necessary. It must be understood that when people cross the Organisation it is not only their own lives they place in danger.'

'You bitch...!' screeches Arturo. 'You bitch!'

And then he launches himself at the girl, screaming with rage. Gina thrusts out her knife arm, and by his own momentum, Arturo impales himself on the blade, right up to the hilt. His expression freezes, transformed from rage to surprise. Gina meets his gaze, watches the light die in his eyes. Then she extracts her knife from his chest, allowing him to fall to the floor.

She hunkers down and methodically sets about mutilating his face.

Gina steers her vespa through the gates of the Villa Santella. Being a solitary girl, raised without the company of children her own age, she has grown up taciturn, content to find her own amusement for most of the time. At the behest of her uncle, Gina has enjoyed a classical education; her loves are art, classical music, and literature. When not reading, sketching, or visiting museums and galleries, she enjoys solitary walks in the countryside, or just riding around on her scooter. This afternoon, she has combined two of the above, riding out into the countryside to sketch a view of Lake Bracciano.

Her little vespa seems a dwarfed incongruity buzzing along the imposing drive, with its huge trees standing to attention on either side. Reaching the forecourt of the villa, she veers off to the left, parking her bike close to the garages. She descends a winding path between terraces of evergreen shrubs and ferns. Balustrades, stairs, and flagstones, all carved from white marble, dazzling under the Mediterranean sun, contrasting with the healthy green of the vegetation. From this emerges onto the rear patio of the villa. A large, kidney-shaped swimming pool glimmers in the sun. A blonde woman lies on a sun-lounger by the pool-side. This is Carisma, an ex-pornographic film artist and her widower uncle's current mistress. Gina vaguely wonders why the woman has adopted the stage-name 'Carisma;' personal charisma not seeming to Gina to be a particular requirement for performing in a pornographic film. Like most of Uncle's women, Carisma treats Gina as though she were a child, a fact to which Gina is completely indifferent. The woman lies motionless, one arm dangling over the side of the lounger. Gina frowns. Something is wrong... She hurries to the woman's side. Carisma's beautiful torso is covered with blood, a bullet hole between her enhanced breasts.

Gina spins round like a cat, her knife in her hand, alert for danger.

Nothing moves. The air, fragrant with spring blooms, is still and silent. She feels exposed out here in the open and crosses swiftly to the tall French windows and steps cat-like into her uncle's study. Uncle Santella is seated at his desk. The desk faces away from the windows, and the leather chair has its back to her, but she can see the crown of her uncle's grey head projecting over the top. He doesn't move. The rest of the mausoleum-like room is empty. Gina does not call out her uncle's name; she does not alert him to her presence. Still keyed-up, she moves round to the front of the desk... Yes, Uncle Santella is dead; he sits erect in his chair, a bullet hole in his forehead.

Across the room, the hallway door opens. In walks Silvestro. He has a gun in his hand, his mirrored glasses and his supercilious smile firmly in place. Almost simultaneously, two hoods appear through the French windows, guns pointed at Gina.

Knife at the ready, Gina stands at bay.

'Drop the knife, Gina,' commands Silvestro. 'We've got you covered.'

Gina weighs up her chances, reluctantly throws down her knife.

'What is going on?' she demands. 'Who killed Uncle?'

'I did,' answers Silvestro smoothly. 'I'm taking over this branch of the Organisation.'

'You? You think they'll let you do that?' sneers Gina.

'"They" ordered it,' replies Silvestro. 'I've been sending back some very unfavourable reports about Don Santella...'

'Lies, I'll bet.'

Silvestro shrugs. 'It doesn't matter. Santella lost a vote of no-confidence. I was ordered to take over. Completely legitimate.'

'So, I have to take orders from you now?'

Silvestro smiles, slowly shakes his head. 'You working for me? That's never going to work, is it...? No, my charming *signorina*, you've become a liability...'

Gina moves like lightning. She grabs the first hood's gun-arm, swings him round. He fires instinctively, and the bullet finds the second hood. And then he convulses, shot himself by a badly aimed bullet from Silvestro. Gina snatches his gun as he falls, fires wildly at Silvestro. He springs for the door, and makes it out unscathed. Immediately he starts yelling for reinforcements.

Scooping up her knife, Gina bolts through the French windows, back across the patio and along the marble path. Tucking the revolver in her belt, sheathing the knife, she jumps onto her vespa and guns the ignition. She buzzes out onto the forecourt, accelerates down the drive. Hoods come running from the villa, firing shots at her. None of them come near the retreating scooter.

'The car!' she hears Silvestro yell. 'Don't let the little bitch get away!'

Through the gates, Gina powers along the road, heading away from the city. Villa Santella stands isolated; groves and orchards line the country road. Gina knows this area like the back of her hand—every dirt track, every bridle path... If she can just shake them off...

Behind her, a Limo screeches through the villa gates; the driver sees her, and turns in pursuit. The black car closes in on her, and a gun-arm appears through the passenger window, fires off shots.

Gina swings across the road to avoid the bullets.

And then a girl appears in the middle of the road ahead, brandishing a shot-gun. For a second Gina thinks herself the target, but the girl waves her out of the way with an imperative arm movement. Gina swerves off the road onto the embankment, tumbling from her bike. She hears the shot-gun roar. Springing to her feet, she sees the Limousine slew across the road, its windscreen crazed. The car crashes into a tree on the opposite verge. A second girl appears: small, dark-haired; brandishing a pistol, she runs up to the crashed car as three dazed men stagger out of it. The girl shoots them dead.

Having carried out these executions, the dark-haired girl turns to Gina, an affable grin on her face. Gina recognises the girl.

'Greta!'

Greta Garbo, no less. Greta and Gina have met before, on an occasion when the Red Army Faction and the Mafia had come into collision.

'Greetings, Gina,' says Greta, speaking in English, their common language.

The girl with the shot-gun joins them. She has a cheeky smile, and short blonde hair like Gina's own, but paler in hue.

'This iss my friend Dissy Hello,' Gina informs her. 'We knew off your predicament, and haff come to rescue you.'

'Why would you do that?' questions Gina. 'Do you want me to join the RAF?'

Greta shakes her head. '*Nein.* I no longer work for that organisation. Dissy and I belong to a new group; vee vant you to join uss.'

'A new group?'

Dizzy speaks up. 'It's a very special group. Exclusive. Our lord and master is very fussy about who he recruits, but he wants you; he knows you're the right stuff.'

'The right stuff?'

'Yep.'

Gina allows herself a rare brief smile. 'Well, there is no future for me where I am; so I might as well go with you...'

Cheering, the two girls embrace her.

Chapter Thirty
Jessie's Trip

The club is called Cyberia, a cyberpunk-themed nightclub in Camden Town specialising in alternative rock music. I say 'alternative rock' but isn't all rock 'alternative' these days? After all, according to one American magazine, the Rock 'n' Roll era is now officially over. Witness the fact that whenever a rock album does actually reach the top of the album charts these days, it's a major news event!

Let's go inside. Once you've been frisked by the security guard and paid for your ticket, you have to venture downstairs to get to where the action is. Through another door and the pounding music, previously muffled, tells you that you've arrived. The walls, painted with imitation grimy brick-work, are adorned with serpent-trails of the pipes and ducting—plastic, but painted to look like greasy metal. Here and there amongst the maze of pipes glowing neon tubes of many different hues add a futuristic touch. In addition to this, several large LCD screens fixed to the walls around the room, screen—silently, of course—cyberpunk anime. On the left of us there are booths with comfy sofas—the chilling out area. Over to the right is the bar, and around it stand tall round tables served with tall stools. The drunk or unwary will sometimes attempt to move one of these stools, but like the tables they are firmly fixed to the floor. And then, facing the bar area, you can see the central arena: the dance-floor, bathed in its technicolour lightshow. It's eleven o'clock now on this warm Saturday night and the club is just starting to fill up. Look around and you'll see we have the usual mixture of students and slackers, goths and punks...

And by one of those improbable coincidences that only happen in real life and in great literature, several distinct groups of characters from this story all happen to be attending Club Cyberia and on this very Saturday night!

Look, these things happen, okay?

In one of the booths, under the pink glow of a neon tube, sit five members of the SEA: to wit, Jessica Harper, Sophie Harris, Gina Santella, Chrissie Wylde and Albertine Sagan. 'Wait a minute!' I hear you cry. 'Don't the SEA have discotheque facilities at their base?' I'm not sure if I've actually mentioned this fact, but yes, you're right. They do have a nightclub. But the SEA girls' club has one tiny drawback: there's only ever them in it. Not always a problem, but tonight the girls require a venue which has its own clientele; tonight, the girls have ventured out for a special reason: for tonight happens to be zero-hour for 'Operation Get Jessica Harper Laid!'

This worthy operation has been launched since the recent shock discovery amongst the girls that Jessica Harper is the only SEA girl not to have had her cherry popped!

Something needs to be done about this.

The girls sit in their booth, drinking vodka and tonics, carrying on as much of a conversation as the intrusive thumping music will allow.

'A bit different to opera, isn't it?' yells Chrissie to Gina.

'*Cosa?*'

'I said it's a bit different to opera!'

'Ah, the music! Yes; yes, it is very different.'

'What was that?'

'I said: "Yes, it is very different!"'

'You should go and dance!' Sophie advises Jessica.

'What?'

'You should go and dance!' louder. She indicates the dance floor. 'That's the meat market, right? You go out there, and you start shaking your stuff! If some guy starts dancing with you, that means you've pulled!'

'Okay.'

'What?'

'I said: "okay!"'

Jessica goes out onto the dance floor.

Two new arrivals appear. It is none other than our Dodo Dupont and Mayumi Takahashi! At thirty years of age you might think they are pushing it a bit, but they're still just about young enough to attend a club like this one. Dodo is wearing boots, hipster shorts, and vest-top, all in black, the shorts wet-look shiny and revealing a pleasing amount of buttock cleavage. Our Mayumi is wearing a black trilby (I don't think I've mentioned this before, but Mayumi likes hats—she is rarely seen out of doors without one), a black suit jacket over a blouse and tie. Eschewing such unnecessaries as a skirt or trousers, her lower half being adorned only with thick black tights and buckle shoes. (And the possible addition of panties.)

Dodo's arrival does not go unnoticed.

'It's Dodo!' yelps Sophie.

'*Cosa?*' from Gina.

Sophie points.

The SEA girls, all smiles, wave madly at the two women. Dodo spots them, is momentarily nonplussed, then smiles and waves back at the four mass-murderers.

The two women head for the bar, and then, armed with drinks, establish themselves at one of the chrome tables.

Jessica had never danced before joining the SEA, but being a girl—and having been cured of her physical awkwardness by Vautrin—the moves have come naturally to her. She's strutting her stuff right now, while eyeing the merchandise populating the dance-floor. Who to choose? She has been advised to go simply by appearance. These people are the enemy, after all; she's not looking to form a long-term relationship with any of them; she just needs someone to go with tonight, a one-night stand, so just pick a boy you think looks cute. Sound advice!

She likes the look of the DJ. Pleasantly scruffy, stubbly, a lumberjack shirt over a Pixies t-shirt. Perhaps she is attracted to him because, being stationed behind his decks, he is not exhibiting the off-putting tacky dance moves of some of the other guys around her. He just nods his head to the music as he sorts through a pile of CDs for his next tune. (Jessica doesn't know this yet, but his name is Curtis and he is still reeling from the loss of his girlfriend.)

Jessica catches his eye, smiles toothily. He politely smiles back.

Albertine now trips onto the stage, winking at Jessica as she starts dancing. Albertine is in dire need of penetrative sex, not having had any—poor thing!—for several weeks. (At least, not unless counting one occasion featuring Dizzy Hello and a strap-on dildo.) Dressed in her usual French school uniform (passing itself off as cosplay for tonight), she is soon being noticed by the other dancers.

The three remaining SEA girls don't see that Dodo has approached them until she leans over the back of their sofa. 'Please set my mind at rest,' she says. 'You're not here to blow up this place, gas everyone, or in any other way cause a massacre, are you?'

'Oh, no!' Sophie assures her. 'We're definitely off-duty this evening. Just here to have fun, the same as everyone else.'

'That's why Mayumi and I are here, too,' says Dodo. 'I just wanted to make sure you weren't likely to spoil our evening.'

'Oh, we wouldn't dream of it!' gushes Sophie. 'And please give our regards to Miss Takahashi. Tell her we love her hat!'

Nodding her head, Dodo departs.

Jessica re-joins her friends.

'You've given up pretty quick!' observes Chrissie.

'I haven't given up,' says Jessica. 'I like the DJ. But he's DJing.'

'Don't worry about that!' says Chrissie. 'He won't be DJing all night. There'll be several DJs taking turns. You've just got to wait till he finishes his set.'

They see Albertine leaving the dance-floor. She has already secured a partner. She marches him out the door, heading upstairs to the toilets, the usual rendezvous for these 'quickies.'

From her table, Mayumi regards the notorious terrorists.

'I would rike to photograph them,' she tells Dodo.

'From what I know of those girls, I should think they'd be more than willing,' Dodo replies.

'Are you going to arrest them, Dodo?'

Dodo shrugs. 'It's not my job to arrest them. I've given Mark a buzz; he knows that they're here. It's up to him what he does about it.'

'Will there be a raid? That would be exciting!' enthuses Mayumi, smiling with her overbite.

'Not sure about that. I think it more likely Mark will want to have them discreetly followed when they leave here. Finding their base is his priority at the moment... Let's go out for a smoke.'

Curtis has finished his set. Procuring a drink, he joins his friends and fellow DJs, who are seated in one of the booths. A newcomer has joined his group of friends. Fat Sarah introduces him to Craig. His name is Robin, and seeing him sitting on his own, doing a 'How Soon is Now,' they had invited him to join them.

Seated next to him, Curt engages the shy, awkward young man in conversation, feeling for him that ready sympathy that comes from having been through similar circumstances. He finds that the newcomer doesn't seem to know much about the music they're playing, so switches the conversation to the general subjects—this inevitably leads him the reveal the recent tragedy in his life.

'...Your girlfriend died?'

'Yeah. She was killed by the Carpenter,' affirms Craig. 'You know, that serial killer who smashes women's skulls in.'

The colour drains from Robin's face. He looks absolutely horrified.

'Yeah, I know,' says Craig, misreading the look. 'Just thinking what her last moments must have been like...I just wish I could get my hands on that bastard; I'd—'

Robin jumps to his feet.

'I need to go to the toilet.'

He departs with alacrity. (And he won't be coming back.)

Moments later, a girl slides onto the sofa next to Curt: the cute girl with the freckles and twin-tails he noticed while he was DJing.

'Hi!' she says brightly. 'Do you want to have sex with me?' (Jessica has been primed by the other girls to get straight to the point. Small talk, they declare, is just a pointless waste of time.)

Out in the smoking area, a small courtyard at the back of the venue, Dodo and Mayumi are seated at a bench sharing a joint. (Because, of course, since the smoking ban, you have to smoke your weed outside.)

'…And so we had to stop this crazy alchemist,' Dodo is saying. 'He'd found the philosopher's stone: the secret of turning base metals into gold. He was planning to ruin the world's economy by flooding the market with tons of the stuff…'

'This is very exciting!' enthuses Mayumi. 'How did you stop him?'

'We raided the place; Mark got into the control room and reversed the polarity on the gold-making whatsit, and all the gold got turned back into brass and copper. Meanwhile, I was fighting with the alchemist up on a catwalk. He flew at me, I ducked, and he went straight over the edge and fell into a vat full of molten metal. After that me and Mark got ourselves out of there, as we usually do, just before the whole place went up…'

Mayumi folds her arms around Dodo. 'You are so brave. You do such exciting things…'

Dodo looks back at Mayumi, at the black eyes behind those glasses; stoned, adoring.

'Christ, I love you…'

'I worship you,' says Mayumi, firmly. 'You are my goddess. You are all woman.'

They kiss, Dodo entwining her long fingers in Mayumi's thick, lustrous hair…

Albertine appears in the courtyard for a post-coital cigarette. Her recent sexual partner trails in her wake.

'Why do you keep following me?' she demands.

'But we haven't got to know each other,' whines the young man. 'I don't even know what you do…'

'Oh, you want to know what I do?' replies Albertine. 'Well, I'm an international terrorist and I recently blew up London Bridge 'ospital.'

'You know, it might be a bit too soon for jokes like that,' cautions the young man. 'What do you really do? I'm a media studies student.'

Albertine claps her hands in mock admiration. 'Oh, 'ow thrilling! When you 'ave written your dissertation contrasting *The Simpsons* and *South Park*, please send me a copy!'

'There's more to media studies than that, you know.'

'Is zat so? Oh yes, of course! Zhere is also Mickey Mouse, is there not? I congratulate you: You 'ave enrolled on ze only Mickey Mouse college course in which you can actually study Mickey Mouse! Bravo!'

Albertine turns her back on him and lights her king-size cigarette.

'Look, can't we just—'

'No, we cannot. Go away. Zis conversation is ended.'

'Is that it, then?' sulks the student. 'You only wanted me for one thing?'

Albertine turns on him.

'Yes, and you were not so very good at zat, were you? Be gone, premature ejaculator!'

Crushed, the student slouches off.

Following Albertine's example, Jessica has escorted Curtis to the toilets. (Although Jessica has opted for the familiarity of the ladies', whereas forthright Albertine had marched her partner straight into the men's.) The club's cyberpunk décor is continued into the facilities, although here the pipe-work is painted on, the brickwork between is daubed with graffiti; some of it the work of the original artist, some of it added by other hands.

Jessica and Curt are in one of the cubicles, industriously French-kissing. Jessie's first ever snog! A bit awkward at first, some mashing of teeth, but she has soon got the hang of it, and now she's loving it. Curtis's hands have wandered down to her buttocks, and he kneads them through the material of her cargo pants.

She's feeling it now, is Jessica; her body is electrified. She feels like she's going to lose control; she *wants* to lose control; no, she *needs* to; she's so turned on it's like she's going to explode…!

But then, the anti-climax; Curtis ends the kiss, and, sighing heavily, removes his arms form around her waist. 'I can't do this,' he says, embarrassed, apologetic.

'Why not?' demands Jessica. 'What's wrong? Aren't I attractive enough?'

'No, 'course you're attractive, love,' Curt assures her. 'You're as cute as anything—It's just that…'

'What?'

Another sigh. 'I lost my girlfriend recently. She was killed by that serial killer; you know: the Carpenter. And the worst thing is, that night, we'd just had a row and she walked out of my flat. That's when it happened, when she was walking home from my place. It's all my fault…'

'That's terrible,' says Jessica. She feels a twinge of genuine sympathy for Curt—perhaps brought on by her relief in learning that she's not the one responsible for his not being able to get in the mood. 'But you shouldn't keep blaming yourself, you know,' she continues. 'You couldn't have known what was going to happen…'

A weak smile. 'Yeah, that's what everyone tells me, but it's easier said than done. You see, when she walked out, I did think about going after her, but then I decided not to; I thought I'd let her stew till tomorrow before making up with her. So you see: one petty, spiteful decision on my part, and it got Tanya killed…'

Jessica embraces him awkwardly. 'I wish I could make you feel better…'

'You're a sweet girl,' says Curt, flipping one of her twin-tails. 'I feel bad about letting you down. I thought I was ready for it, but looks like I'm not—and I haven't got any Viagra on me! Anyhow,' looking at her; 'I'm not sure how old you are, freckle-face. I don't want to do a Roman Polanski!'

Jessica smiles up at him.

'Oh, I'm older than I look!' she assures him (the fibber!)

Curt returns the smile.

'Tell you what!' He reaches into his pocket. 'As a consolation prize, do you want to do some acid?'

'Yes, please!' enthuses Jessica, thinking at least to try one new thing this evening.

Curt produces a small piece of card, perforated into small squares. He sighs. Even this reminds him of Tanya. She used to rib him for taking what she called a 'schoolkids' drug.' He breaks off a tab for Jessica.

'What do I do? Put it on my tongue?'

'Nah, just swallow it.'

She does so. Curt takes one himself.

Three boys corner Sophie in the corridor outside the toilets. The walls here have been painted with a futuristic city skyline at night. Two of the boys accosting Sophie have chin-beards, all three of them have sleazy grins. Sophie judges them to be students; the less politically-correct variety. The first boy leans in, blocking her way with his outstretched arm.

'You're with that French girl and the one with the bunches, aren't you?' he says.

'Yes...' says Sophie. 'What about it?'

'Oh, come on!' says the student. 'We've heard that you girls are all on the pull tonight; you've been grabbing guys and marching them straight up here to the bogs. Well, here we are: you've pulled!'

The other two boys snigger their affirmation. Sophie just smiles.

'You know, this happens a lot in anime,' she tells them. 'You get two or three guys, sleazy creeps like you, hitting on one solitary girl who doesn't know them from Adam—and they expect her to be up for it! I mean, do you really think that's going to happen? Do you really think I want to have sex with all three of you? Or are you going to do "rock paper scissors" to decide who gets me?'

'Why not all three of us?' questions the spokesman of the group. 'You get three for the price of one. You could even have us all at the same time, right? One in the front door, one in the back, and one to suck on. Three times the fun.'

More sniggers of approval at this proposal.

Sophie makes a show of thinking about it. 'Hmm, let me see... No, actually, I think I'll have to say "no" to that one. I'm not up for being the filling in a sex sandwich with you sad-sacks. Excuse me.'

She moves to duck under the outstretched arm, but the student pushes her back against the wall.

'Oh no you don't,' he snarls. 'If your friends are on the market then so are you. You can't mess us around.'

'Oh, I see!' says Sophie. 'This is going to be a gang-rape, is it? Why didn't you just say so all along? What do you think, Gina?'

It is indeed the Italian girl who has just appeared in the corridor.

'Hey! One of your pals!' exclaims the student. 'Even better!'

'The more the merrier!' says the second student. He moves in to embrace Gina—pulling up short when he finds a knife at his throat.

'Lay one finger on me and I will stab you in the neck.'

The student, his face a picture, retreats.

Sophie sighs. 'Oh dear... So much knife crime in London these days. You just aren't safe anywhere, are you...?' To her friend: 'Let's get back to the others, Gina.'

The three students make no effort to stop them.

Jessica is starting to come up. She sits in the booth with her friends. She has told them about the failed sexual encounter and the LSD substitute. ('He's severely depressed about his dead girlfriend, and he takes acid,' remarked Chrissie. 'He'll regret that one when he starts coming down.') It's starting. She can feel it. Glued to her chair, Jessie feels like she is in a plunging elevator. The sounds: the music, the chatter, drift in and out like the tide, rising from a low murmur to crystal clarity. The disco lights, the dancers on the dance-floor, swirl from sharp to soft focus.

And then the song starts to play. It is 'Double Vision' by Vivian Girls, a girl band from New York; Jessica is a big fan. The music, countrified indie-rock; up-tempo, yet beautifully ethereal, wraps its soft wings around Jessica. She is engulfed by a sense of freedom, of burning nostalgia, the endless summers of early childhood... The nightclub lights shift, coalesce, fade out completely... She sees fields of corn basking in the summer sun... And she is high, high above them... She moves forward with the flow of the music, flying over the landscape... Yes, she is flying—flying through the sky... Below her, the storybook landscape flies past her gaze; patchwork cultivated fields, picturesque villages with church spires, vast stretches of woodland, grassy hills with grazing livestock, serpentine rivers, rolling heathland...

And now, sand dunes and tussocks of wild grass announce the limits of dry land, and suddenly, breathlessly, she is out over the waves, the limitless blue sea, flying faster, faster... She rises, leaving the ocean below, and she is passing through an intangible landscape of clouds. Higher still, the sky darkens, the song draws to a close...

And then darkness. Silence. Her eyes readjust. She is back in the nightclub, sitting in the same place on the same sofa. But the people have gone, the music has been silenced. The pink glow-tube on the wall behind her diffuses an island of light; all else is darkness.

'I need you to focus, Jessica.'

That voice. *His* voice.

She turns her head to the left. Vautrin is seated on the sofa at right-angles to herself. They are alone.

'How did you get here?' asks Jessica. 'Where's everyone gone?'

'Everyone is still in the nightclub,' answers Vautrin. 'You're the one who's gone on a trip, Jessica. That's how I'm here. The lysergic acid diethylamide you have taken has opened your mind, enabled me to make contact with you over the astral plane.'

'You sound all serious. Is something wrong?'

'Yes, something is very wrong, Jessica. The portal has closed. At headquarters. We're trapped, myself and the other girls; we can't get out of the base—which means you and the others can't get back in, either. Only you five girls can remedy the situation. You see, the cause of the problem is out there where you are— Now, I need you to listen very carefully, Jessica. I need you to remember what I say, and then to tell the others. Understand?'

'Yes…'

'Someone outside the base is operating a solanite particle accelerator. This has caused the portal to close. You need to find that particle accelerator and disable it permanently. I can't give you the precise location; you will have to find it for yourselves. All I can tell you is that it's somewhere near you in London.'

'We've got to find it and destroy it?'

'That's right.'

'And if we don't, we'll never be able to get back into the base, and the rest of you will be trapped there?'

'Yes. That's correct. I have to go now; this is all the time I have here. Remember what I've told you, Jessica; remember to tell the others…'

Static noise fills Jessie's ears, the lights swim before her eyes. The noise becomes music; a grunge rock song. The lights coalesce into the face of Chrissie Wylde, a look of concern on her features.

'Earth to Jessica…'

'Chrissie…'

She smiles.

'At last! You're back! You totally spaced out there. We were starting to think you'd gone into a coma or something!'

'It was that song…' says Jessica. 'It took me somewhere… I saw Vautrin!'

'You saw Vautrin? That's some trip you're having, girlfriend!'
'Yeah…'

Chapter Thirty-One
Worse Things Happen at SEA

Three o'clock.

Mark Hunters loiters outside the Cyberia nightclub as the patrons drift out. He hasn't ventured inside, judging himself a bit old to be clubbing it. Dodo and Mayumi now appear, arm in arm. Delighted to see their friend, they rush over to him, embracing him gleefully.

'I don't need to ask if you two have been having a good time,' observes Mark.

'I'm surprised you're still here,' says Dodo. 'The SEA girls left about half an hour ago. Don't tell me you missed them?'

'No-no. I've got Fontaine and Collins following them. I'm still here because I was worried they might have left some parting gift at the club.'

'Like a bomb or something? I honestly don't think so. I tackled them on that subject when I first got here. (Did I tell you that?) And they assured me they were off-duty and were not planning a massacre.'

'Yes, but they might've been lying. It comes naturally to those girls.'

'Well, everyone's leaving now and nothing has happened,' points out Dodo.

'True enough, but we'll give the place a once-over, anyway.'

'And what are you going to do about the girls?'

'That depends on what the girls *do*. I'm waiting to hear.'

Stoned Mayumi hugs Mark. 'You should forget all that. Why don't you come home with us? We have a threesome…!'

Mark gently extricates himself from her embrace. 'Thank you, my dear, but I'll have to pass on that kind offer. I'm on duty.'

'You know, you ought to be flattered,' Dodo tells him. 'There aren't many men she'd make that offer to.'

'Flattered, I am,' Mark assures her; 'but still on duty.'

The two women flag down a cab.

'I'll keep you posted,' Mark says to Dodo, closing the door for them.

'Right. Take care of yourself.'

The taxi drives off.

Once again cross the portals of that same luxury hotel in which Mark had caught his first glimpse of Vautrin, and Baxter, the munitions dealer, had met his fate. The SEA girls have booked themselves the penthouse suite for tonight. Money is no object for these ladies!

They have just arrived, and we find them in the vast living area, making themselves comfortable.

'Were we followed 'ere?' queries Albertine.

Sitting on a sofa, she peels off her navy-blue stockings. Trippy Jessica pounces her friend's feet, sniffing and caressing.

'Of course, we were,' affirms Sophie, slipping out of her cargo pants. 'A car followed our taxi all the way here.'

'Well, we knew Dodo was bound to tell Mark Hunter we were at the club,' remarks Chrissie.

'So, what must we do?' Gina wants to know. 'If we stay here, we might be raided.'

'I suppose they might try that…' says Sophie. 'But, you know, I think it's more likely they want to follow us all the way back to headquarters… I know! Let's call Vautrin; see what he says.'

Sophie picks up her smartphone, selects Vautrin's number. 'That's funny. It won't connect.'

'Try one of the others,' suggests Gina.

Sophie tries Flossie's number. No connection. She tries Dizzy, Greta, Juliette, Trudie, Rachel… Same result.

'Your phone must be on the blink,' declares Chrissie. 'Let me try.'

But she likewise cannot connect with anyone at the SEA base.

Gina and Albertine now try with their phones, with the same

negative result.

Albertine looks down at Jessica. "Ave you tried your phone?'

'Embalm,' says Jessica, her mouth full of Albertine's toes.

Albertine extracts her foot. 'Will you pay attention, Jessica 'Arper! None of us can connect with 'eadquarters.'

Jessica stares at her blankly for a moment. Then she says: 'Oh... I wonder if it was real, then?'

'You wonder if what was real?'

'Oh, Vautrin. When I saw him at the club. He said something was wrong. I thought it was just the acid...'

The other girls gather round her.

'You saw Vautrin when you zoned out at the club?' questions Sophie. 'What happened? This could be very important, Jess.'

'I thought I was flying... flying forever...' says Jessica, dreamily. 'Over trees and fields and rivers... Just flying through the summer sky—'

'Yeah, can we cut to the bit where you saw Vautrin?' interrupts Chrissie.

'That was when I got back to the club. It was empty: no people, no music. You'd all gone and Vautrin was there instead... He said he wanted to speak to me...'

'What did he say?' from Sophie, urgently.

'He said that something had gone wrong, and that I should listen very carefully to what he was going to tell me, and that I had to tell the rest of you all about it, cuz it was really important.'

Albertine rolls her eyes. 'Zen why didn't you, nincompoop?'

Jessica shrugs. 'Well, when I got back, I thought it was all just an hallucination; part of the trip. It didn't seem real...'

'So, what did he tell you, Jess?' urges Sophie. 'What did he say was wrong?'

'He said the portal was closed, and that we can't get back into the base, and they can't get out, either...'

Sophie looks at the others. 'Then that's why we can't get through to them on our phones.' To Jessica: 'What else did he say? Was there anything else? Did he say he could fix the problem?'

'No, he said he couldn't fix it. He said the problem was out here and only we could fix it.'

'Only we can fix it? How?'

'He said someone has activated a—what did he call it?—a solanite particle accelerator...'

'Solanite? That's the stuff Vautrin's got those scientists experimenting with,' says Sophie. 'Haven't they got a particle whatsit in their lab?'

'*Si,*' affirms Gina. 'This new device must be causing interference. Did Vautrin say where it was to be found, Jessica?'

'No, he said he couldn't pin-point it, but it's somewhere here in London. We've got to find it and stop it working, he said.'

'And 'ow are we going to do zat?' wonders Albertine.

'Maybe we should ask Mark Hunter,' suggests Jessica.

They all look down at her.

'What do you mean?' demands Albertine.

'Well, he probably knows about solanite experiments from that scientist who escaped, doesn't he? Maybe he's deliberately set this other thing up to stop us getting home...' She looks up at their faces. 'Well, it's possible, isn't it?'

'That acid's done you some good after all,' declares Sophie. 'Yes, I think we need to have a word with Mark Hunter...'

The man in question is sitting in the ground floor bar; the same bar in which we first met Dodo. He has the place to himself, and nurses a scotch on the rocks, wondering what to do next about those girls in the penthouse.

'Can Mark Hunter report to reception, please?' comes an announcement.

Who could that be? he wonders. Headquarters?

He crosses to the reception desk. 'I'm Mark Hunter.'

'Ah, Mr Hunter; I have a message for you. The guests in the penthouse suite have asked if you would be kind enough to go and join them in their suite.'

'Oh, have they, now? Tell them I'm on my way.'

He boards the lift. He isn't too surprised that his presence in the hotel has been surmised. The girls would have realised they were followed home from the club—so it was fairly safe for them to have assumed that either he or one of his colleagues would be on the premises. What he cannot fathom is what they want with him... Once he is in that penthouse, will he be prevented from ever leaving again...?

The lift brings him to the top floor. He knocks on the door of the penthouse suite.

Sophie answers the door, a smile on her face and a gun in her hand. 'Hello! Please come in.'

Mark enters. The girls, stripped down to their underwear, are lounging around the luxury suite. Sophie relieves Mark of his gun.

'Sit yourself down, Mark,' she invites him. 'We'd like to have a little talk with you, if that's alright.'

'Perfectly alright,' replies Mark.

'Take a seat.'

Mark seats himself. Four of the girls look at him intently. The fifth sits on the floor and seems fascinated by her own hand.

' 'Ave you got a solanite particle accelerator?' demands Albertine, coming straight to the point.

'Not on me, no,' replies Mark, surprised.

'But you know where one is?' persists Albertine.

'There's one in your base, isn't there?'

'We mean another one,' clarifies Sophie.

'There isn't another one.'

'Please don't tell fibs, Mark.'

'I'm not fibbing, young lady. After the Peltdown Vale Incident, the solanite energy project was shelved, pending a full inquiry.'

'But we *know* there's a solanite accelerator operating, and that it's somewhere here in London,' insists Sophie.

Mark shakes his head helplessly. 'If there is, it's news to me. Why so interested, anyway? You've got one of your own. Isn't that enough for you?'

'Yes, but this new one is causing interference. It's locking us out. We can't get back into our base.'

'All of you? You mean you're all locked out?'

'No, just us five. Vautrin and the others are still inside, and they can't get *out*.'

Mark smiles at this. 'Well, well, well. So you're locked out and old Vautrin is locked in. That's a poser, isn't it? What are you going to do about that?'

'We are going to find this particle accelerator and destroy it,' declares Gina. 'We know it is located somewhere here in London.'

'Yes, and we'd like you to help us find it, Mark,' says Sophie.

'Now why on earth should I do that?' protests Mark, still amused. 'What with me being your "designated arch-enemy" and all. That would be aiding the enemy. No; cut off from Vautrin and the base, your days are numbered, my dears. Why should I do anything to rectify that?'

Gina marches up to him, puts her knife to his throat. 'Because if you don't, I will slice open your jugular vein.'

'You make a compelling argument. Consider me in.'

'Really?' gasps Sophie.

'I don't have much choice, do I?'

Gina withdraws her knife.

Sophie claps delightedly. 'Oh, good! We knew we could rely on you! Do you know how we can find this solanite accelerator, then?'

'As a matter of fact I do know of a way. Solanite emissions can be detected, even when shielded. When I discovered you lot were messing around with solanite material I went to a Professor Smithers, who has the equipment to detect solanite emissions. I was hoping with his help to pinpoint the location of your base. No luck, though. Your headquarters must be *too* well shielded. But if someone's using solanite material here in London, locating the source should be a doddle.'

'That's wonderful, Mark!' enthuses Sophie. 'If your professor can locate the accelerator, then we can just go in and put it out of action.'

'Sounds like a plan!' agrees Mark, rising briskly to his feet. 'Then

I'll just go'n see the professor right now, and we can get things moving. I shall be as quick as I can!'

He has not taken more than two steps towards the door when he finds three guns and a knife barring his way.

'We've got a better idea,' counters Sophie. 'How about you stay right where you are and you ring your friend Dodo Dupont and get *her* to see the professor?'

'Yes... Yes, we could do it that way,' concedes Mark with a sigh, resuming his seat.

'And just to make certain you don't get any more ideas about leaving us—Girls!'

Sophie, Albertine, Chrissie and Gina pounce on Mark and quickly and efficiently strip him of his clothes.

'*Now* you won't be going anywhere!' declares Sophie.

As the SEA girls admire their handiwork, Mark sits there doing his best to look comfortable in his lean, broad-shouldered nudity. Weighing up the pros and cons, he decides that to cup his hands over his genitals will only look more undignified than to just pretend he doesn't care that they are on public display.

'Look at the hose on that, girls,' says Chrissie admiringly.

'And to think he never uses it,' sighs Sophie. 'What a waste... Ooh, I know!' She turns to Jessica. 'Hey, Jessie darling. Seeing as you didn't get laid at the club, do you want to help yourself to Mark here, right now? We'll hold him down for you.'

Jessica looks up from a detailed inspection of the carpet. She regards Mark thoughtfully, then shakes her head, swinging her twin-tails.

'No... He's a bit old...' she decides. 'Anyway, Trudie wouldn't like it...'

'Trudie?' echoes Mark.

'Oh, yes...' Sophie leans over the back of the chair, folds her arms around Mark's neck. 'Trudie would be *so* jealous if she knew we had you stripped and helpless like this. You see, she likes you, does Trudie...'

'Oh...' says Mark. 'She does, does she...?'

Chapter Thirty-Two

Where is Everybody? (Continued)

'Have a seat, Mark. Get your breath back.'

Having crossed the food court to Vautrin's table, Mark drops into the chair facing him. Vautrin smokes languidly, his eyes hidden behind tinted glasses.

'Would you like something to drink, Mark?' asks Trudie, standing waitress-like at his side, bright-eyed and fresh, and looking not at all like someone who has just run three miles non-stop.

'I wouldn't say no,' replies Mark. 'Something chilled and caffeinated would be nice.'

'Coming up!' says Trudie.

She walks off to the food kiosks.

Mark turns to Vautrin. 'What's going on?'

'You'll have to be more specific, Mark.'

'You know what I mean,' says Mark. 'What's all this? Where are all the people?'

'If you mean the people of London: they're right where they've always been. You're the one who has changed location, Mark.'

'I've changed location…? You mean I'm not in London?'

'You are and you aren't.'

'Look, Vautrin, I'm confused and I'm puffed out, here. How about some straight answers?'

Trudie returns with a large iced coke in a carton with a plastic lid, the lid punctured with a bendy drinking straw. Mark puts the straw to his lips and draws in a refreshing mouthful of the cool, carbonated beverage.

'Okay, Mark. I'll explain as simply as I can,' proceeds Vautrin. 'The people of London are still here; they're all around us: you just can't see them.'

'You're not going to tell me they've turned invisible?'

'Not quite. You see, where you are now is not quite another dimension, but it's not quite your own either. Imagine a place slightly to one side of your reality; just a hair's-breadth out of synch with the continuum you're familiar with. The buildings exist here, so do all physical objects that are not in motion. Everything that grows from the ground exists, too. But, living, moving creatures do not exist here. No people, no animals, birds or insects.'

'Nothing that moves exists? But I've seen cars.'

'Only stationary cars. If someone were to get into one of those cars in the real world, and drove off in it, here it would appear to just wink out of existence.'

Mark ponders this. 'But then, by that reasoning, cars paused at traffic lights ought to become visible,' he decides.

Vautrin shakes his head. 'Not when their engines are still running.'

Mark drinks some more coke.

'And what about the internet? The telephone and television signals? Why are they getting through?'

'Because they're moving,' says Vautrin. 'I told you: nothing that is in motion is visible or accessible here.'

'Say I believe you,' says Mark, after another pause. 'Then how did you do it? How did you pull this off? I mean, I assume I have you to thank for my being here? For my being out of synch with reality, as you call it.'

'You don't remember? No, of course you wouldn't. That's one of the side effects of the transference. Immediate memories are blocked and the recent past all a jumble, right? Yes, believe me, I know how you feel. But don't worry about how you were brought here, Mark. That's not important right now.'

'Okay, then. *Why* have you brought me here?'

'Why indeed?' Vautrin smiles. He leans back in his chair. 'But then, there's another explanation for all this, isn't there? This whole thing could just be an hallucination you're experiencing. In which case, any explanation I offered would be as apocryphal as everything else here.'

Trudie, leaning over Mark's chair, puts her arms round his neck, presses her cheek to his. 'Don't listen to him,' she breathes, pitching her voice loud enough for Vautrin to hear. 'He's just trying to confuse you.'

'And you're on my side, I suppose?'

'Of course I am.' She places her lips close to his ear. 'I'm real. Whatever else is made up here, I'm real. You need to remember that.' She brushes his cheek with a finger. 'What are those little scars?'

'Legacy of a pistol-whipping,' Mark tells her.

'Are you two conspiring against me?' interjects Vautrin. 'You know, I really ought to be jealous. Trudie's very fond of you, Mark.'

Trudie presses her cheek to Mark's once again.

'But then, you're rather fond of her yourself, aren't you, Mark?'

'And what makes you think that?' challenges Mark.

'Intuition. Direct observation,' answers Vautrin. 'Yes... it started, I believe, before you ever even met Trudie that first time at the safe house, didn't it? When you were doing your sleuthing—investigating Trudie's past, uncovering her dark secrets. I think that's when you first started to become preoccupied with her, wasn't it? It's like that old film—is it *Laura*?—the one where the detective investigating the homicide of a young woman becomes obsessed with the victim.'

'And there was that time you captured me,' adds Trudie. 'You said you wanted to help me. I thought that was really sweet of you, Mark.'

'I was concerned about all of you,' says Mark. 'I wanted to get you away from *him*,' nodding at Vautrin.

'Yes, but you came charging to rescue me when you thought I was in danger! You were really worried about me!'

'Trudie, he won't remember that incident,' Vautrin reminds her.

'Oh, yeah. 'Course you won't. Sorry!'

Mark reaches into his jacket pockets for his cigarettes. Coming to Trudie's rescue... So, things *have* happened that he doesn't remember.

'So, what next, Vautrin?' he demands. 'How do I get out of

this place? How do I get back? Assuming I'm not just imagining this whole thing.'

'That's difficult to answer, Mark,' says Vautrin. 'Getting back from here to the real world can be a very difficult and disorienting process.'

'What about you, then? You're here, and I'm sure you wouldn't have come here if you didn't know the way out.'

Vautrin shakes his head sadly. 'Mark, Mark... We're not really here, Trudie and I. I thought you would have realised that by now. Show him what I mean, Trudie.'

Trudie, standing behind Mark, places her hands over his eyes.

'Now you see us...'

She lifts them.

'...Now you don't.'

Vautrin is no longer in the chair facing him. He looks round. No Trudie. He heard her voice a split second ago, but she's gone—the food court is completely empty.

He is alone again.

Chapter Thirty-Three
Chrissie Wylde's World Comes Crashing Down

'Thank you very much! Enjoy your meal!'

Everyone who comes into McDonald's loves Chrissie. The tall and pretty girl, with the long black pony-tail, she provides the kind of smiling and polite service that you would normally only expect to receive in a Japanese McDonald's, not in a surly London branch. You would think Chrissie desires nothing more from life than to serve her customers with fattening, unhealthy fast-food.

'Enjoy your meal! Please come again!'

You would think that, but you would be wrong. Chrissie *does* only have one interest in life, but this interest has nothing to do with hamburgers, bears no relation to glutinous milkshakes, and has absolutely nothing in common with skinny fries—it is something else entirely. And it is this *raison d'être* that energises Chrissie, keeps her smiling through those gruelling peek-period shifts at the fast-food joint.

It is Saturday afternoon when we join Chrissie, and her shift is nearly over.

'Five o'clock. Thank Christ!' says her friend Linda, working the cash register next to hers.

Their relief arrives, and the two girls proceed to the locker room to change. They climb out of their work clothes, and resume their street clothes, these being in Chrissie's case jeans and t-shirt. Chrissie has generous curves as well as stature, and those jeans, when they are pulled up, stretch themselves over two ripe and almost perfectly hemispherical buttocks. Chrissie is renowned for those buttocks; buttocks of an aggressive rotundity usually only to be found on black or Latino women. As Linda has said to her more than once: 'You're wasted here, you know. With those puppies, you should train to be one of those South American buttdancers.'

(Butt-dancing—basically belly-dancing, but with your back to the audience.)

Dressed, the two girls go out into the street.

'Coming to the pub tonight?' asks Linda. 'We're going to the White Swan.'

'Who's "we"?'

'The usual crowd. Well?'

'Depends what Luke wants to do. He might just want a night in tonight. Yesterday he said he thought he might be coming down with something.'

'A cold?'

'I think so.'

'Then you'll soon have it, won't you?'

Chrissie's boy-friend obsession is as locally renowned as is her posterior.

'I really need to get Luke some new jeans sometime,' says

Chrissie, looking at the window display of a men's clothing shop they are passing.

'Can't Luke buy his own jeans?' says Linda. 'He gets more money than you do.'

'But I like buying him clothes! Anyway, I've got better dress sense than he has. I know what looks good on him.'

'Yeah: you!'

They walk on through the afternoon crowd. Chrissie's mobile rings. She fishes it out of her bag. 'It's Luke!'

'Hello, Chris,' comes Luke's voice, congested. 'Looks like I guessed right—I've got a stinking cold.'

'Oh, you poor dear! Well, don't worry: I'll come round and nurse you.'

'Nah, don't do that; I don't want you catching it. I think I'll have an early one tonight, anyway.'

'Oh. Okay. Are you sure?'

'Yeah. Don't worry, babe. Couple of days and I'll be over it, I reckon.'

'What about tomorrow? Can I come and check on you then?'

'Yeah; if I feel better, you can come round.'

'Okay. Are you drinking plenty of liquids? And orange juice? You need vitamin C.'

'No worries; I'm on top of that.'

'Good! Then you just take care of yourself till tomorrow. Love you!'

'You too, babes.'

Chrissie puts her phone away, looking disconsolate.

'He did get that cold, did he?' deduces Linda.

'Yeah. He doesn't want me to come round tonight…'

'When you're ill like that, you're not always in the mood for company. Oh, cheer up, will you? He's not at death's door, and you'll be seeing him tomorrow. Come to the pub with us this evening.'

'I don't know… I shouldn't really be out enjoying myself while Luke's so poorly.'

Linda rolls her eyes. 'For Christ's sake, woman! Do you think he'll want you to sit at home moping just cuz he's sick?'

'I suppose not…'

'Good. So you'll come to the Swan?'

'I'll think about it…'

'Hey, there's Nisha!' She calls out.

Nisha joins them. These three girls have known each other since secondary school. They all share the commendable quality of having quit school after finishing their GCSEs; disdaining those baneful institutions of 'further education.'

'You up for the Swan tonight?' Linda asks Nisha.

'Probably not. I'm pretty much broke till the end of the month. Anyway, I was out drinking last night; don't want to over-do it. You two are both going, are you?'

'I am, but muggins here can't make her mind up. She's pining for her Luke. She can't see him tonight cuz he's got a cold.'

'Chris, you should go out,' advises Nisha. 'No point staying at home moping, is there?'

'Exactly what I said!'

'I'll think about it,' repeats Chrissie. 'Well, this is my street, so I'll see you later maybe, Linda. Bye, Nisha…'

Chrissie returns to her flat. Once inside, she turns on the TV and looks for something to eat. She isn't in the mood for preparing anything elaborate, so she just slides a frozen pizza into the oven.

She has been going out with Luke for over a year now. He is her world, the love of her life; she has reshaped herself to fit into his life, made his interests her own. When she is out with the girls and five minutes happen to pass without Chrissie mentioning Luke, the girls will start to make sarcastic inquiries as to whether she's feeling alright.

She knows this is it. She and Luke will be together forever. She had had a few boyfriends at school, but they weren't the real thing. And yes, admittedly, she'd *thought* they were all the real thing at the time; all of them; but she knows now that really they weren't. Her and Luke are the real thing; she knows it. Those others were just puppy-love.

Chrissie sits down in front of the TV with her pizza, eats mechanically, watches mechanically. A talent show... A quiz programme... The lottery... A hospital drama... Darkness starts to fall, but she hasn't risen to switch the lights on. The pizza, forgotten about after two slices, has gone cold.

And then, with a lightbulb flash, she comes to a decision. She can't leave Luke on his own while he's so poorly! Yes, she'll just pop round to see how he is, bring some things for him! He's bound to be low on supplies if he's too ill to go out. And if she finds him asleep, it won't matter; she can just quietly leave again; or even sit in the living room in case he wakes up and needs anything.

Released from stand-by mode, Chrissie is suddenly full of energy. She cleans her teeth, gets her things together and steps out into the dusk, setting off at a brisk pace. She'll call in at the mini-market on her way to Luke's. She checks her phone. Linda has texted to ask if she's coming to the Swan. Chrissie sends an apologetic reply in the negative.

Yes, what Luke said about not wanting her to catch his cold was just silly! Of course he said it cuz he was worried about her, bless him! She knows that. But she remembers hearing somewhere that when you catch a cold you're only contagious for the first day or so, and by the time you first realise you've got a cold, you've actually already had the bug for a couple of days! So, if Luke's at that stage where the symptoms are really bad, that means he isn't contagious anymore!

Poor Luke! She's never actually seen him under the weather in all the time she's known him. And it's so hard to imagine him like that! He's way too cool, too much of an original to come down with those mundane illnesses. And as for his sex-drive, it seems like Luke is climbing on top of her every five minutes! He just can't keep his hands off her. Not that she's complaining. It's cuz he loves her so much! Chrissie fires up his libido in a way no other girl has ever done for him! Luke has told her this many times and in many different positions—it's because she's so special.

Yes, she hardly ever has her clothes on when she's round Luke's, or when he's round hers. On the bed, on the sofa, bent over a chair, up against the wall; in the bathroom, in the kitchen... He just can't get enough of her! And it's all because they love each other so much. Sex without love is just stupid; it doesn't mean anything.

Chrissie calls in at a supermarket, buys cold remedies, orange juice, chicken soup, and anything else she thinks Luke might be short on.

Armed with her purchases, she arrives at Luke's apartment building. She has her own key, so she'll be able to get in without disturbing him if he turns out to be asleep... Chrissie sighs. She has often suggested to Luke that they should think about setting up house together, but he says he doesn't want to rush into something like that... He's just set in his ways; that's his problem, bless him!

She climbs the external staircase and follows the veranda to Luke's door. She lets herself in. In the darkened hallway she hears the unmistakable sound of sex noises coming from the living room. She smiles ruefully to herself. Watching porn again! Even laid up with a cold he's still watching the stuff. Well, they help him keep up his stamina. And at least that means he's not asleep!

She opens the living room door, blinking in the light. She freezes.

The sex noises aren't coming from the TV: they are coming from the sofa.

Chrissie's stunned mind refuses to accept what she sees. It can't be; it just can't be... Luke and Nisha! Luke, her one and only, between her second-best friend's legs. His back to Chrissie, and, intent on his work, he has not heard the door open. But Nisha knows; Nishi sees her. Yes, she sees Chrissie, and then, looking away and pretending she hasn't, she becomes even more vocal, writhing her body and twining Luke's long loose hair tightly around her hands.

'Harder! Harder...! Oh, mother of God! You're too big! I can't take it! Mercy! Please! Oh God, I'm dying! I'm dying...!'

Chrissie drops the shopping bag and flees.

Out in the street, she staggers, collapses to her knees, crying uncontrollably. Luke. Her Luke. He couldn't. He just couldn't. Luke was perfection. How could he...? What has she done wrong? She tries to think. She's never denied him anything. What has she done wrong? And Nisha. One of her best friends since they were at school together... And deliberately taunting her like that! She saw Chrissie and she was deliberately taunting her...

The awful image of her betrayal is burned into her mind—Luke's bare, wiry back. The pink soles of Nisha's feet.

Chrissie's mind slews around, helter-skelter. Her body shakes. She feels sick.

Luke's bare, wiry back. The pink soles of Nisha's feet.

And is this the first time? Somehow she knows that this isn't. Any suspicion of Luke's fidelity has never entered her head before now. But now... Now she feels as though her eyes have been opened... She recalls other times when he has cancelled on her for one reason or another, often at the last minute...

And what now? What now? She tries to look past this and into the future; but there isn't anything; not a thing... Luke. Her whole life. Her world.

Luke's bare, wiry back. The pink soles of Nisha's feet.

She had never suspected him for an instant. How could she have? Her perfect boyfriend would never do anything like that.

Her perfect boyfriend...

She is standing on the edge of an abyss. The only thing before her is a looming void—a vast nothingness.

Luke's bare, wiry back. The pink soles of Nisha's feet.

Finally, she rises to her feet, wiping her eyes. (Passersby have been ignoring her.) Controlling her shaking limbs, she walks numbly down the street. Has Linda known? Has Linda always known about Luke and Nisha? Was that why she had been so insistent about Chrissie coming to the pub with her tonight? Linda, her best friend... But if Luke has betrayed her, anyone could.

No-one can be trusted anymore. The world is an evil place and full of lies.

Finding herself outside a pub (not the one at which her friends are meeting), she walks inside. Hoping to calm her nerves, she orders a double vodka and coke, takes the drink to an empty table.

Maybe it isn't the end of the world. Maybe she can forgive Luke if he promises not to see that bitch again… But no, how can she ever be sure? If he has deceived her once, he could do it again… But is Nisha the only one…? Have there been others as well…? No sooner does she think this than it seems all too plausible. Luke is so handsome and laid back and charming no girl on the planet could resist him. He's probably been going with loads of girls behind her back…

But why…? Is it her fault…? Has she done something wrong? Has she not been good enough, somehow…?

And now… What…? What is there for her now…? All she can see is that void. Life without Luke seems inconceivable. How can she go on living…?

Two girls sit themselves at her table. This annoys her. The pub is quiet, the newcomers are not people she knows, and there are plenty of empty tables.

'I'm expecting someone…' she says.

'No, you're not,' says the first girl. She has short dark hair, glasses, a kind of spazzy voice. The second girl has blonde hair, also short, and an affable smile on her face.

'He's not worth killing yourself over.'

The dark-haired girl says these words. Chrissie looks at her, startled. How can she…?

'We're here as friends,' proceeds the girl, smiling. 'I'm Trudie, and this is Dizzy.'

'But I've never met you before! How could you…?'

'How could we know that your boyfriend is a lying, cheating piece of crap? We just do. Our master, Vautrin; he has ways of finding out these things. He's known about you for a while now, and he knew you were heading for this crisis. That's why we're here.'

'I don't understand…'

'It's simple, really,' says Trudie. 'We're offering you a way out. It's like you've come to a dead-end, haven't you? Your life can't go on any more; not like it was before. You'd dedicated your life to just one man, and now you've found out he wasn't worth it, right?'

Fresh tears well up in Chrissie's eyes.

'Look,' sighs Trudie. 'You're one of those people who think they're just not complete unless they've got someone else sharing their life with them. That's just how you are. And look where it's got you. So, what are you gunna do? You can either kill yourself, or you could go crawling back to that man and tell him you forgive him. And I'm telling you: that would be even worse than killing yourself.'

'But if I…!' begins Chrissie.

Trudie holds up a hand. 'Forget it. He would never stop cheating on you. He's selfish, he's immature and he's totally hypersexual. One woman is never enough for a guy like that. And don't talk about love. He doesn't know the meaning of the word. He only ever liked your body and the fact that you did everything he told you to do. When you let someone know that they can walk all over you like that, nine times out of ten, they *will* walk all over you. It's human nature.'

'You need to start thinking about yourself a bit more,' speaks up Dizzy. 'Some "enlightened self-interest" or whatever they call it. You've just been basking in the light of that horndog boyfriend of yours. Well, you need to start shining your own light, girl. You've been hiding it under your bush for too long.'

'It's "hiding it under a bushel,"' Trudie tells her.

Dizzy frowns. 'And what the fuck's a "bushel"?'

'I don't know…' confesses Trudie. Turning back to Chrissie; 'Anyway. It's time to let go. He's not worth killing yourself over. You just need to get yourself right away from all this crap. You need a new start. And that's why we're here!'

'You…?'

'Mm-hm. We're part of an organisation. In our group we're all girls, and it's like we're connected, somehow. Our boss Vautrin—who's one guy you *can* trust—he sees those connections; he's the one who's brought us all together. And you're one of us, Chrissie Wylde. You're the last link in the chain.'

'Are you for real?' asks Chrissie. 'I mean, what is this organisation? What do you do…?'

'Whatever you want!' declares Dizzy, cheerfully. 'The sky's the limit! No holds barred. It's time to start shining that light, sister!'

Chapter Thirty-Four
The Raid on the Vallotec Building

Things have been moving fast at SEA's penthouse suite.

First of all, Mark had telephoned Dodo and explained the situation. She had promised to call on Professor Smithers at the earliest reasonable hour and get him to track down the source of the solanite emissions. (Even a stoned Dodo is in full command of her faculties!) Then the SEA girls, feeling peckish (except for acid-tripping Jessica who didn't seem to be interested in food), had ordered room service. A small hours feast and more drinking had followed. Having no desire to starve their prisoner, Mark had been allowed to join in. the repast. Then they had decided to turn in for a few hours' rest, leaving Jessica, for whom sleep was out of the question, watching Netflix with rapt attention. The penthouse suite boasted three bedrooms, and Mark had been allotted one of them. To discourage him from making any escape attempts, Mark had been given two bed-partners: Gina Santella and her knife.

Mark and the SEA girls had slept for several hours, and risen at about eleven, ordering copious amounts of coffee. And Mark had received a call from Dodo. The solanite emissions had been traced to the London headquarters of Vallotec, an independent scientific research group. Mark knew that there was no way a private concern like Vallotec could have legitimately acquired any solanite material, and he was now as keen as the SEA girls to pay a visit to the place. He had instructed Dodo to procure certain equipment necessary for the raid and to bring it to the hotel.

Dodo had arrived in due course; an appraising look and 'I see they're treating you well!' had been her only comment on Mark's enforced nudity. She had brought instructions from Professor Smithers. He had warned that if they planned to destroy the particle accelerator, it was essential to remove the solanite core first. Otherwise, when the accelerator blew, solanite energy would be released into the air of London, and the possible harmful effects of this were not known. Dodo herself had reconnoitred the Vallotec building. The complex was surrounded by a high brick wall and heavily guarded. Force would be necessary, but Mark desired no fatalities and so had instructed Dodo to bring dart-guns, the darts firing a fast-acting anaesthetic. Explosives for destroying the particle accelerator and equipment for scaling the wall had also been procured.

The SEA girls, after a private confabulation, had decided they would take charge of the raid themselves, and that only Mark would come with them—Dodo was to withdraw from the proceedings. Wishing them good luck, the good professor had taken her leave. Mark had insisted that he should take charge of the solanite core once they had secured it, in order to return it to the proper authorities. Vautrin, he had argued, already had more than enough solanite material for his own purposes, and would not be needing any more. The girls had acquiesced to this.

The raid was to take place after dark, so the raiders had still some hours to kill. They had ordered a starchy meal to finish curing their hangovers. Jessica had finally been able to get to sleep. Friendly conversation had followed, the SEA girls chatting freely about themselves, entering into a friendly ideological debate with Mark.

Dusk started to fall. Jessica was roused from her slumber and prescribed a double whisky and plenty of coffee. Sandwiches were ordered. Then everyone took a shower and—Mark included—got dressed.

And then, armed with the necessary equipment, they set forth on their sortie.

Dusk. The raiding party arrives at the rear of the Vallotec building. There is no entrance here, just a tall concrete wall, whitewashed, running the entire length of the perimeter. Across the narrow access road, a facing wall marks the precincts of a disused factory.

'Juliette's father, Rufus Wainwright has an interest in Vallotec,' says Mark. 'I wouldn't be surprised if he was instrumental in enabling them to get their hands on the solanite material. He has plenty of important people in his pocket, and he must be aware of the potential of solanite as a new source of energy. It would mean a lot of money to him.'

'Wainwright's already got a lot of money,' remarks Sophie.

'Men like him can never have enough money,' responds Mark dryly.

The spy and the five girls approach the wall, their first obstacle. From her backpack Gina produces a rope and grappling hook, swings it, throws it. The hook crests the wall, catches, holds. Taking hold of the rope, Gina adroitly scales the wall. Straddling the summit, she affixes a second grappling hook, letting the rope drop down the other side. She descends. The other girls now follow her over the wall, followed by Mark. They are in the Vallotec grounds. Before them are ornamental gardens; flowerbeds, shrubs and neatly clipped hedges, dissected by gravel paths. Beyond these rises the edifice of the main building, its lines modern, functional. Lights show in many of the windows. No-one is in sight.

'I suggest we leave at least one person here to guard our escape route,' says Mark, speaking quietly.

'Excuse me, but *we're* in charge of this operation,' Sophie reminds him. 'And it is my considered opinion that at least one person should stay here to guard our escape route.'

The other girls agree to this excellent plan. Deciding that four people will be sufficient to carry out the raid, Jessica and Chrissie are elected to stay behind. Mark, Sophie, Gina and Albertine set off across the gardens. Reaching an intersection of paths, they spy a uniformed security guard advancing towards them. He espies the intruders, but, before he can take any action, Gina aims her gun, squeezes the trigger. With a hydraulic hiss, the sleep dart finds its target, the guard collapses.

They traverse the gardens without further incident. Two guards stand before the rear entrance doors of the building. Albertine and Sophie take care of them with the tranquiliser guns. The raiding party moves inside; they find themselves in a wide corridor, LED lit, silent and deserted.

'So now we 'ave an 'ole building to search,' breathes Albertine.

'Not the whole building,' demurs Mark. 'Something as big as the particle accelerator would have to be on the ground floor, and considering what they've got in there, the room is bound to be guarded.'

'Then we just look for a door with guards,' summarises Sophie, brightly. 'Come on.'

It doesn't take them long to find what they are searching for. They arrive at an intersection of corridors, and peaking round a corner they see that one branch terminates in a pair of important-looking double doors, guarded by two security men.

'Is that it?' asks Sophie.

'Yes, that'll be the place,' confirms Mark.

'Can we shoot the guards from this distance?'

Mark has another look. 'Nope. They're too far away. Out of range of the dart guns.'

'So, what do we do?'

Silence. Mark glances at his watch, and looking up again, sees three expectant faces staring at him.

'What?' he asks.

'I said: what do we do?' repeats Sophie.

'Why are you asking me? I thought you were in charge of this operation.'

'We are,' says Sophie. 'And as the leader, I'm ordering you to come up with a suggestion,' pointing her dart gun at him.

'Understood. Well in that case, I think our best option is to do what I usually do in these situations: act like we own the place.'

Sophie looks doubtful. 'Does that plan really work in practice?'

'It does for me,' Mark tells her. 'Nine times out of ten.'

And so, playing the odds, Mark and the girls turn the corner and march boldly along the corridor towards guards, guns concealed behind their backs and smiles on their faces. Mark gives the two men a friendly nod. They look puzzled; these people are strangers to them. They exchange looks, and seeing nothing encouraging in each other's expressions, decide something must be wrong, and reach for their sidearms. But too late—they are in range now; Mark and Sophie shoot them with sleep darts.

They pass straight through the doors and find that they have indeed reached their destination. A vast laboratory, the room dominated by a huge horizontal cylindrical structure, from which emanates a steady thrum of power. This is the particle accelerator. Only two white-coated technicians, both men, are on duty, seated at a bank of instruments. One of them, hearing a sound, looks round and sees the intruders. With a cry of alarm, he leaps from his seat and runs for the emergency button on the nearest wall. Sophie fires; the dart hits him in the neck; he pitches forward.

'Stay where you are,' she orders the remaining technician, who sits poised in his seat, fear in his eyes.

'What's going on?' he demands shrilly. 'You've killed him!'

'We haven't,' Mark assures him. 'He's only been shot with a tranquilliser dart. Make this easy on yourself and just do what you're told. We want you to shut down the accelerator and remove the core.'

The technician starts to regain his confidence. 'Why should I help you? You said those guns of yours can only put me to sleep.'

And then he finds Gina at his side, her knife at his throat. 'This can do more than put you to sleep,' she hisses.

'I'd cooperate if I were you,' advises Mark. 'That girl has slit more throats in her time than you or I have had hot dinners.'

'Alright, alright!' cries the technician, now well and truly terrified. 'Just get that knife away from me!'

Gina withdraws the knife, and the now compliant technician turns to the control board.

'Shutting down accelerator...'

The thrum of the machine dies down.

'Extracting solanite core...'

A panel slides aside, a small cylinder appears, attached to metal arms. Mark retrieves it. The cylinder is made of some opaque material, capped with metal at either end. The shard of rock fixed inside it is worth a small fortune.

'And that's it?' wonders Sophie. 'It doesn't look like much.'

'It may not look much,' says Mark. 'But this piece of rock comes from a meteor that crashed on the moon—it's the source of the solanite. Not many people know this stuff even exists.'

'Well, we've shut down the particle whatsit—that means we can get back to our base now.'

'Right. And I can return this to the proper authorities, and so ends our little arrangement.'

They place the core in Albertine's backpack. From her own backpack Gina produces explosive charges and attaches them to the accelerator

'What are you doing?' cries the technician.

'Putting a definite end to your experiments,' says Sophie.

Gina primes the charges. 'All set. We must depart at once.'

They race for the doors, Mark helping the technician to drag his unconscious colleague.

They are out in the corridor, the doors sealed, when the charges blow. The explosion rocks the building. Alarms start to wail. Leaving the technician to his own devices, the four raiders run for the exit. Shouts and the thump of running feet can be heard approaching from the front of the building.

Outside, they quickly cross the gardens to the perimeter wall where Jessie and Chrissie are waiting. Near them lies the unconscious body of another guard.

'Over the wall,' orders Sophie.

Jessica and Chrissie climb the rope first; then Albertine, then Gina. Sophie ascends next. Mark takes hold of the rope, looks up, sees Sophie, straddling the wall, pointing her dart gun at him, an apologetic smile on her face.

'Oh, you wouldn't...' says Mark.

She would. She fires.

Chapter Thirty-Five
The Streets Aren't Safe for a Serial Killer!

Robin Trent had read extensively on the subject of serial killers before deciding to become one himself.

There were some serial killers who said that they didn't feel like they were in control of their actions; that they felt compelled to do what they did. Robin isn't like that. He knows exactly what he is doing. After exhaustive research and weeks of soul-searching, he had come to a decision. One day, he had gone out and bought himself a claw-hammer, not to do any carpentry, but with the express intention of using it to kill someone. (He had read about another killer who had employed the same weapon.) Armed with this, he had gone out onto the streets one night, found a woman who was walking home on her own, and coming up behind her, had struck her over the head with the hammer. He had felt terrified. Fearing he hadn't hit her hard enough, he had struck again and again until he was sure she was dead, her skull split like a melon, blood seeping all over the pavement. After that he had run and not stopped until he had put several streets between himself and his victim. Then he had walked the rest of the way home, looking as calm as he could. The first rush of fear had soon passed, a feeling of elation taking its place. He had done it! He had actually done it! He had attacked and killed a human being!

He knew that he had now taken an irrevocable step; that he had passed beyond the pale of normal existence and entered a new world—an exclusive subculture, inhabited by only a select few. He had destroyed a life, a life he had known absolutely nothing about; a human being who had never done him any wrong. Should he stop now? But to kill just one person would not distinguish him as a serial killer. It would seem almost pitiful to just take on life and then stop. So many people kill another just the once—they kill in rage, for gain, or even by accident. That was nothing to write home about; that was not being a serial killer. No, Robin could not just stop now. And so, he had waited; scrutinising the news media until he was sure no suspicion rested on himself, and then he had gone out and killed again. The same terror, followed afterwards by the sense of elation. After his third victim, the police and press had finally realised they had a serial killer on their hands. The latter had dubbed him 'the Carpenter.'

He was a celebrity!

The killer had now been profiled by the leading experts, and the profiles had rolled out the usual clichéd conjectures: mother issues, childhood trauma, bed-wetting, disastrous first sexual experience, impotence—some of which applied to Robin, some didn't. The culprit's personality they had defined as that of a loner, probably unemployed, unable to meaningfully interact with other people. Robin was a loner, but he had a job and could communicate reasonably well. He felt safe that the police were on the wrong track. Indeed, two or three men fitting the given profile had been arrested and interrogated, but ultimately released without charge.

Robin does not feel detached from his actions, like some serial killers have claimed—but he does feel like a fraud. In spite of seven corpses, he feels like someone just *playing* at being a serial killer and that he somehow isn't the real McCoy. All those killers in America; they are the real thing; but somehow, he isn't; and try as he might, he is unable to shake these feelings.

In short, Robin is a serial killer burdened with Imposter Syndrome.

Even now he believes that if his circumstances improve; if he finds himself some new friends—a girlfriend, even; that he can just stop killing; put it all behind him. This is why he still goes out to pubs and clubs sometimes, hoping to find those right people, that special someone. He knows he has crossed a line, but he feels that he can stop, turn back, return to the old world, and—if one offers itself—start a new existence, and bury the secret of his past deep within him. From his reading he knows that not all serial killers continue killing until they get caught. Some just stop, drop off the radar, and are never apprehended, their activities being relegated to unsolved crimes archives.

So, for Robin, his life as a serial killer is only one compartmentalised part of his life. Sometimes things did overlap, like that horrible evening at that club when he had found himself in conversation with the boyfriend of his last victim. What a moment! Absolute horror had seized him like a vice; he had felt convinced that his guilt must have been written all over his face…

Why are there serial killers? Why do they exist? Why are they more prevalent in the U.S. of A. than anywhere else? It seems as though they are some unfortunate side-effect of modern civilisation. Serial killers are unheard of in primitive, 'undeveloped', cultures. Life in the First World is becoming more and more complicated, and, some will argue, more unnatural; technology seems to be racing ahead at an insane pace. As humans, we were not designed to live in the kind of society we have somehow ended up creating for ourselves, the end result of centuries of 'progress.' But human beings are adaptable, and can usually shape themselves—or *be* shaped—to fit into our complex and unnatural modern society. Those people who just can't fit in become outcasts. Many of these outcasts are happy to exist on the periphery of society; they even feel themselves to be superior on account of this, proud of their subcultural status, distinct from the mainstream. But there are also many involuntary outcasts whose inability to integrate themselves, to interact with their fellow human beings, just dooms them to living lonely and miserable lives… And then there are the ones who go off the rails completely and take their antisocial impulses to the extreme—Spree killers and serial killers who break, erupt like cancer, attacking the organism of society from within. People who break the ultimate taboo: that of robbing other human beings of their lives.

Can First World civilisation be maintained? Can it continue on its present course? Or, are all these serial killers and sexual predators an indication that civilisation is coming apart at the seams? The most powerful and influential nation in the world also has one of the most obscenely high murder rates.

Robin sometimes wonders if he is being too obvious, to clichéd, in only targeting women. Some serial killers will kill anyone; they will break into houses and slay whole families; some will target only children; some will target copulating couples; but the most common target is women, and amongst women, more often than not, it is that perennially vulnerable group, street-walkers who are singled out. But then Robin does have his longstanding issues with women, his crimes are 'sexually motivated,' so perhaps, by targeting women he is only playing his part correctly.

There's another which old cliché often holds true: that behind every serial killer there is a bad mother—either domineering and possessive, or else negligent and promiscuous. Yet neither of these apply to Robin. His woman issues have nothing to do with his mum. No, it was those girls who had mercilessly teased him at school that had done for him.

Robin is on the prowl for another victim.

He is nervous tonight for some reason. Is it time to quit? Will this be the night he gets caught? He is conscious of the hammer in the deep pocket of the jacket he wears. He dreads the prospect of being stopped by the police. What if they decide to start stopping and searching any solitary men they see and who they think look suspicious? Public opinion is enraged with the Metropolitan Police for not having apprehended the Carpenter; they are eager for his apprehension. Who knows what the police might try in order to achieve the desired result?

And yet, compared with atrocities like those hospital bombings, it seems to Robin that what he is doing is pretty small beer. He just picks off the odd individual human being; he doesn't plant bombs and slaughter hundreds with the press of a button…Yeah, with stuff like that going on all around the metropolis, it's hardly worth the police even bothering with him! *His* anti-social behaviour is nothing more than a drop in the ocean. Why don't the police concentrate on finding those terrorists? *That's* what they should be prioritising!

It is only after a killing that Robin feels a sense of power. For the rest of the time he feels weak, vulnerable. One nightmare scenario that haunts Robin's imagination is that a woman he is closing in on will hear his approach before he has chance to strike the first blow, and happening to be trained in self-defence or some martial art or other, will incapacitate him, restrain him, and call the police. Just think of the crushing irony! To be caught by an intended victim. The press would call that poetic justice, and sneer at the weakness of the thwarted serial killer.

Deep in these cogitations, Robin turns a blind corner and walks straight into a brick shit-house, one of the ambulatory kind, organic in construction. Head like a granite block on a thick neck; about six foot five in stature, the man looks like he doesn't possess a single X chromosome. He glares down at Robin.

He speaks. He says:

'Blleuurghh!'

Robin side-steps to pass, but the shit-house blocks him.

'Rrrbluuurgh!'

Robin runs across the street.

'Fuckin' little cunt!' yells the shit-house. 'I'll fuckin' get yer one o' these days! I'll fuckin' remember you, yer cunt!'

Pursued by these threats, Robin doesn't stop running until he has put several streets between himself and his nemesis. Only when he feels sufficiently safe from pursuit does he stop, and, leaning against a lamp-post, tries to control his frantic breathing. Slowly he recovers, his terror abates, and a burning anger begins to rise in its place.

That is it! That is the final straw. Now he'll *have* to kill someone, just to revenge himself for that incident!

Several streets later, Robin finds what he's looking for. A woman walking on her own. There is no-one else about. Robin crosses to her side of the road and increases his pace to catch up with her. She turns down another street. A couple approach from the other direction. He slows down. When they have passed him, he increases his pace again. The woman turns another corner. Robin breaks into a trot to close the distance, his hand clutching the hammer in his pocket. Rounding the corner, he almost runs into someone. It's her; the woman. She is waiting for him.

'Are you following me?' she asks, a quizzical smile on her face. She looks to be in her early thirties, she has thick, permed blonde hair, chin-length.

Fear renders Robin speechless. It's finally happened. The scenario he has dreaded. Caught by his intended victim. What is she going to do?

The woman looks Robin up and down, assesses what she sees.

'You're a shy one, aren't you?'

'Er... yes,' says Robin.

The woman stands under the streetlamp, swaying slightly. Robin suddenly realises she is very drunk.

'So, were you plucking up the courage to ask me out?' she says. 'Thought I might be the one for you, eh? The one you've been looking for?'

'I...'

That smile again; large, even teeth. Robin thinks it the most beautiful smile he has ever seen.

'Okay... Tell you what: there's a wine bar not far from here,' says the woman. 'Want to go there? We can have a chat!'

'A wine bar...?' hesitantly.

'Actually, yeah... You're not really dressed for a wine bar, are you?' she observes. 'Tell you what: let's just find a pub that's still open. How about that?'

'Okay...'

They find a pub that is still open. Robin walks as if in a dream. And then he finds himself sitting at a table with a drink in front of him, the woman sitting across the table from him. The woman's name is Sandra; she has just split-up with her boyfriend.

'Seven years we were together,' she says, sipping her gin and tonic. 'Then he leaves me for some air-head model barely out of her teens. Well, good luck to him. It won't last, and if he comes crawling back to me, I shall take great pleasure in telling him where he can go.'

'You wouldn't take him back...?'

'No way. He's had his chance. So... what about you, Robin? Ever had a girlfriend?'

'No...'

'Didn't think so, somehow—Sorry! That sounded mean. I mean, you're a good-looking boy and all that, but I can tell you're shy. A bit awkward socially, yeah? Don't make friends easily, right?'

'No...'

'What do you do with yourself? Got a job?'

'Yes... in an office...'

'Yeah, I work in an office, too. Who doesn't? So, where do you live? Are you still with your folks or have you got your own place?'

'I've got a flat...'

'Me, I still live in the pad I lived in with Frank... Still getting used to having the place to myself.'

They talk on. Naturally, Sandra does most of the talking. She's drunk and she's loquacious, and she carries the conversation, occasionally asking Robin a question. She talks about her interests, things she's seen on the news, and of course her ex-boyfriend often slips into the discourse.

Robin has always imagined that his ideal girl, when she turned up, would be a teenager. But here is a woman who's perhaps ten years his senior, who is friendly, understanding, humorous... And what's more, she actually seems to like him!

When it comes to last orders, she says: 'I know it's a trite line, but: do you want to come back to my place?'

Panic wells up in Robin. All the time he has been with her he has been painfully conscious of the heavy weight of the hammer in his jacket pocket. (He hasn't even dared to remove his coat.) How can he go back with her to her flat with that thing burning a hole in his pocket? What if she takes off his coat and feels the weight of it, or it falls out? He wants desperately to say 'yes' to her offer, but he just *can't*. Tears well up in his eyes. She'll take it as a rejection. He'll never see her again and he'll be back to where he started…

'It's okay if you don't want to…' says Sandra, sounding like she is wondering if she has misjudged her effect on Robin.

'No, I do want to, really… Just not tonight…'

Sandra brightens again.

'That's okay! I get you: don't want to rush you into anything, right? But, hey, let's meet up again soon. Shall we swap phone numbers?'

'Yes…!'

Chapter Thirty-Six
He Doesn't Look Like a Spy!

Dusk.

Mark finds himself treading the pavement a suburban street. He isn't sure how he has come to be here, but the street seems vaguely familiar. Lights show in the windows of some of the houses, but there is no movement, no noise. How long has he been walking? He can't remember. He hasn't seen a soul. There is something at the back of his mind. Vautrin. And Trudie. Hadn't he met them? Hadn't he been sitting, talking with them; talking about something important…?

Did that even happen? Or had he just imagined it?

Nothing is clear in his mind. Everything is jumbled up. Fragments of memories, fragments of dreams; past and present, reality and unreality; all intertwined. Concentrate. If he can just focus on something; something that has happened, a memory, an event; anything that he can recall with clarity… The raid on the Vallotec building. Yes, he remembers that. Joining forces with the SEA to shut down a particle accelerator and retrieve some solanite. And he had been betrayed. Sophie had shot him with a dart gun. What had happened after that? He can remember nothing… Could it be that nothing has happened? Could it be he is still unconscious under the effect of the tranquilliser dart? Is he dreaming? Will he wake up from all this soon?

And now he hears music, music emanating from somewhere nearby; a moment ago there had been silence. For as long as he can recollect, for an eternity it seems, all he has heard is the sound of his own footsteps. Now there is music. Classical music. Puccini, unless he is mistaken. It is coming from one of these houses. He stops. This is the house. There are lights in the front room, behind the drawn curtains. He knows this house. It means something to him, something important. Has he been here before?

Almost without willing it, he finds himself walking up the path to the front door of the house in which the music is playing. The door is unlocked and he walks straight in, somehow feeling that knocking on the door is not required. The music is louder now, coming from the open door on his left; the living room. He walks in. In the room are four teenagers, two boys, two girls, sitting on the floor around an open pizza box. They look round at Mark without surprise.

'Oh, you're here,' says one of the boys.

'Were you expecting me?' asks Mark.

'Of course we were, old Parsnip,' replies the boy. 'You don't mind if I call you Parsnip, do you, Mr Parsons? At school we only call you Parsnip behind your back, but I think here we can be a bit less formal.'

The other kids laugh.

Parsons? A school teacher? Why did they think he is this Parsons? These four kids; this room; he's seen them before. Images flash before his eyes. Photographs he's seen. Four corpses in a room splattered with blood. Of course! This is the house where Trudie Rayne had been forced to prostitute herself. These four kids are the ones behind it; Martin Hammond and his friends. But how can they be here? They're all dead. Trudie had killed them.

'Are you going to stand there all day?' inquires Martin. 'No need for cold feet. Nothing at all to worry yourself about, Parsnip, old son. We offer a very discreet service here. Nothing gets outside these four walls.'

Mark realises he is being addressed as a client. He'd always known that students from Trudie's school had been coming to this house. But some of the teachers, too…?

'Is Trudie here?'

'Well, of course she's bloody here! She's upstairs waiting. First door on the left, my man.'

Mark turns to the stairs.

'Ah, ah! Hang on a mo'. Haven't we forgotten something?'

'Sorry?'

'Payment in advance, Parsnip old son. One hundred quidlets, if you please.'

'A hundred?'

'I thought we'd already made that one crystal clear—You're a member of staff, so you're not qualified for the student discount. One hundred quidlets.'

Mark finds this whole scenario nauseating—but if Trudie Rayne is upstairs then he needs to see her. He reaches into his wallet and hands over five twenties.

Martin makes a show of counting the notes. 'J good, my man, J good! Up you go, then, old Parsnip. First door on the left.'

Mark ascends the stairs and opens the door indicated. The soft light of a table-lamp illuminates the room. Trudie sits up in bed, holding the silken covers over her chest.

'Hello,' she says, smiling at him.

Who does she think he is? Who is she seeing right now? Does she think he is this Mr Parsons? Whoever she sees, she seems pleased to see him. But perhaps this is just an affectation; part of the service…

'Do you know who I am?' he ventures.

Trudie giggles. ' 'Course I do. You're Mark Hunter, the International Man of Intrigue.'

Thank goodness.

Mark sits himself on the edge of the bed. 'You can see it's me, then? Those people downstairs—'

'—thought you were someone else? Yeah, they would. That's because you were never really here, were you?'

'I don't understand…'

'Don't worry about it! We're together now.'

'Did I see you earlier?'

'Don't you remember? If you think you saw me, then you saw me.'

'Did you bring me here?'

'You brought yourself here.'

'Are we in the past?'

'Past. Present. It's all the same in this place. Want to get into bed next to me?'

'No, I don't.'

'Why not? You've paid for it.'

'Somebody else paid. I just wanted to see you.'

'To talk? Okey-doke! I can do conversation—though that's normally just for the impotent clients. What d'you wanna talk about, then…? I know! Here's a good topic: the monogamy versus polygamy debate. I've been thinking about that one, recently. It'd be good to hear your views on the subject.'

'Monogamy and polygamy? What about it? Are we talking in terms of marriage or just sex?'

'Sex.'

'Okay; what do you want to know? Which one I prefer?'

'No, silly! I mean which do you think is the right one? Which one's most natural for human beings?'

Mark shrugs. 'That's a tough one to answer. It's different for different people, really. A subjective quantity. Different people have different attitudes; different codes of ethics… But if you want my personal opinion, I think that as a whole we human beings are possessed contradictory inclinations in both directions. And that would be what causes all the problems.'

'So, you don't think monogamy is unnatural, then? Something that's been drummed into us by religion?'

'No, I wouldn't say so... Even the religious creeds that advocate monogamy had to have got the idea from somewhere in the first place... I think a lot of people just have a perfectly natural desire to choose one person as their partner for life; to set up a home with them; start a family.'

'Yeah, but then one partner or the other usually ends up cheating, don't they?'

Mark smiles. 'Yes, it does seem to happen a lot. I suppose you could say that as human beings we just want to have our cake and eat it.'

'I think promiscuity's more natural,' declares Trudie firmly. 'Cuz you know, it's been proved that a woman's far more likely to get pregnant if she's inseminated by someone who's not her regular partner—a casual fuck. That's what I heard, anyway.'

'Yes, statistically that is true. That'll be because nature likes diversity in the gene-pool. But then there's sex for reproduction and there's also sex for love. Instinct and emotion both play a part in these things.'

'I think love emotions are fake! I think they're just the smart side of our brain trying to fight the animal instincts; dressing them up with emotions so they look better. It's just the reproduction urge; that's all it is... Even people who don't believe in love and say they just want sex for the sake of sex; it's still the reproduction urge that tells them that. The man just wants to shoot his load, and the woman just wants it inside her.'

Another smile. 'Well, if you're going to strip everything down to basics like that, then yes, I suppose all human behaviour could be reduced to the animal level—you could bring it all down to the commentary of a wildlife programme.'

Trudie laughs at this. 'Yeah! David Attenborough!'

She sits up in bed, folding her arms around Mark, nestling her cheek next his.

'You're different, though, aren't you?'

He can feel her warm breath on his neck.

'In what way?'

'I mean, you think about things. You don't just give in to your instincts all the time…'

'Well, I like to think so. But I'm not perfect. Even the best of us can do the wrong thing, sometimes.'

'And, do you still want to help me, Mark?'

'Well, yes, I do. And do you still think you don't need my help?'

'Yep. I'm fine, I am. See where we are now…This is my past; the life I had before. Don't you ever wonder why I ended up doing this?'

'Of course I've wondered, Trudie. From the fact that you killed them in the end, I assume those people downstairs were forcing you somehow; blackmail of some kind.'

Trudie sits back again. Mark looks at her.

'It's not as simple as that,' she says.

'I don't suppose it is,' says Mark.

'You see… I didn't just give in to them; it was me as well; I gave in to me… Y'see, it all started when they all ganged up on me in their clubroom at school and raped me; that's what they did… But, before that ever happened, I used to fantasize about being taken by force like that.'

Mark shrugs. 'A fantasy is a fantasy. It's safe. You're in control of it. Reality is another matter entirely. You shouldn't beat yourself up over something you fantasized about.'

'I know, but it seemed like I'd wished it on myself; like it was my punishment. You know: "This is what you get for thinking bad thoughts." That's how it seemed.'

'You felt guilty. Victims often try to think up reasons why whatever happened to them was their fault.'

'Yeah, but it wasn't just feeling guilty. I sort of stopped caring… When they told me what they had planned for me, and what they'd do if I didn't go along with it, I just submitted to it… I wanted to see… It was like I was being pushed down this slippery slope and I wanted to see what it would be like if I just kept on going down; right down to the bottom of the pit.'

'It sounds like you were losing your self-respect.'

'I dunno if it was even that. It was the weirdest feeling... I mean, I was carrying on my normal life, going to school and whatnot—living with Mum and Dad; but then I was doing all this as well... I had this secret life... So, what do you think, Mark? Think I was better off here doing this than where I am now?'

'Well, you have your freedom now; or at least you think you do... But where you are now—Vautrin, the SEA—don't you see that it can't last?'

'Why can't it last?'

'It just can't, Trudie. It's not possible. Something like the SEA is bound to self-destruct, and sooner rather than later.'

'Crap! Why should it?'

'It just will. Believe me. You're standing in a very shaky edifice, and I want to get you out of there before it all comes crashing down on top of you.'

Trudie leans in and hugs him again. 'Ah. You're sweet! But even if you were right, even if you could prove that the SEA was only going to last one more week, I'd stay with it for that week. I wouldn't bail out.'

'You have to think about the future sometimes, Trudie.'

'Do you?'

'Of course I do.'

'Then why d'you smoke? If you worried about the future, you wouldn't smoke.'

'That's not the same thing.'

'Yes it is! You live for the present just as much as we do. "You might get run over by a bus tomorrow" and all that... You want to help me, Mark? Or do you just want me...?'

Mark turns and embraces Trudie; a sudden, violent embrace. She pulls him down onto the bed.

Chapter Thirty-Seven

Non-Stop Fucking at the Chalet School

Now I don't know about you, but I think it's high time we paid a return visit to that sterling educational establishment for young ladies in the Swiss Alps, the famed Imrie Academy, and take a look in on its charming proprietress and headmistress. Cynthia Imrie.

We join Miss Imrie in her boudoir. You will perhaps not be surprised to hear that our champion of the education system is usually a late riser. There she is in her antique four-poster, under silk sheets, finally showing signs of life. She rolls lazily over in bed, pats the mattress, and seems surprised to find the bed unoccupied apart from her good self.

Comes a discreet knock at the door and, upon being bidden, a uniformed student enters, wheeling Cynthia's breakfast tray. It is a high honour in the school to be selected to wait hand and foot on the esteemed headmistress, so this particular student must have remembered to turn up for her lessons one day, or something equally remarkable. Cynthia sits up in bed, accepts a cup of tea.

'Thank you, Susan dear,' she says. 'And how are we today?'

'I'm very well, thank you, Miss Imrie. How are you?'

'Just peachy, darling. But I appear to be missing a man. Athletic type; plays tennis. You haven't seen him anywhere?'

Susan's face turns a charming shade of red.

'Well?' demands Cynthia, suspicion clouding her brow.

'I think Miss England wants to talk to you about that…'

Miss England is Cynthia's efficient secretary. In fact, so efficient is this young woman, that Cynthia, without fear or hesitation, leaves almost the entire running of the school to her. Miss England now enters, smartly dressed in blouse, skirt and jacket, ubiquitous memo tablet in her hand, superfluous pencil behind her ear. Her advent is greatly appreciated by Susan, who sees it as an opportunity to beat a hasty retreat.

'Good morning, Miss Imrie,' says the efficient one, in her crisp monotone.

'I'm beginning to suspect that it isn't,' replies Cynthia dryly. 'What's that wretch Benchley been up to?'

Miss England whispers a rapid report into the headmistress's ear. Her face darkens at the news.

'That... That...' She leaves the sentence hanging. Words have failed her. 'Have you got the culprits?'

'Waiting outside, Miss Imrie.'

'Then wheel them in—No. Just the girls first. I'll deal with *him*, afterwards.'

Cynthia climbs out of bed to greet the malefactors, wrapping her nude form in a frilly peach-coloured dressing-gown.

Three shamefaced students enter the room, ousing guilt from every pore; a cosmopolitan trio, one Swedish, one Indian, one Japanese. None of the girls can look directly at their headmistress. Eyes cast down, they wring their hands nervously.

Cynthia silently surveys them for a moment.

'Well, Ronja, Rajni, Risa... What do you have to say for yourselves? Speak up!'

Speak up they do; the first girl bursting into apologies, the second into prayers of contrition, the third into tears.

'Yes, yes, alright,' interrupts Cynthia. 'You can stop your wailing now. And wipe your nose, Risa. I thank you and accept your apologies; but nevertheless, you are still going to have to be punished. There is a line, young ladies, and you have all crossed it, as I'm sure you now realise. To milk a metaphor: you're welcome to my leftovers, but you can't help yourselves to the meal that's still on my table. Do we understand one another?'

More apologies, prayers and tears.

'Good! Now, you must take your punishment and let it be a lesson to you. Five of the best for each of you!'

The efficient Miss England has already arranged three chairs in a row. She has her cane ready. The girls meekly bend over these chairs, and tartan skirts are raised, undergarments are lowered.

'Proceed, Miss England.'

The Efficient One passes along the row and the three culpable and colour-coded posteriors—pink, brown and yellow—receive five whacks apiece, efficiently administered. The infliction of this condign punishment is taken in teeth-clenched silence by the malefactors, but unfortunately Risa, not so tightly-clenched elsewhere, is impelled to release a long and rippling flatulation, the aroma of which soon permeates the room.

Miss England, efficiently anticipating her mistress's wishes, briskly crosses to the window, opens the sash.

'Really, Risa!' protests Cynthia, holding her nose. 'Have you been eating raw fish again?'

The Japanese girl bursts into renewed tears.

'Alright, alright, for God's sake!' snaps Cynthia. 'I've half a mind to let you have five more for letting off that one, but then it would probably only make you fart again and we'd end up being here all day... Alright girls. Be off with you...' She waves a dismissive hand.

Heads bowed, and with awkward gait, the chastised girls depart.

Cynthia's face hardens. 'Now bring in the real culprit,' she tells her secretary.

Paul Benchley, budding tennis pro, fair-haired and rangy, enters the room. He smiles sheepishly.

'Hullo, Cynthie,' he greets her, briskly. 'Lovely morning, isn't it? Warm sun, fresh Alpine breeze coming down from the mountains...'

Smiling a smile that would have set off alarm bells in someone with more intelligence, Cynthia approaches Benchley.

'You've been a naughty boy, haven't you?'

'Ah! Well, you see...' chuckling sheepishly.

'You've been very naughty indeed, haven't you?'

'Well, you know...'

Cynthia playfully tugs Benchley's ear-lobe. Then she digs her long nails into it. Benchley cries out.

'You filthy little worm,' hisses Cynthia. 'Sneaking out of my bed at night and waltzing into the girls' rooms as though they were your own personal harem. Remind me who pays for your training?' She yanks the now bleeding ear-lobe. 'Well?'

'You do,' croaks Benchley.

'That's right. And I expect certain things in return. One of them is at least a semblance of fidelity while you're under my roof.'

She drags Benchley by the ear to the foot of the bed.

'Kneel.'

'Look, now, Cynthie darling—'

'Kneel, you cunt-chasing little shit!'

Benchley kneels.

Cynthia turns to her assistant. 'Miss England?'

The efficient one has the ropes ready, ties them round Benchley's wrists, and then secures them to the bedposts, leaving the sportsman with his arms stretched at full length.

'Cynthie, darling, can't we just talk about this...?' begs Benchley.

'Shut up.'

Miss England now takes hold of the tennis player's shirt, tears it open, exposing his back.

'Cynthie, darling...' repeats the unfortunate man.

Cynthia ignores him. 'Miss England? Begin.'

Brandishing the cane, the efficient secretary proceeds to belabour Benchley across the back. Again and again the blows rain down, raising welts, drawing blood, eliciting cries of agony.

'That'll do,' says Cynthia at length.

Miss England draws back, and Cynthia squats down beside the pain-wracked sportsman. 'Now, I hope you've learned your lesson, darling. And if anything like this ever happens again I shall instruct Miss England to break every finger in your right hand in such a way that will ensure that you'll never be able to hold a tennis racket again. Do we understand each other?'

'Yes...' gasps Benchley.

Cynthia rises, and at her signal Miss England unties his wrists.

'Now lie down here. I'll send the nurse in to patch you up; when I've finished my breakfast, of course.'

Benchley, wincing with pain, climbs to his feet. Casting a look of absolute terror at Cynthia, he flops facedown onto the bed.

Turning a deaf ear to the muffled moaning, Cynthia sits down on the edge of the bed, pours herself another cup of tea.

'Any appointments today?' she asks her secretary.

'Yes, Miss Imrie. Three new students arriving.'

'Ah, yes…!'

After breakfast and a leisurely bath, Cynthia dresses in her usual tweed suit and sets off through the school to her office. She exchanges friendly greetings with the girls gossiping in the corridors. Cynthia, in spite of her occasional severity, is a popular headmistress. In fact, the girls love her.

How has this one-time 'it' girl ended up running a school? Well, it came about like this:

The heiress of a magnate, Cynthia had in her youth led just the wild, dissolute life that was expected of someone of her station. She had spent lavishly: champagne, cocaine, cars, clothes, parties and jewellery. In short, she had unstintingly indulged herself in the approved way for those possessed of empty heads and bottomless purses. But then, one fine morning she suddenly realised she was approaching middle-age and that her purse wasn't so bottomless after all. Her lifestyle and her spending had suddenly caught up with her with a vengeance. Averse to the institution of marriage, she could have found herself a nice rich man to live off; she was acquainted with no shortage of them— but she soon discovered that those nice rich men were by now all looking for younger models than herself. In short, she was approaching that age in which, far from being able to get money from men, she would need to start spending money in order to *get* men.

And money was just what she didn't have.

Contemplating ways to make large amounts of money with the minimum of effort, Cynthia had hit upon the idea of opening a school for the daughters of the disgustingly rich (probably after recalling that she had once attended such an establishment herself.) There was always a demand for these institutions, what with there being no shortage of disgustingly rich people, many of them having daughters who required an education. Cynthia found a location ready-made; a school in Switzerland that had recently gone bankrupt and closed its gates. Advertising for a PA, Miss England had been amongst the first applicants, and a single interview was enough to convince Cynthia that she had found what she wanted. The girl was a treasure. Tremendously loyal, frighteningly efficient, and completely without morals. Miss England had taken charge of the hiring of the staff for the school, selecting from the applicants only people who shared hers and her mistress's lofty ideals and values. And so the Imrie Academy for Young Ladies was soon up and running, and—assisted by their contriving the ruination of several rival establishments—they had quickly become a success, with applicants flooding in from the four corners of the globe. (I think I may have mixed a metaphor here.)

And now, several years on, and things are still going swimmingly. Cynthia revels not only in her revenues and the pleasures for which they pay, but also in her glory as an educator; feeling a tremendous sense of job satisfaction from the knowledge that every girl who graduates from her academy does so having been fully indoctrinated in the lofty standards and ideals of the renowned Imrie Academy.

She now steps into her office, where three new girls are waiting. Cynthia sits behind her desk, and smiles at her new charges. They are three little Asian girls, their smooth faces encircled by the matching black burkas they wear. (Cynthia enforces no prohibition against burkas in her school, as much from appreciating their fetish value as from having no religious prejudices.) The girls sit very primly in their chairs, and regard their headmistress with polite curiosity. The uniformity of the trio is increased by the coincidence of their being exactly the same height. All have flawless café au lait complexions and limpid black eyes, the middle girl's framed with spectacles.

'Delighted to see you, darlings,' says Cynthia. She consults a clipboard. 'Now let me see... Widya, Bulan and Zetty, yes? So who's who?'

By a strange coincidence it now transpires that the three girls are seated in the same order (from left to right) in which Cynthia has just read out their names. The girls continue to regard the head-mistress with silent but profound interest as she proceeds to fit a cigarette into a holder and then ignite it.

'Now, I'm sure you're going to be very happy at our school,' resumes Cynthia. 'You will find that all our students are happy. I can see you're all a bit nervous, leaving your homes for the first time to stay in a new place, far away from your families and in a strange foreign country; but please don't fret. Everyone will make you feel welcome, and I can promise you you'll soon settle in and start to enjoy yourselves.

'Let me just tell you a few things... Just like all our girls, you are all disgustingly rich, so you do not require an education as a means to a career. For you, education is simply an adornment, knowledge, a social tool. I don't expect my girls to work too hard. Feel free to skip any lessons if you've got anything better to do. You're all bright, intelligent girls, so you ought to be able to achieve the maximum results with the minimum of effort.

'Here at the Imrie Academy, our main concern is your psychological and sexual development. Now I see from your records that all three of you have arranged marriages to look forward to when you have completed your education, so you really need to take full advantage of the freedom you will enjoy while you're here. You're pretty little things, and I wouldn't want to see you going to waste. This is a girls' only school of course, but there are plenty of fit young men down in the village who will be more than happy to service you. They'll put you through your paces and teach you the ins and outs of the whole business. Appertaining to this, the school nurse dispenses emergency contraception on demand, or she can fit you with a diaphragm if you prefer. And if an accident does occur and you find yourselves with a bun in the oven, there's no need to get yourselves in a tizzy: our nurse is also a fully-qualified abortionist. Aside from the village bucks, you can of course also enjoy the other girls as much as you like. Now I know this sort of thing may be against the rules where you three ladies come from, but you don't have to abide by silly rules like that; certainly not while you're in my care. You will each find in your bedside cabinets an assortment of sex aids, which can of course be used both for lesbian activities with your fellow-students and for individual self-gratification.

'You see, my dears, as you embark on life, you will find that sex is the be-all and end-all. It is the most intense form of pleasure going and it is also a useful tool for getting whatever you want from a man. Life, my dears, is all about what you can get out of it, and it is the noble aim of this school to start you out as you should mean to go on: living exclusively for pleasure and the gratification of the senses, healthy in mind and body.

'And for you, Widya, Bulan and Zetty, my especial aim for you is to send you all back home to your arranged marriages fully experienced in all sexual activities and fit to perform your conjugal duties to the satisfaction of both yourselves and your husbands—as well as hopefully being as well-versed in all the lies and deception pertaining to covert promiscuous sex that you will be able to revenge yourselves on those despotic husbands of yours if you so choose, by presenting them with sons and daughters sired by insemination from other men's penises...'

'Well!' concludes Cynthia, taking a long breath, and sitting back in her chair; 'I think that's covered everything you need to know! Any questions?'

The expressions on the three burka-framed faces have remained motionless during this lengthy spiel, with the one notable difference that the eyes fixed attentively upon the headmistress are now as wide as saucers.

Chapter Thirty-Eight
For Sale: One Ex-Spy, in Reasonable Condition

A lavish bar with lavish prices. The prevailing colour is mauve: mauve carpets and upholstery, mauve lighting multiplied and repeating itself in mirrored walls. Mark Hunter sits alone nursing his seventh scotch on the rocks. He can feel the effects of the drink, but being blessed with a high tolerance, he is not especially drunk. He doesn't feel any happier for his potations, just a comfortable melancholy.

Mark has been thrown out on his ear—suspended indefinitely. His complete lack of success with reference to the SEA Affair has earned him the disapprobation of the government, of his superiors, and of public opinion. He has failed to thwart any of the group's attacks. He has failed to find their headquarters. (No-one believes him about the house on the Sussex Downs.) He had captured five of the terrorists and after having them in custody and under interrogation, he had allowed them escape. (No mention of the fact that they had initially been abducted at the behest of Rufus Wainwright.) He has failed to positively identify the SEA leader. (Wild theories concerning him dismissed.)

And last of all, his crowning folly. He had liberated some illicitly acquired solanite from a private corporation, only to let it be stolen from his hands by members of the same SEA. A long list of failures. And his failures are the reigning government's failures. It is the government who takes ultimate responsibility. It is the government who has to answer to the public. Net result: Mark Hunter is off the case and suspended without pay.

'Mind if I join you?'

Mark looks up for his introspection. The woman is thirtyish, chestnut hair elegantly styled, dressed in an expensive suit.

Mark smiles ruefully.

'I'm afraid I won't be very good company,' he warns her.

'Oh? And why's that? Down in the dumps?' asks the woman. 'That's what I thought. Sitting there on your own, staring into your glass. Maybe I can help cheer you up?'

'You're welcome to try.'

She slides into the chair opposite Mark. She places her handbag on the table, wafting the scent of her expensive perfume towards him.

'I'm Lucinda.'

'Mark.'

'Just Mark?'

'Mark Hunter?'

'And what are you so sad about, Mark Hunter? Woman trouble?'

'Nope. I'm currently unattached. Work-related.'

'Your job getting you down?'

'You could say that. Suspended without pay.'

'What is your job?'

A rueful smile. 'Believe it or not, I'm a spy.'

'Seriously?'

'Seriously.'

'Well, this is a first. I've met all sorts, but I've never met a real spy before. I suppose you're going to tell me now that the spy work's not as glamorous as it's cracked up to be…?'

'Well, it's not always glamorous, but it has its moments.'

'And what did you do to get yourself suspended?'

'Gross incompetence.'

'Oh. Are you not very good at being a spy?'

'I thought I was good at it until recently. But my latest case has been a disaster from start to finish.'

'What sort of case? Are you allowed to tell me?'

'You wouldn't believe the truth if I told you.'

'Try me. I'm intrigued.'

The woman's smile is warm and inviting. Everything about her is warm and inviting.

'Okay, then. What if I were to tell you that that spate of recent terrorist attacks, from the *Apprentice* massacre to the hospital bombings, were carried out by a bunch of teenage girls?'

A rich laugh. 'I would say you were having me on.'

'Well, I'm not.'

'The papers say anarchists are responsible for those attacks.'

'That's what the papers say. The full story has been suppressed thus far. I think there are even people in the government who just *prefer* not to believe it; they'd like some more realistic culprits to be presented to the clamouring public.'

'Well, could you be wrong about this bunch of teenage girls? Perhaps they're just cranks; you know, claiming to do things they actually haven't done.'

Mark shakes his head. 'Oh, no. They're definitely the culprits. I'm sure of that much.'

'Are they anarchists, these girls?'

'Well, that's a word that means different things to different people. People often say "anarchy" when what they actually mean is "chaos" or "disruption." Anarchy is a political system. These girls I'm talking about have no politics; they just like causing chaos. But in putting out the story that the perpetrators are anarchists—well, it's close enough to the truth not to be an outright lie.'

'But still; schoolgirl terrorists. That's pretty hard to believe. Where do schoolgirls get guns and bombs from? Where do they get the money?'

'That we don't know. One of the girls happens to be very rich, so she may be supplying the funds; but the girls are led by a man. I think he must have access to money, although where *he* gets it from, I don't know.'

'And who is this man?'

'Oh, he's a complete mystery. He just appeared out of nowhere.'

Mark signals a waiter and orders fresh drinks for them both.

'So, what do you do, Lucinda? Judging from your clothes it's something well-paid.'

'I'm the director of a textiles corporation. Not as exciting as being a spy, but yes, it pays well.'

'Well, I have my excuse for being here on my own; what's yours?'

Lucinda laughs. 'That's easily answered: I was looking for a man.'

'And do you normally go about it this way? Just walk into some likely establishment and start looking around?'

'As a matter of fact, yes: that *is* how I go about it. I'm not one for long-term relationships; not at the moment, anyway. When it comes to lovers, I like variety. So yes, I look around a bar or a club, and if I see a man and I like the look of him, I start talking to him. If I still like him after I've heard enough to make my mind up about his character, I invite him back to my place.'

'You're very direct. And I imagine your success rate is much higher than it would be if the genders were reversed.'

'Yes, I have the advantage there. I've yet to meet a man who has declined my offer once I've made my mind up that I like him.'

'And what about me? Where do I stand? Have you made your mind up about me?'

'I have, and I like you very much, Mark.'

Mark sips his drink.

'Would you still like me if I declined going back to your place?'

'I'd be disappointed. I pride myself on understanding people. I think that what you need right now is a change; something new. I think I could be that something new. I'd like to make you happy if I can, Mark, even if it's only for tonight.'

'That's very kind of you, but—'

Lucinda takes his hand, fixes his gaze with her own. In this mauve light, he can't discern the colour of her eyes. 'I'm serious, Mark. If I left you now, you'd just stay here and drink yourself into a stupor and be even more miserable. Don't punish yourself like this. Come home with me.'

Mark finds himself accepting. They talk some more, finish their drinks, and leave.

'Make yourself at home.'

Mark sits on the sofa, while Lucinda goes to fix them drinks. The flat is one of a luxury block; the spacious living room has a cream colour-scheme: wall, carpet, soft furniture, curtains, all in shades of cream. By contrast, the wooden furniture, book cases, cabinets, tables, are all dark mahogany.

Lucinda returns with the drinks, seats herself beside Mark. He sips his scotch, picks up a paperback book from the coffee table.

'Ah, *The Maias*! The masterpiece of Portuguese naturalism. Do you read a lot?'

'Quite a bit, but this is my first Eça de Quieroz. I'd never got round to reading him before. Have you read many of his, then?'

'Most of them, I think.'

'Any others you would recommend?'

'I'd say they're all worth reading. *The Tragedy of the Street of Flowers* is interesting because Eça abandoned it after the first draft and wrote *The Maias* instead, as a sort of replacement. *Street of Flowers* ended up not being published until the 1980s, when the author's copyright expired.'

'Are the two books similar, then?'

'Well, the stories both have a central incest theme, but otherwise, no.' Mark brings himself up short. 'Oops! Have I just blurted a spoiler?'

Lucinda laughs. 'No, you haven't. I'd guessed they were brother and sister.'

'Oh good. I didn't want to ruin the whole book for you...' He sits back on the sofa.

'Anything wrong?'

'I suddenly feel very tired,' says Mark. He rubs his forehead. 'I don't know what's coming over me... Can you take my glass? I feel like I'm about to drop it...'

Lucinda takes the glass, puts it down on the table. She regards Mark intently. He meets her gaze blearily.

'You've drugged me, haven't you?'

'Yes.'

'Fatal?'

'No. It will just send you to sleep.'

'Why?'

'Because that's what my employer wants.'

'Employer?'

'Yes, I'm afraid I lied to you about my vocation, Mark: I'm not a company director; I'm a prostitute. I was hired to pick you up and bring you back here.'

'By whom?'

'Me.'

Rufus Wainwright stands in the bedroom doorway. He crosses the living room, confronts Mark, grim satisfaction written on his granite features.

'Wainwright…'

'Yes, Rufus Wainwright; the man you thought you could fuck around with and get away with it. Well, you're going to disappear, Hunter… I've been waiting for this. I hated your guts from the moment you first walked into my office, and you've done nothing but fuck me around. You've come between me and my daughter, you've threatened me in my own office and now you've stolen the solanite material that cost me a small fortune to get my hands on.'

'Well, as for the solanite, it was the SEA girls who ran off with that. I'm sure if you ask your daughter nicely, she'll give it back—'

Wainwright punches Mark in the face.

'Shut up. There's a vat of quick-lime waiting for you in the truck downstairs. It's how I dispose of people who I want to disappear permanently. But before that, I'm going to take some personal revenge. It'll be a while before that drug sends you to sleep, and I'm going to make sure you hurt a lot before you pass out.'

He punches Mark in the face again. After this, he drags him off the sofa and onto the floor. He commences kicking Mark, who weakly tries to shield himself.

'You smug, smart-mouthed piece of shit,' grates Wainwright, punctuating his words with kicks. 'Humiliating me in my own office; making me look a laughing-stock to my competitors. Do you know how much it cost me to get hold of that solanite? And what have I got to show for it? Nothing!'

Mark, protecting himself from the blows as best he can, feels as weak as a kitten. He can hardly move his arms; he feels a weight pressing down on his head.

Then the front door bursts open. Horizontally, Mark sees Juliette Wainwright and Dizzy Hello enter dramatically, guns pointing.

'Leave him alone, father,' commands Juliette.

'You?'

'Yes, me. Move over to the settee…'

Dizzy squats down beside Mark. Her concerned face swims in and out of focus.

'Don't worry about him anymore,' she says. 'You just go to sleep…'

Mark struggles back to consciousness.

Fragments of dreams swim in and out of focus, entangling themselves with returning memory. He smells carpet; he is lying on a carpeted floor. He has a racking headache. He feels nauseous. His body announces several centres of pain; one side of his face is swollen. He remembers Lucinda. The drugged drink. Wainwright kicking him. The two SEA girls bursting in…

He scents blood. Sitting up, he soon perceives the cause: Across the room, Rufus Wainwright, lashed to a wooden chair, head sunk on chest, mutilated and dead. Rising unsteadily, wincing at the pain in his head, Mark staggers over to the corpse. The clothes are in shreds, the body a mass of cuts and burn marks. The eyes and genitals have been removed and lie in a sticky pile on the carpet.

Juliette had said that the next time she saw her father would be to kill him. She has certainly kept her word… Mark remembers the reports of a ski instructor, found tortured to death in the vicinity of the Imrie Academy…

Lucinda he finds behind the sofa. The girls have spared

Lucinda the fate of her employer; they've been kind to her; they have just shot her neatly between the eyes.

Mark staggers to the kitchen, gulps down a glass of water. He decides it will be a good idea to remove himself from the vicinity of this apartment before the police arrive.

Chapter Thirty-Nine
Sophie's Choice

It is difficult to trace the origins of Sophie Harris's Unfortunate Condition (to use the formal terminology.) It only manifested itself for the first time fairly recently, but it may well have been lying dormant for some time. The symptoms of an Unfortunate Condition are such that they will only make themselves felt in certain very specific circumstances; for the remainder of the time the sufferer is able to lead a fairly normal existence.

If I had to hazard a guess, I would suggest that, as in the case of Jessica Harper's condition of chronic clumsiness and ill-luck, that Sophie's Unfortunate Condition came into being with the commencement of the menstrual cycle.

Sophie Harris is a well-balanced girl from a comfortable middle-class background. Her parents had divorced when she was a little girl and since then she has lived with her mum and younger sister. She attends an all-girls' public school, in which she is a well-liked student; not one of the 'in' crowd, but not a social misfit either. She performs well in class and at sports. In appearance she is a tall girl with an athletic figure, her black hair cut in a 1920s style bob.

It never occurs to her until later, but the fact is that Sophie has never been completely alone with just one member of the opposite sex. Perhaps not a remarkable fact for a girl who lives in an all-female household, attends and all-girls' school and doesn't socialise with boys outside of school hours; but nevertheless, for Sophie this fact turns out to be a very significant one—because the first outbreak of her Unfortunate Condition happens one day at school, when she is called to have a meeting with the careers advisor. The careers advisor is a man.

Sophie sits in the careers advisor's outer office, engrossed in her smartphone as she awaits her turn. The previous girl has just come out and returned to her lessons. The secretary seated at her desk politely ignores Sophie's abuse of the school rules with regard to the use of smartphones during lesson time.

The door opens, and the careers advisor, Mr Hastings, appears. Bald-headed, paunchy and middle-aged, he is not the stuff of schoolgirl fantasies. In her own mind, Sophie instantly dismisses him as old, boring and conventional.

'Come in, Sophie.'

She follows him into the inner office, takes a seat.

Mr Hastings, once ensconced behind his desk, launches into his well-rehearsed spiel regarding career paths, citing her interests and academic skills as pointers. Sophie replies automatically. She hasn't decided on a career as yet, planning to attend university after leaving school. Frankly, her mind is more occupied with an interesting conversation she has been having on Messenger: a dialogue with a Filipino girl of her own age and who shares her love of anime.

And then it hits her. Without warning, it rushes over her like a tidal wave. Her pulses race, her breathing comes rapidly and she feels a burning between her legs. She jams her hands between them, her legs squirming. Jesus Christ! She has never felt so aroused! Her body demands just one thing and demands it imperatively: penetration by a man. Nothing else matters now. Her education, her career—not even anime matters right now. She needs sexual intercourse with a man. She *must* have sexual intercourse with a man.

And there is a man before her. Yes, he is a bald, pot-bellied man, but still a man, and as such has the equipment with which to satisfy her imperative need. Her mind cries out that this is insane, that she can't do this; but her organism will not be denied, and the primal scream of instinct overwhelms the paltry voice of intellect.

Sophie starts tearing off her clothes.

'Take me! For God's sake, take me!' she yells, tears streaming down her face.

'What are you doing?' squeaks Mr Hastings, horrified.

She is naked before him, legs spread in the M position, hands pulling apart the lips of her distended vagina.

'Please!' she begs 'Just take me! Take me!'

'Stop this!' screeches Mr Hastings. 'I'm a married man! I have a daughter nearly your age!'

'I don't care! I don't want to marry you! Just take me, for Christ's sake! This feeling's killing me!'

Mr Hastings yells for the secretary. The secretary rushes into the room. For Sophie, the woman's advent acts like a switch being thrown. Her insane sexual desire evaporates in a moment. She is herself again. Frozen in her girlie magazine pose, she looks from the horrified Mr Hastings to the incredulous secretary. Then, with a shriek, she curls herself up in a ball.

Sophie is sent to see the school nurse. The female nurse is sympathetic, speaks of sudden hormonal rushes, frequent in adolescence, and discreetly advises Sophie to masturbate more often.

This humiliating incident is successfully hushed up by the school and Sophie attempts to put it behind her. Apart from anything else, she is mortified with the thought that she could have been so desperate as to offer herself up to someone like Mr Hastings! Well, it will never happen again. An orgasm last thing at night, another first thing in the morning, and she will be fine.

Unfortunately for Sophie, she won't. No amount of self-gratification can cure an Unfortunate Condition.

As has already been mentioned, Sophie is an anime fan, an otaku. And the chief reason why Sophie doesn't get out much outside of school hours is because she does all her socialising online. She has no like-minded friends at school, but thanks to Facebook she has literally thousands of online friends who share her passion. They exist all over the world these otaku girls, and they form their own cliques on Facebook, often identifying themselves to other otaku by using images of anime characters as their profile pictures. Sophie has friends from all over the world, from India to Argentina, from Kenya to Cambodia. One thing these girls have in common is their single-minded devotion to anime, and disdain of all other visual entertainment forms.

Although there does exist anime geared towards a female viewership, Sophie, like most of her FB friends, has somewhat tomboyish tastes and generally prefers the male-oriented material, fanservice and all.

And of course some of the 'girls' she befriends on FB turn out to be fakers, as Sophie usually discovers when they send her pictures of their very male genitalia on Messenger. Some of the girls like to name and shame these internet pervs when they get sent dick-pics, but Sophie just contents herself with blocking them.

Why, she often wonders, do guys think you'll fall in love with them just from seeing a selfie of their boner? Girls don't really care how big a cock is if they don't like the guy it's attached to; and Sophie cannot help but think that the kind of guy who sends her dick-picks is not going to be the kind of guy she would like to get to know. But so many of them seem to do it! And people say that it's women who like to flaunt their bodies. Well, clearly men are just the same, except that with them it's just one particular part of their bodies that they love to flaunt.

On this half-term morning, Sophie sits at her laptop in her room, busily social-networking, when the front door-bell rings. She goes to answer it. The caller is James, Mum's new boyfriend. James is black and is a lawyer like her mother.

'Oh, hello!' says Sophie. 'Mum's not here, but she should be back soon. She's just taken Wendy to the doctors.' (Wendy being Sophie's younger sister.) 'Come in and wait.'

James sits himself on the sofa and Sophie stands awkwardly before him wondering if she can return at once to her bedroom and her social-networking, or whether courtesy demands she ought to stay and entertain the guest.

And then it happens.

An intolerable feeling of sexual desire takes hold of her, hijacking her body, her mind, her senses. Just like that last time.

'Oh, no! Not again, please!'

She bursts into tears.

'What's wrong, Sophie?' asks James, concerned.

'I'm sorry!' wails Sophie, frantically pulling her clothes off.

'What are you doing?' alarmed.

'I'm sorry! I can't help it, really I can't!'

Naked, she straddles James's lap, starts tugging at his trouser fly.

'Hey! Stop that!'

'I can't!' blubbers Sophie. She pulls out his penis.

'Cut that out! What are you—?'

Dismayed and unwilling though James may be, Sophie still has no problem manipulating his treacherous penis to tumescence.

'I'm sorry! I'm really, really sorry!' moans Sophie, as she deftly lowers herself onto the ramrod straight erection…

She pounds him, she screams, she comes, he comes, she comes again. And they are the most dizzying orgasms Sophie has ever experienced. Spent, she falls into his arms.

Then comes the reaction: with a sudden shriek, she leaps off him, grabs her clothes from the floor and scampers up to her bedroom.

Neither of them mentions the incident. News of it never reaches Sophie's mother. James acts as if nothing happened—seeking neither an explanation or a repeat performance. But Sophie's mind is in a turmoil. Torturing her mind for an explanation, she has arrived at a horrible conclusion. First Mr Hastings, and now James. Those two situations, those two outbreaks, had one key element in common: on both occasions she was alone in a room with a man. And from this she comes to the realisation that those two occasions are actually unique in her life; that she has never before been in a room alone with just one man! She can't even think of a time this has happened in her earliest childhood, and it definitely hasn't in her recent, adolescent years...

Then that must be it. Somehow, for some strange reason, she can't be in a room alone with a member of the opposite sex without losing all control of her body! But that's ludicrous! Whoever heard of that happening? What could be wrong with her? Is she a nymphomaniac? Is it her reproductive urge gone completely haywire?

One thing is certain. She will have to make sure that those fatal conditions are never allowed to occur again; she has to make sure that she will never let herself be alone in a room with a man again.

Time passes. Sophie becomes—like Haruhi Suzumiya—melancholy. In response to inquiries from family and schoolfriends, she always answers that nothing was wrong. She can't tell anyone about her condition; she just can't—not even to her closest confidants; those far-flung friends with whom she communicates online.

But then comes an exciting event which serves to lift her spirits; something new and exciting in her life. Dad has come back to England with his new Australian wife! They have settled in a nearby town, so that the father can be near to his children. She hasn't seen her father since she was six, but she still remembers him.

They come to visit.

It is evening. Sophie feels eager but nervous. She sits in the front room with Mum and Wendy. (James is tactfully not present.) The arrivals are expected imminently.

They hear a car pull up outside.

'It's them!' squeaks Wendy.

'Oh God...'

'Just relax, Sophie!' says Mum. 'It's only your father.'

A knock at the door. Mum answers it.

He looks the same, is Sophie's first thought. Just a bit older, but basically the same. The brown hair, the beard, are just she remembers them. Her greatest surprise is that he isn't much taller than her. She had for some reason imagined that he would still be towering over her, as he did in her childhood recollections.

He is cordial with Mum; he introduces his new wife. Sophie searches for signs of that awkwardness you expect to find between ex-spouses. But no; they seem to be perfectly at ease with each other.

'Hello, Dad,' she says, offering her hand.

'My God, look at you! You're all grown up!' he exclaims, shaking her hand warmly. 'You were still a little girl when I last saw you.'

'I'm growing up, too!' chips in Wendy.

'You sure are, sweetheart,' agrees Dad. 'You were just a toddler last time I saw you.'

Soon they are all sat down, talking amiably: how the girls were getting on at school; what life was like out in Australia… Right now, at this moment, Sophie feels happy. But there is still that something nagging at the back of her mind; that something she can never tell anyone about.

It has been agreed that the girls will spend a weekend with their father and step-mother. And so, on Friday after school, Dad and Stella arrive to pick them up.

'Your mother says you like Japanese cartoons,' says Stella to Sophie, as they drive along. She sits beside her husband while Sophie and Wendy share the back seat.

'Yes, I love them,' confirms Sophie.

'Hey, aren't those things pornographic?' blurts out Dad, concerned.

'Dad!' protests Sophie, laughing. '*Some* of them are, but I don't watch those ones.'

'I'm glad to hear it!' says Dad.

'And what do you like, Wendy?' asks Stella.

'I like *Hollyoaks*!' announces Wendy, proudly.

They arrive at Dad's house, a spacious bungalow on a new estate. The spare bedroom has been fitted with two beds in readiness for the sisters. After being shown the room, Sophie has to excuse herself; she desperately needs the toilet and she hadn't had time to go before they set out. Enthroned, she contemplates the weekend ahead with pleasure. It feels so good to finally see her father again after all these years, and her step-mother seems really nice.

When she has finished, Sophie returns to the bedroom, starts unpacking her bag. Dad comes in.

'Is the room alright, then?'

'It's great, Dad,' assents Sophie. 'Where's Wendy?'

'She's gone with Stella to the supermarket,' answers Dad. 'Stocking up with supplies for the weekend.'

Sophie's heart drops like a stone. Stella and Wendy have gone. They are alone; just her and her dad. She is alone in the same room with a man. Oh, not now. Please, not now. Not here.

The intolerable feeling floods over. She bursts into tears. She pulls her clothes off.

'What on earth are you doing, Sophie?' demands Dad, aghast. 'What's wrong? Are you ill?'

Crying, she throws herself on the bed; Daddy's little girl who isn't a little girl any more.

'Take me, Dad!' she wails. 'For Christ's sake, take me!'

And the poor weak fool; he does just that!

Afterwards, she runs. She just pulls on her clothes and flees the house.

Her father. Her own father. And it was her fault! She had made him do it.

In her wretchedness, it doesn't occur to Sophie to attach any blame to her father; she only blames herself. She had made him do it. She is the one with something wrong inside; she is the abnormal one.

It is now dusk. She leaves the estate behind, and running blindly, finds herself on the periphery of the new town, and then out onto a quiet country road. She only stops when she arrives at a level crossing.

She can't go back. There is no way she can go back to that. She looks at the railway tracks. She has not come here by design; she didn't know she would find a level crossing here; but now that she is here, it feels like she been brought here by fate—she knows what she has to do; she knows there is only one way out of all this.

'It's not the only answer, you know.'

She spins round at the sound of this sudden voice from nowhere breaking into, and contradicting, her thoughts. A man and a girl. The man looks like a retro pop star; the girl younger, pretty, with short, blonde hair.

'Who are you?' she demands. 'What's not the only answer?'

'Throwing yourself in front of a train is not the only answer,' says the man.

'And who says I was going to?' demands Sophie.

The man smiles. 'An educated guess. You've just committed incest with your own father, so you are understandably confused and distraught.'

'How the hell do you know that?' screeches Sophie.

'I know everything about you, Sophie Harris,' replies the man. 'I've been taking an interest in you for some time.'

'I've never met you before. How could you…?'

'I know how you feel,' speaks up the girl. 'I was freaked out when Vautrin first walked into my life. That's his name, Vautrin; and I'm Dizzy. Vautrin turned up out of the blue just after my mum had died, and I was feeling like you are now. And he knew everything about me, as well. He came to help me. And now we're here to help you, just the same.'

'Nobody can help me,' declares Sophie, wretchedly.

'That's just where you're wrong,' says Vautrin. '*I* can help you.'

'How? I've just fucked my own father, for Christ's sake!'

'I know, and you're entirely blameless. *He's* the guilty one. You were compelled to offer yourself up to him. He wasn't compelled to accept.'

'You... you know what's wrong with me...?'

'Yes. You have a condition. Extremely rare—in fact it's a condition that has yet to even be recognised by medical science. But don't worry; there is a cure, and I happen to be in possession of it.'

'But if medical science...'

'With all due modesty, I know a few things medical science doesn't. What you suffer from I like to call an Unfortunate Condition. You do not do what you do because you are hypersexual or immoral—you have an illness.'

'Is that true?' asks Sophie.

'Yes.'

'And you can cure me?'

'Yes. And all I ask for in return is that you come with us.'

'Come with you?'

'That's right. It's for the best, really. You can't really go back to that mess you've just left behind, can you? Even as we speak your father is lying to his wife and your sister—telling them he doesn't know where you've gone, what could have prompted you to run away...'

'Vautrin's offering you a completely new life,' says Dizzy. 'A new start. We've got this place, you see—a secret base. There's a bunch of us girls there and it's awesome; the place has got *everything*. You can watch all the anime you want! You'll love it, I'm telling you!'

'You're both mad! A secret base...?'

Dizzy chuckles. 'I know it sounds crazy, but it's true! We're a sort of club. Vautrin's brought us together. It's like we were supposed to be together or something, but until now, we weren't.'

This is insane. How can she believe these two? And yet they know everything about her; and there is something compelling about them...

Behind her, the crossing barriers descend, the warning lights start to flash.

'Ah! There's a train coming,' says Vautrin. 'I think this is a good time to come to a decision. The choice is yours, Sophie: you can either throw yourself in front of the train, or you can come with us.'

The rattle of the approaching express.

Sophie makes her choice.

Chapter Forty
The Spy Who Stayed in With a Cold

The search for the SEA terrorists is ongoing. The culprits remain as elusive as ever. And as active. So far not a single attack has been successfully anticipated or thwarted. The group's latest offences, almost commendable in their diversity and inventiveness, include taking control of and disrupting traffic signals in the busiest areas of London, causing crossroad lights to turn simultaneously green for traffic and pedestrians, resulting in dozens of fatalities... Fake mail-outs have been circulated; delivered to seemingly random addresses, the mail-outs informing the householders that they are the lucky winners of £20,000, which they will receive on proceeding to a specified address; eager applicants who arrive at these addresses have 10-ton weights dropped on them as they walk in through the door... The distribution of exploding golf balls amongst consignments sent to clubs all around the country has led to an alarming nationwide shortage of dental surgeons...

The public are clamouring for the apprehension of the miscreants.

Daisy Fontaine knocks on the door of the apartment. No answer. She tries the door, finds it unlocked and walks in. She finds her partner, Mike Collins, snoring in his bed. The room is stuffy and close. She opens the curtains and the window. Then she crosses to the kitchen and puts the kettle on. In the sink lies a mountain of unwashed crockery. She rinses out a mug and a pint glass, filling the latter with cold water. Into the mug goes a generous tea-spoon of coffee and a splash of milk. The kettle boils, and she adds the water. Armed with the mug and the glass, she returns to the bedroom, places them on the bedside table. She shakes her partner awake.

Collins groans, rubs his eyes, sits up in bed, eyes his partner with groggy disfavour.

'Whadda you want?' he mumbles.

Grinning Fontaine hands him the pint of tap water.

'Personally: nothing,' she says. 'If it was up to me, I'd let you snore your head off all day. But our great white chief has summoned us.'

Collins makes his favourite noise, chugs down the water.

'How can you be so chirpy?' he wants to know. 'You were knocking it back as much as I was last night.'

'Yes, but I wasn't drinking beer, was I? It's not the alcohol that gives you a stinking hangover—it's all the other crap they put in beer. Anyway, I remembered to drink my two pints of water before going to bed; I bet you didn't.'

'Can't remember.'

Fontaine passes him the coffee mug. 'Shall I get the painkillers? Or will rehydration and caffeine be enough?'

'I'll tell you when I've finished this,' drinking the coffee.

The two field agents make their way through the midday traffic, Fontaine at the wheel of their Ford Capri.

The radio beeps. 'Control to 3-4. You are overdue for briefing.'

Collins picks up the mike. '3-4 here. We're on our way in. We got caught in traffic. Out.'

Fontaine and Collins do not like Lennox.

Lennox has taken over the SEA case since the suspension of Mark Hunter. Lennox is a proud product of the public-school system, a card-carrying member of the Old Boys' Network: arrogant, authoritative, unpleasant, and—as Fontaine has delicately observed—'born with a silver-spoon up his arse.'

'You're forty minutes late,' are his first words as Fontaine and

Collins walk into the office. His conspicuous nose is today conspicuously red; his enunciation congested.

'Sorry, guv. Traffic,' explains Fontaine.

'Sorry, *sir*,' corrects Lennox. 'The reason I've called you in is that I want a renewed effort to locate the SEA headquarters.'

'You want us to stake-out that farmhouse in Sussex?' queries Fontaine.

'No, I don't! That was a false lead.'

'But, Mr Hunter thought—'

'I don't care what "Mr Hunter thought"!' He blows his nose violently. ' "Mr Hunter" is no longer in charge of this investigation; I am in charge. That house has been searched from top to bottom; no sign of occupancy, and no sign of any entrance to any alleged underground base. The whole idea is ridiculous.'

'Yeah but, that scientist, Herriot said—'

'The man was delirious by all accounts. And again, we only have Hunter's word for what he said.'

'Dodo Dupont was there as well,' points out Daisy Fontaine.

'Ah, yes! That television woman: Hunter's accomplice. I don't approve of amateurs becoming involved in Department business; she hasn't even signed the Official Secrets Act! No, I don't believe in this underground base. This group's headquarters must be somewhere here in London. Nearly all of their attacks have been centred on the capital: so, it stands to reason, doesn't it?'

'Yeah, but if their main base is right here in London, then why have they got all those temporary safe-houses scattered about the place?' queries Collins.

'To mislead us, obviously!' blowing his nose. 'But those safehouses could lead us to the main base. How many of them do we know of?'

'Ten, known or suspected.'

'Then here's your assignment: I want you to investigate all ten of those locations. Find out if any of them are currently being used.'

Once again, Lennox blows his sore nose, his watery eyes shedding water.

'That seems like a pretty bad cold you've got,' remarks Collins. 'I'd take the rest of the day off if I were you.'

Lennox glares at him. 'Thank you for your kind concern, Mr Collins; but I am well able to make those decisions for myself. You just get on with *your* job.'

'What job is that?'

'The safe-houses, you ape! You're to check them all out!'

'That'd be a waste of time, sir,' cautions Fontaine. 'They never go back to a safehouse once we get to know about it.'

'And how do you know that until you've checked them all out?' demands Lennox.

'But I just don't think—'

'I don't care what you think, Fontaine. You and your associate here are nothing more than grunts for the Department; you are paid to do the legwork, not to question orders—now get on with it!'

'Yes, guv.'

'Yes, *sir!*'

'What a fucking tosser,' remarks Daisy Fontaine as they drive along.

Collins grunts. 'I know. "Come back Mark Hunter; all is forgiven."'

'Yeah.'

'And now we've got to check all these bloody safehouses,' says Collins. 'Total waste of time.'

'I've got a better idea,' says Fontaine.

'What?'

'Perfect.'

'What's perfect?'

'Hunter's informer. He put us onto a lot of those safehouses in the first place. I reckon we should go'n see him. He might know about something new.'

'Yeah. Worth a try.'

It is a greasy-spoon café. The puny, popeyed, nervous-looking man sits at a table consuming a plate of sausages, beans and chips. He wolfs his food down as though fearful of having the plate snatched away from under his nose at any moment. He nearly jumps out of skin when the craggy-faced man and the small, short-haired woman sit down opposite him.

'Relax, Perfect,' says Fontaine. 'You remember us?'

Perfect looks at them, consulting his memory. His internal filing system is disorderly, but through the familiarity of long use, he can always find what he's looking for.

'You work for Mr 'Unter,' he says, resuming his meal.

'That's right. We've come for some information.'

'I only give hinformation to Mr 'Unter personal.'

'Hunter's been suspended,' says Collins. 'Don't tell me you didn't know that?'

''Course I know! 'E told me 'isself, dint 'e!'

'Yeah, but us, we're still working on the case *he* was working on,' explains Fontaine. 'And we're looking for some info.'

'What you want ter know, then?'

'It's about those girls we're after,' says Fontaine. 'The terrorists. Do you know about any new safehouses they've set up? Or if maybe any of the old ones are being used again?'

'Well... I might know somethin'...'

'Go on.'

Perfect smiles slyly. 'Mr 'Unter; 'e pays me for that kind of hinformation...'

Collins flares up. 'Look, if you know something—'

'Of course we'll pay you,' interrupts Fontaine. 'If you've got something worth paying for.'

'Well, there's this 'ouse in Brixton,' says Perfect. 'Abandoned hoffices. A bunch of anarchos used ter use the place, but they got wiped out by one o' them far-right groups or somethink. Place 'as been empty for months.'

'But not anymore?'

'Tha's right. I mean, I'm not saying for sure it's them girls as you're after. But *someone's* using the place; tha's definite.'

Fontaine looks at Collins. 'Could be worth checking out.'

'That'll cost yer fifty,' declares Perfect.

'Fifty!' explodes Collins.

'Thas what Mr 'Unter always pays me!' defensively.

Fontaine holds up a hand to forestall further argument. 'Alright, alright. Fifty it is.'

Between them, Fontaine and Collins produce the requisite amount of cash and hand it over, vaguely hoping they will be able to claim the money back as expenses. Perfect gives them the address, and they leave him to finish wolfing his meal.

They park across the street from the house. They wait for an hour. No-one goes in, no-one comes out. No sign of life in any of the windows.

'Let's go in,' decides Collins, at last.

They cross the street, mount the steps to the front door. Fontaine tries the door. It is unlocked. Drawing their guns, they step inside. The hallway is deserted. They pause, listen. Not a sound. Covering each other, they rapidly check every downstairs room, moving with a choreographed precision. Nothing. Guns at the ready, they ascend the narrow staircase in the same dramatic style. Nothing on the first floor. They move on to the second. Voices coming from one of the rooms. They flatten themselves either side of the doorway. Words cannot be discerned, but the voices they can hear sound female and young.

The two agents look at each other, trade nods.

They burst into the room, guns at the ready.

'Nobody move!' roars Collins.

There are three SEA girls in the room: Dizzy Hello, Rachel Ramone, and Chrissie Wylde. (Rachel of course knows this place. In fact, this is the very room in which her erstwhile associates the Brixton Anarchist Collective had held its last meeting on that fateful night.)

'Hands up!' orders Collins.

'How can we put our hands up when you told us not to move?' asks Dizzy, questioning the fine-print.

'You can put your hands up but don't make any other moves,'

clarifies Fontaine.

Obediently, the three girls raise their hands.

'Call for back-up,' says Collins. 'I'll keep 'em covered.'

Fontaine takes out her mobile, while Collins watches the terrorists, gun held in both hands. He notices something white clenched in one of Dizzy's raised hands. Something white, covered with pinprick dimples.

A golf ball.

Collins' eyes meet Dizzy's. She smiles, slowly opens her hand.

'Golf ball!' yells Collins. 'Get down!'

He tackles Daisy Fontaine, hurling both of them to the ground. Fontaine's phone skitters across the floor.

'What the hell are you doing?' cries Fontaine, who has banged her elbow.

'She dropped a golf ball!'

They look. It is indeed a golf ball; it rolls gently across the wooden floor. The three SEA girls have made their escape and are already running down the stairs.

'You pillock!' says Fontaine. 'Come on!'

They scramble to their feet and then hurtle down the stairs in pursuit of their quarry, emerging into the street just in time to see the SEA girls piling into a car. Fontaine and Collins rush to their own vehicle. Doors slam, brakes squeal.

'Right,' says Collins. 'Let's go!'

The silver Capri takes off after the other car. Now commences a breath-taking chase which it is far beyond the meagre abilities of this narrator to adequately describe: They weave through the crowded market, upsetting carts of fruit and vegetables... They drive through the plate-glass window two glaziers are carrying across the street... They speed round and round the area of wasteland, kicking up clouds of dirt... The chase ends when an articulated lorry reverses into the road between the two cars. By the time Fontaine and Collins can get past the obstruction, there is no sign of the fugitive vehicle.

'Buggery bollocks,' says chagrined Collins, thumping the roof of the Capri.

(In the unlikely event of this book ever being filmed, special emphasis should be placed on the above chase sequence, and a lot of the other rubbish cut out.)

Several hours later. Our two professionals are still cruising the streets when they receive an emergency call on the RT.

'Director Lennox has activated his panic button. Get over to his house immediately.'

'Right.'

'Looks like he took your advice and went home after all.'

All MI5 operatives have an emergency 'panic button' in their homes. They can alert headquarters if they come under direct attack, or if they cannot leave their house because enemies are lurking outside.

Fontaine pulls up outside the detached Victorian house in which Lennox lives alone. They can see at once that his front door is wide open.

'Doesn't look good,' comments Fontaine.

Guns at the ready, they burst in. The assailants have departed, but they have left their handiwork behind. Lennox has been cured of his cold once and for all.

On the wall above the corpse, a message has been written in blood:

WE HATE LENNOX!
WE WANT MARK HUNTER BACK!
—THE S.E.A.

Chapter Forty-One
A Chapter Which Doesn't End in Sanity

A naked Mark Hunter, semi-distended, answers the door to Dodo Dupont. Carrying a briefcase, Dodo is dressed in her usual tight black pullover and fake-leather trousers. Mark has never seen her in anything else and has long suspected her of having a wardrobe full of identical outfits.

'Good morning,' he says. 'Step inside.'

Dodo follows Mark into the tennis-court sized living room of his penthouse apartment, admiring his tight buttocks. (According to Professor Hunter, women—at least the ones who are interested in men—are attracted to taut, muscular, male buttocks, as being suggestive of powerful thrusting ability.)

A yawning Mayumi emerges from the bedroom, attired like Mark but with the addition of glasses.

'And how are the love-birds today?' says Dodo, smiling.

'We're good,' replies Mayumi, scratching an armpit.

'Yes, I apologise for our casual dress,' says Mark. 'But we've just got up. Coffee?'

'I'd love some,' says Dodo.

Mark goes into the kitchen, and Dodo sits on her usual sofa, placing her briefcase on the glass-topped table. Mayumi seats herself on the sofa across from Dodo. Taking a packet of cigarettes from the table, she extracts one, lights it.

Dodo produces her own cigarette case and follows Mayumi's example.

'So, how's the exhibition going?' she asks.

'It has been well-attended, thank you.'

'Glad to hear it.'

Mayumi is a photographer of great renown. In her own country her name is spoken of alongside the likes of Nobuyoshi Araki, Kenichi Murata and Kishin Shinoyama.

Mayumi has courted some controversy with her latest photographic collection *Kanamara Matsuri* (named after the Shinto Festival of the Penis), which features a variety of Japanese models kneeling reverentially before a large, erect penis. In each image the same upright member, in profile, occupies the left of the picture, and the face of the kneeling woman, also in profile, on the right. One worshipper clasps her hands in prayer, one cries tears of awe and adoration, one smiles bashfully like a schoolgirl meeting her heartthrob idol, one bathes her face in her deity's effluence, one decorates it with ribbons and bows, one with features stern and pointed finger scolds it for misbehaving—and so on and so forth.

The point of controversy centres in the fact that the 'stunt penis' used in the images is actually that of her boyfriend Professor Hunter—and some of the most virulent critics of this exhibition have actually been amongst Mark's male colleagues in the field of psychology! They claim that he has disgraced his profession with his obscene modelling, and have even demanded that he be stripped of his academic honours. Conversely, Mark's female colleagues have been largely very supportive, arguing that the men are just jealous of Mark's prodigious manhood.

Mark now returns with the coffee tray.

'Filter coffee,' he says. 'None of your instant muck.'

This is something of a running joke. Dodo always drinks freeze-dried instant coffee, maintaining it is all she can really afford on her meagre salary as a spy.

Mark places the tray down on the table, seats himself next to Mayumi, and pours for everyone. Dodo accepts her cup.

She takes an appreciative sip.

'Perfect, as always,' she declares.

'Apart from my coffee, what brings you here this fine morning?' asks Mark, lighting his own cigarette. 'I'm guessing there's news of some kind in that briefcase of yours?'

'Oh yes, my briefcase is brimming over with news,' confirms Dodo. She takes up the case, places it on her knees, and flips the catches. She extracts a sheaf of documents.

'We've identified some of the Pantyface terrorists,' she declares. 'Take a look at these.' She places one glossy print on the table, facing Mark and Mayumi. The image is a head and shoulders portrait of a girl in school uniform with a pair of polka-dotted female undergarments masking her face, the leg holes serving as eye holes, and also allowing egress for the girl's twin-tails.

'That's one of the girls from the Hackney safe house,' says Dodo. 'Now, compare it with *this*.'

Dodo places a second photo beside the first. The image is completely identical, save for the girl's face being uncovered. 'This is a school photo of one Jessica Harper, age fourteen. As you can see, she is quite clearly the Pantyface terrorist in the other picture.'

'No doubt about it,' concurs Mark. 'Have you found out anything about this girl?'

'Yes. Her family home was destroyed in an accident a couple of months ago. A gas explosion. Jessica was believed to have been killed in this incident, along with her mother and older brother, but there was a question mark hanging over this; because none of her remains could be identified in the burnt-out remains of the house.'

'And now that we know that she wasn't there, is there any possibility that Jessica could have caused that explosion herself?'

'We're looking into that,' is Dodo's reply. She lays down another photograph. 'Here's another one we've managed to identify.'

Another head and shoulders portrait of a girl with a pair of knickers over her face, these ones pure white. This wearer has blue eyes and long blonde hair. Dodo places a second photo beside it, once again identical save for the facial undergarments.

'I'd say that was a match, wouldn't you?' says Dodo.

'Doesn't seem much doubt about it,' agrees Mark. 'Have you got a name?'

'We have. She's Juliette Wainwright, daughter of the business magnate Rufus Wainwright. She's attending, or is *supposed* to be attending, a girl's boarding school in Switzerland.'

Mayumi, smoking placidly, listens to this conference without speaking. Having idly taken hold of Mark's penis, she stimulates it to tumescence and begins to casually masturbate him.

'So,' says Mark. 'This Vautrin character has assembled a group of eleven teenage girls and has turned them into the infamous Pantyface terrorist group who are currently wreaking havoc across the country.'

'Is it eleven girls?' queries Dodo. 'I thought we didn't know that yet?'

'You're right,' agrees Mark. 'Perhaps I'm jumping ahead here.'

'Eleven girls…' ponders Dodo. 'And what's the connection between them? Only that they knew each other in another world…'

'Did they? Who told you that?'

'Vautrin told me.'

'But you haven't met him yet, have you?'

Dodo smacks her own temple. 'D'oh! You're right; I *haven't* met him yet. It's *me* jumping ahead now!'

'So where are we up to?' wonders Mark, frowning, tapping his chin.

'Good question,' says Dodo. 'Have we had that bit where I can't remember the name for someone who likes teenage girls, and you tell me it's an ephebophile?'

'Oh yes! And then you say: "That's the bunny"!' Mark ponders. 'No, I don't think we've had that bit.'

'What about the bit where I discuss the etymology of Vautrin's name?'

'I thought that was one of my lines?' says Mark.

'No, I'm pretty sure it's mine,' counters Dodo. 'I'm the one who's well-versed in world literature, aren't I?'

'Are you? I thought it was me…'

Mark sits back in his chair, reflects.

Dodo looks at them. Mark Hunter, the popular TV psychologist; and quietly masturbating him his girlfriend Mayumi Takahashi, the famed erotic photographer... Sitting nakedly together just as they've always done... That's right, isn't it...?

No. No, it's not right. Something's off here. Something's wrong. It's all backwards. He should be Dodo... No, *she* should be Mark... No, *I* should be...

Oh! What is it?

'Don't sweat the small stuff!'

Mark looks round. It is now Trudie Rayne's hand that masturbates him. She smiles at him with her most winning smile.

On the opposing sofa naked Mayumi straddles black-clad Dodo. The lovers are locked in a steamy embrace, mouths glued together. And small wonder! Dodo is about to leave for Switzerland, and she won't be back till this evening! Mayumi's going to miss her like crazy!

'Keep looking at them,' comes Trudie's voice. 'Remember: it *is* a male spectator sport!' She tightens her grip, increasing the speed of her manipulation of Mark's penis.

Mark looks. Mayumi rubs her crotch against Dodo's uplifted thigh, leaving a slick trail on the smooth material of her trousers, while Dodo grips tightly her flowing hair, winding it around her long fingers.

'They're doing it just for you,' says Trudie, pulling harder and harder. 'You're a lucky guy really, aren't you? You're just like Vautrin!'

We're not so different, you and I...

Mark ejaculates—Dodo jumps up from the sofa.

'Well I'm off now!' she announces. 'An all-expenses paid trip to a girls' school in Switzerland!'

'Make lots of happy memories,' says Mayumi, handing her her briefcase.

'I will! And I'll bring some back for you!'

Dodo departs.

Mayumi turns to face Mark and Trudie. She bows low.

'Excuse me. I need to have a shit.'

Exit Mayumi. The curtain descends amid rapturous applause

Chapter Forty-Two
Everything You Wanted to Know About the SEA but Were Afraid to Ask

Welcome to the SEA! I am Juliette Wainwright, daughter of the late Rufus Wainwright (sniffle sniffle I miss you Daddy!), corporate overlord. This is the brand spanking new(d) website of the SEA, the Society of Evil Actions! You probably haven't heard of because your illustrious government doesn't want you to know that all those terrorist attacks the UK has been suffering of late have been valiantly perpetrated by a group of fresh young nymphets (aged 14-18) of outstanding physical beauty and personal charm, who are here to usher in a new age of Beautiful Chaos! So, please tell all your friends about our website where we will be posting lots of stimulating articles and some even more stimulating pictures, such as this snapshot of my friend Flossie's big tits. (See image below.) Remember: The SEA – Only a Click Away!

*

MEET THE SEA GALS – A QUICK GUIDE (compiled by Rachel Ramone)
JULIETTE WAINWRIGHT – born with a silver spoon up her arse
FLORENCE FARRADAY – big tits, small personality
GRETA GARBO – bloody awful German accent
DIZZY HELLO – body to kill for; infantile bloodlust
GINA SANTELLA – legs like a monkey's if she doesn't shave them twice a day
GERTRUDE RAYNE – talks like a spaz; thick glasses like a spaz

THE
S.F.A.
GIRLS!
by SOPHIE HARRIS
JULIETTE WAINRIGHT
TRUDIE RAYNE
ALBERTINE SAGAN
GINA SANTELLA
CHRISSIE WYLDE

GRETA GARBO	JESSIE HARPER
FLOSSIE FARRADAY	RACHEL RAMONE
DIZZY HELLO	ME!

CHRISTINE WYLDE – arse that could cause a total eclipse
RACHEL RAMONE – the eleventh one

*

Greetings, Meine Leiben! I am Greta Garbo, former RAF member, und now part off der wunderbar Society off Eaful Actions! In der RAF I enjoyed strafing der vogs in Syria und Afghanistan, but now I much prefer licking out der kunt off my güt friend Dissy Hello, who iss der most beautiful, sexy, intelligent and sophisticated lady int der whole vide vorld! Also, ass I am a Deutschlander, I ferry much like der sausages, und it iss these I vish to talk about. Sausages come int all shapes und sises und int many different colours. Und off these, SISE iss der most important factor. Any colour sausage is güt ass long ass the sise iss LARGE. Ass for der shape of der sausage, it can bend vun vay, or it can bend der uffer; it can haff a kink in it or be totally straight; ass long ass it iss LARGE. So, if you haff vun of these large, meaty sausages, pleasse to send picture of so that I can decide wheffer to purchase or not! Pleasse go to 'contact the SEA' section to leaff your sausage-pics, und remember: der vurst iss yet to come! Und now, time for a song:

> 'Take der last train to Auschwitz,
> und I'll meet you at der station,
> Ve'll haff time for coffin-flavoured kisses,
> before der gender segregation...'

That voss gut! I am feeling ferry horny now, so I must get out my naughty postcards off Adolf Hitler haffing sex wiff Anne Frank dokky-style in the toilets of the Wilhelmstrasse. I vill speak to you soon!

*

Attention! This is the real Greta Garbo speaking! The article above is a counterfeit: It was not written by myself but by my very irresponsible comrade Dizzy Hello. Many of the comments she attributes to me are untrue. For example, the RAF of which I was formerly a member was the glorious *Red Army Faction*, and not the imperialist British *Royal Air Force*; and while it is true that I do enjoy sausages, I have no use for pictures of them, so please do not send; also, I do not possess any erotic postcards featuring Adolf Hitler, with whom I am ideologically opposed. Thank you for reading this.

*

JULIETTE'S TIPS FOR DEALING WITH KISS AND TELL BRAGGARTS! (FIRST IN AN IRREGULAR SERIES) Girls! Does it really piss you off when the boy you've just had a one-night stand with goes around boasting to all his mates that he's made it with you? Personally, I couldn't care less when this happens. But if you DO care, then when not take a leaf out of Queen Cleopatra's book and kill the bastard once you've finished fucking him? And don't worry if you're not a reigning monarch and don't have soldiers at hand to dispatch the miscreant—just do it yourself! In fact, speaking as a true artist, it is my belief that the perfect moment to put the poor guy out of his misery is just when you are at the peak of orgasmic bliss and your (soon to be deceased) partner is shooting his load inside you. Let's look at some ways and means of doing this...

0)First off, doggy style and facedown are both most definitely out; you need to be facing your enemy at the critical moment!

1)Cowgirl. If you're riding your stud cowgirl style a lovely way to finish him off is to blow his brains out with a six-shooter just when HE blows! This is a personal favourite of mine. However, depending on your circumstances and what part of the world you're in, getting hold of firearms may be a problem for you. So if you can't get a gun then a useful substitute is a Black and Decker (or some other brand's) power drill! Just drill into his forehead (or an eye for easy access) at the critical moment.

2)Missionary. Plenty of options in this position, but remember to make sure he isn't pinning your wrists down! You need to have both hands free. One method is to slip a running noose around his neck; do this just before he comes and this will increase the volume of his ejaculation, as well providing your partner with a much more satisfying orgasm before he dies. Another method is to simply apply your thumbs to his eyes and push them in deeply as you reach that peak of ecstasy. And one I'm especially fond of: get yourself a knife (a kitchen knife will do) and slit his throat at the critical moment and your partner will deluge your body with his warm blood just as he's filling you up with his other vital fluid!

That's all for today. Next time I'll be giving you some tips on disposing of the body, and on how to pin the crime on anyone who's annoyed you recently.

*

A quick word about our gallant comrade, Jessica Harper: Jessie is the only member of the SEA who IS STILL A VIRGIN. And what's worse, she doesn't even think this is much of a problem! Not a problem? Being a constant embarrassment to all your friends? I'd call that a MAJOR fucking problem. So PLEASE help us if you can. Jessie doesn't really like doing nudes, but I was able to burst into her room while she was shafting herself with a dildo and was able to take THIS candid shot! (See image below.) So, what do you say, guys? And if you happen to see this girl walking down the street, just jump on top of her and give her one! PLEASE. You'd be doing the universe a favour, and believe me, it's much better than trying to have a decent conversation with her!

*

Jessica Harper here. I know what she means about not

being able to have a decent conversation with me—she means that I only talk about books! That's not true! I can talk about lots of other things as well. So shut up, fat-arse.

*

DOCTOR DIZZY – THE DOCTOR WHO STILL MAKES HOUSECALLS!

Doctor Dizzy here! I'm going to tell you about a recent operation I performed. It was reported in the newspapers, but they didn't tell the full story and they completely forgot to mention my name! The patient Lucius Grapefruit, that TV streaming zillionaire who wanted to start a colony on Mars. Apparently they don't have cancer on Mars, but Grapefruit DID have cancer. But his Mars Project wasn't ready yet, so going to the Red Planet to breathe the healthy air was not an option—he had to go in for surgery instead. Deciding not to be a burden on the NHS, Grapefruit opted for a private clinic. To cut a long story short, Doctor Dizzy (that's me!) decided to take charge of the operation myself. After we convinced the previous operating team to let us take charge, me and my trusty assistants entered the theatre where our patient was waiting. First problem: anaesthetic was out. We'd used all that up in our negotiations with the other operating team. Now, if the patient's not anaesthetised, he tends to start moving around a lot when you're cutting into him, and this can be very distracting. Fortunately, the solution was at hand. Using my trusty chainsaw (no surgeon should be without one!) I quickly amputated Grapefruit's arms and legs to stop them flailing about during surgery! Brilliant! Now it was time to operate on the tumour, which was located in the patient's stomach area. Using the chainsaw again, I delicately probed the area; and we soon found that pesky cancer! It thought it could hide itself behind Grapefruit's pancreas! As if! Once we'd got rid of the pancreas, we made short work of that nasty tumour! The operation was a success! (Although we did lose the patient.) Another triumph for Doctor Dizzy!

*

Dong! Good Evening! This is the News at Ten, and I'm Sir Trevor MacDoughnut wearing a pair of comically oversized glasses.

Dong! The entire Manchester United team were tragically killed today when a fake 'diverted traffic' sign turned them onto a road which led them directly to a precipice and a two-hundred-foot drop into a quarry. Ouch!

Dong! Also in sport, the entire Liverpool away team were killed when, calling in at a service station, their coach's tanks were filled with aviation fuel instead of diesel. Although the coach failed to become airborne it did provide an impressive sight to motorists as engulfed in flame it hurtled along the motorway like a blazing comet at speeds of nearly Mach one. Hot stuff!

Dong! In a related incident, the entire Aston Villa team were killed today when their coach attempted to enter a tunnel which was actually only a painting, artistically daubed onto the sheer rockface. Whoops-a-daisy!

Dong! And on a lighter note, the entire Melmoth Wanderers team were killed today when their coach, halted at some roadworks adjacent to a scrapyard, was picked up by a magnetic crane and dropped into the metal compactor where it was immediately crushed flat. That's gotta hurt, boys!

Dong! The super-sexy terrorist group the Society of Evil Actions has claimed responsibility for all of the above events. (See SEA website for details.) We asked Dizzy Hello, the super-sexiest of these super-sexy girls, why they had perpetrated these crimes. She replied, in her usual inimitable style: 'Well, none of us really like football, you see...'

Dong!

Chapter Forty-Three
All Aboard the Solanite Express!

Mark is at home when he receives the call from Trudie Rayne.

London is presently simmering under an extended heatwave. As Mark sits reading in his living room, his electric fan does its best to combat the heat, but he finds himself envying Dodo Dupont and her air-conditioned penthouse apartment.

If anything can be said to have come out of this period of forced repose, it is that it has enabled Mark to catch up with his reading. It has been mentioned that Mark's apartment houses a treasure-trove of classic literature; and while it is true that many of the great thinkers and historians are represented on his shelves, his favourite reading is fiction, and especially the fiction of the nineteenth century. Dodo has joked with him that this might be considered a guilty pleasure, seeing as many of these books were the popular entertainment of their time—but then, so were Shakespeare's plays!

Tonight, the standard lamp shines its light on the pages of the *Torquemada* tetralogy by Benito Pérez Galdós—a good case in point, for Galdós was a popular author in his day, disdained by the critics; and it was only after his death that the writer enjoyed a positive reassessment and was suddenly lauded as being Spain's greatest writer since Cervantes.

Mark hasn't been entirely idle during his suspension from work. The SEA affair is not something he can just forget about. He had gone down to Sussex on one occasion and checked out those ten farmhouses again, as much in the hope of being taken prisoner as of discovering any new clues. But if one of those farmhouses was the entrance to SEA headquarters and if they had been aware of his presence, they had not taken the bait.

He has learned about the murder Lennox, his replacement as section chief. *His* replacement is now under twenty-four-hour guard. Mark has emailed his department suggesting that the best way to save any further casualties of this kind would be to simply reinstate himself, Mark Hunter, as requested by the SEA girls. He is still waiting to hear back from them about that one.

And now the SEA has gone viral! Everyone is talking about the new SEA website, the main subject of debate being: is it for real or is it an outrageous hoax? Can all of those recent terrorist attacks and assassinations really be the work of a group of teenage girls? The notion is at once stimulating and horrifying. If anything, the SEA's recent attacks on football teams has sparked more outrage than the earlier hospital bombings, given the popularity of the Beautiful Game. But conversely, the girls' having publicised themselves on their website has lent them celebrity status, with the inevitable fan-clubs sprouting up, selling posters and t-shirts, etc... The government, in cooperation with web browsers, has been trying their best to block the SEA website, so far without success.

Mark's mobile rings. Placing the book in his lap, he picks up the device. An unknown number.

'Hello?'

'Is that you, Mark?' A girl's voice, familiar.

'Yes. Who is this?'

'It's Trudie. Trudie Rayne.'

Trudie! 'To what do I owe the pleasure? And how did you get my number?'

'Oh, we all have your number! But never mind that. I'm in trouble! I need your help.'

'You need my help? What's wrong?'

Pause. 'I've started feeling *different* lately. I don't want to be in the SEA any more. It's not the same; it's not like it was. I don't feel like I'm connected to the other girls; not anymore. It's like you said to me that time, remember? Vautrin had some sort of spell over me. Well, I think you're right; I think it's starting to wear off.'

'In that case you *should* leave the SEA, Trudie. Right now. Get out of there. I can help you; I can protect you.'

'Yeah, but it's not that easy. I think the others are suspicious of me. I think they can tell that I'm not one of them anymore; like they can sense it or something…'

'I see… Where are you right now? At your main base?'

'No, I'm here in London. I'm with three of the other girls.'

'One of your safe-houses?'

'Yeah, it's a warehouse in Soho.'

'And you do think you can get out of there?'

'No. I'm taking a risk just calling you up. If they find me—'

'Where is the warehouse?'

'Bateman Street. Can you come and get me out? You could make it look like a raid—pretend to capture me.'

'I can't organise a full-scale raid; I'm under suspension. It'll have to be just me. I'll get over there straight away.'

'Oh *thank you*, Mark. Please get here soon. I've got to go now; the others are coming…'

'Trudie?'

The line goes dead.

Mark calls Dodo. No answer. He tries her mobile and is connected to her answering service. He leaves her a voice-mail saying where he is going and why. Marking the page, he puts his book aside and goes through to the bedroom. From his wardrobe he retrieves his shoulder holster and straps it on. His official firearm he had had to hand in upon his suspension, but Mark, quite illegally, owns a second handgun, one that had been acquired for him by his informer Perfect. Checking the clip, he slides the gun into the holster.

It is just as he has always thought. Vautrin has to have done something to those girls to turn them into what they now are… And the spell on Trudie Rayne is wearing off. Somehow, he knew it would be her; that she would be the first one to start coming to her senses. But if she can't conceal her disaffection from the others, she is going to be in trouble. He can imagine them just turning on her and tearing her to pieces like animals pouncing on an injured member of their pack.

He needs to get to that warehouse fast.

Mark takes a tube to Tottenham Court Road, then threads the busy side-streets of night-time Soho. One area of commerce unaffected by the heatwave is the red-light district; the patrons of this district never being deterred by the weather.

That abruptly-ended phone call worries Mark. Did Trudie manage to ring off *before* her colleagues saw her on the phone, or only *after*? Apparently all of the SEA girls know Mark's number; so they will only have to take Trudie's phone from her to see with whom she was speaking...

He reaches Bateman Street, comes to an access road between two buildings. Following this brings him to an open yard, at the far end of which is his destination: an old warehouse. Unholstering his gun, Mark approaches the delivery doors, and slips in through the wicket gate. He finds the front part of the warehouse to be in darkness, but a single light shines at the far side of the building, beyond towering stacks of crates; and he can hear the vague sound of voices.

Mark winds his way between the stacked crates towards the light. As he nears, the voices become clearer; female voices, raised in argument. He can now see the light at the end of an avenue between piled crates. He approaches swiftly but soundlessly, keeping to the shadows. And now before him appears an open area, a clearing amongst the forest of stacked crates. That single light illuminates the tableau that greets Mark's eyes. The scene is admirably staged: Trudie Rayne is seated on a straight-backed chair, wrists tied behind her. Three other SEA girls stand over her, interrogating her. Leading the interrogation is the sulky-looking girl with red streaks in her hair; the girl Mark had seen with Vautrin at the hotel all those months ago: Rachel Ramone, a former anarchist. Also present is Greta Garbo; and the other girl he recognises as Flossie Farraday. Trudie looks tearful, cowed; the other girls look angry, implacable.

Rachel is speaking. 'Did you tell him where we were?'

'No,' insists Trudie. 'I didn't have time. Please; just let me go...'

'You don't walk out of the SEA,' sneers Rachel. 'What's wrong with you, anyway?'

'I don't know. I just don't feel the same. I don't like this anymore.'

'And so you decided to grass us up to Mark Hunter?'

'I wasn't grassing on you! I just want to see him. He said he wanted to help me…'

Rachel snorts. 'It's not Mark Hunter you need to see, girl; it's Vautrin. He'll soon bring you back to your senses. But I'm thinking maybe we should just kill you now and have done with it. I don't trust you anymore; I don't like you, either.'

Greta and Flossie voice their agreement.

'Nobody move,' orders Mark, stepping out of the shadows, gun at the ready. 'You three: step away from Trudie. Keep your hands up.'

'You fucking bitch!' spits Rachel. 'You did tell him!'

Glowering, the three girls back away. Keeping them covered, Mark advances until he stands between them and Trudie.

'Are you okay, Trudie?' he asks.

'Yeah. They hadn't started hurting me yet.'

'They're not going to, either. You're leaving with me.'

'Take her,' invites Greta. 'She no longer beliefs in the causse. She is no further use to uss.'

'She's come to her senses,' says Mark. 'You could say she's recovered from her illness. But you, Greta, and all you other girls: you're still sick.'

Mark feels the muzzle of a gun pressed to his back.

'I'm really sorry about this, Mark,' comes the voice of Trudie. 'But, you see, I'm still sick, too. Be a sweetheart and drop the gun.'

Mark drops the gun. Trudie walks round to face him, smiling an apologetic smile. The other girls' smiles are not so nice.

Maybe they were right to suspend me, thinks Mark, glumly. I didn't see this coming. I know what these girls are like and I still went and trusted one of them.

'I thought you needed my help,' he tells Trudie, accusingly.

'I know you did and I'm sorry,' says Trudie. 'But tricking you like that seemed the best way to get you here.'

'Well, you've got me here; now what?'

'Ah! Well, we've got a surprise for you.'

Trudie picks up Mark's gun and joins the other girls.

Rachel moves over to a nearby crate that is being used as a table. Lifting a cloth, she picks up a rifle of a type that Mark has never seen before; a futuristic-looking weapon, all polished metal and crystal glass.

The four SEA girls suddenly have black shades in their hands; they don them as though they are protective goggles. Trudie, Flossie and Greta stand behind Rachel, who levels the weapon at Mark.

'What's all this?' demands Mark, rather feebly. 'You brought me here just so you could shoot me? You could have done that anywhere.'

'We're not going to shoot you,' replies Rachel. 'Not the way you mean. This thing doesn't fire bullets; it's a little device Vautrin made his scientists put together for him. It fires a concentrated beam of solanite energy.'

'A solanite ray? And what are you going to do with it?'

'What do you think? We're going to shoot you with it.'

'So you *are* going to kill me.'

'It won't kill you, silly!' says Trudie.

'Actually, it *might* kill him,' Rachel corrects her. 'But Vautrin doesn't think it will.'

'Then what is it supposed to do?' inquires Mark. 'Make me glow in the dark or something?'

'It'll send you on a trip,' says Rachel. 'At least, that's what we think. It's an experiment, yeah? And we've chosen you to be our guinea-pig.'

'Well, I'm very flattered to be chosen and all that,' says Mark. 'And much as I'm normally more than eager to help forward the cause of scientific discovery, if it's all the same to you—'

Sensing that this monologue is just leading up to Mark attempting a runner, Rachel forestalls him in this by firing the gun.

'All aboard the Solanite Express!'

A dazzling beam of light shoots from the gun and envelops Mark.

A mesmeric lightshow of psychedelic frequencies; swirling arcs of primary and secondary colour, bend and coruscate with liquid movement. Strange modulations of sound fill the air; an audio echo of those pulsing pinwheel lights. Visible sound and audible colour; shifting waveforms and frequencies embracing against a backdrop of timeless vacancy. Mark stands alone amongst them; plucked from the flow of sequential time, he is alone in unknown space. They surround him, these radiophonic patterns of light; they overload his mind and senses. His brain reels; he staggers. A single thought solidifies in his mind. He has to get away from them. He stumbles forward, barely in control of his limbs. Such things as direction, destination, mean nothing here. He senses a surface beneath his feet; he feels his body respire; but perhaps the atmosphere and dimensions are merely illusory—they will vanish if not maintained by his perception of them. His head swims with the effort; the ground seems to pitch and toss beneath him. His vaguest of thoughts disturb the delicate equilibrium. On wades he through the miasma of light and sound, both raising in pitch, in intensity, as though intent on obstructing the intruder. It is everywhere and all around him, this unknowable chaos. He can't escape from it. He clutches his head and screams—

He finds himself in a street. Or rather a vague simulacrum of a street, incomplete, landscaped over a black nothingness. A neon cityscape of floating signs surrounds him, a barrage of sexual invitation:

GIRLS GIRLS GIRLS

REDLIGHT CLUB

STRIPTEASE

HOSTESS BAR

POLE-DANCING

HOT ASIAN BABES

Behind the signs, dimmer squares of light, a semi-defined backdrop of lighted windows on invisible façades.

Mark stands in the middle of the road. Blasts of air, motion without temperature, sweep by him on either side, buffeting him with distorted sound. Two lanes of invisible traffic, and he stands marooned between them. He must get off the road, but the blasts of air and sound are constant, suggesting no abatement, no safe moment to cross. Impelled by a need to move, he strikes off blindly into the intangible traffic flow. A blast of air strikes him, spins him, knocking him off his feet. He rises, staggers on. Another blast of sound and kinetic energy hits him. Another. And then he is off the road onto the pavement.

Now he is amongst a crowd of vaguely-defined people; featureless black shadows. They all move in one direction. From this amorphous mass issues a sound suggestive of a thousand voices; a susurration of overlapping words, from which not a single comprehensible syllable can be distinguished.

Mark blunders into the crowd. He knows that the direction they are all moving in is not the direction in which he needs to go. Their journey is not his. Opposing the flow, he ploughs through them; the shades are insubstantial, yet he *feels it* every time one of them passes through him. The pavement seems to stretch on forever, the crowd is endless.

A sign beckons, a familiar red circle:

UNDERGROUND

There is no visible building, no entrance, just that floating sign. He cuts diagonally through the crowd of shades, and blessedly freed from it, passes beneath the sign.

He doesn't see the stairs. His foot strikes thin air, and he pitches forward, falling; down, down, down…

Darkness and oblivion enfold him.

Chapter Forty-Four
For the Good off the Causse!

Many books have been written about Greta Garbo, the famed Red Army Faction activist and the youngest person ever to make the front cover of *Popular Terrorist*. Some of these books have been written by hacks; some have been written by social scientists; some have been written by adherents to Greta's cause; the one thing all of these publications have in common is that they all claim to be the definitive and authoritative account of Greta Garbo's short (so far), but eventful, life. However, as the various books contradict each other on many key points, someone has got to be telling fibs here.

Let's see if we can make some sense of it all.

One fact that all the accounts agree on, and that seems to be certain, is that Greta was drawn into the RAF (Red Army Faction) by her older brother, Franz, whose membership of the organisation is an undisputed fact. As to how this came about, however, the various sources disagree. Franz's allegiance to the RAF was unknown to his family, with whom he still resided—so why would he want to draw his own sister into such a dangerous world at such a young age? Some assert that this simply illustrates how insanely irresponsible fanatics like Franz are; others say that Franz was forced by circumstances into drawing his sister into his world.

One version has it that Greta walked unannounced into her brother's bedroom one evening and discovered him in the act of manufacturing a bomb. Franz had then sworn her to secrecy, explained what he was doing and why he was doing it. Far from being shocked to learn her brother's secret, Greta had been enthralled, and had eagerly offered her services to assist her brother's cause.

Personally, I'm sceptical of this account. Franz was a member of a highly organised terrorist cell with safehouses and workshops; I find it hard to believe he would have been reckless enough to have stored the materials for the manufacturing of explosive devices in his own family home. Another version, cited by two of the more reliable authors, seems to me much more credible: this being that on account of his terrorist activities, Franz would often have to leave the house at late hours, sometimes sneaking out after the family had retired for the night. And Greta, who liked to stay up late in her own bedroom, became aware of these surreptitious comings and goings. And from all accounts a naturally curious girl, Greta had started following her brother on these excursions to ascertain the reason for them. Had she just thought her brother might be meeting up with a girl or girls? Or had she suspected from the start that her brother was involved in something more sinister? She must have had to have followed him numerous times before she could have discovered anything conclusive. When had she realised the truth? What could she have witnessed? One version has it that following her brother on one of these nocturnal expeditions, she saw him meet up with some colleagues, and had trailed them to a government building which they had broken into to plant a large explosive device. Greta had then either witnessed the explosion at first hand, or else, following her brother from the scene before the event, had simply heard about it on the news the following morning. Either way, she would have known her brother to be one of the perpetrators of the attack.

Allowing the above story, or something like it, to be the truth, how had Greta gone from discovering her brother's status as an anarchist terrorist, to actually becoming a member of the group herself? In answer to this, one version states that after the bomb incident, she had simply confronted her brother with her knowledge, and, full of nothing but admiration, had begged leave to join the group and fight alongside him. Another, more dramatic but less plausible, says that Greta had followed Franz on another occasion, and been led to a secret meeting at a warehouse, where her presence had been discovered after she had sneezed inopportunely; and again, being confronted, she had requested admittance to the group. Either way, Greta, in spite of her young age, had been duly enrolled into the organisation. Her acceptance must have surely been thanks, in no small part, to her brother's influence. (But then, as the girl would have already known too much, Franz's colleagues would have considered that the only other alternative would have been to kill her.) Whatever the reason for her admission, it seems that having a cause to fight for had stirred up all the adolescent girl's enthusiasm and imagination, her defiance of established authority—she had soaked up the group's anarcho-communist doctrine like an eager sponge. (In other circumstances, this enthusiasm and her marked facility for retaining information would have served her well in the sphere of education.)

A couple of the more sensational accounts claim that Greta and Franz had entered upon an incestuous relationship after becoming comrades-in-arms. One of the more scholarly authors has refuted this claim, and I am inclined to agree with her. It is certain that Greta revered her brother; he was her hero, her idol. But to go from that to sharing a bed with him is not an inevitable step. (And besides, we've already had one example of sibling incest in this chronicle, and we really don't need another one.)

What seems perhaps far more plausible, is the claim that another member of the group, a young man named Karl, had, unbeknownst to his comrades, taken advantage of Greta sexually, claiming this activity to be part of her 'initiation' into the organisation. Speculation perhaps, but it is a certain fact that this man Karl was later found stabbed to death in an alley. Attending this fact is the belief that it was Franz who murdered Karl, having discovered his colleague's abuse of his sister. (Greta, in her naïveté, may have simply told her brother what she and Karl had been doing.) Either way, it is firmly believed that the stabbing of Karl was an execution carried out by his own people.

However, with or without her virginity intact, Greta soon rose to prominence within the terrorist cell, her boundless zeal matched only by her technical skill. She found she had a natural affinity for electronics and explosives. On this subject her brother had taught her everything he knew, but the pupil soon outstripped the master. (That Franz wasn't as good with explosives as his little sister was proved conclusively a year later, when he blew himself to atoms with one of his own devices.) Greta became the darling, the poster girl, of the RAF. She was ruthless in her dedication, and at the same time malleable and obedient; she never questioned the orders of the senior members of the group.

The attacks she was instrumental in carrying out, all the world knows about. They were showcase acts of terrorism, culminating in the sensational toppling of the Brandenburg Gate. In spite of her close attachment to her brother, it is understood that Greta showed little emotion on learning of his death. She may have grieved privately; but publicly she merely said: 'He died for the cause.'

Everyone knows of the media sensation little Greta Garbo became, but this notoriety came with one major drawback: with her face all over the internet, television screens, and in magazines, remaining incognito became a virtual impossibility for the girl. A year or so later the inevitable happened: she was captured by the security forces after a spectacular raid on an RAF safehouse to which she had been tracked. No less sensational was the televised trial. Greta had stood in the dock handcuffed and unrepentant, proud of her achievements. The remorseless jury rejected the plea of diminished responsibility put forward by the defence counsel (a plea to which Greta herself had always objected); she was found guilty on all charges and the judge decided that an example should be made of her, awarding her a heavy prison sentence.

All good things must come to an end, and many thought that her trial and imprisonment had put a period to the colourful story of Greta Garbo. But then, in life as in great fiction, there are always developments which just cannot be anticipated…

Cut to:

BELSEN MAXIMUM SECURITY JUVENILE DETENTION CENTRE

…home to some of the most hardened young offenders in Western Europe.

There's our Greta, standing on the edge of the prison playing field, dressed in the regulation drab grey. The playing field extends to the outer wall—a lofty rampart, topped with spikes, guard turrets at each corner. Behind Greta rises the featureless, dispiriting architecture of the prison building. A game of football is in progress on the field; some prisoners are watching the game, cheering on the players, while others stand in small groups, talking and enjoying their brief period out in the open air. Guards stand at intervals, rifles slung over their shoulders.

Greta stands alone enjoying this crisp, sunny day; stretching herself, breathing in the invigorating air. Today happens to be her first day of (relative) liberty after having endured two weeks in solitary confinement—her first chance to stretch her legs and look at the blue sky… And to think, it had been such a minor incident that had resulted in Greta's punishment! Nothing more than this: One day in the prison refectory, a boy sitting opposite Greta, and with absolutely no provocation, had started to mock the glorious Cause in front of the girl's face. And quite naturally Greta had been compelled to retaliate by shoving her fork into the eye of the disrespectful one. Anyone would have done the same. However, the prison authorities had taken a dim view of the situation, and hence Greta's being consigned to the solitary cells.

The boy and girl inmates at Belsen can mix freely for meals, work and exercise, but the cellblocks themselves are gender-segregated: a west-wing for the boys, an east-wing for the girls. This segregation extends to the guards assigned to these wings: male guards for the west-wing, female guards for the east. And while this may have limited the opportunities for sexual congress between the young inmates, it was common for some of the male guards to bribe their female colleagues into allowing them access to the east-wing after lights-out. Greta herself had been the subject of these nocturnal visits on more than one occasion. Whenever these had happened, she had learned to just lie back and think of the Cause. (As for female guards venturing into the west-wing cells for the same reason—well, this has been known to happen, but with much less frequency.)

Right now, a girl called Hilda walks up to Greta, who is performing some limbering up exercises.

'Good to see you back,' greets Hilda.

'Thank you,' responds Greta, swinging her arms. 'I am also pleased to see you, Hilda.'

'So, how was solitary? Did it get to you?'

'Not at all; it was very beneficial,' replies Greta. 'It gave me much time for quiet meditation and reflection on the Cause. I can now return to the struggle renewed.'

Greta has not made many friends since coming to Belsen. Being the most open and honest of girls, she finds it very difficult to conceal the contempt she entertains for many of her fellow inmates—most of whom are just young criminals only interested in personal gain, and blind to the pressing social issues which so urgently need to be addressed, and which are the reason for the Cause. And so, she shuts herself off from the other detainees, while they for the most part consider her to be arrogant and elitist, and they are quite happy to have nothing to do with her.

Hilda is one girl Greta has allowed into her closed world. Hilda has always been a big fan of Greta, and Greta is not so churlish as to cold-shoulder an admirer. And with a course of indoctrination, Hilda could become a useful convert to the Cause!

'Return to the struggle?' echoes Hilda. 'That won't be for a while, will it? Fifteen years before your parole comes up.'

'Perhaps I will not require to wait that long,' replies Greta.

Hilda's eyes widen. She drops her voice. 'You're not planning to escape?'

'Plans have been made,' affirms Greta.

'Well, if you're going to get out of here, I'd do it sooner rather than later if I were you,' advises Hilda. 'Meyer is gunning for you.'

Ceasing her calisthenics, Greta knits her brows. 'Meyer? Who is this Meyer? I know of no Meyer.'

'You *do* know him,' Hilda tells her. 'You stuck a fork in his eye.'

'Ah! The impudent one. Was that his name? And what is this Meyer's grievance with me?'

'You stuck a fork in his eye.'

'He chose to mock the Cause before me. He should have anticipated retaliation. Otherwise, he should not have spoken as he did. Regardless, I have served penance for my infringement of the rules and assault upon his person by spending two weeks in solitary confinement.'

'Yeah, I don't think that's going to be enough for Meyer. The eye you stabbed went rotten—they had to take it out.'

'He has another eye, has he not? He can still see. If I lost an eye, I would be grateful for still having the use of the one I had left.'

'Yeah, but not everybody is as philosophical as you,' says Hilda. 'Seriously; you should really be careful, Greta. That guy's out to get you.'

'I thank you for your advice, Hilda,' says Greta. 'But it now becomes redundant. Meyer is approaching us at this very moment.'

Hilda follows Greta's gaze. A group of boys are indeed marching purposefully towards them, led by a youth conspicuous for both an eye-patch and a murderous expression.

'Run for it!'

'There is no need for me to retreat. It is better for us to resolve this situation immediately,' says Greta, undaunted by the advancing boys. 'Greetings, Meyer!'

'Don't you "greetings" me you fucking little bitch,' grates Meyer, coming to a stop a few feet away from his victim. He points to his eye-patch. 'Look what you did to me!'

'You must look to yourself for the responsibility,' Greta tells him. 'You spoke words you should not have spoken.'

'You little bitch,' spits Meyer. 'So you're right and everyone else is wrong?'

Greta nods her head. 'That is so.'

'And I'm not entitled to my opinion?'

'Of course, if you keep it to yourself.'

'You fucking little—I'm going to kick your stupid face in!'

'I am ready for the attempt.'

The two combatants square up to each other; the six-foot boy, and the five-foot girl. Spectators form a ring around them.

But before the first blows can be exchanged, an interruption occurs, and not a minor one. The sudden scream of airborne missiles, and then one of the guard towers explodes; all eyes in the exercise yard turn to watch the pillar of smoke rising from the now roofless structure; even as they watch, the second bursts into flame. A klaxon wails. Guards run hither and thither, shouting contradictory orders. The eyes of all the inmates are fixed on the perimeter wall, as the sound of rotor-blades draws nearer. And then a helicopter gunship appears over the wall between the two rising columns of smoke.

Breaking away from the group, Greta sprints across the exercise yard towards the perimeter wall. This attack is not unexpected for her; she knows what she must do. The helicopter, now inside the prison compound, hovers like a large and heavily-armed insect. The gunship's forward canons open up, sweeping the yard. Screams and yells as inmates and guards alike run from the deadly hail.

'No you fucking don't!'

Greta snatches a glance over her shoulder. It is Meyer, enraged, barrelling towards her. He lunges, grabs her, Greta spins him round—and Meyer takes in the back a round of ammunition intended for herself.

She drops the corpse and runs on. The guard who had fired—one of the 'either very stupid or very brave' variety—rushes to intercept Greta. A pile-driver to the stomach, a chop to the back of the neck and he is down. She relieves him of his gun, continues towards her objective. The 'copter has now touched down. The door slides open, two men appear, open fire with assault rifles, covering Greta's advance. Another guard makes an ill-advised attempt to intercept Greta. She guns him down.

Greta reaches the helicopter, jumps inside, assisted by the two men. The door is slammed shut, the machine lifts off, clears the perimeter wall and, flying low, soon disappears.

Hilda lifts herself up from the ground to which she had thrown herself for cover. She has witnessed the entire escape, witnessed and admired.

'That's one hell of an exit, girl...'

'Greta; I want you to meet the man responsible for your escape: Herr Vautrin!'

Greta clicks her heels and bows.

'I am very grateful to you, Herr Vautrin.'

The helicopter had landed in a forest clearing thirty kilometres from the prison, whereupon it had been swiftly covered with camouflage netting. Here Greta had been given a change of clothes and the group had transferred to a small truck and had driven twenty miles to a private aerodrome, and here Greta had boarded a light aircraft, fuelled and ready for take-off. In flight they had observed both police helicopters and military jets—part of the coordinated search that had been quickly instituted for the escaped terrorist. The pilot had been hailed by the searchers, but with the plane's registration and flight-plan being both legitimate, there had been no reason to associate the aircraft with the escape plot, and they had been allowed to continue.

The aircraft had finally touched down at a farm just under a hundred kilometres from Berlin, and from here Greta had been driven the rest of the way to the city.

Now they are in a warehouse RAF depot. A large number of group members have gathered to celebrate the success of the spectacular jailbreak. Amongst her cheering comrades is one man who is a complete stranger to Greta: a man apparently in his twenties, with shades and long sideburns. She is struck by his appearance; the man returns her look of frank curiosity with a friendly nod of the head and a charming smile.

Müller; an RAF veteran wheels his chair forward. He has been confined to this conveyance since being crippled by a Special Forces bullet back in the 1970s.

'Allow me to introduce you,' says Müller. 'This is Herr Vautrin, a comrade from England. It was he who acquired for us the helicopter gunship which was so essential for your escape.'

Again, Greta clicks her heels and bows.

'You have my gratitude,' she says.

'It was my pleasure,' responds Vautrin. 'I was very anxious to get you out of that prison.'

Greta feels an immediate attraction to Vautrin—unusual for her. With his laid-back beatnik good-looks he reminds her of her lamented brother, Franz; perhaps it is this which attracts her...

'We were all anxious for your liberty,' says Müller. 'Now you can rejoin your comrades in the continuing struggle.'

A small party has been organised for the occasion of Greta's liberation. Several crates have been placed together to form a table on which there is a plentiful supply of food and drink. Greta partakes of some food, but confines herself to soft drink. She never touches alcohol. She responds civilly to the effusive congratulations of her comrades, but soon drifts away from the party. She is not a social animal. She pauses at an open crate. A batch of newly-acquired sub-machine guns nestle in the straw. She takes out one of the weapons and inspects the mechanism with a practised eye.

'You know you're just a figure-head to them, don't you?' speaks a voice.

Vautrin stands by her side.

'You think so?' says Greta, more interested in the gun.

'I do. Before I came along with my escape plan, they were quite happy for you to languish in Belsen. You see, imprisoned, you were a martyr to their cause. They thought you were of more use to them there, than at liberty and at the top of the Wanted list.'

'But you did not wish me to remain a martyr?'

'Of course not. That would have been an appalling waste.

When I suggested it, your colleagues agreed to my escape plan—but really only because they saw it as being a spectacular showpiece and therefore good publicity. That's what they're all busy celebrating now: not your liberation, but the success of the escape plan; they would have been just as pleased if it had been anyone else they'd sprung from prison. Doesn't that annoy you, Greta?'

'No... Why should it? The Cause is more important than the individual. If it is the spectacle of my escape that is most beneficial to the Cause, then so be it. And why do you criticise the plan? It was yours, was it not, Herr Vautrin?'

'Yes, it was my plan; but I didn't do it for them; or for your Cause. I had my own selfish reasons for wanting to liberate you from that prison.'

Greta frowns, looks at him. 'Your own reasons?'

'Yes. You see, I kind of misrepresented myself to Müller and the others. In fact, I lied. I don't belong to the UK branch of your organisation. As far as I know, there *isn't* a UK branch of your organisation.'

Greta's frown deepens, suspicion clouds her eyes.

'Then who are you? What do you want of me?'

'I want you, Greta.' Vautrin removes his glasses, fixing her with his feline green eyes. 'You see, I'm setting up a little activist group of my own. It will be composed entirely of girls, this group; girls who I believe deserve a chance to spread their wings, to express themselves freely. These people here: they've got you running on a narrow track; you need to break out of it.'

'I believe in the Cause...' begins Greta.

'You believe in freedom; that's what you fight for, isn't it? But what about your own personal freedom, Greta? You'll never have that with these people.' Vautrin cups her chin in his hand, gently lifts her head so that her eyes meet his. 'I'm offering you a new start. You'll make new friends; real friends who will treat you as a human being. These people here, they all just patronise you. In spite of all your skill and expertise they still deny you any advancement in rank or responsibility, don't they? If you asked them, they would probably say it was on account of your youth, but really they're just jealous of you. You owe these people nothing, Greta. The only one of them who really cared about you and respected you was your brother. You know this, don't you? Deep down, you know this.'

'Yes…' Greta gazes into those eyes.

'Then break loose. Come with me.'

'With you…' They remind her of her brother's, those eyes.

'Yes, come with me to a new life…'

'Yes…' Like her brother's eyes… Even though his eyes weren't green…

Vautrin holds something up, interposing it between Greta's eyes and his own. A black, metallic object; an ammunition clip for the machine gun she has been inspecting…

'Comrades!'

The terrorists look round from their revelry.

Greta stands before them, arms behind her back. 'I have an announcement to make. After due consideration, I have decided it is time for me to move on. Herr Vautrin has made me an offer which I have just accepted.'

'An offer?' demands Müller. 'What are you talking about?'

'Simply this: a parting of the ways, Herr Müller. I have valued my time as a member of this organisation, but now I regret that now I must say good-bye. A new Cause beckons to me.'

The object concealed behind Greta's back is revealed—locked and loaded. Without further preamble, she depresses the trigger, methodically fanning the assembly with a hail of high-velocity bullets. When the echo of the gunfire subsides, all are lying dead on the floor, Müller slumped in his wheelchair.

Solemnly, Greta salutes the corpses of her comrades.

Chapter Forty-Five
Has Anyone Seen Mark Hunter?

I know what you're thinking. I know, because I've been thinking exactly the same thing: it has been far too long since we've seen anything of Dodo Dupont. This absence of the good professor from this history for an appalling ten chapters (not counting

Chapter Forty-Two, this being one of the stops on the Solanite Express and therefore not featuring the genuine Dodo Dupont), is an unforgivable neglect of our principal female protagonist. What precisely *is* the professor's status? I call her (or perhaps I haven't called her; I can't remember) Mark Hunter's assistant, but in fact, being old friends, the duo are on a footing of complete equality. Dodo doesn't work for the Department, so she is neither Mark's subordinate nor partner—when she participates in one of the agent's assignments, it is of her own free will. (Apart from on that first occasion, of course.) But then, the working relationship of our heroes doesn't really come into it when assessing Dodo's prominence (or lack of) in this history: this story has been more about Mark because Mark has become more deeply involved than Dodo in the events as they have unfolded. But having said this, I can now assure the reader, and without giving away anything in the nature of 'spoilers', that Dodo, making her return right now, will remain from here-on a key figure in the proceedings as the events of this story build up to their crisis point.

I think of no better way to return to Dodo Dupont than to look in on her bedroom. We're all agreed on this, right? It is morning and Dodo, awoken from slumber, climbs out of bed, being careful not to disturb her partner Mayumi, who is still asleep. The first thing Dodo does—after stretching, breaking wind and scratching one well-thatched armpit—is to check her mobile. No message from Mark. She walks through into the living room. A grey sky frowns over London, and rivulets of rainwater paint a dismal pattern on the surface of the glazed outer wall.

Dodo and Mayumi had gone to the theatre the evening before. And as it is generally considered good etiquette to put one's mobile device on silent when attending such an entertainment, it hadn't been until after the show that Dodo had discovered Mark's message telling her about the call he had received from Trudie Rayne. Upon reading this message, Dodo had seen instantly what Mark had chosen not to see: that the call was obviously a trap. After ringing Mark without result, she, along with Mayumi, had proceeded straight to the warehouse in Soho. They had found the place unlocked but also unoccupied. Next, they had tried Mark's flat. Nobody home. After this, they had had no choice but to go home themselves and turn in for the night, but they were both worried.

She tries Mark's home number now. It rings but is not answered.

She puts on the coffee percolator and returns to the bedroom. She gently wakes up Mayumi.

'Mark's still not answering,' she announces.

'That's bad. What must we do?'

'I honestly don't know,' confesses Dodo. 'If the SEA girls have got Mark, it's a question of where they've taken him. Is it to some other location here in London, or all the way back to their main headquarters? At the moment, I just don't see how we can even go about looking for him.'

Fortunately, the answer to this problem is waiting for Dodo when she next checks her email inbox. Activating her phone again during breakfast coffee, she discovers she has received a message from the SEA. This in itself is unusual—the SEA have never emailed Dodo before. The message reads:

Dearest Dodo,

Don't worry about Mark. He's in safe hands. If you want to learn more—and we're sure you do!—come to our top-secret headquarters at once! All you have to do is go to that farmhouse on the Sussex Downs, the one where you found the wallet. See you soon!

lots of love, the SEA Girls

P.S. Bring Mayumi with you!

Dodo shows the message to Mayumi.

'So, what do we do?'

'Well, if we want to see if Mark's alright, we'll just have to do as they say,' says Dodo. 'Although before I put my head in the lion's mouth, I'd like to check Mark's flat again first, just to make sure they're not having us on and that he's not safe and sound at home.'

'And if he's not there we go to Sussex?'

The two women dress hurriedly. They drive to Mark's flat, to which Dodo has a spare key. No Mark, no message. That's it then—they will have to head south. Once out of the traffic nightmare of London, they make good time down the southbound motorway. The rain follows them.

'Will Mark be okay?' asks Mayumi.

'I'm hoping he will be,' says Dodo. 'I mean, I know what those girls are capable of, but they seem to have this kind of twisted affection for Mark, their "designated arch-enemy"—'

'And for you; they like you, too!'

A smile. 'Yes. And me. So yes, I don't think they would have arranged that elaborate trap, if all they wanted to do was kill Mark. What I'm hoping is that they're just having a good laugh at poor Mark's expense for being so gullible and believing that story of Trudie's…'

'This makes the second time he's walked into trap like this,' says Mayumi. 'There was that time with the prostitute; he walked into trap then, also.'

'Yes, but I don't think Mark was so much to blame on that occasion,' answers Dodo. 'He knew he'd made an enemy of Wainwright, but he couldn't have guessed just how deep it went. He'd just assumed that that man's revenge would have been satisfied by getting Mark suspended from his job. And it sounds like that woman who picked him up sold him a convincing story.'

'Does Mark always get picked up by women in bars?'

'I don't think he makes a habit of it, love. But then, until he got suspended, he wasn't in the habit of sitting drinking by himself in fancy bars.'

'We don't see him so much since they suspend him; I think he's avoiding us.'

'That's what I've been thinking, as well. I think he wants to lick his wounds in private, or something…'

Finally, they arrive at the farmhouse. Uncheerful at the best of times, the solitary house looks especially forlorn under the heavy grey cloud; the muddy brown brickwork darkened by the rain to even more melancholy shade. Dodo pulls up close to the front door.

'Come on, then,' says Dodo. 'I'd have liked to have left you out of this, sweetheart, but those girls have insisted on your presence.'

'That's okay,' Mayumi assures her. 'I wanna help, anyway. Let's rescue Mark!'

Dodo squeezes her arm. 'We'll do our damnedest,' she smiles.

Inside, the house looks as abandoned as it had the last time Dodo was here. No sign of a welcoming committee.

'Where is the secret entrance?' Mayumi wants to know.

'That's just it. We couldn't find it last time we were here.'

'Then how do you know it is here?'

'Well, the girls told us to come here, didn't they? And they knew we found that wallet here last time.'

'What wallet?'

'The wallet belonging to that scientist who escaped from the SEA base.'

'Oh yeah. The guy who blew up.'

Dodo pushes open the double doors of the back room.

'In here. This is where Mark found the wallet.'

'And you check the floor for trapdoors?'

'No point. There's a cellar underneath.'

'You check the cellar?'

'We did. There was no sign of a secret entrance.'

'Then maybe this is the wrong place,' suggests Mayumi.

'But we were told to come here,' Dodo reminds her.

They step back into the front room.

'Maybe it was a trick,' persists Mayumi.

'You mean we were brought here on a wild-goose chase? That's possible, of course...' Dodo raises her voice. 'But if, on the other hand, those little brats *are* here and they're just having another laugh by messing us around, how about they stop now? We came here at their request, remember?'

As if in response to this the double doors behind them slam shut, eliciting satisfyingly startled reactions from the two women. Now comes the unmistakable sound of a lift car ascending. The sound stops. The doors swing open again, gently this time, revealing two bright red metal doors where before there had been a room. The doors slide open, revealing a brightly-lit lift car, untenanted.

Mayumi examines the lift through her glasses. She looks up at Dodo. 'I think they want us to get in lift,' she pronounces.

'I think they do,' agrees Dodo.

They step inside. The doors close. The lift descends.

'We're going to the secret base?' questions Mayumi.

'Looks very much like it.'

The lift comes to a halt. The doors open. Standing before them in a white, futuristic corridor is the reception committee: Vautrin, flanked by all eleven of the SEA girls. Friendly smiles all round.

And no sign of Mark.

'Professor Dodo Dupont,' greets Vautrin. 'It's a real pleasure to meet you at last. I'm Vautrin.'

Dodo and Mayumi step from the lift.

Vautrin turns to Mayumi.

'And Takahashi-san. Honoured to meet you also. The girls are all great admirers of your photography.'

He bows to the Japanese woman; she returns the gesture.

Dodo surveys the man—or being—she has heard so much about, but has never actually met until this moment. Young, good-looking, laid-back, confident; just the kind of roguish pretty-boy to turn the heads of a bunch of teenage girls—but has he turned their minds as well? How has this Svengali managed to convince these girls to join his lunatic organisation? Has he really worked some spell over them, as Mark believes? And will he attempt to use that same influence upon herself? She will have to be very wary with this man. But then, perhaps as adults Mayumi and herself are safe; perhaps he can only work his mesmerism on the impressionable semi-formed minds of youths.

And the girls: here they all are. Fawning over Vautrin like

groupies around a rock-star. It has to be more than just the pheromones of an alpha-male that draw them to him.

She decides to come straight to the point. 'Where's Mark?'

'Not here, I'm afraid,' answers Vautrin.

'You told me he was!'

'Did we? When we invited you here, I think we just said he was safe. Let's go to the girls' recreation room. We can talk more comfortably there.'

Dodo acquiesces. Vautrin leading the way, they move down the corridor, Greta and Jessica clinging to Mayumi's arms, Sophie and Dizzy to Dodo's.

Dodo looks around her. 'Just how big is this place?'

'I'm not entirely sure,' confesses Vautrin.

'You're not sure? You built this place, didn't you?'

'No.'

'Then who did build it?'

'I don't think anyone built it. It's just here.'

'And how about that lift?' Dodo wants to know. 'How can it suddenly appear in a room that was empty a moment before?'

'When it's not needed it's not there,' shrugs Vautrin. 'We have another lift for vehicles that descends from the barn next to the farmhouse.'

They walk into the rec room. Dodo is not altogether surprised to find the walls decorated with photographs of her good self.

'My pictures!' cries Mayumi, delighted.

'You're going to love it here!' promises Sophie, hugging Dodo round the waist. 'We've got a guest suite all prepared for you. It's great! It's got everything you'll want!'

'We didn't come here for a sleepover,' protests Dodo.

'Ah, but we insist you remain our guests for a short while,' says Vautrin.

'Look, I came here to find Mark!'

'I know. And you'll be our guests until it's time for you to join him.'

'And why can't we see him now?'

Vautrin shakes his head. 'Not possible, I'm afraid. Not yet.'

'But you know where he is?'

'Yes and no.'

Dodo growls. 'Straight answers, please. You lured Mark to that warehouse in Soho, and you captured him. So where is he?'

'We lured him to the warehouse, yes; but we didn't take him prisoner.'

'Then what did you do with him?'

'Something very interesting. You know that I have some scientists here, working under my direction on solanite experiments?'

'The Peltdown Vale team; yes. What's that got to do with Mark?'

'I'll explain, if you'll let me: Under my guidance this team has constructed a device, a rifle, which fires a concentrated beam of solanite energy.'

'And?'

'We zapped Mark with it!' declares Dizzy, brightly. 'Well, Rachel did.'

'What!' Dodo grabs Vautrin by the collar. 'You maniac!'

The SEA girls close in around Dodo. The air becomes thick with their sudden hostility. Had anybody but Dodo dared to lay hands on Vautrin, the assailant would have been torn to pieces in an instant.

'Let go of him,' orders Juliette.

Dodo obeys. She doesn't have just her own life to think about.

'What's happened to him?' she insists, addressing Vautrin. 'Has he disappeared?'

'As I said, he's not accessible to you right now,' insists Vautrin. 'But we have him under observation.'

'What's happening to him?'

'You could say he's gone on a journey—'

'A first-class ticket for the Solanite Express!' chips in Dizzy.

'—A metaphysical journey. When he arrives at the terminus; that will be when you can see him.'

'You don't have to worry,' Trudie assures Dodo. 'None of us would let anything bad happen to Mark.'

Dodo relents. 'I suppose I'll have to play this your way, if I ever want to see Mark. Well, as we're your prisoners—'

'Guests!' insists Dizzy.

Dodo looks at Mayumi. 'Sorry I dragged you into this, sweetheart. But it looks like we're going to be here for a while.'

'That's okay,' says Mayumi. 'This place looks fun!'

Chapter Forty-Six
It Happened Like This

'Here comes Chambers,' announces Mark. 'He'll be taking the plans to Marshall. Or what he thinks are the plans. We know that Chambers has gambling debts from Hammond's casino. When Marshall's man Woodhouse approached Chambers to steal the submarine plans, Chambers saw this as his way out. It should have been simple: Chambers' brother was director of the project. All Chambers had to do was get hold of the keys and have copies made. Simple. But there was one problem: Chambers is a coward. He just couldn't nerve himself to carry out the robbery himself. That was where Mills came in. Chambers knew Mills was secretly seeing his brother's wife. The solution: blackmail Mills into stealing the plans. That should have made things easier; Mills had legitimate access to the office; no-one would suspect him. Unfortunately, the night Mills arrived to steal the plans, Dr Chambers returned to the office unexpectedly. There was a fight; Mills killed Dr Chambers. Now, Chambers wanted the plans, he wanted the money, but he never wanted his brother killed. Result: Chambers, when he found out what had transpired, lost his head and killed Mills. Chambers then tried to frame his brother's wife for the murder; she had always despised him, so he had no qualms about doing that. Unfortunately for Chambers, in his rage he had killed Mills before learning where he had hidden the plans. Luckily for us, we found them first. We replaced them with our own fake plans and left them for Chambers to find. And now Chambers is taking the plans to Marshall, where he thinks he'll be paid and that it will all be over. But what Chambers doesn't know is that Marshall is in cahoots with Hammond's casino. The poker games were fixed so that Chambers would lose heavily. Now they've got him where they want him, they're not going to let him go so easily.'

'So we move in and grab the lot?' asks Dodo.

'Not quite yet. We know Marshall is using his toy emporium as a cover for smuggling secrets out of the country, but there's somebody else above him; we don't know who that person is.'

'You think they'll show up tonight?'

'I'm hoping they will. There's a very good chance.'

Mark and Dodo stand at the window of an empty second floor room, directly across the street from Marshall's toy shop. The room is in darkness. Below, in the street the illuminated bow window of the toy shop spills its light across the pavement. Agents Daisy Fontaine and Mike Collins are covering the back of the target building.

'Here comes someone,' murmurs Dodo.

Mark scans the street below with his field-glasses.

'Well, well, well. If it isn't our friend Spooner.'

'He's not the mastermind, surely?'

'No, I don't think so. Spooner is just another pawn in the game. As Sir Malcolm's private secretary, he would be very useful for them to have in their pocket. They got at him through his cocaine habit. He was introduced to the stuff at a nightclub known as the Golden Fleece. The Golden Fleece is owned by Hammond. It was all arranged from the start. Spooner would do anything to avoid the scandal that would follow if his drug habit was made public.'

'Someone else coming,' observes Dodo. 'A woman.'

Mark applies himself to the field-glasses again. 'I don't believe it! Mrs Chambers!'

'Don't tell me she's behind all this!'

'She must be the one! Yes! It all makes sense now!'

'Not to me it doesn't!'

'Explanations later,' says Mark. 'We've got to move fast. Mrs

B won't have forgiven Chambers for trying to frame her for the murder of Mills. We've got to move in.' He picks up his RT. 'Collins. We're moving in. You and Daisy move in from the rear, but keep out of sight until we need you.'

'Roger.'

Mark and Dodo leave the empty building and cross the street to Marshall's toy shop. A bell tinkles when they open the door. Marshall's caters for the adult collector of models and toys rather than for children; Victorian teddy bears, china dolls, model vintage cars are on display; on a central table, a model train set has been set up in its own miniature landscape. Electric candles in wall brackets discreetly light the shop. A man appears from a back room.

'I'm sorry, sir, madam; we're closed.'

It is Woodhouse. Mark walks up to the counter, smiling.

'I know it's late, but I just had to come by and inquire after my Pup.'

'Your pup, sir? A stuffed toy?'

'No-no, a Sopwith Pup. 1918 vintage, RFC markings.'

'Oh, I see! A model aeroplane.'

'That's right. I brought it in for repairs. Some of the struts had been damaged.'

'Well, if you'll bear with me, sir, I'll just consult the ledger.'

Woodhouse lifts a large leather-bound tome from under the counter.

'Your name, sir?'

'Hunter. Mark Hunter.'

Woodhouse scans the page. 'Hunter... No, I don't see anything... When did you bring the item to us?'

He lowers the book, sees his customer covering him with a gun.

'No noise. Just lead the way through to the back.'

'What's this about?' demands Woodhouse.

'Just take us to where Mrs Chambers is,' says Mark. 'Nice and quietly.'

Dodo lifts the counter flap; they follow Woodhouse through a door, along a passage, into a storage area. An interrogation is in progress. Chambers sits on a straight-backed wooden chair, menaced by Mrs Chambers, Hammond and Marshall. Spooner stands off to one side.

'What is it, Woodhouse?' snaps the widow. 'I told you—'

Then she catches sight of Mark and Dodo. A gun appears in her gloved hand. Mark and Dodo dive behind two rows of shelves; Woodhouse, not so fast off the mark, finds himself the recipient of the bullets intended for the intruders.

'Now look what you've done!' roars Marshall, as Woodhouse crumples to the floor.

'Fontaine! Collins!' yells Mark, firing off a shot. Everyone dives for cover. Fontaine and Collins burst in through the rear entrance. More shots. Taking advantage of the confusion, Chambers pounces on his former sister-in-law, wrestles with her for the gun.

Hammond takes a shot in the shoulder, drops his gun, falls to his knees. Marshall breaks cover and runs for a side door. Fontaine moves in to intercept him. Marshall fires, the bullet takes Daisy Fontaine between the eyes.

'Daisy!' cries Mark. He watches in disbelief as his colleague falls down dead.

It wasn't supposed to happen like this.

Marshall disappears through the side door.

'I'll get after him!' cries Dodo.

In a daze, Mark follows her. Through the side door a stairwell. Rickety wooden stairs climbing several floors to the garret. Mark, at Dodo's heels, bounds up the stairs.

Daisy Fontaine is dead. What Mark feels is more than just shock at the suddenness of the tragedy. It is all wrong. Why would Fontaine have run to intercept an armed man instead of just bringing him down with a leg-shot? She was a trained operative. She just wouldn't have done something that stupid. It is all *wrong*—like watching a film you think you've seen many times and know backwards, but then suddenly one of the performers says or does something you know they weren't supposed to; that they'd never done before. The kind of impossible occurrence that could only happen in a dream.

But this isn't a dream, is it?

Mark tops the last flight of stairs. Dodo is already across the cluttered garret and climbing out through a dormer window in pursuit of Marshall. Mark climbs out after her. Outside the window, a narrow shelf of flat roof; four floors below, the street; the night is cold. Ahead, he sees Dodo, climbing up onto the neighbouring roof; further ahead, Marshall, silhouetted against the sky as he negotiates the building's sloping roof.

Mark crosses the flat roof, grabs the ledge, pulls himself up onto the next roof. He moves unsteadily along the tiles of the inclined roof, avoiding a skylight. Ahead he sees Marshall. The crook has come to the edge of the next flat roof. A chasm yawns between this building and the next. Marshall looks back, sees his pursuers closing, and, taking a short run-up, clears the gap. Landing on the gable, he pulls himself up to the apex of the roof.

Dodo doesn't hesitate; she jumps straight after him. Mark drops onto the flat roof, runs straight at the gap and leaps. He slams into the gable, his hands fail to grip the summit, he slips.

'Dodo!' he cries.

He is slipping further. He can find no purchase on the slate tiles. Dodo has stopped, is looking back at him.

'Help me!' yelps Mark.

He has slipped to the edge, his legs dangling over the abyss. There is no cornice, no guttering to grab hold of. Dodo just stands there.

'I can't help you, Mark,' she says, her voice sounding odd, colourless. 'We don't exist on the same plane of reality. We inhabit different worlds. So you see: I can't help you.'

'For God's sake, I'm going to fall!'

'I'm sorry, Mark. I just can't help you...'

And Mark falls.

Chapter Forty-Seven
Bathing with the Enemy

Fanservice time again.

We join the SEA girls and their honoured guests in the base's communal bath; a Japanese bath, the size of a small swimming pool, sunk into the floor. For those of you who don't know how these things work, with a Japanese bath you first do all your soaping and rinsing from a tub on the tiles outside the bath and only then, when you're squeaky clean, do you get into the water. A Japanese bath is for soaking in, not for wallowing in your own dirt. As said, Dodo and Mayumi are present, along with all of the SEA girls, with the single exception of Trudie Rayne, who is currently 'away on business.'

Our professor of psychology and our acclaimed photographer squat on two of the tiny plastic stools, submitting to being soaped and sponged by two of the SEA girls; Sophie administering unto Dodo, while Dizzy performs the same office for Mayumi. The remainder of the SEA girls are already in the bath.

'...No, I wouldn't say my worldview has changed drastically since I was a teenager,' Dodo is saying in response to a query put to her by Juliette. 'But, yes, my opinions have evolved over the years. I'd say that nearly always happens—whether you cultivate your own opinions or if you just copy other people's. To be honest, looking back I'm deeply embarrassed about some of the bullshit I spouted back when I was your age.'

'So you're saying you think that us girls won't think the same way as we do now in ten years' time?' challenges Juliette.

'Well... I hate to be pessimistic, but I'm not sure that any of you lot will still be around in ten years' time.'

'Oh, Dodo!' reproves Sophie, pausing in her diligent scrubbing of Dodo's back. 'That's not a nice thing to say!'

Dodo shrugs. 'Well, what do you think? Where do you all see yourselves in ten years' time?'

'We don't think that far ahead,' answers Dizzy, pouring water over Mayumi to wash away the soap-suds.

'I *can't* think that far ahead,' confesses Sophie. 'I just can't picture that in my mind. I can think about what I might be doing tomorrow or next week, but I just can't see much further than that.'

'Maybe you can't visualise your future because you know subconsciously that you haven't got one,' suggests Dodo. 'Or at least you know that the lives you're living now can't possibly go on for much longer... You're like the depressive who can only cope with the present by blocking out the future, living one day at a time.'

Rinsed off, the two women step into the hot bath and sit themselves down amongst the SEA girls.

'Why are you wearing your watch?' asks Dizzy of Jessica.

'That's alright; it's waterproof!' announces Jessica, proudly displaying the timepiece in question.

'Yeah, most watches are waterproof,' says Rachel. 'But we still usually take them off when we get in the bath. So do you, usually.'

Frowning, Jessie looks at the face of her watch, as though it might tell why she has elected to wear it in the bath—but as usual, it only tells her the time.

Dodo and Mayumi have now spent two days in SEA captivity. Apart from the loss of their liberty, they have had nothing of which to complain; in fact, the two women have been treated like royalty. A sumptuous guest suite has been allotted to them. The wardrobes are liberally supplied with clothes to fit both women. There's even a cupboard full of hats for Mayumi. They have been served the best food, and the SEA girls have gone out of their way to keep the women entertained. In short, the SEA girls are the most agreeable bunch of sociopaths with whom Dodo and Mayumi have ever been forced to spend time.

But a constant source of worry for Dodo is the question of Mark Hunter's whereabouts. Where is he? Vautrin has assured Dodo that she and Mayumi will be reunited with him soon, but on separate occasions has said 'he will be joining us' and 'you will be joining him.' Is Mark going to be brought to the SEA base, or will she be taken to wherever he is now? Is he somewhere within the confines of the base already? The corridors of the complex seem to be endless; Dodo and Mayumi have been adjured not to wander too far or they will find themselves lost.

Just what is happening to Mark? He has been subjected to a dose of alien radiation, according to Vautrin. Nobody really knows the effects of solanite; it is an unknown element. While scientists were experimenting with the stuff at Peltdown Vale, a whole building had disappeared. But now those scientists are apparently to be found right here in the SEA complex, working in captivity. (Dodo and Mayumi have not been allowed to see them.) What is the connection between solanite energy, Vautrin, and this base? Vautrin has spoken of Mark being on a 'trip'; a metaphysical journey aboard the 'Solanite Express'. Does this mean he is at rest somewhere, lying in a bed in some room, dreaming whatever it is he is going through? Or is he actually in motion; physically involved? Vautrin refuses to elaborate on this question, and whenever Dodo attempts to broach the subject with any of the SEA girls, they will immediately change the subject. (Dizzy had gone so far as to clamp her hands over her ears and start singing: 'I'm not listening to you! I'm not listening to you!') Dodo has been forced to resign herself to await events with as much patience as she can muster. She is a prisoner in this place; she will just have to play the game Vautrin's way for now.

She relaxes in the hot water of the bath, Mayumi by her side, the other girls all around. They are an interesting study. She has spoken to them all individually as well as collectively while she has been here. Vautrin has clearly brought his personality to bear on all of them, but whether it is to the extent of hypnotism, or just an abundance of charisma, she still isn't sure. These girls, who had until recently led completely separate lives, are somehow connected; they are linked, claims Vautrin, by some invisible thread of causality. And Vautrin, whose mind can apparently reach out to some astral plain beyond the limits of conscious human minds, had discovered that connection and brought the girls together.

'Another question, Dodo,' says Juliette. 'Do you agree that there's no such thing as an unselfish act?'

'Well, you would have to deny such concepts as generosity and consideration to others, wouldn't you?' replies Dodo.

'I don't deny those concepts. I say that generosity and consideration are selfish themselves.'

Dodo shrugs. 'Well yes, if you want to look at it that way, you could assign selfish motives to just about any human action short of sacrificing your own life on the spur of the moment. If you buy a friend a present, something you know they will like, you could be said to be doing it as much for yourself as for them.'

'Because you want to hear their gratitude to you,' says Flossie.

'Not necessarily even that,' counters Dodo. 'The very act of performing a generous deed makes us feel good; that could be called the primary selfish motive.'

'You talk of buying your friend a present,' says Albertine. 'I would say it is more selfish when you buy zhem something zat *you* like—a favourite book or CD—instead of getting zhem something you know zhey would like. You are merely selfishly imposing your tastes and preferences on others.'

'I think that sort of thing can be less to do with selfishness, and more with the egocentric expectation that other people are going to like whatever it is that we like,' answers Dodo. 'It's a common enough human failing; we've probably all been guilty of it. Often, we just can't take into account the fact that everybody has different tastes, and—sticking with your book or CD example—that what might be sublime music or literature to you, might do absolutely nothing for the next person. As human individuals, we can't help measuring other people by our own yard-stick.'

'And that's what makes you different, Dodo!' declares Dizzy. 'You can get into other people's heads; you can understand where they're coming from. Christ, I bet you even understand me!'

Dodo smiles. 'Understanding you, Dizzy Hello, would be one hell of an achievement.'

Dizzy claps her hands gleefully, clearly taking this as a

compliment. Giggling all round.

'There's nothing wrong with being selfish, anyway,' remarks Rachel. 'It's just natural, isn't it?'

'Well yes, but "Natural" isn't necessarily "right," you know,' argues Dodo. 'Things that are acceptable in the animal kingdom might not be acceptable for us, because we're burdened with intelligence, a conscience; with civilisation we have built up codes of ethics, dos and don'ts of moral behaviour. For example, you could say it's perfectly "natural" to be a coward, to run away from danger; but our intelligent and moral side tells us that cowardice isn't a good thing, especially when it involves saving our own skins at the expense of other people's.'

'Sade, when he was talking about that sort of thing, always talked about "Nature" with a capital "N,"' says Juliette. 'He thought everyone should be true to how Nature made them.'

'And that's kind of ironic, really. Sade was virulently anti-religion, yet you could say he was almost deifying nature by speaking of it with a capital "N" like he did. But then, the Sadean philosophy is basically about establishing your worldview, deciding all your thoughts and actions based upon how you feel about these things when you're at the peak of sexual arousal.'

Dizzy looks confused. 'I don't get it. When I'm really turned on, I look at things the same way as I do the rest of the time. Doesn't everyone do that?'

'No, that will just be you, Dizzy,' Dodo tells her.

'Hey, I've just realised something,' speaks Chrissie: 'We're one person short? Where's Greta?'

Everyone looks around.

'She's not here,' says Sophie.

'Yeah, but she *was* here,' insists Chrissie. 'And I never saw her get out of the bath.'

Other voices concur—Greta did indeed originally form one of their number in the bath. So where is she now?

A general search is about to be instituted, but then, bursting out of the water like a cork, appears the girl herself. She noisily exhales the pent-up breath from her lungs.

'So! How long?' Greta directs this question at Jessica.

'How long what?' asks Jessie.

'How long vos I able to remain submerged!' snaps Greta. 'You vere timing me, *ja*?'

'Timing you…?' Jessica transfers her confused look from Greta to her wristwatch. And then, enlightenment spreads its radiance across her features. 'Oh yes! *That* was why I was wearing my watch in the bath! I was supposed to be timing you! Silly me!'

Greta's Scowling visage suggests stronger terms than 'Silly me!' to describe this act of remissness on the part of Jessica.

The guest suite.

The main room is airy, furnished in a modern, comfortable style. Doors on the left and right give access to bedrooms. The chamber on the right has been occupied by Dodo and Mayumi; the one left is apparently waiting for Mark Hunter. A third door gives access to the *en suite* bathroom. Adorning the rear wall of the living space, a splendid framed painting, *The Rape of Europa* by Félix Vallotton, oil on canvas. (Dodo had assumed this painting to be a reproduction, until art expert Dizzy Hello had assured her that it was in fact the original. 'It's a fake one they've got hanging in the Cunts Museum,' meaning '*Kunstmuseum*.')

We see Mayumi stretched out on the sofa reading a magazine. The doors swoosh open and Dodo enters.

'I can't find bloody Vautrin anywhere,' she announces.

'And there is still no news about Mark?' asks Mayumi.

'No there isn't, and I'm getting fed-up of waiting. I'm wondering if we shouldn't start thinking about escaping from this place. They just keep us hanging on with these vague promises that we'll be "seeing Mark soon."'

Dodo drops onto the sofa next to her partner.

'Maybe we should look around this place,' suggests Mayumi. 'See if we can find Mark.'

'Yes, that's another idea. This place is big enough to get lost in, so we've been told. Plenty of room for them to be hiding Mark somewhere.'

And then it happens. A hissing sound. Dodo spins round and sees thick white gas seeping through the key-hole into the room. This is all the more surprising given that the sliding door had been innocent of any key-hole until a moment before.

'They're gassing us!'

Shielding her nose and mouth with her arm, Dodo rushes for the door. The sensor-operated door, which normally opens automatically, fails to perform its usual office, remaining stubbornly closed.

Coughing, Dodo backs away from the door, re-joins Mayumi, who hugs her for protection.

'They're killing us!'

'No, it's a knock-out gas,' coughs Dodo.

Now, whether Dodo is enough of an expert to have determined this fact from the odour of the gas, or if she merely seeks to reassure her lover in what actually might be their final moments, I cannot say. Either way, she fortunately happens to be correct. The two women, overcome by the fumes now filling the room, fall back onto the sofa, locked in each other's arms; incapacitated but still amongst the living.

Chapter Forty-Eight
In Which Dodo and Mayumi Wake Up in a Strange Place

An unfamiliar ceiling. An unfamiliar bed.

Dodo gathers her thoughts, swiftly arranging them into chronological sequence: SEA headquarters—the guest suite—the white gas filling the room. Yes, that was the last thing that happened; the final memory before oblivion. Dodo takes in her new surroundings Where is she now? A bedroom, modestly sized and furnished; such as you would find in any ordinary flat or house. Daylight filters in through the drawn curtains. Mayumi lies by her side, still sleeping. She carefully draws back the covers and swings her legs out of the bed. On a chair, hers and Mayumi's clothes, carefully folded. On top of the clothes, Mayumi's glasses, also carefully folded. Dodo stands up, inspects the pile of clothes. Yes, it is their own clothes; the same they were wearing when they were overcome by the gas.

She moves over to the window, pulls back the curtains. She sees a street; a narrow thoroughfare flanked by a row of fairly modern terrace houses. Of traffic and people, she sees none.

Returning to the bed, she gently wakes Mayumi.

Her eyes open, focus on Dodo. She smiles sleepily.

'Hey...'

'How do you feel?' Dodo asks her, stroking her cheek.

'Okay...' She looks around. 'Where are we?'

'In a house, it seems. I've no idea where.'

'We not in SEA base anymore?'

'Nope. Wherever we are, we're above ground.'

'How rong have we been asleep?'

Dodo looks at her watch. 'It's morning. So, for several hours, apparently.'

The two women dress.

'Whose house are we in?' asks Mayumi.

'I don't know. As it must have been the SEA brought us here, it might be one of their safehouses; and that could mean we're back in London. Let's go and see who's home.'

They find no-one downstairs. They check every room in the house: living room, kitchen, bathroom, bedrooms; the house is fully furnished, but there are no signs of occupation.

'You know, this house has never been lived in,' declares Dodo. 'You can sense it as much as you can see it.'

'Just been built?'

'Could be. But then why is it furnished?'

They check the kitchen. The cupboards contain crockery and cutlery, but no food. The fridge is plugged in and working, but devoid of contents. They try the taps of the sink. The water supply is connected. The kitchen window looks out on a paved yard;

beyond that, a wall; beyond that, the back yards of another row of houses.

'Everything's connected,' observes Dodo. 'Water, electricity... But if the SEA were using this place, you'd expect it to look lived in; at least you'd have thought there'd be food in the kitchen... Let's go outside and see if we can find out where we are...'

There is a telephone in the hallway. Dodo picks up the receiver, listens.

'Dead.'

They step out into the street. The house proves to be one of a terrace identical in appearance to the row across the road. The street is deserted; no people, not even a parked car. The air is still, the silence deathly. At one end of the street the houses terminate abruptly; beyond, open countryside, as far as the eye can see. At its other extremity the street opens out onto a paved town square, overlooked by a large structure which looks to be a municipal building of some kind.

'Well, we're not in London,' remarks Dodo. 'You can't hear any traffic; not even in the distance. This must be a village or small town, I'd say. But where the hell are the people? There ought to be someone about...'

'Maybe it Sunday,' suggests Mayumi.

'Then we would have to have been asleep for several days, and the state of my legs tells me we haven't. Let's try the neighbours.'

They knock on the door of the adjoining house. They wait. No answer. Dodo tries the door. It opens.

'Hello?'

Receiving no reply, they venture inside and find themselves in a living room identical to the one they have just left—completely identical.

'Okay, this is weird,' says Dodo. 'Every stick of furniture exactly the same.'

They inspect the kitchen, the bedroom, bathroom; every single detail is a duplication of the neighbouring house.

'Come on.'

They run across the street, check out several of the houses

opposite. The pattern repeats itself; the interior of each house is as identical as the exterior.

'This must be a new town,' declares Mayumi. 'No-one's moved in.'

'That's one theory,' acknowledges Dodo 'The houses look new enough; but the architecture doesn't. It looks more 1950s to me.'

'The retro look.'

'It's not a very appealing retro, is it? Post-War austerity… Come on, let's try that town hall, or whatever it is.'

They set off along the street. The silence persists; nothing moves. They arrive at the town square. Its centre-piece is a war memorial; and amongst the buildings facing it: an old-fashioned public house, the George and Dragon; a quaint-looking post-office-cum-general store; and the large administrative building. Further streets, with identical rows of terrace houses, radiate from the square.

'There's something weird about this place…' says Dodo. 'Something's missing…'

'People,' supplies Mayumi.

'Something else, too… I know what it is! No grass or trees. Look! You'd expect a plot of grass or some flowerbeds around this war memorial, and none of the houses we've seen have gardens; just bare back-yards. There's not a blade of grass anywhere.' She points an accusing finger at the municipal building. 'And *that's* wrong, as well. From all we can see, this looks like a very small village—so why such a large administrative building? It doesn't look right.'

'Why did they bring us here?' wonders Mayumi.

'Good question. What game are those girls playing with us now? And are they watching us from somewhere? They must be, mustn't they?' In a louder voice: 'Well, are you here? Okay; you've got us confused; now, how about showing yourselves? Game over!'

They wait, Dodo with impatiently folded arms. No SEA girls oblige them by appearing.

'Looks like they haven't finished toying with us yet,' says

Dodo. 'Come on; let's try that town hall.'

The doors of the building are unlocked. They pass into a vestibule. An unpleasant smell greets them.

'Ugh!' from Mayumi, holding her nose. 'Smells like rotten meat!'

Dodo looks grim. 'I think I know what it is… Where's it coming from…?'

A pair of important-looking doors stand on their left. Dodo opens one of the doors. The stench is immediately much stronger. Mayumi is about to follow her in, but Dodo gently pushes her back.

'You stay here, sweetheart. I think I know what's in here and it isn't going to be pretty.'

'Okay,' acquiesces Mayumi, content not to witness anything which might offend her Japanese woman's refined sense of beauty.

Dodo enters the room, closing the door behind her. A conference room, oak-panelled, thick carpeted, dominated by a sturdy oak table supplied with tall-backed chairs. The bodies are lying on the floor. Six of them, in army uniforms; an officer and five squaddies. They have all been shot, and from the state of decomposition Dodo surmises they have been left lying like this for at least a week. Shielding her nose, she makes a cursory examination of the bodies, looking for any clues. She finds nothing: no papers of identification, gun holsters empty.

She returns to the vestibule and acquaints Mayumi with her discovery.

'If they're genuine army soldiers, then this place could be a barracks town,' hypothesises Dodo. 'That might explain the uniformity of the place. If it is a barracks town, then the SEA must have somehow taken over the place.'

'Why would they do that?'

'I wish I knew.'

'What should we do now?'

'I think leaving would be a good idea,' answers Dodo. 'The SEA obviously want us in this place for some reason; if we try to leave, the girls may show themselves.'

They emerge from the town hall, and proceed back down the same street of houses. At the far end, the terraces end abruptly, interrupted by a road. A tall hedgerow borders the road on the opposite side; beyond this, open fields.

'This looks like a ring-road circling the village,' she observes. 'But I can't see any road leading away from it. Look—the hedge follows it all the way around; as far as we can see, anyway.'

'Do we have to climb over the hedge?' asks Mayumi.

'Let's walk along the road a bit. Maybe we'll find a checkpoint.'

They proceed along the road. It soon becomes clear that the road does indeed encompass the entire village. The hedge tall that borders it remains unbroken. No gate and guardhouse; nary a stile or farm track.

Dodo stops. Mayumi does likewise.

'This is insane,' declares Dodo. 'This hedge goes right around the village like a perimeter fence. How the hell does anyone get in or out?'

'It's crazy,' agrees Mayumi.

'And another thing: over that hedge, green fields and trees. This side of it, not a single blade of grass. It's like nature is being kept at arm's length.'

'So, what do we do now?'

'We'll have to climb over the hedge. Maybe we can force a way through it.'

Dodo advances towards the hedge. Mayumi is much surprised to see her suddenly spring backwards with a yelp, landing on her rear suspension.

'What's up? Did you see something?' from Mayumi, confused.

'No, something hit me; it was—Hang on a mo."

Rising to her feet, she steps forward, cautiously this time, arms extended, palms forward. Her hands meet resistance, her palms begin to tingle with pins-and-needles. She pushes harder; the resistance increases correspondingly.

'It's a bloody forcefield!' she cries, incredulous.

'Oh! I didn't know they make them!'

'*I* didn't know they made them.'

Mayumi joins her, touches the invisible barrier with her palms. 'It tingles!'

'Yes, it's definitely a magnetic barrier of some sort; it's not just a transparent solid wall.'

'Does it go right round the village?'

'That's what I'm assuming, but let's check anyway…'

They follow the course of the perimeter road, running at a jog-trot, stopping at times to feel for the energy barrier. It is always there; right at the edge of the road, just in front of the hedge. At one point, Dodo tries pushing her whole body against the energy field; but the more she pushes, the more resistance she encounters, the stronger becomes the static electricity pins-and-needles sensation.

'I wonder how high it is…' says Mayumi.

'High enough,' asserts Dodo. 'You know, it might even be a dome, covering the entire village.' She puts her hands on her hips, surveying the sky, imagining the invisible barrier that hems them in. 'This has got to be Vautrin's doing… No-one on Earth made this forcefield.'

'So… we stuck here…'

'Yes, until Vautrin or some of those girls decide to show themselves.'

'You think they watching us?'

'They've got to be… I don't see any surveillance cameras—but then, that could just mean they're well-hidden…'

Mayumi has turned to face the nearest street, another one of those double-rows of terrace houses, radiating, like the spokes of a wheel, from the village square. 'I see someone!' she exclaims.

Dodo spins round. 'Where?'

'In the square. He just run round corner. I think he see me.'

'He? It wasn't one of the girls?'

'No, it was a man.'

'Vautrin… Or maybe Mark?' suddenly excited. 'Yes! Vautrin said we'd be joining Mark soon! Maybe this is it. Come on!'

Calling Mark's name, Dodo tears up the street, Mayumi keeping up as best she can. Dodo emerges into the square, just in time to ses a figure duck around a corner by the chintzy post office.

A man in a brown suit.

'Mark!'

She dashes across the square, turns into the yard behind the post office.

And there he is. Mark Hunter. Brown suit dishevelled, tie askew, several days growth of beard on his chin—but indisputably Mark.

Dodo grins broadly, sighs. 'Mark! Thank Christ; I—'

She stops. Something is wrong. Mark just stands there, not moving, looking at her blankly.

'Mark, are you alright?'

No answer.

Mayumi appears.

'Hey!'

Mark reacts neither to her presence or her greeting.

'What wrong with him?' asks Mayumi.

'I dunno… They've done something… What have they done to you, Mark? You know who we are, right? Dodo and Mayumi, yes? Your best friends?'

That dose of solanite energy, thinks Dodo. What the hell has it done to him? Scrambled his brains?

She walks up to Mark, slowly, half-fearing he will bolt again. 'Let me help you, Mark. I can help you…'

She reaches out, touched his arm.

He shakes her off.

Dodo recoils, hurt. 'Mark? What's wrong? It's me: Dodo…'

Mark looks at her, accusation lighting up his weary eyes. 'I know you…' he says. 'You killed me…'

Chapter Forty-Nine
A Serial Killer is Forced out of Retirement

Islington City Council. The housing department. The usual open-plan office. I don't think I need to describe the set-up: I'm sure that many of you reading this book, either having nothing better to do, or else still vainly hoping for something better to do, work in office environments just like this one. We have the usual line-up of characters: the ubiquitous office clown, not nearly as funny as he thinks he is; the handsome bachelor who's having an affair with the supervisor (she of course being married); the young 'Work-Related Activity Group' mental-health case who serves as office dog's-body; the vague, colourless secretary who appears devoid not only of a sense of humour, but much in the way of any personality at all...

And then there's the retired serial killer. He, I admit, is not usually to be found amongst stock characters in your average open-plan office—but this particular open-plan office does happen to boast one of these originals (a fact unknown to all apart from the retired serial killer himself.)

It's our old friend Robin Trent of course. Yes, he's finally doing well for himself is our Robin! I knew you'd all be glad to hear this—because, let's face it, he's had a pretty rotten life up until recently. But things have taken a turn for the better, and here he is now in his new position; a more responsible, and better-paid position than the one he held before, back in his Carpentering days. Here he is, sitting at his desk, filing some correspondence on his computer, his last task before finishing up for the day.

'Oi, Robin!' It's the office clown, at the adjacent desk.

'Yes?' says Robin.

'Did you hear about the dyslexic pimp? ...He bought a warehouse! Ha, ha!'

Robin smiles wryly.

'Geddit? Cuz "Warehouse" looks like "whorehouse" written down!'

'Yes, I get it,' Robin assures him. 'Very good, Clive.'

'Have you finished with those inquiries, Robin?' asks the chief, across the room.

'Nearly done, Beth.'

'Good. Then I think we're on top of everything for once. Let's call it a day.'

'It's a day!' says Clive, inevitably.

'You really should be doing the stand-up comedy circuit, Clive,' says Beth. (A dangerous suggestion—I am sure there are a great many stand-up comedians in existence who have embarked on their careers in comedy upon having had it suggested to them; and failing to realise the suggestion was a sarcastic one.)

Robin saves his files and shuts down his desktop. Everyone is getting their things together, getting ready to depart.

Clive stops at the desk of Vera the Vague. 'Man walks into the doctors with a lettuce leaf sticking out of his bum,' he says. 'Doctor says, "That looks nasty." Man says, "You think that's nasty; that's only the tip of the iceberg!" Ha!'

Vera looks up at him blankly, unsmiling.

'Geddit? Cuz he had an iceberg lettuce up his bum...'

The blank look continues.

Wrong person, wrong joke, thinks Robin, exiting the office.

What is the secret of Robin Trent's success, you ask? What is it that has enabled to kick his unfortunate antisocial habit? The answer: Meeting the right woman! Her name is Sandra. You remember Sandra: the tipsy lady Robin was following with intent to kill that fateful night, but ended up going to the pub with instead. Sandra has proven to be the best thing that ever happened to our Robin Trent. All that time he has wasted trying to connect with teenage girls, when really it was an older woman that he needed! Sandra—warm, compassionate, responsible—is the ideal woman for Robin. Robin was a lost, little boy crying out for help. Sandra is the one who has answered that call. She has made a better person out of Robin. His social skills have improved, and along with them his confidence and self-esteem. On the surface at least, he is now a completely new man!

In addition to the new job, Robin has moved out of his shoebox flat into Sandra's much roomier apartment. She has introduced him to literature, and got him reading proper books. She has passed on to him her love for classical music… In the majority of relationships it will be the weaker, more malleable, partner who will re-shape themselves to fit into the other partner's life—and here it is grateful Robin who has happily reshaped himself to fit into Sandra's life.

All that time he had spent trying to recapture the teenage years he had wasted! The past is the past; you can't change it or relive it. He's an adult now, and he should be living an adult's life.

And as for the sex, it's absolutely amazing! Robin would have told you it was the best sex he had ever had, if he had ever *had* any sex prior to this. Sandra is the veteran and she has been using all her skill and expertise to teach Robin the ropes. (Robin is pretty much the polar-opposite of Sandra's ex, and she is enjoying the experience of being the partner holding the whip-hand.)

But what about the Carpenter, I hear you cry? What about the serial-killing? Oh, *that!* Forget about it! It was just a phase! Robin is over it. He has hung up his hammer and given up playing at being a serial killer. He never really considered himself the genuine article anyway. Frankly, he's just embarrassed about the whole business.

Does Sandra know? Has he told her about his past activities? Now, that's just a stupid question—of course he hasn't. Understanding Sandra may be, but even Robin, and in spite of his sociopath's desire to find someone who will approve of his criminal behaviour, is savvy enough to predict that telling Sandra of his having been a serial killer who has taken the lives of seven women, is not news that would be greeted with sympathy or approbation—even if it is society that's really to blame!

No; Robin has kept quiet about his past activities, and I don't blame him.

But does he worry about his past catching up with him? Actually, he doesn't. After a month had passed, and it had started to become clear that the Carpenter killings had stopped, there was the usual media speculation. Had the killer left the country? Had he been imprisoned for some other, lesser, offence…? But then, with no fresh leads, and what with everything else that's been going on in the metropolis of late, media attention has shifted away from the Carpenter, and now Robin is fairly confident the police have stopped even looking for him.

People like Robin can often be ludicrously sanguine about these things.

Robin is on the tube train, an overpacked oven of overheated bodies, homeward bound. He can't wait to get back to Sandra. There's this juicy story all over the news he's dying to talk about with her: scandalous goings-on at a girls' school in Switzerland; the headmistress has been arrested, the school closed down.

The train arrives at his station, he flows with the crowd up the escalator and is oozed out into the heated open air. A short walk to the middle-income apartment block, and he is home. He lets himself in as usual. The living room is empty, the television playing to itself. None of the customary sounds and smells of cooking emanate from the kitchen. Strange. Is she not back? No, she must be; the television is switched on. Has she just popped out for something? He calls her name. The call elicits no answer. He looks in the kitchen. No sign of preparations for dinner.

Kicking off his shoes, he goes through to the bedroom. No Sandra. He tries the bathroom: unlocked and unoccupied.

He finds Sandra in the spare room, kneeling beside some boxes of Robin's belongings; belongings he has never needed to unpack since the move. Sandra has opened the boxes. She looks at him with an expression he has never seen on her face before: a look of horror, of accusation, of hurt betrayal.

Robin feels that proverbial cold hand close its fingers around his heart.

'What are you doing?' he asks, keeping his voice calm with an effort.

'The police were here earlier,' is Sandra's reply.

The cold hand squeezes harder. 'The police? What did they want?'

'They were asking about you,' replies Sandra in a dull voice.

'Me? What about me?'

'They wanted to know about you. When I met you. How long I've known you. How long you've been living here with me. If you ever like to go out on your own at night.'

Robin smiles weakly. 'What sort of questions are those? What are they investigating?'

'The Carpenter. That serial killer. They told me something. About dates. The Carpenter stopped killing a couple of months ago—around the same time I first met you.'

'So what? That's just a coincidence. It doesn't mean anything. You don't think I was the Carpenter, do you?' (Forced laugh.) 'Come on, Sandra: you know me.'

'I *thought* I knew you. What about these?'

She picks up a scrapbook from one of the boxes.

Cold hand again. Those scrapbooks. Why hadn't he thrown them away? In common with many others of his kind, before actually becoming a serial killer himself, Robin had been fascinated by the subject, eagerly reading up on and collecting all the information he could find upon serial killers and their activities. He had filled several scrap-books with all the press-cuttings about serial killers and sexual predators he had collected.

And now Sandra has found them.

'That was just a hobby I used to have,' he explains weakly. 'I know it's a bit morbid, but I was interested in that sort of thing back then. Lots of people are.'

'You never mentioned it to me.'

'It was old-hat. I was embarrassed about it.'

'It wasn't just a hobby, was it, Robin?' persists Sandra, her voice starting to break. 'I wish it was; but there's something else I found…'

'Look, if it's about those magazines—'

'It's not the dirty magazines. I can understand you having them. It's this.'

She pulls a claw-hammer from the box, looks at him, her eyes imploring.

The hand now squeezes Robin so tightly he can hardly breathe. The sight appals him. *The hammer.* How the hell did it end up in that box? He threw it out, didn't he? He threw it out! Didn't he...? His mind races to remember... It was the time of the move, he was sorting through his things, sorting through his life... He was *going* to throw out the hammer; he knew he had to get rid of the thing; but he remembers he couldn't quite decide how to go about it... He didn't want to put it in the bag with his household rubbish, in case the police for some reason decided to search his trash; he didn't want to dispose of it in a way that could be connected with him... He had thought of slipping it into a public bin at night, but was worried about CCTV cameras. Then he had considered hurling it into the Thames, or burying it in a park somewhere... But which scheme had he fixed on? What had he finally done? The answer is there before him, in Sandra's hand. He hadn't done anything. In the hurry to move, the excitement of the opening of this new chapter in his life, he must have just dropped it in a box with all his other dubious possessions and then gone and forgotten about it.

'It's just a hammer,' he says, finally.

'The Carpenter killed those women with a hammer like this.'

Another feeble smile. 'Everyone has hammers, don't they? It's just part of a DIY kit.'

'Then where's the rest of the DIY kit? One hammer's not much use on its own.'

'It's probably in one of the other boxes.'

'It isn't; I've looked. And what about this?' She points to the hammer's claw. 'The claw bit: it's been filed down; the edge has been sharpened.'

'That was how it was when I bought it.'

'I don't believe you, Robin,' says Sandra, shaking her head. 'You're the Carpenter, aren't you?'

'No!'

Her voice cracks. '*Aren't you?*'

Robin hangs his head. Tears stream down his face.

'Oh my God... It *is* you... I've been living with you all this time, and you...'

'But I'm *better* now,' blubbers Robin, wretchedly. 'I *was* the Carpenter, but I'm not anymore, am I? You made me better.'

Sandra ignores this. 'That night, when we first met: you were following me... You were going to kill me, weren't you...? That was why you were following me...'

'Why can't you leave it alone?' wails Robin. 'I've changed, haven't I? Ever since I met you I've been better; I've been a good person...'

'And what about those seven women you killed? I'm I supposed to just forget about them as well?'

'It's the *past*. I was sick then. I'm better now.'

Tears forming in her eyes, Sandra shakes her head. 'No, Robin. You're still sick...'

'Don't say that, Sandra,' pleads Robin. 'Don't abandon me; don't turn on me. You're everything to me, now. I need you, don't you see?'

'You need help, Robin; I see that...'

'You're not going to tell the police, are you?'

'Of course I'm going to tell the police!' screams Sandra, her forced calmness finally deserting her. 'What else can I do? Can't you see, this is over? You expect me to just carry on like before, knowing you've killed seven innocent women? To just forgive that?'

'I couldn't help it... It was those girls teasing me at school... I told you about that... You said you felt sorry for me; you said you hated those girls for what they did...'

'I did feel sorry for you; but, for Christ's sake, it doesn't make it okay for you to go around killing people!'

'Stop it, Sandra! Stop talking about that! You're ruining everything! I've been happy, and now you're ruining everything!'

'Stop whining, for Christ's sake! I'm calling the police!'

'No...'
'Yes!'
'NO!'

With an inarticulate roar of baffled rage, Robin pounces. He snatches the hammer from her hand, strikes her over the head with it. Robin pushes her to the floor, straddles her—his expression is bestial, insane.

'You've ruined *everything*!'

He smashes the hammer into her face.

'You've ruined everything!'

He smashes again. Bone crunches, a jet of blood sprays him.

'You've. Ruined. EVERYTHING!'

Again and again. The face is smashed to a pulp, shards of bone puncturing flesh, smashed brains, blood spreading across the carpet.

Finally Robin desists. Breathing hard, tears streaming down his blood-spattered face, his ears ringing, his breath coming in great gulps.

As the rushing in his ears dies down, he slowly becomes aware of another sound; an urgent and insistent hammering at the front door of the apartment...

Chapter Fifty
Being a Continuation of Chapter Forty-Eight

'You killed me...'

'What are you talking about?' demands Dodo. 'How could I have killed you? We're both here, aren't we?'

'We're here...' looking around; 'but that doesn't prove anything...'

Dodo looks at her friend. His usual vitality is absent—drained away; his whole demeanour is changed: he seems vague, detached... What have they done to him?

She places her hands firmly on his shoulders.

'Look, it's me, Mark—Look at me. I'm here; I'm real. I don't know what you've been through, but it's over, now. I'm here, Mayumi's here... Try to think clearly...'

Mark shakes off the persuasive embrace. 'No! You're not real—Different plane of reality... Vautrin said—'

'Vautrin's playing games with your mind!' shouts Dodo. 'He irradiated you with solanite energy. That night in Soho; at that warehouse you went to. Do you remember that?'

'Solanite...? Don't remember...'

No, he wouldn't remember, realises Dodo. Memory loss seems to be a symptom of exposure to solanite energy. That scientist Herriot had gaps in his recollection.

She fixes Mark with her most encouraging smile. 'Come on, Mark... What's all this rubbish about saying I killed you, or tried to? Why the hell would I do something like that?'

The scowling look of accusation returns.

'No! You betrayed me! You killed me!'

It is at this point that Mayumi takes a hand. She walks straight up to Mark, signalling Dodo to step aside, and, in the best Japanese tradition, she slaps him hard around the face.

'*Baka!*' she snaps. 'We're your friends!'

Mark reels from this manifestation of friendship, stunned, subdued.

'Try to focus, Mark,' Dodo tells him. 'I can't imagine what you've been going through, but I think it's over now, and you're amongst friends.'

'Friends...' Mark rubs his jowl, shoots a puzzled look at Dodo. 'Why did you let me fall?'

'Let you fall? What are you talking about?'

'We were chasing Marshall across the rooftops. I slipped. You let me fall.'

'What are you—No, I remember: You mean the Chamber Case; Marshall took off and we chased him across the roof-tops—But that was *last year*, Mark. Yes, you slipped and you did nearly fall off; but I pulled you up, didn't I? Marshall got away, but I saved you.'

'You didn't save me. Not the second time it happened...'

'The sec—Mark, the same thing can't happen twice. If you've just been reliving that night, it must have been a dream or an illusion or something; part of the solanite trip.'

'Trip...?'

'Yes, you've been on a trip on the Solanite Express; that's how Vautrin's girls described it; but I think you're out of it now, Mark. You've got off at the last stop and you're back in the real world. Look, what you need is a good stiff drink; there's a pub around the corner...'

And to implement this sound advice, Dodo takes one arm, Mayumi the other, and they lead the now passive Mark back into the square and straight up to the doors of the George and Dragon. Fortunately, and unlike the kitchens of the houses, the pub proves to be fully provisioned; provisioned with drinks although not with a bartender, so they serve themselves—a vodka and coke for Mayumi, whiskies and soda for Mark and Dodo.

Refreshed with the liquid stimulant and his friends' small-talk, Mark starts to seem more himself. They now set about comparing notes.

The first thing that emerges is that Mark has no more idea than Dodo or Mayumi of their current location; it is unfamiliar to him; he only recalls having been here a short while before his friends found him. Has he in fact only just arrived in this place? Or has he perhaps been here all the time, but seeing other places, believing himself to be in other places?

Dodo explains to Mark the events which have led to Mayumi and herself finding themselves in this location.

They then try to piece together what has happened to Mark. This proves difficult, as Mark can remember very little. Not only does he remember nothing about having gone to the warehouse in Soho, his memories of the several weeks prior to that evening seem also to have gone astray. The last event he can recall with any clarity is the raid on the Vallotec building, two months previously... Recent memories are a vague jumble; walking the streets of a deserted London, chasing an elusive Trudie Rayne, fragments of conversations with Trudie and with Vautrin; and the reliving of past events, but with roles exchanged, important details altered…

Question: has Mark been here in this village all the time, walking around in a dream; hallucinating? Or had he physically been transported to some other place, and has only just now returned to reality?

'How do you know I have returned to reality?' challenges Mark. 'Maybe it's you two who have joined me. We might be inhabiting the same unreal world.'

Is that possible? wonders Dodo. If Mark, after being dosed with solanite, has been moved to some other place, could this village be part of that other place? The village certainly seems unreal. Even discounting the forcefield, you still have a village, bizarrely uniform and inexplicably empty, surrounded entirely by a tall hedge, with no roads leading in or out of it.

'Hang on a minute,' says Dodo, 'No, that doesn't work. We would have had to have been dosed to solanite radiation, like you were. We weren't; I know that much. We were just knocked out with common-or-garden knock-out gas.'

'Maybe you were exposed to solanite rays while you were out,' suggests Mark.

'No, because our memories are fine,' points out Dodo. '…But, you know, maybe there's another explanation: We were at the SEA base. That place seems to exist in some other plane of reality. Maybe the base is some kind of gateway between the real world and the one that you were sent to—Yes! So, then maybe when you thought you saw Vautrin and Trudie; maybe it *was* really them! Back at the base, they disappeared for a couple of days; said they'd been away on "business." That's all they'd tell us…'

'There you go, then,' says Mark. 'Maybe this *is* the dream world, and Vautrin has just brought you both here to me…'

'If this is a made-up world, why does it have six dead soldiers in it?' Mayumi wants to know.

This is a good point.

'We need to think about how we can get out of here,' says Mark, after an interval.

'Yes,' agrees Dodo. 'Vautrin obviously brought us here to meet up with you, Mark. That's done. We've met. Maybe him or some of the girls will show up soon. Or maybe that forcefield has been dropped and we can just walk out of here.'

'If "here" really exists...' cautions Mark.

'Don't start that again!'

'Sorry. I still feel... disjointed. I'm fairly certain you and Mayumi are both real, but I'm not sure about anything else. I still don't know if I can trust my five senses.'

'It's going to take you a while to get over all of this,' Dodo tells him. 'You've really gone through the wringer. I mean, look what that scientist Herriot was like—' She breaks off. 'Christ! You're not going to explode like he did, are you?'

Mark smiles. 'No. I'm pretty sure what happened to Herriot was due to something Vautrin had done to him, and not the result of exposure to solanite. I don't think I'm in any danger of blowing up.'

'Yeah, that makes sense. Some kind of biological booby-trap. The rest of that team are apparently still alive and well, somewhere in the SEA base.'

'Apparently? You haven't seen them?'

'Nope. Vautrin wouldn't let us.'

Mark rubs his prickly jaw.

'I'd like to take a look at this forcefield,' he says.

'You can't; it's invisible.'

'*Examine* it, then. If, as you suggest, it's no longer there, we can get out of here and find out just where we are.'

finishing their drinks, they exit the pub and make their way to the edge of the village. A quick, cautious check informs them that the energy barrier is still in place.

'I can't smell the countryside,' announces Mark. 'I suppose the barrier must be keeping it out.'

Dodo tells him about the complete lack of vegetation she has observed in the village. 'The only explanation I can think of is that this is a barracks town,' she concludes. 'That would explain the rigid uniformity of the place and those dead soldiers in the town hall. The only thing I can't figure out is why there's no checkpoint; no roads in and out of the place.'

'A road out of here wouldn't have anywhere to go,' speaks up a new voice.

They spin round. Vautrin stands before them, having apparently materialised out of thin air. Trudie Rayne is with him, dressed in her usual school clothes. She clings lovingly to Vautrin's arm. Mark feels a twinge of jealousy.

'Hello, Mark,' says Trudie, smiling at him. 'Had a good trip? You're out of it now.'

'I was wondering when you'd show yourself,' Dodo tells Vautrin. 'Have you been here watching us all the time?'

'No. Only just arrived.'

'Mind telling us what this place is?'

'A venue I acquired.'

'What do you mean that a road leading out of here would have nowhere to go?'

'I mean just that, Professor Dupont.' He holds up a box-like control device. 'I'll demonstrate.' He thumbs a button.

And then the sky falls in.

That's how it seems to Dodo Dupont. She staggers. Mayumi screams. The sky has been blotted out by some huge object. Her brain races to process what she sees—to make sense of the impossible. Rock. That's what she sees rock. Right above their heads, it is like a huge meteor that has appeared from nowhere and now hangs frozen in the sky above the town.

But then she sees that it is not just the sky that has gone but the countryside as well. The bucolic scenery beyond the forcefield has been an illusion, dispelled at the press of a button. The truth has now revealed itself: they are standing in a huge natural cavern. The whole village is. The cavern is illuminated by a huge grid of arc-lights suspended from the ceiling. Beyond the precincts of the village stand other structures, previously concealed: generator houses, storage tanks, pipelines.

High in one face of the cavern wall, a glassed-in observation platform suggests some sort of control room beyond.

Dodo finds her voice first. 'What the hell is this place?'

'A nuclear bomb shelter, Professor,' answers Vautrin. 'We're currently deep underground. This facility was built in the 1950s, during the cold war. It's purpose, in the event of a nuclear attack, was to provide shelter for the government, the military top-brass, senior civil servants—all the country's VIPs. The idea behind the construction of this replica village was to give some sense of normality to the people sheltering down here; something comforting and familiar, rather than having to adjust to a completely enclosed complex like our SEA base.

'A nuclear attack perhaps seems unlikely in the current political climate, but this shelter is nevertheless still maintained by the army, in case it should ever be needed. As for me, I stumbled on this place completely by chance. Exploring the limits of the SEA complex, I discovered an exit into a cave. I followed the cave out into this cavern. I immediately saw the possibilities of this place, so I had the girls move in and take over from the army. It wasn't difficult to achieve this; the facility had only a small staff. The forcefield and hologrammatic landscape were not parts of the original design; I added those myself. Quite a neat little deception, wasn't it?'

'You know, I'd always heard rumours of the existence of a place like this,' says Mark. He has adjusted more quickly than his two friends to the sudden change in their surroundings. 'I'd just never been able to find out if they were true...'

'Your security clearance can't be high enough,' says Vautrin. 'But how are you, Mark? I should have asked this sooner. Have you recovered from your experience?'

Mark looks at him. 'I'm really out of it then? I'm back in reality?'

'Back in the reality you came from, yes.'

'Why did you do it?' demands Dodo. 'Why did you have to put him through all that?'

'An experiment,' answers Vautrin. 'Anyway, you can't expect me to treat Mark nicely all the time. We are on opposite sides. Considering he's my nemesis, I haven't been that hard on him at all.'

'Just one quick trip on the Solanite Express,' says Trudie.

'And what was the point of all this?' pursues Dodo. 'This little deception? Just a practical joke?'

'Well, I needed someone to test my holographic landscape on… But yes, watching you trying to make sense of this place has been quite diverting.'

Trudie glides over to Mark, caresses his stubbly jaw.

'Do you remember?' she asks, her voice just above a whisper. 'I was there with you; that was really me, you know—not just an illusion…'

'Yes. I remember,' answers Mark, looking at her.

Watching the exchange, Dodo frowns.

Vautrin claps his hands.

'Well, there's no need for us to stay here now,' he says. 'Why don't we go back to the complex? It's quite a walk, but not too far.'

'What do you intend to do to us now?' Dodo wants to know.

'Do? Nothing. I suggest you return to the guest suite with Mark; give him some time to rest up and recover from his experiences.'

'And then you'll just let us leave?'

Vautrin shrugs. 'You can make a daring escape, if you prefer.'

Vautrin leading the way, they set off across the floor of the cavern, leaving the subterranean village behind them.

Chapter Fifty-One
The Prosperities of Vice

'I don't know what you think about the "nature or nurture" debate,' speaks Juliette. 'I'm inclined to side with the "nurture" theory myself. I think in most cases, any abnormalities a human individual develops are a result of their upbringing, their environment; those childhood experiences etch themselves onto the unformed mind, shaping, and perhaps warping, that individual's personality. But, having said that, I do consider myself to be one of the exceptions to that rule. I firmly believe I was born the way I am. This self-evident flaw in my personality was with me from birth; no—it was with me when I was still evolving in my mother's womb. And I don't believe heredity can be held responsible for this aberration, either. None of my parents or grandparents ever exhibited any of my peculiar tendencies. Yes, of course my Daddy is cold and ruthless; but that's not the same thing as my sadistic nature; his vices are just greed and selfishness. Yes, it was just some freak, some accident, that caused my mother to incubate and give birth to a monster. I say "monster" because that is what most people would say of me, yourself included, no doubt; but I prefer to think of myself as being an "original."

'Nobody really recognised my peculiarity during my formative years. At that age, any early manifestations of my condition were probably dismissed as being nothing more than the instinctive unthinking cruelty of a small child. That phase of childish destructiveness is perfectly natural, and is a stage that most individuals grow out of through education and with psychological maturity. With myself, the opposite occurred. My cruelty became more refined as my intelligence developed—and I developed very rapidly; I was a most precocious child. As I entered adolescence, my pleasure in committing acts of cruelty became entwined with my emerging sexuality, became one with all those exquisite feelings of bodily gratification. (Although, if you believe with Freud that even prepubescent children have an elementary sexuality, then you could argue that my pleasure was of a sexual nature from the beginning.)

'The first person I killed was my mother. This happened when I was eight years old. My father and mother did not love each other. She was an heiress; he had married her for her money and position. For Daddy, the marriage was just another business arrangement. I was the only fruit of their unhappy union—I like to think I was a rape child; I have no proof to back this up, but the idea of being conceived in an act of sexual violence amuses me; and I can well imagine Daddy venting his rage on my mother in this way... So, as I say, it was an unhappy marriage, and by the time I was eight, my parents had long since stopped even pretending to like one another, but for various reasons they had decided not to separate—to keep up appearances in public. When not in London, we lived in the large country house my mother had inherited. I should explain that my mother was a weak, neurotic creature, completely cowed and dominated by my father. I despised her for this weakness as soon as I was old enough to understand it. I would say and do everything I could to torment her and aggravate her condition.

'She had had several lovers, my mother; their presence in the house my father contemptuously tolerated. (My father never brought home a mistress. I think that then—as now—he had no time for "relationships" or "affairs," and simply satisfied his organism with visits to prostitutes.) At the time of her death, my mother's current lover was an American called Harvey. I decided I would steal this man away from my mother. As I say, this happened when I was eight. I was already aware through my dealings with some of the servants that I had power over men; naturally I exulted in this power. But this was the first time I put that ability to deliberate use. Whenever I was alone with Harvey, I would flirt with him shamelessly, hugging and kissing him, rubbing myself against him with a thin pretence of innocence. To give Harvey his due, he did resist at first. I don't think he had a paedophile bone in his body until I began to work my charms on him. Of course I ensnared him in the end—I had him eating out of my hand. And I timed the *dénouement* perfectly: Mother walked into the room one day to find me fellating Horace. She went into hysterics at the sight, and I, I just laughed in her face. I told her that Harvey loved me now, not an old hag like her; that he would be spending his nights in my room not hers... Oh! The look on my mother's face, before she turned and fled the room, is one I shall always cherish... The sequel was inevitable. Mother was later found in her bathroom—she had slit both her wrists. I was very pleased with this result, but I felt that the situation still needed something else; a finishing touch... So I went to my father in a fit of childish tears, told him that Harvey had been abusing me, and that mother had killed herself because she had found out about it. Just as I had anticipated, Daddy quietly had Harvey killed. I think I danced around the house with joy when I heard about this happy result...

'I was a spiteful, vindictive little thing, wasn't I, Karl? But that was just childishness; children are such selfish, heartless creatures. Since then I have matured into the cool-headed, rational sadist you see before you. Is that what you like, Karl? Do you like me as I am now? Or would you have preferred to have known the younger me?'

Karl, the young man to whom this question is addressed, does not answer. Karl cannot answer. His lips have been tightly sewn together.

This one-sided conversation takes place in the front room of Karl's chalet. Karl is a ski instructor, young, handsome and vigorous, and frequently visited by girls from the nearby Imrie Academy. His visitor tonight is Juliette Wainwright, but the activities being pursued are not those which Karl has come to expect in his dealings with Miss Imrie's girls: pinned to the polished floor of his own front room, as Juliette delicately tortures his helpless body, while at the same time favouring him with this account of her formative years.

Juliette admires Karl's genitals, which she holds cupped in her hands. The cupped hands are nowhere near Karl's crotch, as the genitals in question have been detached from that place of origin. But worry not—Juliette possesses a full medical and surgical kit, and she has performed the amputation using sterilised instruments and has also staunched the wound left in the young man's crotch. She doesn't want him bleeding to death on her before she has had her fun.

'It's a shame the blood escapes when you remove it,' she

remarks, contemplating the sorry-looking genitalia. 'If it had remained distended then I could have pleasured myself with it. Oh, well!'

And, dismissing the subject, she tosses the hairy mess over her shoulder.

Inarticulate groans from Karl.

'Now. To return to my story: so, at the age of eight, I had already been responsible for causing two deaths; but my first personal killing, the first one at which I was actually a witness, transpired a few years later. I was on holiday in France at the time. Out walking in the countryside, I met this boy, a local boy; he was about my age, plebeian, reasonably good-looking. He probably told him his name, but I've long since forgotten it. (I should say, I was already fluent in speaking French at this time.) Well, after the inevitable sex, the boy offered to take me rock climbing. There was an escarpment close by that he said we could scale. I agreed to the enterprise and we reached the escarpment. He started up first, saying that I should watch his movements and then follow him. However, being no novice at rock-climbing, I decided to take another route and doing this actually reached the top before him, much to his annoyance! I sat there on the summit, laughing at him for being beaten by a mere girl, urging him to get a move on. This goaded the poor boy into action; and that was when he got himself into difficulties. I don't know if, in his haste, he took a course different to the one he had intended, or if he was just unlucky; but he reached out for this outcropping, and then, when he threw all his weight on it to pull himself up, the rock started to come loose! Now, it happens there was a ledge close to this spot, and I could have easily climbed down onto it and assisted the young man out of his difficulties. But—and this was completely on the spur of the moment—I decided not to. He called out for help, and I put on a show of being too distressed by his predicament to even do anything. And then, as the rock he was holding started to break away, he looked up at me, this boy did; his eyes terrified, pleading. And then the rock came loose and he fell to his death. I'll never forget that look; to this day it often comes before my mind's eye as my body experiences an orgasm.'

While speaking, Juliette has been drawing a scalpel around the circumference of Karl's upper arm. (The right arm, if you're interested.) She now makes several incisions and peels the skin from the arm like a glove. She begins to draw the scalpel along the denuded arm, irritating the exposed nerve-endings.

Muffled screams of agony from Karl; his body writhes.

'Yes—I know what you're thinking: that wasn't really a personal, "hands on" killing, was it? I'd simply let the boy fall to his death. A passive murder, I suppose you could call it. I didn't actually get my hands dirty. Well, I'm sure you will be pleased to learn that my first more intimate, "hands on" killing happened not very long after that event. She was a girl at the school I attended at that time. She was not a girl I particularly disliked, or who disliked me. But she had something I wanted. A CD album, it was; nothing more. I desired it because it was limited edition with a bonus DVD and a slipcase signed by the band; it had only been available via the band's website and had sold out before I even had knowledge of it. I coveted that CD, and it annoyed me intensely that this other girl had possession of a copy and I hadn't. I offered to buy it from her; she stubbornly refused; perhaps she thought the ridiculously inflated prices I offered were not meant seriously; although I suspect it was more that she enjoyed the feeling of ascendancy over me her possession of this CD gave her. Well, whatever the reason, I couldn't convince her to part with it, so one night I broke into her house. I climbed through the window into her bedroom. I found her asleep in her bed. I took one of the pillows from under her head, and jumping on top of her, I smothered her with it; yes, I deliberately murdered her. Ah! The feeling of her body as it writhed helplessly under me, struggling for life, growing ever weaker; and then the relaxation as she finally expired—Oh, it was exquisite! When it was over, I just put the pillow back under her head, found the CD I wanted and left. And then, a few months later I got bored with my acquisition and sold it on eBay. Can you believe it? It just shows how the emotion of coveting something is a much more intense and long-lasting emotion than that of possession of the desired object. The satisfaction of possession soon begins to wane.'

Juliette has cut open Karl's abdomen. She now introduces her hand into the cavity and begins to extract his slippery wet intestines.

More screams muted by the now-bleeding sewn-up lips.

'So that was it. My first "hands on" killing. And of course, since then, I've just never looked back. I've learned to savour the moment; to protract the tortures, the victim's pain. It's the same as sex really: disappointing when it's over too soon... Oh, and of course I should mention Marquis de Sade; the Divine Marquis. I felt like I'd met my soul-mate when I first read him. His great works became my bible. Everything he said rang so true. The Misfortunes of Virtue. The Prosperities of Vice. The inversion of established morality. Yes, Sade was the ultimate rebel... And that brings us pretty much up to date. I've now found myself a school that is not run by reactionaries or hypocrites, and here I am! Of course, dear Cynthia, our headmistress, doesn't share my sadistic nature, but she is still a shameless hedonist, and I can identify with that.

'I know you've been servicing the girls for some time now, Karl. I'm sure they won't thank me for robbing them of this source of gratification. But, what with you living all alone out here... Well, you made such a tempting target. But then, you're not the only stud around here; there are plenty of other eager boys down in the village; so the girls won't lose out by your tragic demise... I'm curious, Karl: have you reached the stage of final despair yet? That awful moment when you see no way out but death? When you are forced to accept the inevitable...? Or are you still clinging to some vague hopes that you will actually survive this evening? That I might relent, or that some happy accident might occur that saves you? Do you really still want to live? After you have been deprived of your manhood; the one thing that makes you useful?'

Muffled groans and imploring tearful eyes are her answer.

'Yes, yes; I understand—not much demand for a handsome

young ski-instructor who can't fuck, is there? Well don't worry; I'm getting bored now, as well. I'll put you out of your misery...'

Juliette makes her way back up the mountainside to the school. The front door of the main building is always considerately left unlocked after dark, so as not to impede any nocturnal excursions the girls might need to make—another example of Cynthia Imrie's consideration for her students.

What would Miss Imrie say if she knew what Juliette had been up to tonight? She is a broad-minded lady, and she knows of Juliette's proclivities; nevertheless, she might consider that Juliette has gone a touch too far on this occasion. She would cover up for Juliette if the police came snooping around; she wouldn't rat on the girl. However, she might still consider Juliette had become a liability as far as the school and its reputation is concerned, and might have her quietly removed from the student roster and sent back to England. This would be a shame. Juliette likes it here at the Imrie Academy; the relaxed non-goal-oriented atmosphere, the way the other girls all look up to her, obeyed her every command... Yes, it would be a shame to have to leave; so best not to tell Miss Imrie about tonight's activities!

Juliette makes her way up to her room. She has a bedroom to herself in the east wing—except that tonight she doesn't have it as much to herself as usual, because when she walks in and turns on the light there is a man sitting on the bed. He smiles at her and says 'Hello.'

Juliette is not easily thrown, but this throws her. She stands nonplussed. The man is a stranger—good-looking, dark hair with a fringe, long side-burns; dressed in a polo-neck sweater and cords. Her mind seeks for an explanation to account for this male presence in a female academy, and comes up with only one.

'Are you Miss Imrie's latest beau?' she asks. 'If so, I suggest you go back to her, or we'll both be in trouble.'

'I'm not your headmistress's lover,' replies the man smoothly. 'I'm here to see you.'

'Does Miss Imrie know you're here?'

'No. Nobody does.'

'What do you want? Are you the police?'

The man smiles. 'Now why would you ask that? A guilty conscience, maybe? I'm not surprised after what you've just been up to. But no, I'm not with the police.'

'What I've been up to?' says Juliette. 'How would you know what I've been up to?'

'I know almost everything there is to know about you, Juliette.'

Juliette frowns. 'Is this blackmail? You want money?'

'Wrong again. Just relax and let me explain myself, Juliette. Please sit down.'

'Thank you for the kind offer,' says Juliette sarcastically, seating herself on her desk chair.

'I should introduce myself first: my name is Vautrin.'

'Made up name. And you're English? You sound English.'

'Well, I came here from England, yes.'

'You came all this way just to see me?'

'Yes. I've come to you with an idea, a proposition.'

'What sort of proposition?'

'A new life, basically. A new start.'

'And what if I'm quite happy with my current life?'

'Even if you were, you could well find what I'm offering more appealing to you. Anyway, after your little escapade tonight, it might be a good idea for you to get away from here. I know you've done this kind of thing before, and I'm sure you were careful not to leave any evidence... but the police might still come sniffing round here. That fellow has a certain reputation locally, which links him to this school.'

'I'm not worried about the police. They can't touch me.'

'Maybe not, but anyway, please listen to what I have to say before you make any decisions.'

'Oh, alright. I'm listening.'

'Good. I want to assemble a group, an organisation; that is my desire. I've chosen you as my first recruit.'

'What sort of organisation are you talking about? I'm not a

political animal.'

'Nor am I. What I'm propounding is an activist group with absolutely no political or religious agenda. A group entirely moulded around the self-gratification of its members; committing spontaneous actions based on spontaneous impulse.'

Juliette smiles. 'You mean a group that commits terrorist acts just for the sake of it?'

'Yes, exactly that. Many existing terrorist groups really only do that anyway, even though they may claim to have long-term goals in mind. We will just be being more honest about it. Destruction for the sake of destruction. Beautiful chaos.'

'It sounds nice and all that, but are you serious? I mean, I like the idea, but how are you going to set it up? Do you have funding, equipment? Where are you going to find the other recruits?'

'Answering the last question first, I've already found the recruits. You see, I can sense things. Connections. On an ethereal level. I've found a thread; this thread has led me to you. There will be ten others, all connected by this same thread. All teenage girls like yourself.'

'Do I know these girls? Are they here, at the school?'

'No. You haven't met any of them. But you're still connected. I'm not sure as to how or why... Perhaps, even though here you have yet to meet, in some other world, a mirror image or a might-have-been, you have always been together. All I know is, I sense this connection. You must each be approached at a different precise time. You are the first link in the chain.'

'And how do you sense these things, Mr Vautrin? Are you psychic?'

'Yes, I think I must be.'

'So you've got eleven girls. What are you going to do then? Have you got a secret base all ready for us?'

Vautrin smiles. 'That's precisely what I've got.'

'Really? Underground? Impregnable? Futuristic? Like something out of a spy film?'

'Got it in one!'

Juliette laughs outright. 'This is crazy, but for some reason I believe you. I think the fact that you're even here makes me believe you.'

'I would never lie to you, Juliette. Come with me. You already exist on the periphery of the society you were born into. It's time for you to step out of it all the way; abandon the mainstream completely; you might as well. You could have more fun than you ever imagined.'

'Well, there is one blot looming on my horizon: my corporate father and this drip he wants me to marry…'

'That's nothing. You can get away from all that. Kill them both if it will make you happy.'

'And what's your place in all this? Will you be our lord and master? Will us girls have to obey your every command?'

'No, not all. You'll all be free agents. My role will be more that of a patron than a commander-in-chief. Support and encouragement are what you'll get from me.'

'And why are you doing this?'

'Because I want to.'

'Mr Enigmatic, aren't you…? And where is this secret base of yours?'

'Back in England.'

'And I suppose you want me to slink away in the night? I won't be able to say good-bye to the girls, Miss Imrie?'

'I'm afraid not. To them you will have disappeared off the face of the earth.'

'And this evil society of yours: has it got a name?'

Another smile. 'We'll work on that…'

Chapter Fifty-Two
The Chimes of Big Ben

'What we need is a missile base on the moon,' says Lambert, sitting back, feet on the control desk. 'Then we could take out any country that starts giving us aggro.'

'Policing the Earth from a missile base on the moon is not

feasible,' replies Denver, without looking up from his computer screen. 'The moon is too far away. For a rapid response, the missiles would need to be in orbital satellites.'

'That's pretty much America's "Star Wars" project, isn't it?' says Garrow, sipping her coffee. 'But those weapons they've got in orbit that are supposed to be there to protect the Earth from outside attack—easy enough to turn 'em around to fire the other way.'

Our disputants are manning the control room of a coastal missile base. A huge screen covering one wall displays a grid map of an area of the East Coast and North Sea, a red circle indicating the installation's location. Manning the control room of these missile defence bases is a routine job, and the crew are not conspicuously key-up for action.

'Well, I know who I'd fire them at,' declares Lambert.

'Let me guess: the Middle East,' sneers Garrow.

'Damn right. Wipe out the wogs, you wipe out the problem.'

' "What's an Arab, daddy?" ' pipes Denver, quoting an old 9/11 joke.

Says Garrow: 'You're a twat, Lambert. The IS and that lot; they're not the problem. Now the Russians: *they're* the ones to worry about.'

'It's about keeping Britain safe from terrorists,' maintains Lambert. 'That's what matters. Look what's been happening in London recently—'

'Yeah, those attacks are being done by that SEA group, not the Islamic State, you prick.'

'Oh, come on! You mean you really believe that shit? A bunch of kids doing all that stuff? An internet hoax. It was the wogs alright.'

'Then why would the government say it wasn't them?'

'Obvious. We have to be oh-so-careful not to offend the Muslims, don't we? So, just blame it on this made-up bunch of girls.'

'Lambert, that makes absolutely no sense at all,' declares Denver. And then: 'The bastard! He's attacking me with velociraptors!'

'Denver, I don't think you should be using the main defence computer to play your stupid RPG,' says Garrow.

'I can clear the screen soon enough if there's an emergency. Don't worry.'

'Seriously, you don't believe all that stuff, do you?' insists Lambert. 'Society of Evil Actions? Teenage girls? It's a joke. It's got to be.'

'The government haven't denied it,' points out Garrow.

'Yeah, but they haven't confirmed it, either. I'm telling you, it's just internet cranks. It's got to be! I mean, where could a bunch of fucking schoolgirls get hold of guns and high-explosives?'

'You can buy anything online, these days,' remarks Denver.

'I know it all sounds mad,' allows Garrow. 'But it's mad enough to be true. The world's gone bonkers since 9/11.'

Noises somewhere outside. Muffled cracks.

'That sounded like gunshots!' from Garrow.

'Someone practising,' suggests Lambert.

'I'm not sure… Listen. It sounds like there's some commotion out there…'

Footsteps running down the corridor towards them.

'Someone's coming. Look busy,' says Lambert. 'And get your fucking RPG off the monitor, Denver!'

The doors burst open. The three officers spring to their feet, saluting commendable unison. Unfortunately, their effort is a wasted one, as the newcomers are not superior officers. They are in fact four teenage girls; two in school uniform, two in casual clothes. Three of the girls hold pistols, the fourth a machinegun. The intruders are none other than Juliette Wainwright, Dizzy Hello, Greta Garbo and Trudie Rayne.

Salutes stupidly frozen in place, the three officers stare at the intruders in disbelief.

'No fucking way…' breathes Lambert.

'Hands up!' orders Juliette. 'Back away from the controls.'

Hands raised, Garrow, Denver and Lambert back away from

the controls.

They *are* real! thinks Garrow, stupefied. And they're here! Those SEA maniacs! The stories were true—they were all true.

The girl with the machinegun levels her weapon at them; they are now safely out of the range of the missile control boards.

'You're them, aren't you?' says Garrow. 'The SEA!'

'At your service!' replies Dizzy. And she opens fire, ripping into Garrow, Lambert and Denver with a hail of bullets. The soldiers drop like broken puppets.

Dizzy exhales a deep sigh with satisfaction. No—no matter how many times she does it, she still always gets that warm, tingly sensation in her perineum!

'Okay, Greta: do your stuff,' says Juliette.

Greta busies herself at the controls. The map on the wall-screen switches from the coast to an overview of London. Further adjustments and it zeroes in on Central London.

'Locking on first target,' says Greta. '…Target locked. Locking on second…'

Alarms cry out, red-alert beacons flashing in concord. More shouts and gunfire outside.

'We've still got time,' declares Juliette. 'Carry on, Greta.'

'Locking on third target…'

The Albert Embankment, across the river from the Houses of Parliament.

Curtis strolls aimlessly along the Embankment, hardly looking where he is going. He has taken to doing this, whenever his lonely bedsit becomes too much for him. He will just set off like this through the streets of the city, walking wherever his legs take him, wrapped in a blanket of depression and isolation.

In the intervals of these walks, Curt will spend days shut away indoors, doing absolutely nothing. Complete *ennui* has set in; no activity appeals to him. Man delights him not; no, nor woman, neither…

If he thinks of reading a book, he will be put off from even attempting the task by the possibility of not enjoying it. Likewise, he might consider listening to some music, or watching a DVD—the same thoughts will stop him from doing this. With these thoughts barring him from all minor diversions, he will spend hours at a time just lying in his bed, the duvet over his head.

He has cut himself off from the world around him, from his entire life. He no longer reads or watches the news. He has stopped his nightclub DJing. He has stopped seeing his friends. He ignores their texts or emails. On a few occasions someone has knocked on the door of his bedsit, he has not answered.

And of course, he thinks about Tanya.

The case is the usual one: he just hadn't realised just how much he needed Tanya until she had been taken from him. She had been the one thing that stopped the world from crashing in on him. All he does now is torture himself with the regret that he hadn't gone after her when she had walked out that night; with mortification that the last words he'd ever spoken to her had been 'fuck off.'

At first, he had thought he could carry on as normal; he knew that carrying on as normal was the recommended thing to do in these crises, so that's what he had done. For a while this had worked well enough; but then depression and lethargy had taken hold, and he had started to isolate himself.

He vaguely looks at the people around as he strolls along the embankment. How can they carry on as though nothing is happening? All those terrorist attacks... Serial killers like the one who had killed Tanya... The world is going to hell in a handbasket, and people just carry on as though nothing is happening. Carry on with their normal lives. It's obscene.

Curtis will walk for hours like this, choosing his path randomly, eyes ahead, rarely looking to the left or right. When he has had enough, he will turn his steps homeward, always completing the journey on foot regardless of how far he has wandered. He shuns the close proximity to other people he would inevitably experience on the bus or the tube...

He becomes dimly aware of an approaching sound, increasing in pitch; the sound does not alarm him, he just takes it to be a jet fighter flying low.

Then comes the explosion, loud and imperative.

Ahead, some distance away, in the direction of Blackfriars: a fireball mushrooms into the air.

Curt freezes in his tracks, infected by the panic from the people around him. He stares at the plume of black smoke rising into the clear blue sky.

A crash? A suicide bomber?

That shrill mechanical sound fills the air again, off to the left. This time Curt sees it all. His eyes lock on a black arrow streaking through the sky. Hideously real, it smashes into the side of St Stephen's tower; an explosion like thunder; fire and smoke erupt. Big Ben rings discordantly, sounding its own death-knell. Curtis stares as the summit of the tower topples, falls onto the Parliament building with a deafening crash, throwing up a huge cloud of dust and debris.

The screams around him become hysterical.

Jesus Christ! Jesus fucking Christ!

Freezing shock and terror grip Curt. He staggers, almost fainting. Around him people are screaming, swearing, running around, wondering where death is going to strike next. Another missile screeches from the sky. Another explosion, off towards Trafalgar Square.

Curtis drops to his knees, covers his face.

This is it.

It's the end of the world. It's the end of the fucking world—

'Three hits!'

The four SEA girls' eyes are on the electronic screen. Three red lights flash on the map of London; three red lights indicating that the missiles they have launched have reached their allotted targets. Caught up in their elation, the girls do not observe Garrow, lying in a pool of her own blood, dying but not yet dead, her face contorted as she reaches slowly, with tremendous and painful effort for the gun in her belt holster. Unclipping the holster, she grips the butt, slowly pulls out the weapon, aims it with arm unsteadily extended, at the back of the nearest girl, the girl with the long blonde hair. Tightening her hold on the grip to steady her aim as much as she can, Garrow squeezes the trigger.

A report, and Juliette stiffens, hand clutching her breast. The others stare at her with expressions only slightly less surprised than that of Juliette herself. Juliette collapses without uttering a sound, and in falling reveals the prostrate woman officer on the floor behind her, still holding the gun unsteadily.

For a moment, the three remaining girls are stunned, like statues.

Dizzy reacts first. With an animal scream she grabs her machinegun, swiftly crosses to where Garrow lies and empties the entire clip into the woman. Her body dances spastically under the metal hail, spraying blood in all directions.

After this, a pregnant silence.

Trudie drops to her knees, lifts Juliette, arms around her shoulders. Juliette's head lolls; her eyes wide open but vacant, unseeing; the brain behind those eyes has ceased to function. Blood trickles from her mouth. The lucky bullet has gone straight into her heart, destroying that vital pump and killing her almost instantly.

Juliette. The formative link between Trudie's old life and her new one... That day she had found the girl sitting on the bed in the room; she had opened up a new life to her in that matter-of-fact way of hers... And now...

      She can't be dead. This isn't supposed to happen. None of them should die. They are indestructible.

'She's dead...' says Trudie, blankly. 'She's... She's dead...'

Dizzy, her immediate rage satisfied, looks bewildered, says nothing.

'Come,' says Greta briskly. 'Ve haff to get out off here...'

Chapter Fifty-Three
Life is Beautiful

Back in the guest-suite, the first thing Dodo and Mayumi had done was to strip Mark naked, propel him into the bathroom, commanding him not to return until he had thoroughly cleaned himself up. In due course, Mark had returned from this exile, cleansed and refreshed in person if not in mind. Thereupon, Mayumi had stripped off her clothes and proceeded to give Mark a thorough foot massage—which is to say she had given Mark a massage using her feet, Oriental style.

And then, after a much-needed meal, Mark had retired to rest.

Today, since waking from protracted slumber, he has spent a lot of time just lying there on his bed, ruminating. He doesn't seem out of it any more, reflects Dodo; that detachment, that abstraction, has passed. He is lucid, aware of his surroundings. When you speak to him he answers in his usual cheerful voice. But he seems disinclined for long conversation. What is he thinking about, lying there? How to stop Vautrin? How to escape? Or is he just brooding about that girl Trudie Rayne? Something happened between those two...

The SEA girls, all of them, have gone out 'on a job.' It must be something big to require all eleven of them. This has placed them, considers Dodo, in a morally ambiguous position. They ought to have tried to stop the girls from even setting out, knowing that whatever this 'job' was, whatever it entailed, it would almost certainly result in a calamity of some kind. But what *could* they have done, just the three of them?

'She's dead, isn't she?'
  'Yes.'
  'What happened?'
  Dizzy tells him.
  They stand in the recreation room, Vautrin and the ten remaining girls. The girls, just returned, are sombre, subdued.

'Can't you *do* something?' demands Sophie.

Vautrin shrugs. 'I can't roll back time or bring the dead back to life.'

'Why didn't you warn us this was going to happen?' from Dizzy. An accusation more than a question. 'You can see things, right? The future.'

'I can see certain things, Dizzy. I could never have predicted a chance occurrence like this… But come on, girls! The mission was a success! Better than we could have imagined. You won't believe this, but the rocket that hit St Stephen's tower caused it to fall onto the House of Commons. The cabinet were in session. They're all dead! Every single one of them. You've effectively wiped out the entire government! It's unprecedented! There's total chaos out there! Just watch the news reports; you'll see!'

He looks at the girls, hoping for some reaction to the news. Nothing. No elation. No glee. Sophie, Flossie and Jessica are quietly crying; Trudie and Chrissie are also visibly upset. Baffled anger is written on the faces of Dizzy, Rachel and Albertine; Gina and Greta's expressions are unreadable.

'It doesn't bring back Juliette,' says Sophie.

The atmosphere has shifted. They have expected something from Vautrin; some miracle that would bring Juliette back to them. He has disappointed them; for the first time in their acquaintance he has disappointed them by not being able to do this.

And now, because of these events, something has changed. The balance has been upset. The girls are no longer an indestructible unit. Vautrin is no longer a super-being.

'You can't let this get you down,' urges Vautrin. 'Juliette wouldn't have wanted that.'

No response. The girls just look at him, look at him with eyes no longer register that submissive, canine veneration.

Vautrin turns on his heel and leaves the room.

A laboratory. Computers, work benches with chemical and electrical equipment stand at one end of the room; the massive grey bulk of a particle accelerator at the other.

Before this device stands a group of lab-coated scientists, in conclave.

'So it's decided?' Professor Norton, bald, bespectacled; the restless, gleaming eyes behind the lenses, dart rapid at the haggard faces of his team.

Murmurs of agreement.

'Yes, we've got to do it,' says one. 'This has gone on too long. It's got to end.'

'Right. He wants transference—we'll give him bloody transference.'

'Anything could happen,' cautions another.

'Anything's better than this nightmare,' answers the first.

A knock on the door, and Dodo walks into Mark's room. He is lying on his bed, hands behind his head, staring sightlessly up at the ceiling.

'The girls have come back,' she reports. 'But only ten of them.'

Suddenly alert, Mark raises his head, looks at her. 'Ten?'

'Yes; one of them didn't make it: Juliette Wainwright.'

'What happened?'

'I'm sketchy on the details. The girls weren't in the mood for talking. They raided a missile base somewhere—that was all I could gather. I don't know what they did there; blew the place up, maybe.'

'Or fired some of the missiles.'

'Well, whatever they did, one of them didn't get out of there alive. And now they're not in the mood for celebrating. Juliette getting killed seems to have completely floored them. I've never seen them like this.'

'This could be the beginning of the end,' says Mark.

In the recreation room, some of the girls are drowning their sorrows. Others have drifted off to their own rooms. Ignored by everyone else, Albertine and Dizzy are engaged in a blazing row;

trading insults and barbed sarcasms.

Jessica wishes they would just shut-up. Their argument's stupid. Like them—stupid. Deciding that the oblivion of alcohol might be a good idea at this time, she moves over to the drinks table where Rachel stands fixing herself a drink. Jessica picks up a vodka bottle. Unscrewing the lid, the bottle somehow slips from her hand; it falls onto the carpeted floor, spilling as it does so, then starts glugging out its remaining contents into the pile.

'Fucking clumsy bitch!' snaps Rachel.

Jessica doesn't respond; she stares at the spilt bottle in horror. Now she raises her hands; fingers splayed, they shake visibly.

No.

She runs from the room.

'…Reports of panic-buying in supermarkets across the country. The nation is in shock, glued to its television sets. Authorities have repeatedly stressed that the deaths of the Cabinet and Shadow Cabinet members has not destabilised the infrastructure of the nation. They are urging people to remain calm…'

This nightmare has to end. That's how they all feel.

How long have they been kept here? They have lost all track of time. Their world has become just this damned laboratory and the rooms where they are allowed to sleep.

They had woken up here, with no idea of how they came to be here, many of them strangers to each other. And then that madman Vautrin had appeared. He told them they had been experimenting with solanite, the new element found in a meteor which struck the moon; conducting tests at a place called Peltdown Vale. During one of these tests, there had been an accident which had somehow transferred them here; put them in his hands. That was the story he had told them. Vautrin wanted them to continue with their researches, but now under his guidance. They were prisoners in an underground complex, he had explained; they would not be allowed to leave; they could hold no communication with the outside world.

At first they had refused to work, demanded their freedom. Vautrin's response had been to summon those psychopathic girls of his—and acting on a signal from their leader, they had just gunned down all the 'non-essential personnel'—the office workers and cleaning staff—laughing and joking while they slaughtered.

After this, the scientists had set to work.

They had worked, but they had also plotted; and they had decided that one of their number should try and escape. Herriot had been chosen. He had made it out of the lab, and they had never seen him again. They had started to hope, but then Vautrin had appeared and informed them that Herriot had indeed made it to the outside, but had immediately fallen ill and then died a very undignified death. They could expect no rescue; and the same fate would await all of them if any of them were to be so reckless as to escape from the complex. In here, you live; out there, you die.

And what was the purpose of these experiments? Vautrin had always been vague about this. Transference. Transposition. The barriers between one reality and another. What did he want to achieve? To cross over? To bring different worlds together? Create a new universe of nightmare and insanity?

Norton knows he could be making things a lot worse with what he is about to do, but that glint in his eyes announces that he is way past caring. He is still enough of a clinical scientist to be objectively aware of this; that he has cracked, reached that point beyond despair. They all have.

Well, one way or another, it's going to end. Right now.

Every ounce of solanite material has been placed in the accelerator.

He turns the controls up to maximum.

Dodo switches off the TV. (Dodo is still unsure as to in what kind of pocket universe or sub-dimension the SEA base exists; but wherever it is, they can still pick up Freeview.)

'Well, they've done it this time,' she remarks, wonderingly. 'They've wiped out the whole bloody government. Jesus Christ.

And I bet they didn't even plan on that happening, either. They couldn't have known which way the clock-tower would fall when it was hit.'

'But they not celebrating,' says Mayumi, sorting through photographs she has taken of the SEA girls during her stay at their headquarters. (Mayumi is not one to let these national catastrophes get in the way of her art.)

'Nope, they're not celebrating. Because Juliette was killed. That's all they care about. Last I saw, they were all busy drowning their sorrows. Most of them, anyway.'

'Maybe now is a good time to get out of here.'

'That's what I've been thinking.' Dodo looks at the closed bedroom door. 'I think now *would* be a good time to get out of here. If only we can get Mark out of his brown study.'

'He's not in study; he's in bedroom.'

Dodo smiles. 'It's an expression, sweetheart. I mean he's just lying there, deep in thought.'

'Why?'

'He's got a lot to think about. He's been through a lot.'

'Tell him it's time to go.'

'I ought to. The trouble is, I've got a feeling he won't want to leave here without that girl Trudie Rayne; he's got her stuck in his head.'

Jessica runs.

She runs through the endless white corridors of the base, taking every turning she comes to, wanting to lose herself.

The bottle had slipped from her hands… A stupid accident; the kind which had happened all the time to the old Jessica… Falling over, breaking things, blowing up her house and her family… And now it's coming back… She thought she had left that old Jessica behind forever… But the magic Vautrin had used must be wearing off… It's coming back… It is the end for her…

Finally, exhausted from the effort, Jessica stops running. Catching her breath, she continues at walking-pace. How far has she gone? This base seems to go on forever; even Vautrin doesn't know how big it is. She hasn't seen a door for some time, she realises. Just blank white walls; an endless, pointless proliferation of corridors.

She turns a corner. The corridor now before her terminates with the barrier of a pair of red doors... The entrance to the bunker village? She could have sworn she has been running in completely the wrong direction to get to that place.

Maybe it's another lift up to the surface...

Jessica approaches the doors; they smoothly and silently part for her, and beyond them the clinical walls become the rough-hewn walls of a cave... Then it *is* the underground village? There's a cave there before you get to the bunker... Or maybe it's some new exit! One Vautrin either doesn't know about or hasn't told them about...

She steps into the cave. The doors close behind her, shutting out the artificial light. Darkness now surrounds her, but not complete darkness. There is luminance somewhere ahead. She walks on. She can feel cold air. And a smell; not just the smell of damp rock, but another smell. Vegetation.

Is she near the surface? But that would be impossible; the SEA base is way underground... Isn't it...?

She walks on, towards the light, the fresh air.

A turn of the cave, and she sees before her the cave mouth; an irregular shape framing the light of day. She breaks into a run—and then she is outside. A vast plain grassland stretches away in all directions. The sky is of a pastel mauve. In the hazy distance, mountains. And silence; complete and utter silence.

These are not the Sussex Downs. This isn't even England. The strange sky, the scent of unfamiliar vegetation... This is somewhere else.

In the middle-distance, directly before Jessica, one man-made object stands incongruous. A building. Modern, several storeys, it looks like it might be an office building; empty, abandoned. Jessica knows immediately that this building is as out of place as she is; it doesn't belong in this landscape any more than does she herself.

She advances onto the heath; the grass is light and springy. She looks back: the cave from which has emerged is set in an outcrop of rock, with cathedral-like spires reaching into the pale sky. She looks ahead again, beyond the lonely building, into the distance.

She has nothing to go back for. She strikes off across the undulating moor under the purple sky.

Vautrin suddenly staggers, clutching his head in pain. Fighting the nausea, he looks wildly around him. Unaccustomed beads of sweat form on his face.

No! What's happened? What have they done? If they've—
No!

Clenching his fists, tightening his jaw, he lurches along the corridor, slowly fighting off the nausea, gaining strength and balance.

He comes upon Rachel Ramone and Sophie Harris, locked in feline combat, spitting obscenities, scratching, biting. Vautrin wades in and pulls the combatants violently apart.

'Stop fighting and come with me!' he snarls.

It is the sheer surprise that makes the girls forget their grievances and obey. They have never seen Vautrin angry before.

They fall into step behind him as he hurries onwards through the corridors.

'What's wrong?' asks Sophie.

'The end of everything unless we're in time!' answers Vautrin savagely.

They reach the laboratory. The particle accelerator is shaking, vibrating with unchecked power; the humming sound, climbing ever higher, fills the room. The scientists stand in a group watching the device. They turn and face the newcomers, challenging them with their haggard exultation. Sophie and Rachel level their guns at them.

'What have you done?' roars out Vautrin, raising his voice over the noise.

'Set the whole bloody shebang to overload,' replies Professor Norton with a grim smile, likewise pitching his voice. 'You can't stop it! I've locked the controls!'

'How much of the solanite material is in there?' roars Vautrin

'Everything. The whole bloody lot.'

'You irresponsible—! Do you know what you've done?'

'No, I don't,' confesses Norton, cheerfully. 'But anything's better than suffering what we've all been suffering in this place. And who knows? Maybe we'll end up somewhere nice!'

He laughs exultantly.

This annoys Sophie. She shoots Norton through the head.

And, as is often the case, that first shot sets off a general massacre. Rachel shoots dead a scientist who wasn't doing anything in particular; and then the two girls are gunning down the entire scientific team, picking them off one-by-one like targets in a shooting gallery.

'Stop it, you idiots!' cries Vautrin, over the screams and gunshots. 'We've got to get out of here! The thing's going critical!'

The hum of power has now risen to an ear-splitting pitch. If the girls even hear him, they ignore him, intent on picking off the scientists, who, forgetting their previous resignation, still vainly try to avoid the bullets. Lab-coated corpses, red on white, litter the floor.

Vautrin just leaves them to it, and flees the room.

He has barely made out into in the corridor when comes a blinding, kaleidoscopic flash of light. He staggers, falls.

And then silence, abrupt, heavy.

Vautrin slowly rises himself.

He sees a wall. There, where the laboratory doors had stood moments before, now only a blank wall.

'What are you doing here?'

The speaker is Flossie Farraday. Her question is directed at Chrissie Wylde, who is in the act of pouring herself a drink. The two of them are alone in the common room.

'What do you mean, Flo?'

'What I mean, *Chris*,' (voice dripping acid) 'is what the hell are you doing in the SEA? Why are you even here? That's always bothered me; you being here.'

'What's your fucking problem?' demands Chrissie, nettled. 'I'm *here* because Vautrin chose me, same as he did you and everyone else.'

'Yeah. And you were the last one, weren't you? Vautrin must have been really running out of suitable candidates by then, mustn't he? He must have been really scraping the bottom of the barrel by the time he got to you.'

Chrissie erupts. 'Fuck you, you fucking bitch! What's with the fucking attitude? Why shouldn't Vautrin have chosen me? He chose you, didn't he? What's the fucking difference?'

Flossie smiles contemptuously. 'Vautrin rescued me from a life of misery; that's the *difference*. Same goes for all the other girls. Do you know what my life was like? My family hated me. Everyone at school hated me. I was bullied everywhere I went. Christ, I can't even understand now how I even lived through all that… And what about *you*, Chris darling? What was *your* crisis? What kind of unbearable life did *you* have to be rescued from? Hmm… Oh yeah: your boyfriend dumped you. That was it, wasn't it? Your boyfriend dumped you. Big fucking deal.'

'He didn't dump me, he cheated on me,' retorts Chrissie. 'What's your fucking problem? Just because I didn't have a life of misery like you? Get over yourself.'

'You shouldn't be here. Vautrin made a mistake. It should have been you that got killed today, not Juliette. So why don't you just get the fuck out of here?'

'And why should I? If you've got a problem with me, you can talk about it with Vautrin, can't you? You can't just tell me to go.'

'I don't need to talk about it with Vautrin—and I *am* telling you to go. Fuck off.'

'Sorry. Not happening.'

'Fuck. Off.'

'Fuck off yourself! Christ—you think you're the only person on the planet who's got a hard-luck story? *You* fuck off; fuck off somewhere and wallow in self-pity, you fucking toffee-nosed doe-eyed fucking bitch!'

Flossie launches herself at Chrissie. Perhaps she doesn't like the 'doe-eyed' comparison; she goes straight for the jugular, claws out. Chrissie meets the attack, repels and retaliates—and then, like enraged cats, they are tumbling about the recreation room floor, frenziedly punching and kicking.

The course of this murderous Catherine-wheel brings its components into collision with the legs of the drinks table; a handgun, left there amongst the bottles and glasses, falls to the floor. Chrissie sees it. Kicking Flossie from on top of her, she grabs the gun. Flossie, on her feet, is already lunging at her; perhaps she sees the gun, perhaps she doesn't. Chrissie fires. The bullet makes a neat red hole in Flossie's forehead, and a much larger one when it comes out the back.

Reaction sets in. Chrissie kneels on the floor, chest heaving, staring mutely at the corpse she has just made.

'You shouldn't 'ave done zat.'

Chrissie looks round. Albertine stands at the other end of the room near the door; she has her own gun, and holds it two-handed, levelled at Chrissie.

'She attacked me,' protests Chrissie. 'She went psycho on me. You saw it, didn't you?'

'I saw you fighting. She did not attack you with a gun.'

'I just picked it up and fired. I wasn't thinking.'

'You *should* 'ave thought.'

Chrissie realises Albertine is about to fire. She makes her move. Two shots ring out. Chrissie's shot strikes Albertine in the arm. Albertine's blows the top of Chrissie's head off.

The French girl drops to her knees, face contorted with pain, her forearm a wet, splintered mess.

And now Dizzy enters the room, her own gun at the ready. Her eyes sweep the room, taking in the carnage.

'What's going on?' she demands of Albertine. 'Did you do this?'

'Chris shot Flossie. I shot Chris. She got me in the arm.' This report uttered through gritted teeth.

Dizzy walks up to her.

''Elp me,' pleads Albertine. 'Zis pain is killing me. Find Vautrin…'

'Vautrin can't help you.'

'Get me to the medical centre…'

'Uh-uh. You're not going anywhere.'

Standing over her, Dizzy places the muzzle of her gun against Albertine's head.

A shift in reality.

For a moment, Trudie sees herself standing in an empty street, on her way home from school… It is the same feeling, the same feeling she felt that day, just before her world changed…

Lying on her bed in her room. Her room in SEA headquarters. She has slept in this room nearly every night for many months now, but it suddenly seems a strange place to her, this room. This isn't her room. Her room is her bedroom in her parents' house in London. This room… this room is somebody else's…

What is she doing here?

This isn't me.

Who is she?

How did all this happen?

Then the past few months suddenly come crashing down on her—a fast-forward of all the insanity, of depravity and atrocity. The horror of it pins her to the bed; holds her prisoner, a captive audience to the reality of all her crimes, passing in review before her mind's eye. She sees it all—memory spares her nothing; burning bodies pitch from crumbling buildings into flowing rivers of blood.

Lying there she clenches herself, forces back a sudden bowel movement.

No. No-no-no. This can't be real; it just can't be. This is just some insane nightmare… Vautrin. The SEA. They can't be real. Doing all those things, killing all those people… Not me. I didn't do all that… It's like Mark has always said. That Monster Vautrin has been keeping her under a spell, an enchantment. And now that spell is wearing off—for real this time...

Mark. He cares for her. He wants to help her. She remembers a conversation, a moment of intimacy, that might have been a dream. Mark is here right now. Over in the guest-suite with Dodo Dupont and Mayumi Takahashi. She has to go to him. He will protect her; he will help her... She knows she can never go back to her old life—she has gone way too far for that—but Mark, he can do something; make a new life for her, can't he? A new life in some distant place... He will help her; he's the only one she can turn to...

Mark. Only a few corridors away from her. It isn't her fault what she has done. Mark has said that all along. She's a victim here; she has been brainwashed... Mark... She has to go to him now! It's her last and only hope...

Meretricious hope easing her fear, she rises from her bed, puts on her shoes, leaves the room belonging to the girl she has been sharing her life with. The corridor is silent. The atmosphere of the place feels strange, altered... Perhaps it's just her...

She heads off in the direction of the guest suite, building hope upon hope. But then, at the first intersection she encounters Dizzy Hello. The girl is advancing towards her, has seen her; it is too late for Trudie to retreat without arousing suspicion...

For the first time since she has been here, Trudie is scared of this girl, one of those former comrades and bedfellows... Dizzy Hello is one of the sickest, most out of control of them all; she always had been—even before Vautrin; an insane, bloodthirsty animal...

Just walk past her. Don't look at her. It will be fine...

Without having broken her step and doing nothing more than acknowledge the other girl with a brief nod, Trudie maintains a bland expression and a casual, unhurried demeanour. Dizzy doesn't seem particularly interested—she looks preoccupied. But just as they draw level, just as Trudie thinks she is going to be able to pass the girl without being challenged:

'Hold it.'

Trudie stops. She forces herself to turn and face the girl.

'Yes...?'

'Where are you going?'

Trudie tries to keep her voice level. 'Nowhere. I was just—'

Their eyes lock. Something passes between. The collision of two auras no longer in harmony. In that pregnant moment each reads something in the other's eyes. Dizzy's narrow.

'Traitor.'

She raises her gun.

Dodo walks into Mark's room. The spy lies on his bed, smoking a contemplative cigarette.

'I think we should get out of here,' says Dodo, without preamble.

'Escape, you mean? Do you know the way?'

'Yes, I know where the lift to the surface is. Mayumi and me have had the run of the place for several days, remember.'

'If we leave, I'm taking Trudie with us,' states Mark.

Dodo sighs. 'I knew you'd say that. And what if she doesn't want to come?'

'I'll convince her, I'm sure I can.'

'Mark. Even if you can, don't you think the other girls might object? Not to mention Vautrin. We should just try and sneak out without being seen; now's the time.'

'I'm not going without Trudie,' says Mark.

'Oh, *Mark*. You're obsessed with that girl; you've got her stuck in your head. I've never seen you like this before.'

'I know,' apologetically. 'It's not like me at all, is it? But I just can't get her off my mind. I have to—'

A gunshot.

Mark springs to his feet.

'They're killing each other!' he cries. He rushes past Dodo.

'Mark!'

'I've got to find Trudie!'

He races out into the corridor. Dodo, throwing a 'Come on!' at Mayumi, follows.

Round the first corner they find two corpses: Greta Garbo and

Gina Santella. Gina's knife is in Greta's chest, Greta's bullet in Gina's. Mark runs on; Dodo pauses to scoop up the German girl's gun.

The recreation room. Three more bloody corpses: Albertine Sagan, Chrissie Wylde, Flossie Farraday.

Trudie. Don't be dead. Please don't be dead.

'Where can she be?' demands Mark.

'Let's try the girls' quarters,' says Dodo. 'They're this way; not far.'

They run on. A long stretch of corridor. A girl appears at the far end, running.

'Trudie!'

'Mark!'

Thank God! Mark runs to meet her, sees fear and relief chase each other across the girl's countenance. Arms outstretched, she hurries towards him—

And then a shot rings out, and the embrace, defined in two mind's eyes as an imminent event, becomes only a hopeless dream. Trudie Rayne clutches her chest; a surge of red over her white blouse. She falls.

Mark stops, horrified.

Dizzy Hello stands at the end of the corridor, gun raised. She takes aim at Mark. But Dodo Dupont is before her. Her well-aimed shot takes off the top of the girl's blonde head. The corpse pitches backwards.

Mark is now on his knees beside Trudie. Her hand grips his weakly. Those eyes, behind the thick-lensed glasses, meet his, entreating him…

And then the hand goes limp, the eyes glaze over.

Something freezes over inside Mark. Dimly, he is aware that Dodo and Mayumi are standing by his side.

'Mark…'

The light begins to fail. The white walls of the corridor are turning to a sunset orange.

'What's happening?' from Mayumi.

'I don't know…'

A figure appears at the end of the corridor. Vautrin. He comes towards them, staggering, leaning against the wall for support as though the corridor were tilted at an angle. He looks pale, ill, drained of energy. Has he been shot? wonders Dodo. She sees no sign of a wound.

Close to the dead girl and the kneeling man, he comes to a stop, leans back up against the wall, exhausted.

'So, here we all are,' he says hoarsely, managing a feeble laugh.

'What's wrong with you?' asks Dodo. 'Are you injured?'

Vautrin shakes his head.

'The interface is severed,' he says. 'I'm fading out.'

'Because the girls are dead?'

Vautrin speaks with an effort: 'That would make sense, wouldn't it? The girls' belief that they wished me into existence… And now there's no-one left to make me real…'

'No-one left? Are they all dead?'

'I think so. I'm not sensing any of them anymore.'

'What's happening to this place? It's like it's shutting down or something.'

'There was an overload in the solanite particle accelerator. My tame scientists rebelled on me; they did it on purpose… The whole lab is gone… It's spreading… This place is going and I'm going with it. I'm connected to this place…'

He looks down at Mark. 'Looks like you've won the game after all, Mark, doesn't it?'

Mark looks up at him.

'…Ah yes…' says Vautrin. 'Perhaps nobody's one after all… You could never have saved her, Mark…'

He leans his head back against the wall. His body is fading; becoming transparent before their eyes.

'This is it… I'm going…'

'Going where?' from Dodo.

Another weak smile. 'I wish I knew…'

'Just who are you, Vautrin?' demands Dodo.

'Oh. just someone passing through… Goodbye, Dodo…

Goodbye, Mark...'

And he fades out of existence.

'Is he dead?' wonders Mayumi.

'Dead or gone,' says Dodo.

The light fades fast. The corridor walls turn from sunset orange to deep brown; darker, darker—and then they find themselves in pitch darkness. The temperature suddenly drops; the air is now damp, chill and metallic.

'What's going on?' demands Mayumi, gripping Dodo's hand.

Dodo fishes out her lighter, ignites it. The flickering light reflects the surface of uneven rock walls. They are in a cave.

'I guess this means we're back in the real world,' she says. 'Vautrin's base must have mapped itself over these natural caves...'

Trudie's body is still with them, lying on the cave floor. Mark rises to his feet, looks at his friends in the flickering orange light. He manages a smile.

'Back in the real world,' he agrees. 'Now all we've got to do is find a way out of here...'

Epilogue
An Advertisement

BEAUTIFUL CHAOS - PORTRAIT OF ELEVEN KILLERS
A Psychological Study
by
PROFESSOR DOROTHEA DUPONT
Illustrated with Photography
by
MAYUMI TAKAHASHI

ON SALE NOW!

Printed in Dunstable, United Kingdom